SACRED VALLEY: BETRAYAL

A supernatural horror novel
by Shaun M Jooste

Inspired by the Silent Hill game franchise

OTHER NOVELS BY AUTHOR

THE CELENIC EARTH CHRONICLES
The Windfarer
The DragonRider
The Sadgi

CONTENTS

This novel is dedicated to my wife and children for all your great love, patience, support, and encouragement while writing the story.

Also, a dedication goes to George Boeree, former professor of Shippensburg University in Pennsylvania, for allowing me to use your name and the relevant articles utilised in Hollowbrook Elementary's Library.

PREFACE

For those of you who don't know, Sacred Valley: Betrayal is a rework of my original horror novel, Silent Hill: Betrayal released in 2016. I'm not going to go into much detail as to what happened: you can check my author blog or the Celenic Earth Publications site.

In summary, Konami removed the permission I believed I had to use the Silent Hill name to write my own stories. I decided not to stop working on these novels and simply give a new name to the town. What was born was new lore, which introduced new names and a history of the town.

It gave birth to something entirely new, which I am calling an alternate universe to the one Silent Hill is in. With the concept of the multiverse running rampant in our own world, I decided to make use of it for Sacred Valley. So, there's still minor mention of Silent Hill in this story, but only as an alternate dimension.

I've also had the opportunity to edit my work after years of working as an expert editor for content agencies. I was ashamed to see how many errors I had made, but I'm glad for the opportunity to rework this book. Please note, I kept it in UK English, as that's the localisation in my country.

And so, without further ado, I present the reworked Sacred Valley: Betrayal horror novel.

Shaun M Jooste

PROLOGUE

HOT PURSUIT

Trevor McKenzie moved softly in the bed, the sheet shifting over the nude woman beside him as he stirred gently in his sleep. The sun had not risen yet, leaving the two lovers peacefully enjoying their embrace, only the restless wind outside hinting at what was to come.

His short brown hair bristled against the large white pillow that he shared with the auburn-haired woman in his arms. The double bed was in a rustic room that needed a lick of paint a few years ago, as did the rest of apartment 202 of South Ashbourne Heights.

Trevor's face turned into a grimace, his thin eyebrows arching on his pale forehead. His right arm gripped the edge of the bed as he bared his teeth in pain and anger. His left shoulder jerked, causing the woman to lift her head in fright. His groans turned deep, sounding like the dark growl of a rabid hound.

"Trev?" the woman called softly, too afraid to wake him. Despite this, she moved to touch his chest, causing him to sit up in a sudden frenzy and grip her upper arm tightly. She pulled back, alarmed by the blackness in his eyes and the odorous sulphur emitted by his hoarse breathing.

"Sacred Valley," he groaned in a dark masculine voice with a subtle feminine undertone within it.

Kathy Georgeades panicked and tried to yank her arm from his vice grip. When she realised she could not break free, she arched her back over the bed, ignoring the sheets that fell off her upper body. She reached for the glass of water on the bedside table and twisted her body back to him. The water splashed over his face, making him jolt his head away from her and release her arm.

She moved off the bed, standing on the floor and watching him for further signs of violence. He was drying his eyes with his hands, his chest appearing to be breathing more gently than it had during his possessed episode. Kathy reached down for the gown on the floor by her feet and covered her nudity. She cleared the long red hair over the back of the gown and tied the sash over her belly.

"What… what happened?" Trevor asked, looking at her in surprise.

"You had a nightmare," Kathy responded. "I'll go make us some coffee."

Kathy walked out without giving him a chance to respond. He clasped his face in his hands in a vain attempt to wash away the remnants of his bad sleep. He tried to remember anything from the dream, something that would trigger what had caused him to get such a fright. The only fragment retained were the words 'Sacred Valley' in the guttural outcry.

He needed to get out of the apartment for a bit. Get some fresh air, away from the bad memories; away from everything that reminded him of what had happened…

Trevor found his favourite pair of black jeans, some black socks with his boots, and threw on a grey tee before donning a red and green checkered shirt. As he passed the wardrobe along the wall, he looked in the mirror on its door. His short brown hair was soaked from the sweat during his sleep, his green eyes glistening with the fog of its wake.

Grabbing his cellphone from the bedside table, he moved out of the room. Trevor moved down the passage, spotting Kathy's feet by the toilet through the bathroom door that was slightly ajar. He moved past her and slowed his pace as he entered the open-plan lounge kitchen area.

He looked up at the ceiling. The fan was on, even though he recalled switching it off before. Trevor felt the chills up his spine as he watched the blades turn. He almost expected it to unhinge and fall from the ceiling, waiting for the extra supports he had placed there a few months before to suddenly snap and pull the fan down again.

Yet the blades continued spinning, taunting him with every sound they made, cutting through the thick, humid air.

"Trevor?" Kathy asked from behind him, making him jump. He hadn't even heard her flush the toilet. She stepped back at his reaction, looking into the lounge area to see what had alarmed him.

"I thought I switched the fan off last night," he clarified, rubbing his forehead.

"You did, but I put it back on moments ago. It was getting musty in here."

She frowned at him, cautiously stepping past him to the kitchen area. Trevor watched the fan spin for a moment longer before stepping into the lounge, taking a seat opposite the passage from the room. He stared at the blank television screen.

Just above the television screen was a painting of another red-haired woman sitting in a nurse uniform on a bed. When he moved in, Trevor had found many paintings in the room and sold many of them off, but this particular one had caught his fancy. Kathy had always hinted that it was because the woman in the painting resembled her. In the corner of the painting, the name 'Roseline' was inscribed.

Trevor remembered that he had tried the same thing once, inspired by the apartment's previous tenant. Despite his best attempts not to, he looked in the corner of the lounge by the window and saw the painting hidden behind the wall unit. The blond hair was visible from the part of the painting that protruded. It instinctively made Trevor look up at the fan again. The whirring of the blades started to sound like the grinding of gears.

"I told you before," Kathy said gently as she placed the coffee mugs on the low coffee table in the centre of the lounge, "it isn't healthy for us to stay here, especially after what happened."

"I know," he replied as she sat down beside him. "I'll start looking for a place today."

"You said that last time," she retorted. He smiled and then looked down at her arm.

"Did I do that?" Trevor asked, pointing at the bruise forming on her arm.

"Don't worry about it," she replied, reassuringly smiling and pulling the gown sleeve down. "You weren't in the right frame of mind."

He nodded, but Kathy could tell by his expression that he would not so easily forgive himself for hurting her. She reached for his coffee and aimed to hand it to him when his phone rang.

Trevor looked tentatively down at his pants pocket, deciding whether to answer. His mind was still cloudy from the bad sleep, so he accepted the mug of coffee while letting the phone ring to its conclusion. Kathy simply watched him, unsure of what to say to him.

His phone had hardly ceased calling when Kathy heard her phone ring from the room. Unlike Trevor, she moved to answer it. Trevor watched her lithe body move down the passage until she was out of sight. He closed his eyes to savour the rich taste of the coffee and then threw the cup down instantly.

The liquid from the mug poured over the dirty lounge carpet. He leaned forward, turning the cup upright to inspect the contents. It looked and smelled like coffee, but when he had tasted it, he could have sworn it had a hint of....iron. As if he had tasted blood from a flesh wound.

"Trevor, it's Jay," Kathy said as she returned to the lounge with her cellphone in her hand. "He says he needs to talk to you now."

"I don't want to talk to anyone right now," he said, waving the phone off. "I'll call him tomorrow."

"He says it's urgent, love," Kathy replied, placing the phone into his hands. "He says it's about.... her."

Trevor looked into her eyes and immediately knew who she was talking about. His ring finger itched where the wedding ring used to be, but he ignored it. He put the phone to his ears and heard the sound of sirens in the background.

"Jay, what's going on?"

"Trev, get the hell out of there, man," Jay replied on the other side. "The cops are coming."

"Why?" he said, standing up suddenly. Kathy stared at him wide-eyed, wondering what had caused him such consternation.

"They know, man," Jay replied. Trevor struggled to hear his words through the noise of the sirens.

"How the hell could they know?" Jay said, and then whispered to Kathy to get dressed. She took the cue and ran back to the room.

"Some forensic report that came up. They found new evidence."

"You told me the case went cold," Trevor said, breathing deeply as he tried to hold down the panic within him.

"It had," Jay replied. "It did. Then some therapist's report rocked up at the station. Someone's spilt the beans."

"Who?"

"Well, it isn't me," Jay replied. "So unless you've been seeing a Doctor Emily Hoffman…"

"I haven't," Trevor interjected. "I've been staying away from any form of counselling."

"Then it can only be Phillip, man," Jay said. "Unless you've told Kathy."

"No, but I don't think she's stupid," Trevor said. "It wouldn't be her; she wouldn't betray me."

"Listen, we can discuss this later," Jay said. "We're on our way to you now, leaving the station. Get going."

Trevor cut the call, not bothering to say goodbye. He ran to the room and got into his wardrobe. He grabbed a blue extra-large sports duffle bag and threw some clothes into it. He reached under his shirts on one of the racks and took his wallet with his cash, cards, and driver's license.

Kathy was done getting dressed and had stashed some items in an overnight bag. He could tell by her expression that she had many questions on her mind but chose to keep them for later. She reached for her car keys and threw them to him as they left the bedroom.

When they reached the lounge, Trevor stood aside to let Kathy through first. As he turned around to do so, he saw the 'Roseline' painting lying on the floor next to the television stand. He looked up at the wall… his painting was there in its stead, the woman smiling down at him. The name 'Caroline' was bleeding down from the upper corner. He could have sworn she wore a smirk he had not painted.

"Trevor!" Kathy called from the door she had already opened, reaching to him with her hand.

He ran towards her, grabbing her hand. As he closed the door with the other hand, clutching his bag, he saw the ceiling fan shift and fall to the floor. His heart pounded, his breath caught in his throat, as Kathy jerked him away towards the stairs.

The stomping down the steps beat the hammering of his heart in his head. He tried to listen past the noise for the sound of the sirens. All he could hear was his feet on the timber treads and landings.

They reached the ground floor and made their way to the front double doors of the lobby. Out of habit, Trevor swung his glance towards the mailboxes hanging securely against the wall. He stopped in his tracks as Kathy's hand left his, her momentum carrying her forward before she also stopped.

"We don't have time for this," Kathy said hastily. Trevor looked at her, wondering how much she suspected or actually knew. She seemed in an awful rush for someone who didn't know what was happening.

"Hold on, there's something in my box," Trevor said as he walked towards the red object sticking out from the small opening of his mailbox.

He pulled out a red paper that seemed singed at the edges. It was blank on the initial side, but as he turned it over, two words were written over the centre:

Sacred Valley

He saw a strange symbol on the upper right side of the paper. He started studying it closer when Kathy's tug on his arm reminded him that he was being hunted by the police.

Storing the paper in one of the upper zipped sections of the duffel bag, he made his way out of the apartments to Kathy's car waiting in the parking lot. He opened it and hopped into the driver's seat. He heard the sirens in the distance as he started the car into action, Kathy slamming the passenger door closed as he tossed the duffel bag into the back seat.

The blue two-door hatch car reversed out of the bay, spun around, and sped towards the street. Trevor watched the traffic approaching from both directions. As the parking lot threshold approached, he saw the police cars coming from the right. Kathy clutched his right leg in dread.

Trevor watched the traffic carefully. As the car roared onto the road, he kicked the gas pedal down to over-rev the vehicle and then released it again. The car's back end spun out, allowing them to drift into the right lane. The traffic in the left lane swerved to miss him, causing one of the sedans to nudge the back of the hatch. Trevor fought with the steering wheel to correct the balance and then raced towards the highway.

A swarm of police cars followed in pursuit. Trevor watched in the rear-view mirror as one of them caught up to them, the forest trees enclosing either side of the highway. He tried to make out the driver of the closest police vehicle, but it was still too far behind.

"You must be wondering what's going on," Trevor finally said, using the conversation to fight the excessive tension building up inside of him. They had cleared most of the traffic and seemed to have a clear road ahead of them now.

"I assume it has something to do with Caroline's death," Kathy replied, unsure of her assessment.

"Something like that," he agreed.

"But I don't understand," Kathy finally stated, "I thought you said she committed suicide."

"She did," he replied. Trevor opened his mouth to say more, but the words got caught in his throat. He swallowed hard and tried again, but what he needed to tell her would not come out.

"Ok," Kathy said, rubbing his leg, "whatever it is, it can wait until we are out of this mess."

Trevor looked at her to offer a smile in gratitude and then looked past her to see one of the cops alongside them. He saw the names "J. Nixon" and "F. Johnson" written on the door of the police vehicle, although Trevor only spotted one man in the car. The cop reached for the loudhailer's radio.

"Pull over your vehicle now!" the officer shouted, then nodded back toward the other cops. He made a motion of swerving the steering wheel of the police car.

"What's he doing?" Kathy asked, bewildered.

"Trying to help us," Trevor said when he understood what the officer wanted him to do. "Hold on tight."

Trevor gripped the steering wheel hard and swerved the car first right and then left towards the cop's lane. He made sure to slam into the side of the police car and then hit the front again when the officer slowed down.

The cop car spun around, and its back end hit one of the other cop cars. This caused a chain reaction of police vehicles that hit each other, either off the road into the forest or into the oncoming traffic lanes. Trevor sped away into the morning light just as he noticed a mist moving in from the forest.

Officer Nixon turned his car around again and chased after Trevor. Kathy looked back and saw two other police vehicles that had survived the accident following him.

"I don't think we'll lose them on the highway," Kathy said stated.

"I'll turn off at the next exit," Trevor said, watching as the sirens of the three vehicles behind him flickered dully in the thickening mist. "Is there a map book in your car?"

Kathy bent towards the back seat and scrummaged around on the floor. After a moment's search around the confectionary packaging and litter, she pulled the book onto her lap. She opened it up, quickly searching for their area. As soon as she located the correct page, her finger traced the road they were on.

"No," she said softly, her finger standing still at the next exit on the map.

"What is it?" he asked, puzzled at the tone in her voice.

"Nothing," she said hastily, looking back at the police vehicles. "I just need to find another exit."

Trevor was about to question her when a green road sign appeared on the left of the road. He swallowed hard as he saw the destination.

"Trevor, don't," Kathy pleaded. He looked at her once and then in the mirror. He saw the turnoff ahead.

"Everything has been leading me to this," Trevor finally said, "all the nightmares these last few months."

"I thought you've moved on?" Kathy asked.

"So did I," Trevor said, turning the car suddenly into the exit. "I love you, Kathy. But I need to know why she killed herself."

"Isn't it obvious?" Kathy replied.

"Caroline wouldn't kill herself over us. At least, not the Caroline I knew."

"You know…. Sometimes a woman's true nature comes out when she is really betrayed."

Trevor shared another glance with her. Once again, he wondered just how much she knew.

"Why Sacred Valley?" she asked under his striking gaze. "What will Sacred Valley provide that you cannot find elsewhere?"

"My dreams, the messages to my phone, the red paper in my mailbox," Trevor replied. "I don't think it's a coincidence."

"But Caroline is dead," Kathy tried again. "Who could give you answers there?"

"Didn't you tell me that Phillip was transferred from Dunst Hospital to the Ashenfall Hospital in Sacred Valley?"

"Yes, but what does Phillip have to do with this?"

Trevor went quiet, leaving Kathy to stare at him in confusion. He looked in his mirror at the turnoff from the highway just as the police reached it.

Officer Nixon stopped his car at the turnoff, causing the other two to stop too. He reached for the radio and turned to their channels.

"I'm going in after them," he told the others. "Wait here."

"But this road has been abandoned for years," the woman on the radio replied. "The bridge has collapsed. There's nothing in there."

"Then block this road," Officer Nixon said. "Be ready to stop them if they double back."

"Affirmative," the woman responded.

Trevor relaxed his foot on the pedal, making Kathy look back into the mist. She only saw one vehicle's siren following them on their dark road to Sacred Valley. The road started climbing, and Officer Nixon maintained a short distance behind them.

"It feels so strange to be going back to Sacred Valley," Kathy said, feeling more at ease to speak.

"When was the last time you saw the place?" Trevor asked.

"I went to school here," she responded, looking down and playing with a charm bracelet on her wrist. "I felt at home there, more than with my parents. I had some good friends."

"That sounds great," Trevor smiled. "We could use some good friends right now."

"And you?" she asked in return. "When last were you here?"

"I came to the resort some years back," he replied. Kathy noticed that the question seemed to trouble him. "We came in by ferry to the Silvercrest docks by the resort, so I never really got to see the town properly."

The radio suddenly lit up and made a momentary noise. Trevor and Kathy both stared at it as the radio's light flickered and the signal dial started tuning up and down its width. Trevor reached down to switch it off and received a static shock when his fingertips touched it.

Trevor looked back up and caught a glint of a sign higher up on the road. The mist curdled into a denser mass, obscuring the words on the sign from his view. Yet, before the sign had vanished, Trevor swore that he had seen the town's name on it.

"Trevo…" a female voice on the radio crackled, making them look at it again. "Don…to Sacred Va… Stay away. Don't Lo..k for me. Please Tr…. St… away."

"Trevor, look out!" Kathy shouted, pointing to the road ahead.

A large topless man stood before them. The light of the hatch glinted on the strange metallic object situated over the man's head, his wounded muscular torso shimmering in the eerie mist. He was fading in and out of view when suddenly the mist lifted slightly and revealed a huge boulder in the road ahead.

Trevor swerved, trying his best to avoid the rock. He attempted to over-rev the gas again, making the car's tail spin out too much. The officer in the police vehicle slammed into the side of their hatch, sending their car into somersaults over its sides and slamming into a barrier near the edge of the road…

ACT ONE

THE WILD DOGS OF JUSTICE

1

NIGHTMARE

Trevor stirred his aching body, groaning as he attempted to open his eyes. He could feel a sticky fluid on his cheek and the side of his neck, and his body was awkward. He tried to move, but the pain made him exhale quickly and remain still.

He finally managed to open his eyes. He was lying against the car door, his neck slightly bent against the headrest of his seat. He was looking up at the passenger door and realized that the car was lying on its side. Running his fingers on his neck, he felt a pool of blood that had collected there.

He tried to move again and then noticed something shift on his belly. Seeing a golden band, he picked it up for closer inspection. He saw the links meant to hold charms and realised it was Kathy's charm bracelet. All of its charms were missing.

It dawned on him suddenly that Kathy was not in her seat. He jerked up, only to grimace in pain again and lie back down. Taking it more slowly, he moved until he could see over his seat into the back of the car. It was empty too.

Trevor looked out the windscreen to see if he could spot any movement, but all he could see was mist. It seemed much denser than before, and he could hardly see past the car's nose.

Placing the charm band in his shirt pocket, he gathered his strength and courage and moved towards the passenger door. It took him a few minutes, but he finally managed to extricate himself from the vehicle. He stood beside it on the road, squinting into the mist in an attempt to spot Kathy. His eye caught the police vehicle that had chased them in the opposite lane.

As he reached it, he peered in through the smashed side window. No one was in there or any sign of where the officer had gone. Trevor was about to step back when he spotted a police radio built into the dashboard. He reached his hand in and retrieved the receiver.

"Hello?" he spoke into it, hoping it was already set to the correct frequency. "Can anyone hear me? Hello?"

No one responded. Trevor did not even receive any form of static. He checked the power levels and saw by the green light on its side that it was still fully charged. He dropped the receiver, feeling there was no further use in trying.

Turning around, he saw the large sign looming ahead of him. It had two spotlights attached to the top of it, but even with all its luminescence, Trevor still had to walk further forward to read it. When he walked far enough to see the big white words written on the green sign through the fog, he read:

Welcome to Sacred Valley

It sent chills down Trevor's spine. Something had wanted him here, and until recently, he had thought it was Caroline. He thought back to the car radio that had turned itself on, remembering the voice that had spoken to him. He had tried making out the voice among the crackling noise and was almost certain it sounded like Caroline's.

Yet, as he stood before the town's welcome sign, he was no longer sure of anything anymore. Too many questions pounded into his head. Is this where his dreams were leading him too? Who was the man with the strange metallic object in his head? Where was Kathy? Where was Jay?

"Pull yourself together, Trev, old man," he said softly, shaking the last cobwebs out of his head. "This is no time for hysteria."

He felt into his pocket for his cellphone and pulled it out, glad it had survived the crash. The phone's light flickered momentarily and then cast an eerie glow into the mist. He checked the battery power, which there was enough of. Yet the signal was non-existent. The signal bar showed an SOS symbol, meaning he could only make emergency calls.

And this felt exactly like an emergency.

Trevor dialled the emergency number and waited as the phone rang. He was about to hang up again when someone answered.

"Hello?" Trevor tried.

For an answer, all he got was a low growl. He thought for a moment that the growl sounded very canine, but realised it was much deeper; like the core of a burning fire.

He hung up. He needed to move. He looked back down the road away from the town and wondered if Kathy would have tried to head back. Walking back down the road towards the rocky boulder, he kept a look out for that strange metallic-headed man he had seen. Once he passed the boulder, he saw that he had more than weird men to worry about.

The road broke off abruptly. Trevor walked to the end of the road, knelt on his knee and peered over the edge carefully. There was nothing there except an endless abyss. Not even the mist penetrated that darkness. His head reeled from vertigo, and he fell backwards away from the cliff.

"This is insane," Trevor said aloud, if only to hear the sound of something other than the nothingness surrounding him. "I must be dreaming. This can't be real."

He got up and walked back to the vehicles. Once again, he wondered where Kathy could be, and for the first time, he allowed the other subconscious thought to pass through. If she had woken up next to him, why did she not wake him? Or at least wait for him. And where was the officer? Surely the officer would have checked that he was alright and strove to wake him.

He suddenly felt very alone and even more certain that this was a dream. Even so, he could not just remain there waiting. His impatience would get the better of him. He stepped onto the road, taking his first deliberate path into the town of Sacred Valley.

Trevor checked his phone after feeling like he had been walking for hours. The time showed that it had only been fifteen minutes. Just as he started worrying that he had gotten lost, he spotted the bulk of buildings ahead of him and realised that he had finally reached the town itself.

The buildings looked abandoned. They had suffered the abuse of vandalism and graffiti some time back. Still, Trevor could not spot anything modern about them. Even the writing on some plastered walls had faded away in some places.

Just as he saw a convenience store on his left, he realised he had reached a four-way crossing. He moved to one of the pavement corners to see if he could spot names for the streets. Even though he did not know Sacred Valley's roads that well, he hoped that, should he get lost, seeing the names would help him find his way back out again.

The road he had been heading down was Hawthorne Avenue, and the road crossing it was Kingsley Street. He made a mental note and looked down either side of Kingsley. The mist covered everything, and he couldn't see very far. In the moment's loneliness, he had no idea where he should be heading or what to do.

He heard a flutter of wings and looked up to see a black crow land on a lamppost. It stared down at him from his perched position. Trevor felt uneasy under its gaze and decided to move further down Hawthorne.

Watching the buildings he passed for any signs of life, he noticed more crows landing on the trees to the right. They remained closer to Kingsley than in the direction he was heading, which made him feel slightly better about gaining distance from them. As he faced the front again, he scratched his forehead, which started itching.

"What the hell?" Trevor said, looking down at his fingers. He crossed the tips over each other, feeling the softness of the substance. "Is this ash or snow?"

He looked up, trying to spot the source of the drifting items. Spinning around, all he could see was more of the mist falling into the city, realising that he had been walking in it since he awoke from the car crash.

Turning around again to keep heading away from the crows, he spotted a faint light to the left. Trevor sprinted towards it, hoping for his first signs of human life. Seeing the sign 'Café 7to5' on the roof of the building, he made for the large glass windows that emitted the light from within.

He knocked on the glass frame, hoping to catch someone's attention. Smudging his face against the pane, he looked inside. Despite the light being on, there was clearly no one inside the public area or behind the counter, which would have served the patrons. At the right end of the counter, he saw something circular drawn in red on the wall. It looked like dried blood.

Trevor tried the door and found it locked. Whirling around, he looked for anything to smash the windows with. At the base of the closest tree, he saw a large round stone, big enough to throw with enough momentum. He rushed to pick it up and aimed it at the window.

Trevor.

His arm remained still above his shoulder. He looked back to the road in the direction of the crows. He could have sworn that he had heard Kathy's voice. Keeping the stone in his hand, the fingers barely reaching each other over its bulk, he moved slowly towards the crows.

Trevor...

There it was again. This time Trevor was sure it was her. He saw a shape in the mist, and it bolted away from him. Trevor impulsively ran towards it. He saw the trees with the crows looming ahead of him and made sure to stay away from them.

He reached Kingsley Street and looked left down the road. It was quiet again, except for some squawks from one or two crows. He moved down Kingsley, keeping an eye on both sides of the road for any sign of the mysterious figure. He spotted several benches on the pavements and some more trees, but the figure had vanished.

Trevor stopped as an alley appeared between two buildings. It looked dark and foreboding, and he was about to move away from it when a trail of blood running down the side of a building in the alley caught his eye. Inspecting the trail further, it looked like someone had run their bloody fingertips along the wall down its length into the darkness.

A large feminine cry rang out into the mist from the alley, causing Trevor to run into it with abandon. The mist seemed to vanish, replaced by the smothering darkness, as he followed the alley with the little light that was left. Another cry made him hasten his pace, with the darkness now seeming to choke the air out of his throat. The more he moved into the alley, the more the grip appeared to hold around his neck, making him cough and splutter as he rushed to get to Kathy.

The pathway ended, and he knocked his knee into the corner of a brick wall. He cried out, falling down to his other knee. He hardly had time to deal with the pain when he heard a soft, wailing noise. As his head spun from the aching throb in his knee, he looked around in the darkness, trying to spot its source.

Trevor reached into his pocket for his phone, removing it and waking its light. He shone it into the alley around him, moving it around and back again as the wailing noise seemed to get closer. It sounded very much like a baby crying softly, but there was maleficence to it too. He wasn't too sure if it was wailing or laughing darkly anymore.

Then he saw it. It was crawling slowly towards him. At first, everything about it appeared normal, besides the fact that it wasn't wearing any clothes. Its eyes shone white in the wan light of his phone. The baby halted its crawl and then lifted its upper body up, its arm reaching towards something above it.

Trevor lifted the phone up in trepidation. As the light moved up the baby's arms and past the fingers, it revealed shoes and then legs suspended in the air. He moved his back into the corner more snuggly, hoping it would somehow protect him. The phone's light revealed a blue skirt covering the waist of the person above him and then the slim uncovered belly.

He moved over the torso, covered by a loose green top, and lit the face. The woman's dead eyes stared in his direction, the blood around her mouth having dried already. It took him a moment to realise that she had a noose around her neck and was suspended from the brick slab above them.

When the phone's light caught the floor, Trevor stood up in a panic, ready to run back out of the alley. It was now filled with babies blocking his path, but something was intensely wrong with them. Their expressions had warped into demonic faces with fangs protruding from under their lips. Their fingers had long claws jutting over the floor as they all crawled towards him.

Without thinking, he lifted his hand to throw the stone towards them when he realised he no longer held it. He bent down to feel for it on the ground, but it was nowhere to be found. He looked at the babies again just as they jumped up at him and started devouring his neck, arms and legs, Trevor's cry being the one to fill the alley now…

2

SAVING GRACE

Trevor woke up with a start, bolting upright from his seat. The light glared into his eyes, and he recovered for a moment. Rubbing his eyes, he slowly opened them and took in his surroundings.

He recalled this place. The wooden counter stretched from the wall on the right across the length of the building, with the serving area behind it. Wooden tables littered the seating area around him, with the odd assortments having been abandoned long ago.

Following the line of bar stools at the counter, he saw a pinball machine at the end of the right wall. A service hatch on that side of the counter also seemed to lead into a hidden kitchen area at the back.

A red-painted image on the wall above the serving hatch helped him recall where he had seen the building. Trevor was unsure if he had been dreaming before, but he had seen the same symbol on the wall when he stood outside Café 7to5, banging on the windows.

He felt older than he was and aching in every joint as he moved closer to the symbol. It had two concentric circles on the outer perimeter and three smaller circles in the centre; two below and one above. Within the outer concentric symbols were ancient letters that looked like a cross between the Hungarian and Norse alphabets.

These letters were divided by an eye at the top, what seemed like justice scales to the left, an object with a trident at the bottom and a strange symbol on the right that he could not identify. Trevor also noticed that the Hungarian letters had been mirrored and not facing the right direction.

There were other small images around the inner circles. Still, it was the

Hungarian rovásírás that Trevor was the most familiar with. If there was one thing that Caroline loved about him, it was his passion for ancient mythology and languages. She had, of course, leaned towards ancient philosophy more but could not help but indulge in his tales of mythological places and creatures.

Trevor traced his fingers on the four mirrored Hungarian words.

"It's a cult symbol," a female voice said suddenly, making Trevor spin around and fall against the pinball machine. He pushed himself up in an upright position again, his heart pounding in his chest.

"Sorry," he apologised sheepishly. "I didn't know I had any company."

She smiled in acceptance of his explanation. She was standing behind the counter, on the darker left-hand side at the other end. As she moved towards him, he saw short blond hair barely touching her shoulders and magnificent green eyes shining brighter than the wan light in the café should have allowed.

Her pale skin was complemented by a light yellow jersey that was tight enough on her upper body to reveal her medium-sized breasts but not sufficient to show the size of her belly. Trevor could just make out her curvy waist over the edge of the counter, which was covered by blue jeans and a brown belt.

"That is called the Holdközépont, or Lunar Nexus roughly translated," she explained, nodding towards the red symbol on the wall. "It's not the only symbol of its kind here in Sacred Valley."

"Where does it come from?" he asked, turning to look at it again. "What does it mean?"

"It's derived from some cult that once existed here," she explained, "in the early days of Sacred Valley. The group believed it had some mystical power, although I dare to think that if it existed, the power would have long gone."

"What kind of power?"

"Well, the two outer circles are supposed to represent resurrection, and the three inner circles are the present, past and future. It has some mystical connection to the moon. I've read somewhere, though, that it should never be drawn in blue or black."

Trevor looked suspiciously at her for a moment. Now he wondered not only where she had come from but also how she knew so much about the symbol.

"Were you a member of that cult?" he asked carefully, sitting on a bar stool.

"The Twilight Covenant?" she replied, snorting in laughter after that. "Oh, heavens no. Although I am intrigued by them. It's part of my reason for being here. I've been studying this mystical town since its fall, ever since they abandoned it to the fires that still burn beneath it. The cultures that stayed behind, the religious beliefs…I'm very much into it all."

"I'm all for studies into the mystical and mythological," Trevor acknowledged but still watched her sceptically. He had little interest in the town's history then, though. "Do you know what the four names in the circle mean?"

"I can only guess that the power of the Lunar Nexus was the magick invoked onto the four people whose names are within it," she replied, sighing softly. "I'm afraid there are still too many mysteries to solve."

Leaving the last words lingering on her lips, she looked at Trevor intensely as if they were to have some importance to him. It made him uneasy, so he returned to the symbol and placed his right palm on it.

"Well, whatever power it had before definitely seems gone now," he told her, returning to the counter. "I don't even feel a tingle."

"You never told me what you're doing here," she said as he remained standing on his side of the counter. "I haven't seen someone roam these streets in years."

"It's a bit complicated," he replied, avoiding her gaze.

"I'm sure you can dumb it down for me," she smiled, leaning forward onto the counter. He couldn't help but notice how her breasts pressed on the wooden surface and blushed when he realised she had caught his observation.

"I guess, if I had to use the symbol's philosophy," he replied, looking back at the sigil, "then I could say that my past has come back to haunt my present, and I'm here to find the answers that will determine my future."

"Ooooh, very cryptic," she said appreciatively. "You seem like a very intelligent man. One would think smart enough to stay away from here. Mr....?"

"Trevor," he answered. "My name is Trevor."

"Nice to meet you. Jeanette."

He looked into her eyes for a moment, taking in the beauty that was hidden at face value. She had some light freckles over the bridge of her nose and cheeks, which could only be spotted with keen observation. Her fingers were small and thin, now wrapped between each other as she clasped her hands on the counter.

"Jeanette, have you seen any creatures on the streets?"

"Why? Are you going back out there?" she asked incredulously.

"I came here with two others," he said, revealing his immediate goal. "I need to find them."

"I've heard some strange noises recently," she replied, nodding in thought. "The town has pretty much been asleep until you arrived. I was about to make my way back to the church when I found you lying inside here."

"You never saw any crazy demonic children crawling around, did you?"

"Come again?" Jeanette asked slowly.

"Don't worry," he replied, looking towards the street. "Ever since I got here, it's felt like I've lost my mind. You mentioned a church?"

"Yeah," she said, reaching for the back of her pants pocket. She unfolded a street map onto the countertop. Trevor realised by the title at the top that it was a map of Sacred Valley.

"This is where we are," she informed him, pointing at a spot on

Hawthorne Avenue. Then she moved her finger down to the corner of Hartley Street and Hawthorne. "That's the church. I stay there mostly. You know, feeling safe on holy ground and stuff."

Trevor reached for the map, but she pulled it away from him. She folded it back up and returned it to her pocket. Reaching under her side of the counter, she pulled another one and handed it to him.

"I'm sorry, but maps are hard to find," she informed him. "You better hold onto it. Otherwise, you might get lost."

"I'm pretty good with directions," he told her proudly, tapping his head. "This memory has not failed me yet."

"Oh, you cute little man," she replied tartly. "You have so much to learn still."

"What do you mean?"

Her response was interrupted suddenly by a loud banging on the entrance windows. Trevor whirled around, almost falling off his seat. A large man clad in bulky clothes was hitting his fist against the window while looking over his shoulder at the street.

"Jay!" Trevor shouted and ran for the door. He clipped the handle with the side of his hand, but it would not open. Trevor looked up and saw a latch on the side and a bolt on the top frame of the door. He quickly released them and let Jay enter, shutting the door just as hastily behind him.

Jay had collapsed to the floor as soon as he had entered the café. Clearly, he was out of breath and had no strength left to stand. Trevor reached down and helped him up, taking him to one of the sofa seats by the window closest to the pinball machine.

Jay's police uniform was dirty. Trevor could almost not read the label that said "J. Nixon" on it. His bulky form was more from his muscular weight than the bulletproof vest hidden under his jacket. His black bald head glistened with sweat as his chest rasped for air. Jay coughed to clear some phlegm that had entered his throat.

Trevor turned to the counter to ask Jeanette to get some water, but she had vanished. The counter was desolate, not one semblance of her former presence as evidence of his sanity. Having no recourse to any aid, he jumped over the counter, ignoring the service hatch, and looked around for water. The access to the kitchen was bolted closed from the other side, so he hastily searched under the counter on the shelves.

He soon found a small brown bottle with a white label and a green cross. Searching around the bottle, he saw a small inscription that identified it as the property of the Ashenfall Hospital. At the back of the bottle, he saw bloody fingerprints, and from the look of it, Trevor could tell it was fresh.

Not wasting any further time, Trevor rose over the counter again and returned to his fallen friend. He turned Jay's face up, popped the bottle lid open, and drained the liquid down Jay's throat, making sure not to drown him.

Jay coughed a bit more and then cleaned his mouth with the back of his hand. He looked up at Trevor with blinking eyes until his sight cleared up again.

"What the hell was that?" Jay asked, sitting up as he regained his strength.

"I'm not sure," Trevor responded, looking at the empty bottle. "It seems to pass as medicine here."

"Well, whatever it is, it gives one hell of a regenerative boost," Jay said. "I feel better than when I woke up in this haunted town."

"Hey, how come you never waited for me?" Trevor asked suddenly. "Or woke me from my car?"

"I would have if I knew where the hell you were, Trev," Jay responded as they stood up. "Or me, actually. Before the accident, we were riding up the hill. After I woke up, I was lying in an alley. I have no idea how I got there."

"You me both," Trevor replied, scratching his head. "What were you running from?"

"Something is flapping around out there, man," Jay responded, his eyes widening as he remembered what waited outside.

"You're afraid of birds?" Trevor asked for his own amusement.

"It's not a bird," Jay responded. "There's something wrong with it... with how it sounds."

"Why? How does it sound?"

"Geez, how do I explain this?" Jay said, pulling a handkerchief from his jacket and rubbing the moisture from his face and head. "I'm unsure if it sounds like a demon or a child crying."

Trevor stepped back, his mouth opening in fear, any further words stuck in his throat. His back hit the counter, and he looked up at the Lunar Nexus. The lines were no longer dormant on the wall but now had a soft glow that pulsed to the beat of some invisible heart.

"What's that?" Jay asked, pointing at the symbol. "What the fuck have we stumbled into, Trev? Some satanic ghost town?"

"You know I don't like it when you swear," Trevor reminded him.

"Sorry, man," Jay replied, raising a palm in apology. "I'm scared shi..... out of my wits. And this is definitely not the Sacred Valley I remember."

Trevor looked at the glowing symbol some more, feeling rather hypnotised by the soft pulse. For some reason, he felt compelled to place his hand on the centre of the sign.

"Trev," Jay said, watching him as the hand drew closer to the epitaph. "Trev, man, what are you doing? That thing looks evil."

Ignoring him, Trevor moved his hand even closer. His breathing had become deep and long, and he felt like he was meditating. When the skin of his hand touched the wall, a strange language entered his head, and his vision went red. He could not release the wall, or it would not release him. He could feel his blood boil inside him, and his veins swell as if his very life was being squeezed out of them.

And then he calmed down. Trevor felt a supernatural energy fill him. He no longer felt sore or in pain, and his joints felt less stiff than before. As his sight returned to him, his hand still on the wall, he stepped back and felt the new energy coursing through him.

"Are you ok?" Jay asked slowly, walking up to him.

"Yeah," Trevor replied. "Actually, I feel great. I can't remember the last time I felt this strong. Ever since...."

He went quiet. Jay did not have to guess what he was about to say. Ever since Caroline's suicide, Trevor had been a different man, as if a part of him had been stolen. Yet now, Jay could see a glint of his old self returning.

"Give it a go," Trevor offered.

Jay walked to the Lunar Nexus, switching glances between it and Trevor. He raised his hand carefully while Trevor observed the Lunar Nexus with renewed interest. He saw a change in the symbol, one that he had missed before. The four Hungarian inscriptions of the names he did not know had vanished.

Not only had they vanished, Trevor realised just before Jay's hand reached the wall, but the one on the top left had been replaced with a mirrored version of his own name: ꓬH3MƆH.

"Jay, no, wait!" Trevor shouted and bolted for him.

It was too late. Jay's hand touched the Lunar Nexus just as Trevor reached him. Trevor grabbed his arm, which sent a jolt of electrical energy through Jay into Trevor. Trevor soared backwards through the air like a man jolted by an electrical fence and crashed into the opposite wall.

Regaining his senses, Trevor stood up and watched as Jay released his hand, looking like he had the stature and strength of a hundred men. Trevor could tell that Jay felt the same energy coursing through his veins and rushed to look at the Lunar Nexus. It had a new inscription at the bottom left: 14ΛƆƆ.

"What's wrong?" Jay asked, looking at the new name with him.

"You see those words?" Trevor replied, pointing to each. "It says 'Trevor' and 'Jason'."

"Is that a good or a bad thing?" Jay asked.

"I'm sure we'll find out soon enough," Trevor replied. He studied it once more, frowning deeply as he did so.

"Ok, man, you gotta stop with the cryptic expressions," Jay said, frustrated.

"Sorry, Jay, I'm just puzzled," he said, turning away. "I could have sworn the previous names were written clockwise in the circle, but our names are appearing anti-clockwise."

"Look, I don't know about you, but I suggest we spend less time studying ancient hieroglyphs…."

"Hungarian…"

"…and devise a way out of this joint. Ya feel me? We have to get the hell out of here."

"I can't leave without Kathy," Trevor declared.

"Of course not," Jay sighed. "So what should we do?"

"Kathy mentioned to me in the car that she went to a school here in Sacred Valley," Trevor said, thinking aloud. "If I'm guessing right, she would have gone somewhere familiar, possibly where she would feel safe. Our best bet is that she's at the school."

"Ok, but first things first," Jay interrupted as Trevor reached for the map Jeanette had given him. "We gotta head to our cars, man. My weapons and supplies are there. We might need it."

"Yeah, I think I left my bag in the car, too," Trevor agreed. "After that, the school."

"Indeed," Jay said. "Do you have another one of those maps?"

"No, I think this was the last one," Trevor replied quickly. "You can check behind the counter, though."

While Jay went around the counter through the service hatch, Trevor inspected the front door. He tried to pierce the mist with his sight, but it was still too thick to even see the road past the pavement. Soon enough, Jay was at his side again, not having found any maps.

"You ready?" Trevor asked more to himself than his friend.

"I don't think so, but let's just do it," Jay replied, wringing his hands together in anticipation. Trevor opened the door, and they headed out.

The streets were as silent. The mist fell languidly from the sky and had not lessened in density. They could still hardly see in front of them. As Trevor moved forward, he just made out the end of the pavement and, after that, the street.

Their steps echoed dully on the pavement while crunching on the soil where tree roots had lifted the pavement slabs off. They moved back up Hawthorne towards Kingsley, Trevor keeping an eye out for the opposite side of the road despite being unable to see it. He recalled the nightmare he had had vividly now and waited for the sound of crows.

He only heard the soft rustling of leaves in the slight breeze that pervaded the air and their feet clopping along the pavement slabs. Trevor wished they had found some weapon in the café that they could have used on the way back to the cars. He thought to keep a lookout along the shop walls for any item that could be used.

He had hardly glanced to his right when he saw another medicinal bottle by the closest building. It was lying on the outer sill of a window that had been boarded up with planks on the inside. He moved towards it and placed it in the front jeans pocket.

Jay kept looking cautiously around as Trevor re-joined him, and they moved forward again. They had reached the intersection of Kingsley and Hawthorne when the sound they had feared finally arose. The flapping wings were distant, but there was no mistaking their approach.

"That's odd," Trevor said quietly.

"What is?" Jay asked.

"I had a dream about walking these streets earlier," Trevor explained. "In the dream, the crows were flying away and leading me towards something, though."

"Ok," Jay said, standing still and watching toward the sound. "And so?"

"Well, now they're coming towards us."

"What do you think it means?"

"I have no idea," Trevor replied, awaiting the crow's appearance.

As it got closer, they could hear the flutter of more wings. It became clear that it was not just one but a murder of crows. As the sound augmented into a fluttering chorus, the first group appeared like a dark cloud before them. Trevor instinctively raised his hand defensively, stepping backwards down Kingsley, and then gaped in utter shock as they transformed.

Their small bodies gurgled outwards in mid-flight as their new chubby forms broke out. The feathers flew off their bodies to join the falling ash as the skin of the falling babies pushed further out. Trevor was about to scream for Jay to run when their mouths revealed sharp fangs, and their nails became hardened claws.

Jay needed no motivation and attempted to run toward their vehicles further up Hawthorne. He had hardly reached the middle of the intersection when the next wave of crows accosted him. The crows transformed into babies and fell with rabid teeth on his face and arms, making the officer fall. His bulk banged hard on the floor with a thud while he writhed under the demonic toddlers.

Trevor opted to run back to the café, knowing full well that there was nothing he could do to save Jay. He ignored the subconscious thought that he was being a coward just as much as he ignored the babies that fell past his head and landed on the pavement behind him. He felt a small wave of relief when he saw the path back was clear just before another cloud of darkness washed between him and Café 7to5.

There was nowhere to go. The wailing babies were behind him, with crows soaring before him and from the street on the right. He had buildings to his left. His fear choked and paralysed him, making him unable to lift his hands up to protect himself. The crows before him became falling babies with long fangs that bit into his neck and arms...

2: Saving Grace

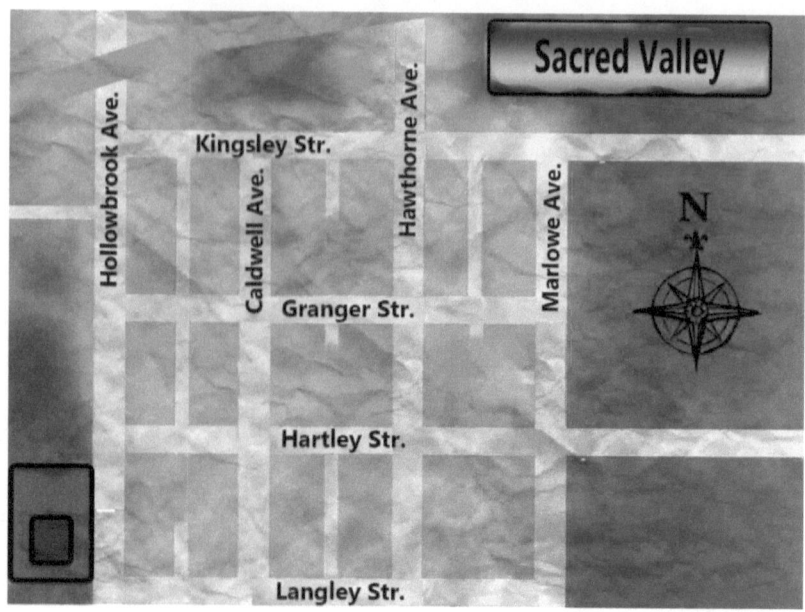

3

MYSTERIES IN THE MIST

Trevor opened his eyes slowly. He used his elbows against the floor to push himself up and then into a sitting position. Jay was lying unconscious against the counter on the floor to his right, and to his left was a pinball machine. When his sight adjusted and his senses returned, he realised they were back in Café 7to5.

From his seated position, he turned his head around and up, fixing his gaze on the glowing Lunar Nexus above them. It was still pulsing as before, with their names blazing with soft fires within the outer circles. The letters became embers of red ink as the fire died down, eventually dying down to its original form; mere writing on the wall with a soft glow.

Jay stirred and looked up at Trevor before surveying the area around them. He joined Trevor in sitting up and rubbed his eyes. Trevor examined him. Where blood, wounds and gashes should have been from the attack, his body looked fresh and untouched. He inspected his own body and realised it was the same. It was as if they had never ventured outside in the first place.

"What happened?" Jay asked sleepily, inspecting his own body for wounds too. "How did we get back here?"

"I don't know," Trevor replied, looking up at the Lunar Nexus again. "Jeanette mentioned something about that insignia having to do with resurrection."

"Who's Jeanette?" Jay asked.

"Some cult researcher I met in this café before you arrived," Trevor indicated. "I think you scared her off."

"Was she hot?" Jay smirked. It made Trevor smile, which in turn lightened the tension and confusion in his head.

Trevor realised his jeans were uncomfortable in the seated position and stood up. He felt inside his jeans pocket and retrieved the health bottle he had found on the streets before the demonic attack. Jay jumped up in shock.

"That can't be, man," Jay said, pointing at the bottle. "You found that thing outside there after we had left the café already."

"I know," Trevor said, placing the bottle back in his pocket. "None of this makes sense, trust me."

"Ok, so what do we do now? We need our bags. I need my gun."

"Well, I…."

Trevor's eyes caught the kitchen door over Jay's shoulder. He moved towards the counter to ensure his eyes were not deceiving him. Jay followed his gaze and joined him in staring at the door.

"What's wrong?" Jay asked.

"When you burst in here before, I had tried that kitchen door to look for something to help you. Some first aid kit or something. It was locked."

The door now stood slightly ajar. Trevor lifted the service hatch and moved towards it. As he opened it further, the timber creaked on the hinges, letting Trevor walk into the dark kitchen. He saw the light switch to the right and flicked it but to no avail.

The light from the dining area behind them helped Trevor at least see where he was walking. There was a large counter in the centre of the room, with cupboards suspended from the ceiling corners around the perimeter walls of the kitchen. On the door's opposing wall was a stove that looked like it had been unused for years, with a counter that ran the length of the wall on either side. An old frier lay dormant next to the stove with mature oil inside.

On the door's wall, another counter with three deep wash basins was at the far end. Where they ended, there were sets of drawers and cupboards along the floor all the way up to Trevor. They set about searching the drawers and cupboards, hoping to find something they could use against the beasts in the mist.

After searching in the darkness, Jay found a carving knife in a drawer next to the closest basin. The entire length of it was made of stainless steel, even the handle. He took it out and moved to the door to inspect it in the light. There were cuts along the edge that had rusted slightly, but it was still sharp. He sucked the wound on the fingertip he had tested it on.

"Any luck?" Jay asked Trevor, who was inspecting the plumbing by the basins after having failed to find anything along the stove's wall and the suspended cupboards. All they contained was food that had a living ecosystem of fungi residing over it.

He tested one of the copper pipes near the further basin and found a loose one. He pulled and tugged, trying different angles before finally kicking it loose. He tested the pipe's weight and balance, which was the length of his arm from wrist to shoulder. It felt heavy enough to do some serious damage.

"Let's go," he said, joining Jay as they left the kitchen and feeling his back pocket to make sure the map was still there. The medicinal bottle remained in his left front pocket, and his cellphone in the right.

They passed the Lunar Nexus on the wall and made for the door. Trevor opened it more cautiously than before, listening for the sound of fluttering wings or wailing babies. It felt like forever before they ventured out onto the pavement.

"Is there no other way?" Jay asked.

Trevor pulled out the map, and they studied it. The end of Hawthorne Avenue, where the cars were, could only be accessed through the Kingsley intersection. He placed the map back and held the copper pipe in a ready position. As he moved towards Kingsley, Jay lifted the knife up too.

The misty streets were as silent as before. Trevor saw the window sill where he had acquired the health bottle before, but it was empty now. It took them longer than before to get to the intersection, always keeping their ears and eyes open for their former attackers. When they reached the place where they had fallen, they found a bare pavement.

Jay moved to the road and knelt where he had been attacked. He inspected the fresh blood stains on the tarred surface and felt the liquid with his fingers. It was still relatively warm.

"This place is fucked up," Jay said, standing to see a glaring Trevor. "Sorry, man."

"Maybe if you spend more time trying and less time cursing," Trevor offered, looking around again.

There was no sign of the birds or babies. No clouds of darkness tainted the mists that surrounded them. Once again, the rustling of leaves was the most they could make out in the abandoned town.

Trevor wasted no more time surveying the streets. He moved forward on Hawthorne. He spotted the convenience store to their right but ignored it, anxious to return to their vehicles.

After some time, they finally made it back to the accident scene with no fatal events or attacks. Trevor made for his car while Jay ran for the police vehicle. Jay easily accessed the car's boot, where his bags and weapons were, but Trevor had difficulty climbing over the top of the car to get to his duffel bag in the back seat.

"Would you like a baton to replace that pipe?" Jay asked as they met between the vehicles, placing their bags on the road.

"Nah, keep it for now," Trevor replied, swinging the pipe to and fro. "I have a feeling this pipe might really hurt something."

"Alright then," Jay replied, frowning in doubt and placing the baton back in his bag. "Listen, I've only got one pistol, but here are some other fun toys for you."

Jay clipped a new mag into his Ruger LC9 pistol and then holstered it on his hip. Kneeling down, he dug into his bag and pulled out some items, which he threw to Trevor. The first was a long black torch with a wide lens. Trevor tested it, noticing how the strong light managed to penetrate the mist quite well. From where they were, he could just make out Jay's name on the side of the police vehicle.

The next items were two police-issued two-way radios, one of which Jay strapped to his belt. This was accompanied by two sets of batteries for Trevor, which he slipped into a side compartment of his bag. Jay ran his hand through the bag some more and, being at a loss as to what else he could pass on, simply zipped the bag up and strapped it on his back over his shoulders.

"That's it?" Trevor asked, wondering what else was in the bag.

"Yeah, sorry, man," Jay apologised. "When I called you to get out of the apartment, the last thing I could have prepared for was a haunted town with strange monsters in it."

"Fair enough," Trevor replied. "Ok, let's head back in. We need to find Kathy and get out of here."

Trevor and Jay were closing in on the Kingsley and Hawthorne intersection again. Trevor had wanted to use the torch, but Jay had advised against it for the time being and encouraged saving batteries. As they got closer to the intersection, Trevor raised his pipe, and Jay unclipped his pistol before lifting the knife before him. Ammo was another resource he could not afford to waste, but he wanted easy access to his Ruger just in case.

Trevor halted his progress, looking at the hazy lights that shimmered in the mist to their left. Without uttering a word, he walked towards it with Jay following him. The convenience store had reinforced glass windows along the Hawthorne and Kingsley lengths on either side. Trevor was sure they would have some difficulty breaking in. Fortunately, as they tested the old double doors, he discovered they wouldn't have to.

The mist had not entered the store, and Trevor felt relief in his eyes with the light that enabled them to see clearly inside. He lowered the pipe in his hand and passed through the turnstiles in line with the tills on his left. He felt excited as he entered the aisles of shelves containing the shop's products and sighed when he realised that his exhilaration was premature.

As with the food in the Café's kitchen, most of the shop's products had expired. Jay investigated the tin food and noticed that their usefulness had passed too. Trevor watched as Jay lingered by the tins, wondering if the officer actually considered taking a chance to eat it anyway.

Leaving Jay to find his own equipment, Trevor investigated the medicine aisle. Most of the items had been sold or trashed, but he found a first aid kit on a lower shelf. After placing it in his bag, he spotted a small long syringe with some liquid. The needle was covered with a plastic cap, and a white label on its side stated that it was a medicinal ampoule. It joined the kit in his bag.

Trevor looked for an aisle with D-I-Y items for any tools or weapons, but he realised that this was a small store and only stocked the basic items. Jay soon joined him with gasoline tins in his hands.

"What on earth would you need those for?" Trevor asked as Jay placed them in his bag and strapped it on his back again.

"You never know," Jay replied. "Fuel always comes in handy, even if it means we get to burn those fuc..... monsters."

Trevor understood the logic. He moved to one of the tills, pulled the map out, and placed it on the till counter. Jay joined him in studying it as Trevor tried to find the best route to Hollowbrook Elementary School.

"We could just go back down Hawthorne until about Hartley and then to Hollowbrook Avenue," Jay offered.

"Yeah, I was thinking the same thing," Trevor replied. "There's something in Kingsley I want to show you, though. So maybe we could head down Kingsley to Hollowbrook and then straight down to the school."

"That can work, too," Jay replied. "Can you see if there's a police station anywhere?"

Trevor studied the map while Jay looked at the entrance doors. He looked for any large buildings marked as a police station and then looked at smaller buildings. He spotted the Sacred Grove Church, which reminded him of Jeanette, before looking up at Jay.

"No, nothing. But there are two bridges that head somewhere off this map, maybe to another part of Sacred Valley. It could be that side."

Jay moved to the map and looked at the indicated bridges.

"Yes, you're right," Jay said, pointing at the lower bridge off Hartley Street. "If I remember correctly from the guys in Ashbourne and Dunst that used to be sent out here occasionally, the police station is just off that road. There's also a small hospital out there."

"Ashenfall Hospital?" Trevor asked.

"Yes, I think so," Jay nodded in response. "You're not thinking of heading out that way, are you?"

"If Kathy isn't at the school, she would be at the hospital. She told me once that Phillip had been transferred there from the hospital in Dunst."

"Shouldn't that be our first target, then?"

"Hollowbrook Elementary is closer," Trevor said after considering the options. "We will save ourselves a lot of time if she is at the school and not the hospital. With those creatures roaming the streets, she would want to get to safety as soon as possible."

"Alright, then we stick to the school," Jay agreed.

Trevor looked down at his right hip as the two-way radio started crackling. Jay's radio also sang into chorus, leaving them to fiddle with the frequency and volume knobs in an effort to find the cause. No amount of tinkering altered the sound that emanated from the radios.

They both jerked their heads to the door as it rustled. Something was banging against it. Jay immediately raised his knife just as Trevor lifted the pipe. The rattling on the glass door grew louder as the object banged against the reinforced surface, and then suddenly, it went quiet.

Deciding not to waste time waiting, they moved towards the entrance doors. They saw blood smeared on the outer glass surface, but the creature that had caused it was nowhere to be seen. Trevor reached for the handle of one of the doors when one of the glass windows closest to the till they had been standing by abruptly smashed inwards.

There were two crows with bloody faces. Despite their aviary forms, they wailed like the demonic babies Trevor expected they would turn into. The birds searched the area until they spotted their quarries. They flew in the men's direction, their squawks and toddler cries echoing sickly through the shop. The closer they got, the more the radios on their hips screeched.

Where Trevor felt frozen again by fear, Jay ran forward to attack. He wielded his knife above his shoulders, shouting out what sounded like a war cry to intimidate the beasts. As the first crow fell upon him, he slashed the air and cut at the wings and neck. The knife struck its mark, making the bird fall to the floor, crying out in pain and transforming into a baby.

Jay was focussing on the second bird as Trevor came to his senses. He ran to the fallen creature, watching as it struggled to change. It still had feathery wings and body, but the head was that of the baby. As Trevor lifted the pipe above his head, it scowled up at him in pain.

The pipe remained there. He just could not bring himself to smash a baby's face. Trevor wondered if it would have been easier if the baby had shown its demonic side. Still, the face only showed normal gums in its mouth and no wicked eyes.

The crow appeared to regain its energy. Having failed to transform into a baby, it returned its head to that of a crow. It was about to jump back on its feet when Trevor brought the pipe crashing down, smashing into the bird's skull. Feeling the adrenaline and exhilaration pumping through his body, he kept pounding it again and again until the bird lay crushed on the floor with the blood seeping over the tiles.

He turned to see that Jay had also dispatched the other crow to its death. The radios had fallen to silence, hanging dormant on their hips once again. Checking out the window to see if any more were approaching, he quickly signalled with his free hand that they head for the doors.

They were out in the mist heading for the intersection again. Jay followed Trevor's lead as he passed the Hawthorne threshold into Kingsley proper. Trevor moved with trepidation towards the alley he had entered in his nightmare, with Jay following in curiosity.

Trevor found the buildings on the left pavement, hugging the walls so that at least one of the sides was eliminated from risk. They kept an eye out for more crows, hearing a flutter here and there before the sound vanished again into the dense mist.

"I don't suppose you'd venture a guess as to where those crows are coming from," Jay asked quietly, "or why they're here?"

"I have no idea," Trevor responded. "But they remind me of a legend I once heard about."

"Well, would you care to share?" Jay asked when he realised Trevor had stopped moving.

Trevor was standing at the point where the alley led off from the pavement between the buildings. He quickly peeked around the musty corner of a building to look into it. Not only was the mist hampering the view, but the alley's darkness was not helping much either. It was almost as if light refused to enter it.

He pulled the torch off the belt on his left hip and flicked it on, shining it down the alley's length. The darkness appeared denser than the mist, and the torch only broke a portion of it just ahead of him. Feeling more secure that he would at least see what he would be walking on, he headed in with the pipe raised again.

Jay followed without question. Trevor heard some rustling, a clipping sound, and a gun cocked. It made Trevor feel insecure about his protection in comparison. However, he needed to see if the body was still hanging at the end of the alley.

It followed the same route as before, except he could see less than his dream had permitted. The building walls were hidden from his view as the torchlight focussed ahead of them. Trevor heard another click and spared a moment to look back. Jay had also unclipped his torch and was walking backwards behind Trevor, using the torch to spot any trouble following them.

Jay bumped into Trevor when he came to the end of the alley. Too afraid to look up at first, Trevor shone his torch around the corners, watching for any signs of the demonic babies. There were none, nor any signs of blood or violence. Resigning himself to his initial reason for entering the alley, he moved the torch up.

Despite his expectations, the sight of the hanging noose still made his throat constrict in fear. He swallowed hard, inspecting the rope that dangled from the overhead slab. It had blood smeared on it, but no body. Where he had seen the corpse before was simply a paper rolled in the centre of the noose.

Trevor used his pipe to strike the rope and dislodge it. He reached up and caught it while Jay switched glances between him and the alley. Trevor turned his torch to paper and saw an advert for 'The Charming Petstore' with images of various animals. Trevor initially assumed that these were the animals the store possibly sold until he realised it could not be.

The butterflies drawn around the name of the store he could still accept, but a pet store that sold a bear was rather harder to fathom. Hearts were drawn at the upper right corner, with the largest having an arrow through its centre.

His cursory study of the advert was cut short by the radios crackling again. Trevor hastily stowed the pamphlet in the same section of his bag where he had placed the red Sacred Valley page from his mailbox. Both of them shone their torches back up their alley, pipe and gun raised.

The crackling grew louder on the radios, causing Trevor's spine to chill and his heart to race at the same time. His hand clutched the pipe so hard that the copper bit into his palm. He looked at Jay for a moment, who seemed to have the composure of a rock: steadfast and strong. He did not seem swayed by the noise, but Trevor reached down to switch his radio off, becoming more unnerved by it the louder the noise rose.

Jay's radio continued to scream when they saw movement ahead. It was low down on the ground, and for a moment, Trevor thought it was a demonic baby. As the creature moved closer, he realised just how wrong he was. The sight of it made him lower his pipe, the ghastly image making him take a step or two back.

A quick glance would have fooled anyone that it was merely a shaggy dog. Its fur was drenched as if the mist had washed it with its foulness. Jay's torch revealed the nauseating brown of decayed blood with the matted fur trailing down two of its legs, the front left and rear right. The other two legs had no fur at all, though. The skin was pinkish flesh, leading to the initial illusion that the fur had simply been removed.

Parts of the hound's fur had been scorched by fire, and where the bitter lesions were exposed, the tissue and flesh bulged out in small diseased mounds. Minute rivulets of blood and pus flowed over the mounds and back into its body, ensuring that none of the precious fluid was lost.

Trevor dropped the pipe, the clank on the ground making the hound raise his head and growl at them. The ends of those furless legs did not end in paws. The front fleshy leg had a human hand at the end of it, and the rear had a human foot. Instead of a knee joint, the front arm had an elbow.

Jay started shooting as the hound ran for them. Trevor watched as Jay missed the first two shots, but the three that followed hit the mark. The hound cried out in pain, falling against the wall to their left. The beast closed its eyes momentarily, but the matted fur shifted at the places where it had been shot. It seemed like the flesh underneath it was rolling around until the bullets fell onto the floor beside the beast.

It stood up again. Jay lowered his gun, watched incredulously as it growled again, and ran towards them in a disturbing limp. He offloaded bullets again, Trevor finally backing into the end of the alley as the hound jumped on Jay's chest and made him fall onto the bag on his back. The gun fell out of his hand towards Trevor's feet just as Jay reached for the pipe and held it against the beast's neck.

It was yapping at his face, the foul teeth inches away from biting a huge hole in it. Jay struggled against its unearthly strength, his bulky muscles no match. Its fur was leaving red stains on his uniform as he tried to move his feet to attempt to kick it off him. The hound's human hand was strangling Jay's throat.

Shots rang through the alley, and the hound looked back towards the street. Trevor stood with the gun raised, waiting to see if his shots had had any effect. The only noticeable impact it had was to anger the beast further. It ran towards Trevor, allowing Jay to stand up and chase it. Trevor aimed again, grappling between fear and survival, his hand shaking the pistol and disorientating his sight.

He knew Jay would not make it in time. The hound was almost upon him, and Jay was still too far behind with no matching pace. Trevor gulped as he stepped back again, his feet catching each other as he tripped to the floor and onto his bag. The hound jumped up and pounced onto him with all fangs out.

Suddenly, it stopped moving and slumped down. Jay's radio went silent to join Jay's halting footsteps. Trevor's hands were both on the gun's grip, raised up into the hound's mouth. Its curdled blood was dripping down his hands and arms, but he was too stunned to move.

He had not heard the shot go off. Instinctively, as the beast had fallen on him, he had lifted the Ruger up and pulled the trigger just as its fangs fell over it. The bullet had torn through the back of its head, leaving it to drop dead over him.

Jay helped move the corpse. Trevor handed him the gun and accepted a hand to pull him up. He used the back of his loose checkered shirt to clean his hands and arms as much as he could, watching to make sure the hound didn't stand up again.

"Are you ok?" Jay asked, watching him in concern.

"Yeah, a bit shaken, but ok," Trevor replied.

"How much training do you actually have with a gun?" Jay asked, realising that it was one thing he did not know about his lifelong friend.

"That was my first time," Trevor acknowledged.

Jay looked down at the blood-stained pistol for a moment. He turned it over in his hand and pulled the magazine out, inspecting the amount of ammunition left in it. He tossed the spent mag aside and replaced it with a full one. He reversed his hold on the Ruger, handing it over to Trevor.

"What are you doing?" Trevor asked before accepting it.

"You need the practice," Jay responded, shaking the gun towards him. "I can manage without it since I've been trained in melee combat too."

"Not against monsters, though."

"Fair enough," Jay smiled. "But from what I've seen so far, you need it more than me. You'll love it, though. It's very compact and has a loading indicator, there by the chamber."

He took the Ruger, followed by the holster, strap and an extra box of ammunition that held ten rounds. Once he had attached the strap and holstered the pistol, taking his trusty copper pipe back in hand, they used the torches to find their way back out.

They were glad to have more light in the streets, even though the mist still didn't allow them to see very far. The torches were almost useless in its thickness this time, so they switched them off. As they progressed further down Kingsley, Trevor listened for any sound from his radio, becoming accustomed to it signalling the presence of anything evil or supernatural near them.

They spied the turn off into another street on their left. Trevor tried to remember the name, but his memory was a bit jaded with everything that had happened since the convenience store. As they progressed past it, he pulled the map from his back pocket and folded it open. The bare light through the mist was just enough for him to make out the words.

"Uhm, Trev," Jay said suddenly, Trevor walking while looking at the map. "You may want to see this."

Trevor pulled his studious gaze from the map to look ahead of them. They had just cleared Caldwell Avenue. He squinted into the fog, trying to determine whether the rest of the road was perhaps just hidden by its white mass. He reached up with his copper pipe and pushed it against his duffel back on his back until he found a slot he could slip it into. With both hands holding the map, he approached the edge of the tarmac.

Just as by the crashed vehicles, the road was broken. He could not see if the road continued on the other side of the gap, but the buildings on both sides of the road still continued on. Yet over the road's edge, it dropped down a cliff into a dark abyss. Trevor looked on either side and saw that they could not use the pavements to get across either.

Trevor left the pipe attached to the slot on his bag, enjoying having free hands for a change. He rubbed his right palm while they headed back to Caldwell, feeling the effects of gripping the weapon too hard. They cleared the road into Caldwell when Jay broke the silence.

"You said that those babies reminded you of a legend."

"Oh yes," Trevor replied. "I completely forgot."

"So what legend, man?"

"It's actually part of an ancient lore that I'd read about in a book somewhere, although I've never seen versions like these sick beasts," Trevor indicated. "There was a creature known as Tiyanak which haunted these villages on an island. It was said that they resembled babies at first and would lure victims out with their cries.

"Once the babies were found and held, they would reveal their vampiric or demonic forms and feed on their victims."

"How does that relate to these babies we have been facing, except for the demonic part?"

"They were also said to turn into crows from time to time to help them travel to their next feeding areas or to escape attacks."

"Ah, yes. That sounds more like them."

"That's not all, though," Trevor said, looking down at the ground. "That dog we faced. There is also a legend about a girl living in a village with her father. The village was very isolated, so the only men she could be suited with were the village's men. The girl refused to marry any of them, though."

"Ok," Jay said, confused, standing still to focus on the tale. "What does that have to do with the hounds?"

"One day, a canine came along that she believed was worthy of her love."

"Oh man, that's gross."

"Yes, well, she married the hound, and they had ten offspring. Half of them were pure canines like the father, but the other five became known as the original Adlets."

"Is that what we faced?"

"It looks the same," Trevor confirmed. "Half human, half hound. The lore continues with the girl's father getting irritated with having to feed the litter. He moved the canines to an island and told the canine father to return to their shore daily, where the food would be waiting for them.

"So one day, the girl's father had an idea. Instead of placing meat in the bags, he placed rocks. After the canine father collected the bags, he swam back towards the island. The rocks made him sink and die before he got there."

"That's cruel," Jay said as they carried on walking down Caldwell.

"It's nothing compared to what the girl did to avenge him. She commanded her litter of Adlets to eat off her father's hands and feet, and then devour him."

"Ok, that's definitely worse. What happened then?"

"She sent her canines off into the wild to care for themselves, and they were lost to the shadows, never to be seen again. There have been rumours of them being spotted in dark forests or caves though, the five original Adlets forming their own tribe."

"And you think these hounds are the Adlets?" Jay asked.

"I'm not sure, but the resemblance is uncanny," Trevor replied.

"Well, instead of calling them demonic baby crows or half-human hounds, let's just stick to Tiyanaks and Adlets."

Trevor nodded in agreement but stopped walking when he heard a soft crackling on the radio again. They looked around them, unsure of which direction it was coming from. They stood back to back, circling each other and waiting for the creature to appear. Jay took out his baton while Trevor unclipped the holster.

"Go sparingly," Jay warned. "The ammo in that mag and the box are our only bullets."

Trevor closed the holster and reached up over his shoulder for his pipe. Jay's radio started screeching louder as the creature approached, and soon enough, Trevor could see the Adlet before him. Jay turned to stand beside Trevor, ready to take the hound out.

Catching the Adlet and Jay by surprise, Trevor ran forward. He clutched the pipe boldly with both hands, resembling a baseball player getting ready to hit a home run. The Adlet stared dumbfounded at the charging human before bolting forward to meet the attack. As the hound jumped into the air to bite into him, Trevor swung into its rising belly.

The sickening crunch of breaking ribs made Jay bend over from nausea. The Adlet was writhing in pain on the road, its head jolting to each side while the human hand rested on its hurting belly. Trevor stood over it triumphantly, his legs on either side of its twisting head. He raised the pipe perpendicular to the road and brought the lower end straight into its gaping maw.

The pipe pierced through its skull, ending any further movements. The hound lay still as Trevor placed a heel on the beast's neck and plucked the pipe from its head.

"What the hell was that all about?" Jay asked, looking very impressed.

"I need to get used to killing these things," Trevor replied, "otherwise, I will spend more time being afraid than actually looking for Kathy."

Jay watched momentarily as Trevor continued down Caldwell, seeing a new stride to his steps. The pipe looked too comfortable in his hands now; Trevor was ready for anything.

4

DUSTY MEMORIES

Trevor and Jay strayed towards the right side of Caldwell Street, angling towards entering Granger Street, closest to the Petstore. They both kept their weapons ready, waiting for any more Adlets or Tiyanaks to attack. Still, not even the radio made any sign of creatures approaching.

As they walked past one of the residential houses to the right, Trevor spotted a doghouse on the lawn. He made a wide circle away, fearing a dog might break from it any moment. He continued facing it, though, as Jay went on ahead. Although the canine unit seemed empty, Trevor had no courage to inspect it for useful items.

Trevor caught up to Jay, his eyes focused on the pavement again. He saw the turnoff into Granger just as the radio started crackling softly before returning to silence. It caused them to slow their pace, watching the road and misty sky for any signs of darkness.

They turned into Granger just after they passed a broken white picket fence on the corner. Trevor caught a glimpse of another cut in the street just as they crossed over the road. He moved to the edge, noticing that Granger seemed to continue past the abyssal gap. Yet once again, nothing appeared to assist them in bridging it except the buildings on either side.

"Can I see that map?" Jay asked, to which Trevor nodded. "And a pen?"

Jay inspected the street map once the items were in his hand. Trevor watched in interest as Jay marked the area where they had crashed their vehicles with an 'X'. He then proceeded to do the same where the road ended in Kingsley and finally at their current spot in Granger.

"I think it's best we mark where the roads end," Jay said, handing both items back to him. "This town is starting to feel like a maze, and I would hate to get lost in it or double back."

"Good idea," Trevor said as he looked for the alley in Kingsley where he had seen the pamphlet with the Charming Petstore advert. He quickly drew a noose on the end of the alley and tucked the items away in his pocket.

Jay looked to the left pavement and saw a wide building whose right end was adjoined with another building just where the crack in the street started. A sign installed under the roof's eaves read "The Charming Petstore." The walls had once been mantis green, but the years of decay had not been good to it. The green had nodes of rusted brown on it with drips of stained carmine red from the window sills.

Trevor removed the street map, and Jay joined him in studying it. Trevor wrote the word "Petshop" on a building just off Granger before putting the map away.

"Hey man, what are you doing?" Jay said, wondering what he had seen.

"Remember that page I found in the alley?" he asked, to which Jay nodded. "It was referring to this pet shop."

"Ok, but what does it have to do with anything?"

"I'm not sure," Trevor confessed. "Maybe nothing, but since we're here, we might as well go look."

"Alright," Jay agreed, not having a better idea to present.

Trevor tested the knob on the wooden frame of the glass door and found it unlocked. They both entered slowly, the only light within coming from the low light outside through the grimy window panes. The assortment of battered and corroded animal cages piled up against the windows further distilled this indirect light.

Failing to find a light switch, they resorted to using their torches to inspect the shop. Trevor recalled the image of the bear on the pamphlet and hoped very much that a live bear was not hiding in a dark corner somewhere.

"What are we looking for?" Jay asked, inspecting the shelves on the left wall where various animal food bags had long since expired.

"Anything that could be useful," Trevor replied, moving through one of the two aisles with shelf stands on either side. He passed by a variety of animal magazines to the left, from the basic care of domestic cats and dogs, to the more advanced care for exotic reptiles, fish and birds.

Jay's radios crackled softly.

They turned around in their respective areas, listening and watching for any movement in the dark shop, when a stirring on the street caught Trevor's eye. An Adlet was walking past the shop window, sniffing the ground with its canine face.

Trevor whistled softly to Jay and indicated with the side of his hand by his neck that Jay kill his radio's sound. He nodded in understanding and switched it off, the only remaining sound being a low growl from the Adlet at the door. Trevor panicked as it looked up through the door's glass and instinctively thrust the torch's light under his checkered shirt, diving for the end of the aisle.

He sat against the wooden shelf support and dared not look around it back at the door. Despite his earlier bravery against them, he did not want to be cornered in a shop by them. The open streets felt like a better arena.

The low growl stopped and was replaced by the Adlet's claws on the pavement. Trevor glanced down the other side of the aisle, where he could see the front door directly and noticed that the hound was heading back into the mist. The fog covered it, and it was gone from view.

Trevor switched his radio on and heard the crackling die away into silence. He pulled the torch out from under his shirt, revealing the shop's counter at the back of the shop before him. As he stood from the ground, he saw a door behind the counter with something scrawled on its surface.

"Is it gone?" Jay whispered from behind the last aisle where he had been inspecting the shelves along the wall. Trevor could barely make out his head on the floor.

"Yeah, I think so," Trevor replied, deciding to keep his radio on for a change. He shone his torch at the insignia on the door, moving around the counter to study it closer.

"What did you find? Jay asked, joining him.

"It's a triquetra," Trevor responded.

"A what?"

"It's a symbol of a triple deity," Trevor responded, following the lines with his fingers. "In Christian religions, it represents the triple unity of God in the Father, Son and Holy Spirit; in pagan religions, the Triple Goddess in God's female forms."

"Ok, so it's a good sign," Jay commented.

"Not in this case," Trevor replied, earning a low sigh from Jay. "Like the inverted crucifix or pentagram, this symbol has also been turned upside down, representing the serpent's triple nature."

"The devil also has a triple nature?" Jay asked.

"Well, various theories have been applied," Trevor shrugged. "One is that it symbolises Lucifer, Lilith and the child they would one day send to the earth. You see how the inverted symbol has a single point showing down?"

"Yes?"

"It is said that, where God's image has a point shown up representing choosing his son as our salvation above all else, the inverted one reflects Lucifer's choice to send his son as a last resort."

"Why only as a last resort?" Jay asked.

"It is said that he fears his son may overthrow him, should he conquer the earth and the heavens. Like in ancient mythology, it happened to many deities and their children."

"You know way too much about these supernatural things," Jay responded. "At what age did you lose your virginity again?"

Trevor ignored the quip and studied the inverted triquetra further. The three loops of the image had indentations in them, two in the upper loops and one in the downward loop. A fourth indentation was at the centre, where the three arcing loops crossed. He felt the central one with the tip of his finger, discovering just how circular, shallow and smooth it was.

"Hey, here's something on the counter," Jay said quickly, turning to hand it to Trevor.

"It's a poem," Trevor said after a cursory inspection.

"Maybe if you read it out loud, it will open a door or something," Jay offered.

Trevor looked at him dubiously, making him feel like an idiot for thinking it. Yet, he could not defy some logic to the thinking, and so he read it out loud if only to eliminate the solution as an option:

"Four inanimate objects, once beloved, now lost.
Where the ends of roads, albeit but one,
Shatter into the fiery abyss.
The keys to the door to the first host.

The fur and claw be south on the thorny sheet.
While the coloured wing, right where the crown lies.
Cupid marked his target towards the hart of an alley.
In a tree beyond the rising crane drips the sickening beat.

Four inanimate objects, once lost now found.
Placed in their beds, as above, so below.
Except for one, connecting them all,
In the centre, its love shall abound."

"Fur and claw," Jay said after they had a moment to take in the words. "That sounds like those Adlet dogs out there."

"Maybe," Trevor said, still in thought.

"And was Cupid always like a baby in the images?" Jay offered some more. "It could be those baby demons."

"Possibly, although we could just be grabbing at straws," Trevor replied, casting his eyes over the words again. "I don't see how killing more Adlets and Tiyanaks will help us open this door."

"Ok, what could it mean then?" Jay asked.

"Well, there are some things in this poem that seem very specific," Trevor finally said, moving hastily to the counter and opening the map next to the poem on its wooden surface. "For instance, 'thorny sheet' and 'hart of an alley', with heart incorrectly spelt."

"You think it refers to an alley in the streets?" Jay asked, looking at the map by the light of Trevor's torch.

"Bingo, yes," Trevor replied, pointing to the map. "Hawthorne could be the thorny sheet. Hartley could refer to the hart of the alley."

"Ok, and is there an alley in Hartley?" Jay asked as they both looked at the street in question.

"Yes, there is," Trevor smiled triumphantly. "Now, just to determine what the crown and crane refer to."

"I'm guessing Kingsley has to do with the crown," Jay suggested. "I have no idea about the crane, though."

Trevor studied the map some more. Nothing on the map gave a clear indication of what the crane meant. In frustration, he folded the map into his pocket and tucked the poem into the same slips for notes as the red Sacred Valley page.

"You know what?" Trevor said, switching his torch off and heading back around the counter. "We're getting side tracked. We're heading to the school to find Kathy, not going on some mysterious treasure hunt. Just forget…"

As he passed the corner of the counter he stopped in his tracks. Even by the mere light from the streets he caught sight of a small object that he had somehow missed before. He clicked his torch back on and shone it on the thin, circular band, with hooks where some items used to be.

"Oh no," Trevor said, holding the object up. "Please say it isn't so."

"What?" Jay asked, taking the thin band from him and cleaning the dust off it. Trevor had taken the poem out and was inspecting the words again.

"When I was with Caroline, I had given her a charm bracelet," Trevor elaborated, handing the poem to Jay. "On the band, there were four items: a bear, a butterfly, an arrow and a heart."

"Oh I see," Jay remarked, noting the words in the poem. "Furry claw, coloured wings, cupid's mark and sickening beat."

"Someone's toying with me," Trevor said, packing the note and band away in his bag. "I know people blamed me for Caroline's suicide. Even her family thought I killed her and falsified the suicide. And now the police are after me."

"So you think this is personal?" Jay asked quietly.

"I'm starting to," Trevor replied. "The voice over the radio in the car, the red note in my mailbox with 'Sacred Valley' on it and now Caroline's charm bracelet; it all leads to one conclusion."

"Someone's out to get you," Jay finished for him.

"Not just out to get me, but messing with my head. Haunting me. Well, I'm not going to play this game."

Trevor stormed towards the door, leaving Jay to remain at the counter and look at the symbols on the door again. Jay was still somewhat unsure about Trevor's hypothesis, but they had nothing to go on at that point. He agreed with his friend though. The need to find Kathy and get out of the town was the first priority.

Yet, something was still niggling at Jay's nerves. He feared that their presence at Sacred Valley had more to do with other reasons relating to Caroline's death. Jay hadn't made the time to discuss the evidence the police had found against Trevor and how it related to Caroline's death. And, after the brief sightings Jay had had in the mist of a man with a strange metallic object on his head, he had his suspicions of who was toying with both of them.

5

CHARMING KEYS

Trevor moved towards the shop door, walking through the aisle along the wall that led straight to it. His mind was so rattled from finding Caroline's bracelet, evident in his feet stomping on the hard ground. As he closed in on the glass door, his anger subsided briefly as he remembered the Adlet that had inspected the door before. It made him slow his stride when a glowing book on the shelf to his right made him stop completely.

The shelf's entire length stored literary novels that may have been contemporary at one point many years ago. There was a mixture of hardcovers and paperbacks, without concern for genre division. Only one of them had a red glow that Trevor had seen before, and upon closer inspection, he confirmed what he suspected it might be.

The Lunar Nexus was inscribed over the jacket of the hardcover. The book's jacket was leathery in texture and purple in hue. He ran his right hand over the Lunar Nexus, wanting to feel if the Lunar Nexus itself had a different feel to it. As he did so, the same warmth and blinding red light took him over, and he stood there as the energy revitalised him and filled every nerve in his body. As soon as the Lunar Nexus worked through him, he dropped the book and collapsed.

"Trevor!" Jay shouted, running to his side. He tugged at Trevor's arm and then rolled him onto his back in an attempt to wake him up.

The Lunar Nexus on the book caught his eye. He remembered seeing it in the café before. Still, he doubted its purpose after their names had been written in the outer circles. He took a closer look at the Lunar Nexus, not needing a torch to read the glowing runes in the circles and noticed that their names were still burning softly inside it.

"What happened?" Trevor said as he groaned.

"You fainted after touching that symbol, man," Jay replied, hitting the book's spine until it spun under the shelf to the next aisle. "You ok?"

"Well, I feel stronger and healthier, just like I did at the café, but that blinding light was too much for me this time," Trevor confessed. He stood up, correcting his duffel bag's position on his back. He pulled the pipe out from the side, indicating his readiness to leave.

His anxiety set in again, expecting the Adlet from the street to appear from within the mist at any second. The silence of the radio did not comfort him as much as he thought it might. The pipe in his hand was not as reassuring as he hoped it would be. Yet, he feared for Kathy, for this mess he had brought them into, and so set out with unwarranted confidence.

He felt more than heard Jay's presence behind him. The creak of the door seemed to travel down the street. Trevor could feel that he was gripping the copper pipe too hard again, but he didn't care.

Not seeing any sign of the Adlet around them, he moved away from the broken part of the street towards Caldwell. Having looked at the map enough times, he knew there was another street he could use to get to Hollowbrook. If Kathy found a way to get to the school, he could too. If not, then he would just need to look elsewhere for her.

They entered Caldwell, Trevor setting a facer pace for both of them. He kept to the right pavement, hoping to turn into Hartley Street as soon as possible. The road was pleasantly quiet and seemingly uninhabited until Trevor's radio started crackling. They both stood still and started walking backwards until they realised it only caused the radio to grow louder.

Soon they could hear the fluttering of wings behind them in Caldwell, causing them to bolt in the direction they had been heading. Their feet joined the cacophony of screeching crows and the squealing radio that pierced Trevor's ear as if it was attached to the side of his head. He was sweating profusely, wondering if they would be able to outrun their demonic hunter, when he realised they wouldn't get any further.

Caldwell's road came to an abrupt end. There was an impassable gap ahead of them, just like in Kingsley and Granger, before the road continued towards Hartley. Trevor realised that there was no option but to fight.

Too preoccupied to shut the radio off, he turned around, holding the copper pipe high. He saw a dark shape emerge from the mist ahead of him just as an Adlet approached Jay from the right. Jay reversed the hold on his knife, angling the tip down in preparation. With Jay focussing on the hound, Trevor resigned himself to battling the Tiyanak alone.

The crow transformed as the momentum carried the baby form down upon Trevor. He swung sideways at the creature, sending it wailing down to the tarmac. He heard a loud cry as Jay attacked the Adlet, walking forward to finish the fallen Tiyanak off.

Trevor stopped again as he saw more shapes walk out of the mist. Two more Adlets approached from behind the fallen baby, yapping at each other's bleeding maws like two starving dogs about to fight over the only bone available. The one on the left took charge and bit into the Tiyanak's neck just as it turned back to a crow, lifting it up in its teeth while swaying it from side to side before crushing it with its vice-like jaws.

Trevor turned to tell Jay to run. He had killed the Adlet he had been battling, with the corpse lying bleeding on the floor. Trevor noticed, however, that the stainless steel blade was still stuck in the beast's mouth, with Jay trying to wrestle it out. Trevor was about to help him with it when more fluttering made him turn around.

The crow slapped into his face just as he lifted his pipe to hit it. It clawed on his face, leaving deep cuts on the cheeks and forehead. He could feel the marks burn as if sulphur had been poured on them before he managed to grip the body of the crow and thrust it off.

"AHHHHHHHH!"

Trevor spared a moment to look at Jay and found that he was down on the ground with one of the two Adlets Trevor had seen moments before biting into his leg. The Adlet that had killed the crow was now charging at

Trevor, who lifted the pipe and brought it vertically down on its head. It sounded like the skull had cracked, but the hound simply shook it off and charged again.

While the Adlet continued to gnaw at Jay's ankle, another Tiyanak crow transformed into a demonic child. It dove from the sky onto him, its fangs gripping into Jay's neck and shoulders. Jay lost the voice to scream louder, went deathly quiet and then slumped to the tarmac.

Trevor brought the pipe up into his Adlet's chin, sending the hound's head rolling over and falling to the ground. Before it could move again, he ran over and shoved the end of the pipe through the beast's skull. Just as he removed it from the soggy remains, blood the hue of rust dripping on his shoes, the bulk of another Adlet hurtled itself into Trevor's waist. It felt like his ribs had fractured as he collapsed to the floor.

The Tiyanak flew up from the road towards Trevor just as the Adlet rolled off him. With the pain seething into his sides, he tried to reach for the gun in his holster as he had no hopes of raising that pipe again. It had fallen to the road somewhere, further than the Adlet was. The Tiyanak soared down like a hunting eagle when some other Adlet jumped in the air and crushed it in its maw.

Trevor tried to stand, but the pain in his ribs was just too much. The gun was too firmly holstered with the clip down on it. His fingers fumbled as his eyesight began to blur. The two Adlets looked down at him, growling in pleasure as they sunk their teeth into his neck from either side....

His screams echoed in the darkness. He bolted into a sitting position, staring wildly at the shelves surrounding him. His chest was heaving heavily as his throat burned from the thirst he suddenly felt. His stomach groaned from hunger, making him realise that he had not eaten in a long time. With weariness he had never felt, he felt like he could have just laid himself down to sleep for aeons to come.

A soft glow on the ground caused Trevor to reach for the book that had slid under the lowest suspended shelf. As soon as he had the leathery cover firmly in his hands, he placed his palm on the Lunar Nexus. It sent the rejuvenating warmth through his body again.

He heard and felt his ribs snap back into place. The tiredness seeped away like an ebbing wave turning back to the shore. His thirst and hunger vanished, too, as if his desires to sate those basic human needs had vanished. Trevor felt whole and complete again, as if he had never faced those demonic creatures a moment ago.

The glow of the Lunar Nexus faded and died out like the last vestiges of a fire that finally died down. Trevor touched the Lunar Nexus symbol, not receiving any warmth from it at all. Whatever power it had had before was gone and would not be able to revitalise him anymore.

Trevor stood up and looked for Jay. He was back in the Charmed Petstore, but there was no sign of the officer. The copper pipe that had dropped out of his hands was also no longer with him, and he assumed it was still in the street where he had fallen. Trevor was in no mood to either find out or venture down Caldwell to retrieve it.

And as concerned as he was that Jay was still trapped at the end of Caldwell, he knew there was nothing he could do to save him. Jay's fate was his own, and Trevor could only look forward to saving Kathy now; if she was still alive.

Trevor took the Ruger out. He wasn't taking any more chances with saving ammunition. With the fading of the Lunar Nexus, he was unsure he would survive another attack. True to Jeanette's interpretation of the symbol, it seemed to revive him whenever he was killed. He didn't want to take the chance that it would fail to do so now that the symbol had gone cold.

Glad to find that the bag was still attached to his back, he checked his pockets. His phone was still in there with the battery at three-quarter power, and the signal was still lost. The map and pen were also still in his rear pocket. He marked the end of Caldwell where the road had ended, between

Granger and Hartley, and then inspected the streets.

Trevor saw that, pending any further abrupt road gaps, he would need to head down Granger back all the way to Hawthorne before turning right and heading to Hartley. He could then venture all the way down Hartley to Hollowbrook, failing which the final street he could use at the lower end of the map was Langley.

Stashing his goods but keeping his gun at hand, he moved back out onto the streets. He passed over Caldwell, trying to see down to the part where the gap was, but the mist was too thick. His radio signalled softly that the creatures were still roaming nearby, so he picked up his pace further into Granger.

He stayed on the right pavement, hugging the building walls again while searching for Hawthorne Avenue. There was a dip in the pavement as an alley broke to the right between buildings, but Trevor was not prepared to enter one alone again. He bypassed it without even looking down into it.

Trevor slowed down when he reached Hawthorne, about to turn right into it when a movement in the mist caught his attention. The radio was pleasantly silent, but the shadow on the road betrayed the stranger's presence. Trevor played around with the radio's volume control and then the power switch, making sure that it was actually working, when he discovered that the radio was not at fault.

"Jay!" Trevor exclaimed as soon as his appearance was clearer, running forward to embrace him in greeting. "Where the hell did you come from?"

"That café," Jay responded as they split apart. "I woke up on the floor under that Lunar Nexus again."

"That's great," Trevor said, feeling truly grateful while also feeling guilty that he would have left Jay behind. "And the Lunar Nexus? Did it die down?"

"Die down?" Jay frowned. "Why would it die down? No, it was still burning fiercely."

"That's strange," Trevor commented.

"There was something different about it, though," Jay offered, reaching into the top pocket of his jacket and handing Trevor a small note. "It had a new name on it that wasn't there last time. I noted it down in case it meant something to you."

Trevor looked down at the note, reading over the mirrored letters:

ᚾ4Ɏ⌀ϯ

"It's Kathy's name," Trevor finally said. "She's activated the Lunar Nexus, which is good. It means she's alive. Where-about on the circle was it?"

"Top right," Jay replied. "Do you think it means something?"

"I'm not sure yet, but I will let you know once I figure it out," Trevor replied, renewed determination swelling with the news of her name. "For now, let's get to that school."

Trevor noticed that the knife had been replaced by Jay's baton in his hand. He clutched the Ruger harder in his hand as if that lent some more security. They both moved down Hawthorne together, Trevor feeling even more determined not to get killed again. The fading of the Lunar Nexus on the book really bothered him, and he feared the consequences.

They had just set into their pace when he realised they would go no further. Hawthorne ended sooner than Caldwell had. Trevor spun around, raising the pistol with the grip held tight. He eyed the road down the sight of the barrel, waiting to see if this end was swarming with creatures just as much as Caldwell had.

The mist was quiet, and nothing seemed to stir. Trevor lowered the gun slightly, about to tell Jay they needed to find another way, when a motion to the right caught his peripheral attention. It was an Adlet on the edge of the broken road, and it seemed like it was alone.

Yet the motion of the hound bothered him. The radio on his hip started whining louder as it moved closer, so he switched it off. The head of the Adlet was jerking from side to side, like a dog playing with a chew toy. It was growling playfully, ignorant of the presence of the two men behind it.

"Hey!" Trevor shouted to get its attention, raising the gun again.

The Adlet dropped the object it had been ripping with its teeth and focussed on them. The growl changed to a more dangerous sound as the half-human hound moved to run towards them. Trevor didn't wait for it to get closer and offloaded bullets into its head. It yelped and fell down, needing four shots before it finally collapsed dead to the floor.

The blood and pus from the cancerous mounds drooled onto the road by Trevor's feet. He kicked its head to make sure it was indeed dead. Getting no response, he moved to the object it had been toying with. He knelt down, inspecting the torn teddy bear.

"The furry claw at the end of the thorny sheet," Jay said behind him, looking over his shoulder. "Is that what the poem was referring to?"

Trevor didn't bother answering. He had spotted a hole torn in the belly of the bear. He probed inside the hole, feeling something solid inside of it. His fingertips struggled to grasp it from within the bear's stuffing. Eventually, he pulled out the item he had expected it to be. He turned the silver bear charm around in his fingers, recognising it instantly.

"It's one of the charms I gave Caroline," Trevor informed Jay. "There's a small scratch here at the top that I use to toy with in idle moments. It's definitely hers."

"I'm sorry to hear that," Jay responded with sincere sympathy. "Look, we need to get to this school and find Kathy, man. I'd hate to see this place when the sun sets."

Trevor looked up at the sky, suddenly wondering how late it was. It felt like they had been in Sacred Valley for hours, if not days, but there had been no indication of a change in the light levels. The mist did a good job of cutting everything out, even a glimpse of where the sun was.

He stood up and retrieved the map and poem. He read through the cryptic words indicating the location of the four charms and then checked the areas of the map where he assumed the other charms would be. Where Jay was now more compelled to find Kathy and leave, Trevor felt bound to find the other charms.

"The last chance we have to get to the school is down Marlowe," Trevor finally said to a tensely waiting Jay. "If we cannot go down that road, then I have no idea how we're going to reach her."

Jay led the way back up Hawthorne to Granger, and they turned right towards Marlowe. They heard some fluttering to the left, which then died down again. It made Trevor realise that his radio was still off, so he quickly reached down to click it on again. The radio crackled softly but died down as the Tiyanak moved away from them.

Continuing further into Granger, Trevor spotted an alley to their right between the buildings. It was dark inside the alley, much like the alley in Kingsley where the noose was. Jay also noticed the alley but moved forward in an effort to avoid it. Trevor turned towards it when he saw a medicine bottle at the corner of one of the buildings abreast of the alley.

"Let's check it out," Trevor ventured.

"Why?" Jay asked. "Does the alley lead to the other side?"

"Who knows, there might be a way through."

Jay shrugged and moved in with him. Trevor had to turn his torch back on as the darkness seemed to overpower the mist again. He raised his gun with the other hand near his torch, making sure he was ready to shoot at a moment's notice. Yet the radio remained silent, giving them hope that the alley was void of any malevolence.

Just like Kingsley's alley, this one was also cut short. Something shimmered in the dance of the torch's light, and Trevor instantly moved towards it. He caught the glint again and bent down to pick the arrow up. Beside it against the wall was a bow to complement the arrow.

"Wait, this doesn't make sense," Trevor said, harnessing his pistol. He retrieved the poem again, reading the reference to the arrow. "' Cupid marked his target towards the hart of an alley'."

"You could still have been right about Hartley," Jay offered, leaning over to point at the map. "Just like an arrow, this alley is pointing in its direction."

Trevor could see the logic in his argument. He was about to inspect the arrow further for clues when the radio started crackling again with the return of fluttering wings.

"Oh no," Jay said softly, brandishing his baton bravely.

"Take this," Trevor said, throwing the torch at Jay.

With the poem stowed away again, Trevor instinctively notched the arrow into the bow and lifted it in aim. The action immediately brought memories of how he once showed Caroline how to hold a bow properly and aim while keeping her environment in mind. It had been one of the cornerstones of their relationship, and it was almost as if she was right there with him.

The crow seemed to take note of Trevor's aim and dodged from side to side while he kept the bird in view. He felt exhilarated using the bow, the same energy he had when he first took up his hand-crafted bow at a young age. When the moment felt right, he released the arrow and watched as it crossed the torchlight towards the Tiyanak.

The crow moved at the last moment, and the arrow's head slammed into the wall, ricocheting onto the floor. Jay didn't give the bird time to recover and rushed forward to meet it. His growing experience with the dark creatures was starting to show as his baton smacked into the body of the Tiyanak with a sickening beat.

Trevor watched for a moment longer as Jay strangely kept hitting the bird on the floor. Dropping the bow, Trevor moved past him back towards the street. Jay returned his torch in passing, and he shone it on the floor where the arrow had fallen. The shaft was lying against the wall where it met the floor, but the head had fallen to the side.

He lifted it up to the torch, inspecting it carefully. Running his fingers on the end where the shaft had been connected to it, he felt something in the hollow hole. His finger was too thick to pry the object, so he tipped the two lower ends and tapped it on the floor. The arrow charm fell out.

"Ok, so that's two of four," Jay said. "It seems we're running into these items whether we want to or not."

"Maybe," Trevor responded, not so sure of their luck. "Come on, let's get to Marlowe."

They moved out, Trevor leaving the bow, shaft and head behind while stashing the arrow charm with the bear charm. When they reached the street, they turned right into Granger, heading towards the final road that could lead them to Hollowbrook Elementary.

There were no further interruptions or calls from the radio as they wended into Marlowe, turning right in the hopes that they could finally enter Hartley or Langley. Not having been in the street yet made Trevor more apprehensive.

The grip on the gun increased further; not due to any creatures arriving or warning signs, but rather the anger at having found another broken gap in the street. Trevor stormed down the width of the gap, hoping to find a way past it, when all he encountered was a huge fence blocking the way down to the waters below.

"You know," Jay said as he joined his side, "we've basically been all over the part of this town we have access to. And we haven't found Kathy. So wherever she is, there must be a way there."

"If only we can find it," Trevor said, his voice full of despair.

"Can I take a swing in the dark here?" Jay asked, with Trevor wondering if there was some pun intended.

"Swing away," Trevor replied sardonically.

"Those charms are clearly not coincidental," Jay mused. "We're obviously meant to find them all. For whatever purpose, I don't know yet, but that's the only assumption I can make."

"Fair enough," Trevor said.

"So I suggest we go up Kingsley, find the charm there, and then look for this crane."

"Well, it's not like we have anything better to do," Trevor finally said, pulling the poem out again. "The butterfly is at the right end of Kingsley. We can head up Marlowe; it will take us straight there."

They proceeded up as planned, the quiet streets making them feel lethargic and complacent. Trevor had his pistol hand beside his hip while Jay held his baton just as casually. Trevor was feeling tired, and his thirst was starting to return again. As they walked towards Kingsley, he kept an eye on the buildings to the left in an attempt to find any shops that may contain edible food.

"You know what's strange?" Jay said as they neared Kingsley. "The concentration of creatures seems to be greater near the Petstore than here. It's like something is pulling them there."

"Or trying to keep us away," Trevor offered. "Maybe Kathy's through that door in the store, and something's trying to stop us from finding her."

"Or someone," Jay finished.

They finally entered Kingsley and walked to the right. They had hardly gone forward when the road broke down into the abyss again. Trevor took out his map and marked all the streets they had failed to cross since the pet store. It confirmed Jay's words that there was no clear path to Hollowbrook Avenue.

Completing his cartographical objective, he studied the area for the butterfly charm. They split up to either side of the road, hoping something would reveal the path to the mystical item. Trevor inspected every inch of the pavement, wishing a creature would present the answer. Yet no Adlet or Tiyanak made the radio cry out, or the cloudy mists stir.

They met in the centre of the road again, staring across the gap for an answer. Trevor noticed that the mist was thinner here, and he could see more of the river span than before. There was another part of Sacred Valley over the water. He wondered for a moment if Kathy had gone there instead.

A movement at his feet made him look down. Minute blue wings fluttered over the edge of the road. Trevor knelt down to get a better view. Dropping his bag, he lay forward on his belly until the tarmac pressed into his ribs. Jay automatically held his foot down on Trevor's leg to give him more support.

The underside of the tarmac was riddled with broken and corroded steel rods that had once served as reinforcement and tension bars for the road. In the midst of this cobweb framework was a butterfly nest. The host of butterflies swarmed around it, making it hard for him to see if there was a charm among them.

He carefully reached up for his torch on his hip just as Jay knelt down to hold Trevor more securely. The light trickled against the twigs, leaves and flapping blue wings until he caught something that shimmered in their midst.

Ignoring the pressure in his head from dangling upside down, Trevor bent his waist so that he could lean more forward. He felt Jay change his grasp on his legs to account for the adjustment. His fingers breached the nest as he parted some of the more predominant leaves, causing the butterflies to move slightly away in observation.

His fingers were just out of reach. If he could reach a hand further, he would have been able to pull it out. Trevor twisted his hip slightly to gain more depth, his fingertips scaling forward until he had the soft metal in the grasp of his pointing and middle fingers.

Suddenly the radio began to crackle. Trevor looked up to Jay on the road, wondering what creature was approaching them, when a hand reached up from beneath the broken tarmac and tangled reinforcement to grab Trevor's arm. A paw with steel claws reached up to clutch the tension bars for support as the hand pulled further on his arm. The furry face of the Adlet moved forward until its nose was in Trevor's face, growling as it stared deep into his eyes.

Jay reacted by pulling on Trevor's legs. Trevor moved slightly up, the arm with the charm held in its hands being tugged as he was pulled from both sides. While the Adlet used his hand to hold onto its quarry, it used its human and canine feet to claw further along the underside of the road.

Trevor tried to use his other hand to push himself up and away from the beast. The torch in his hand knocked against the tarmac, causing it to fall out of his hand and crash against the hound's forehead. It bounced off it, spiralling past the mist and into the abyss.

The hound was stunned for a moment, its grasp slacking enough on Trevor's arm that he could rip it free. Jay moved him up more quickly as the Adlet recovered and scampered up the side of the road like a spider climbing its web. It was almost upon him again as Trevor reached up to his hip, offloading bullets to its head as soon as the sight of the Ruger was aligned with the beast's head.

The swift movement to retrieve and fire the pistol had caused the charm to slip from his enclosed palm while the Adlet dodged the line of fire by moving its head to the side. Trevor watched in fright as the silver object fell down, holding his breath while his heart raced to a fast beat.

The Adlet opened up its maw to collect the charm with its bite. The charm fell onto its teeth as Trevor offloaded two more bullets. The first went over its head between its raised ears, but the last connected solidly between its eyes. The Adlet slumped back with a look of shock on its dying face, the radio softening to silence with every passing second.

Trevor thought all was lost. He waited for the hound to join the torch into the abyss, but the Adlet remained dangling before him. Its feet were tangled among the web of tarmac and reinforcement. The human hand somehow still grasped onto the tension bars it had used to pull itself up. And in the open maw of the hound, among the filthy sharp fangs, he saw the butterfly charm resting against the upper palate.

"Jay, no, wait!" Trevor shouted as his friend attempted to pull him up again. "I see it. Lower me down."

"You're crazy, man," Jay responded, grasping Trevor's leg as he continued to help him up. "We'll find another way."

Trevor felt so angered in his exhilaration and trepidation that he lifted the gun to aim it at Jay. The officer looked at the Ruger and then at Trevor, halting his haul up from the side of the road.

"Let…me…down," Trevor said, seething the words between his teeth.

Jay seemed to consider responding. Trevor could tell that Jay was struggling with the situation and wondered if he thought about letting him fall into the chasm. Yet Trevor was determined to get this pendant. He had worked too hard to obtain it just to let it go.

Jay gave in to his request as he lowered him back in again. Trevor hitched the pistol to his hip again so that he could have both hands free. His chest was abreast of the Adlet's dangling belly now, and his hands could reach past its neck. He listened carefully to the silent radio, hoping it would steel his resolve.

He ran his hands along its neck to check its response. Expecting a forest of fur, he was surprised to find human skin on its neck up to its mane that fell from its jawline and the back of the head. The Adlet did not stir, nor was there a pulse in the neck.

This did not ease Trevor's tension or apprehension. He lowered his hand to its teeth, Jay holding him around the ankles at the edge of the road. He kept his fingertips just outside of the hound's mouth, too afraid to take it one step closer to the charm. Trevor closed his eyes and took a deep breath, opening them again as he reached in.

The charm was in his hand. The Adlet remained still, blood dripping slowly from the top of its head into the abyss below them. Trevor breathed a sigh of relief before turning up to give Jay the signal. His friend looked down at him for what felt like a very long moment in reflection before acceding and returning him to the top of the road.

"Thanks," Trevor said, cleaning himself off and strapping his bag back on just as Jay moved with his face towards his.

"Pull a gun on me again," Jay said ominously, "and it will be the last thing I'll ever let you do."

Trevor watched as Jay stormed back down Marlowe. He wanted to speak up to in some way account for his behaviour. Yet, the words choked in his throat. He had had no time or patience to explain to Jay, while dangling off the road above a deathly chasm, that he really needed the charm. Trevor decided he would just let Jay cool down and make it up to him in time.

"Have you worked out where this damn bird charm is?" Jay asked in an irritated tone as Trevor caught up to him.

"Which bird charm?" Trevor asked in confusion.

"Wasn't there something about a crane?"

"The last charm I gave her was a heart," Trevor informed him, growing agitated at the thought of obtaining a real heart and fearing wherein it might be. "The reference was made to a tree beyond a crane."

"Well, I have not seen any cranes, and we've been basically everywhere that these fucking streets allow us to go," Jay responded and then noticed Trevor's expression. "Don't you even dare tell me to stop swearing."

"Maybe we're looking at it wrong," Trevor said, holding back his retort. "Perhaps it's not a bird, but some other type of crane."

"Of course," Jay said suddenly, the realisation abating his anger slightly. "There's a bridge down here somewhere, right?"

Trevor took out his map quickly, and they both had a look. Just after the gap in Marlowe, Hartley extended into a bridge leading to the other side of Sacred Valley over the river beneath it towards Lake Silvercrest.

"Yes, but it's on the side that we can't get to," Trevor announced, putting the map away again.

"Maybe we don't need to," Jay pondered. "Maybe we just…"

His words were cut short while they passed the Granger intersection with Marlowe. Jay squinted towards the right pavement. He moved to it without a further word, passing Granger completely as he approached a fence blocking a lawn area on Marlowe.

As Trevor followed him, he realised what had caught Jay's attention. A Gingko Biloba tree stood in the middle of the lawn, with broken park equipment buried in the sand on the outer ends of the property. Trevor frowned, wondering how they had previously missed a tree of such height and stature. They must have missed it simply because they had not been looking for it.

The upper foliage of the tree was so broad that it hugged the building walls on two sides, the other two sides being reserved by the tarmac of Granger and Marlowe. Jay found a gate hanging on its hinges and moved through it to the tree.

Trevor soon joined him in investigating it, but they didn't have to look long. On the side of the tree facing the corner of the two walls of the building, they found a large knot in the tree where three branches broke off to form the upper foliage area. In the seat of the knot was a heart, cuddled by the bark of the tree that had grown over the sides of it.

At first, the appearance of a heart in the tree had taken Trevor back, but what was more striking was that the heart was still beating. It seemed to pump whatever life fluid the tree fed on into the xylem tubes of the branches. Yet, the beating of the heart was not a tune that Trevor was familiar with; rather, it pulsed along to its own sick song.

"All yours," Jay announced, reaching down to the side of his right boot and handing Trevor a small switchblade.

Making sure his radio was still on, he moved closer to the heart of the tree. He ran his fingers through the muscles, which felt as sick as the beat sounded. Trevor held the blade tip on the heart, taking a deep breath before driving it in. He widened the slit until he could delve inside with his fingertips, acquiring the heart charm much quicker than the others.

Feeling like it was almost too easy, Jay and Trevor both looked to the streets for trouble. The radio still remained silent, not helping much in allaying their fears. Yet, no creature made its way from the streets into the miniature park area. Trevor suddenly remembered the Adlet that had attacked him from under the road. With renewed trepidation, he looked up into the tree.

His sight was blocked as something fell softly over his face. He brushed it aside hastily, stepping away from the tree. He heard Jay's footsteps near him and followed them until they found the gate and were again on Marlowe.

Looking back, they saw what had befallen them. The Gingko had dropped all its leaves, and the branches looked pale and forlorn. The tree had a more stony appearance now as if it had been dead for years. With the final leaf touching the ground, Trevor realised that nothing was coming after them.

"Come on, let's get back," Trevor instructed, moving back towards Granger.

"Hold on," Jay said, looking down as he contemplated his next words. "We need to split up."

"Why?" Trevor asked carefully, wondering if it was due to his actions in Kingsley.

"We can't go on like this," he responded. "We need more supplies. I want to cross that bridge to get to the Police Station, maybe call in some reinforcements. Even if we find Kathy, we still need a way out of this forsaken town."

"I understand that," Trevor said, "but can't that wait until we actually have Kathy."

"No, that might take too long. I want to make the call now already before it's too late."

Trevor knew he was partially lying but also understood that arguing with Jay would not alter his resolve. Jay had his own personal reasons for wanting to split up, so Trevor decided to give him his space.

"How are you going to get there, though?" Trevor asked, pointing at Marlowe's gap. "There's no way through."

"I'll find a way," Jay responded, "even if that means swimming across the river."

"Fair enough," Trevor replied, starting to unclip the Ruger's holster.

"No, you keep that," Jay told him. "There should be some weapons at the station. I've got the baton until then."

Trevor was urged to try and stop him one last time but then just extended his hand in greeting. Jay considered it and then shook it heartily before offering one final smile to ease the tension between them.

"Good luck finding Kathy," Jay offered.

"Thanks," Trevor replied. "We'll get you at the station."

With a final nod in agreement, Jay left. Trevor watched him walk up Marlowe, the mist curling and swirling around his form as his body became a shadow. He turned to give one last wave, then vanished into the fog.

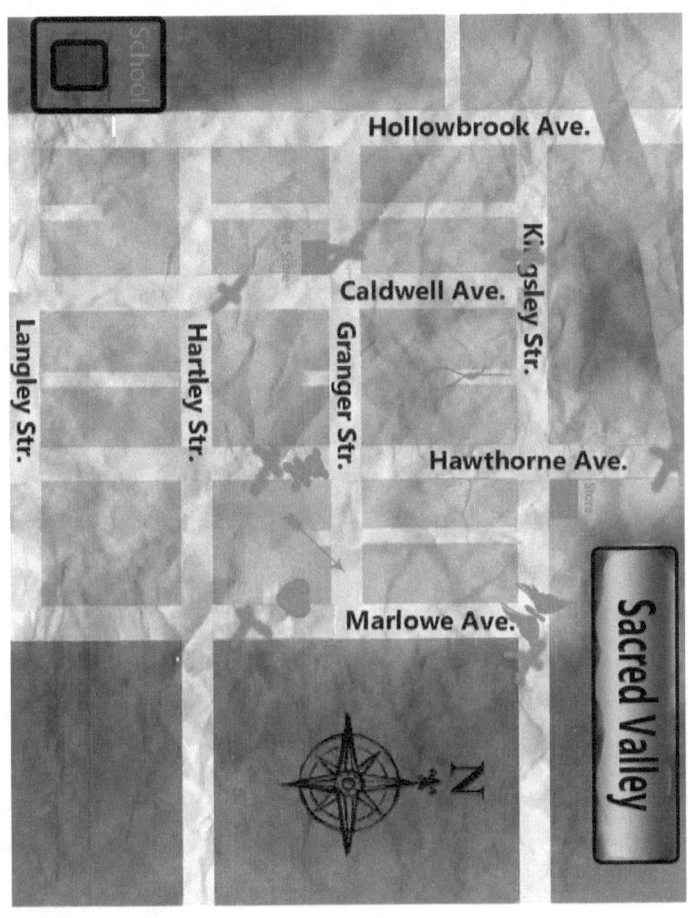

6

HOLLOWBROOK ELEMENTARY

Trevor tried to stubbornly refuse to admit that he missed Jay's company on the way back to the pet store. It was easy enough while Granger was empty and void of any evil. Still, as soon as the radio made even the slightest of noises, he realised how brave one could pretend to be with someone at your side.

Despite the occasional warning of creatures nearby, Trevor made it to the pet store without incident. He had learnt to move in a direction that silenced the radio again and thereby realised that he could use the radio as a noise compass to detect where the beasts were located.

As he approached the shop door, he did a quick ammunition check and realised that he had already used half of the Ruger's magazine. He still had the box of ten in his bag, but he was unsure how long that would keep him. He made a mental note to look for more or find another melee weapon to replace the lost copper pipe soon.

Entering the Charming Petstore, he took out the cryptic poem and approached the door behind the counter. The inversed triquetra was still on the door. Trevor reached for his torch and remembered with a sinking feeling that he had lost it in his battle with the Kingsley Adlet for the butterfly charm. Not dissuaded, he took his phone out of his pocket and switched it on.

By the soft light of the phone, he reread the last part of the clue:

'Four inanimate objects, once lost, now found.
Placed in their beds, as above, so below.
Except for one, connecting them all,

In the centre, its love shall abound.'

Trevor went for the immediate win and placed the Heart charm in the centre notch of the triquetra. He waited patiently, shining his phone on the intersection of knots as the door's wood reached out and melded with it. The charm was now set flush in the wood, with the other three indentations still hollow.

"' As above, so below'", Trevor read out loud once he returned to the poem on the counter.

An idea occurred to him. He took out the map and stretched it out beside the poem. With his pen, he marked the places he had found the remaining charms. The Butterfly had been on the upper end of Kingsley, while the Bear and Arrow had been on the lower ends of Hawthorne and the alley.

He turned back to the symbol with the charms in his hand. As the Butterfly had been so far removed from the others, he assumed the charm would go into the single knot facing down. His success was rewarded with the Butterfly being accepted into the wood.

As Hawthorne was to the left of the alley on the map, Trevor placed the Bear charm in the upper left knot. The wood moved forward to absorb the charm but then moved back out, causing the Bear to fall out of the indentation. Trevor reached forward and caught it quickly, afraid to lose it in the darkness.

"Oh yes, of course," Trevor said, returning to the map and turning it upside down like the triquetra. Now, with Kingsley at the bottom like the Butterfly charm, Hawthorne was to the right of the alley. Trevor placed the Arrow in the left knot and the Bear in the right, the door accepting both.

Trevor heard the lock on the door click. Without being touched, the door creaked open of its own accord. He folded the map and placed it with the pen in his back pocket while holding the poem in his hand momentarily.

"I guess your use has expired," Trevor said, about to crumple it up and throw it away. Yet, it nagged him that he might need it again in the future.

Stepping on the side of caution, he placed it in the notes section of the bag.

He finally walked through the door into a small courtyard in the back. There were other doors leading to other shops and rooms, with a passage leading to an alley to the right. As the alley seemed like the only way out, Trevor headed that way just as the door closed and locked itself shut.

The mist seemed thicker in the alley than in any other areas he had been. It took a moment for Trevor to realise it was more than that. The sky had turned darker while the falling mist continued to flow. It was harder to see ahead of him, but he did not let that deter him.

At the junction where the passage met the alley, Trevor had a choice of turning right back to Granger or left to Hartley. With the hope of finally entering the latter, Trevor chose left. He took his Ruger to hand, checked that there was a bullet in the chamber and headed to the street.

It felt like his luck was changing. His feet stepped onto Hartley with no evident gaps in the street. With a jubilant heart, he started to jog to the right, hoping to reach the school quickly and without interference. However, his hopes were cut short when the radio began to whine.

It did not rise in crescendo as usual but went straight to an outright roar. Trevor tried to move in different directions to get an indication of where it might be coming from, but the sound remained at the same pitch.

Suddenly the road ahead of him towards Hollowbrook was covered in hordes of shifting movements. It seemed like the whole town's beasts were descending on him at once. Trevor turned around and ran down Hartley, hearing the pounding of paws and flapping of wings behind him. He picked up speed until the noises behind him softened.

His foot slipped, and he fell over the edge of the road that burst in front of him. He reached out and caught a protruding steel bar that jutted out of the road, looking down into the darkness of the abyss beneath him. He pulled himself up quickly, standing on the road again as the darkness approached before him.

To his right, an Adlet ran through the mist and jumped on him. Trevor fell on his bag but twisted so that his feet propelled the hound over him onto the tar behind him. Recovering quickly, he rose up and aimed the pistol at the dog's head.

Fluttering wings in the darkness ripped his attention away as a Tiyanak attacked him from the left, tearing into his forearms with their claws. Trevor exclaimed, dropping his arms down momentarily and then looking up as the Adlet attacked again. Trevor raised his gun and started firing. Just as the Adlet jumped, a bullet clipped into its forehead, and it fell dead to the ground.

He turned around quickly, hurrying to find the crow, when he saw another two Adlets facing him. They were growling deeply, their groans more akin to the burning pits of a volcano than to actual hounds. They both barked simultaneously and ran for him.

Trevor shot at the one on the left first as it was closest. The bullet hit into its body, and the beast fell to the floor in pain just as Trevor shifted his shots to the right. The crow slammed onto his bag, turning into its toddler form and biting into his neck just as he reached over and hit it with the butt of his gun. It fell off to the road, its body slamming hard with the surface. The Adlet jumped onto him, and he fell backwards onto the Tiyanak, the baby wailing in pain as he rolled over it.

The Adlet was yapping at his face as he raised the gun under its chin and fired into it. He rolled the dead body over and rose up from the baby. It struggled to change into a crow again, but Trevor wasted no time letting it. It was squirming grossly on the floor as he offloaded two bullets into its demonic head.

The injured Adlet had regained its feet and composure. Trevor aimed and shot, receiving only a click from the weapon. He looked at the red loading indicator, realising with a sickening feeling that he had spent the ammunition in the mag. There was no time to reload with the single box of ammo he had left, but the Adlet had no sympathy for him. Almost as if the creature realised his predicament, it opened its yap in a wide grin and ran for him.

Helplessly he watched as the Adlet approached him. Trevor was almost tempted to let it take him in the hopes that the Lunar Nexus would resurrect him, but he was not confident enough to take the chance. There was only one thing he could do, and as the hound jumped, he struck the pistol into the side of its head.

He enjoyed the crunching sound against the skull. The beast fell on its side on the road, writhing in pain. Trevor walked towards it like an agent of death, staring down at it in pleasure. He raised his foot and brought it down hard on its head, watching as the skull gave in and the hound died. Not satisfied with its stillness, he kept crushing its head until it was a stew of gunk on the floor.

Something was wrong. The radio should have died down, yet its whining had only subsided. He suddenly remembered Jay's thoughts that the creatures seemed more active closer to the pet store. As if in affirmation, he saw a crowd of Adlets stepping out of the darkness from Caldwell's side of the road. This was complemented by a fluttering of wings from Hollowbrook Street.

He decided the only way to survive the onslaught was to run. Ignoring the crows ahead of him, he ran for Hollowbrook Street, making sure to turn towards any opening among the cloud of beasts flying towards him. As the Tiyanaks fell down to him, he dodged and parried, using the barrel of the Ruger to hit any aside that were able to attain their prey.

For what felt like long minutes, he ran with the sound of claws on the tar behind him. He finally made Hollowbrook and turned left, knowing very well that if there was a break in the road, it would be the end of him. Yet, he hoped with sheer determination to live that there was a way, so he kept running. He broke through the dark Tiyanak cloud and raced through the mist with the armies of evil behind him.

After a long sprint, his chest rasping, he finally saw Hollowbrook Elementary to his right. He looked back and frowned, wondering where the creatures had gone to. His radio started winding down until there was only a faint crackle left. He slowed his pace to a brisk walk and reached the school's boundary wall just as the radio finally fell silent.

Trevor stood motionless before the school, looking at his bleeding arms. He was terribly exhausted, hungry and thirsty. His thirst suddenly reminded him that he still had the one medicine bottle found on Hawthorne outside Café 7to5. He dropped the bag and searched for it, instantly flipping the top off and downing the liquid.

The medicine rejuvenated him only slightly. He was still hungry and a bit weary, but the bleeding on his arms seemed to subside. He considered using the first aid kit to patch it up but decided not to waste it. He had yet to learn what awaited him in the school, but he would need the kit later if it was anything like the streets.

With the bag on his back again, Trevor moved to the school's double doors. The name "Hollowbrook Elementary" was emblazoned on a side wall. Trees marked the front lawns, hiding him from any street view and vice versa. Trusting that the radio silence meant no evil was around, he reached for the knobs on the front doors.

Something was glistening upon the ash on the concrete slabs before the school. The ash was as white as snow around the school as if it was untainted compared to the rest of Sacred Valley. Trevor reached down for the shimmering object and swallowed hard when he realised what it was.

This time, another charm bracelet lay in his palm with its charms in place. Only three objects were linked to the golden band. The first was a golden paintbrush with the tip plated in white gold. The second was a treble clef made from steel but plated in gold. The final charm was an open book, with the outer covers made of silver but the inner page side made of wood.

"Kathy," Trevor whispered, standing up with the bracelet in his hand.

Finally, he had confirmation of where she was. He was unsure whether she had dropped it so that he could find her, or if some violence had caused it to fall off. It had been a gift from him, representing the three cultural aspects she loved the most. Each one was a personal passion of hers, which she had spent much of her life cultivating. It was akin to Trevor's love for ancient mythology and mystical lore and the aspects that had brought them together in the first place.

Trevor dared his first steps into the school foyer, placing the charm bracelet with his notes in the bag's front slip. The door's closing echoed through the front passages of the school, announcing his entrance. He tested the knobs again, feeling reassured that it still opened. He moved through the lobby to another set of double doors and into a passage perpendicular to the lobby.

To the left was a reception desk with an open front portal. The air was musty, but Trevor felt relieved that no mist filled it. It was dark with no lights on, but his sight could pierce the darkness much better than the street or the dark alleys.

As he moved forward, he realised it was because of a light coming from within the reception area. Once he reached the front reception desk, he saw it was not from the reception itself but rather from a room behind it. The door was hanging from the top hinge alone, but Trevor could see from the opening that the room had suffered some damage.

He walked into the reception area and inspected his surroundings. The light from the office behind it assisted Trevor in seeing some of the contents on the desk and the surrounding walls, but there was one object which did not need any illumination to help it glow.

The Lunar Nexus shone brightly against the wall the reception shared with the room behind it. It pulsed like it had in Café 7to5, and Trevor immediately noticed Kathy's name in the top right of the concentric circles. The bottom right remained empty, with Trevor and Jay's names still burning in the top and bottom left.

Trevor was hesitant about the Lunar Nexus before, but now he could not wait to reach it. He stumbled over papers and books on the floor until his palm pressed against it. As before, a wonderful warmness spread through his veins, sating his hunger and thirst while drowning a rising need to empty his bladder.

This time the Lunar Nexus not only satisfied his basic human needs but also healed his wounds. He could not look down for the burning red light in his sight, but he could feel the scratches and pains leave his body. When his vision returned, and the Lunar Nexus pulsed calmly on the wall again, he moved closer to the office light and inspected his body. Not even a scar remained from the attack on the streets.

"I need to get me one of these when I return home," Trevor thought out loud. "If I return home."

Having dealt with his physical ailments, he spent more time inspecting the room further. The counter by the open portal was cluttered with papers and documents. He ruffled through them momentarily, a single note near the computer's keyboard catching his attention. He used the office light through the doorway to read through it. It was a note from the school nurse indicating that the infirmary had been restocked with medical supplies. Trevor made a mental note to find it once he left the reception.

Trevor searched the drawers next, which were situated in the back corner next to a printer. Most of the things were stationery and loose personal items, but he found a few phone chargers in the last drawer. Checking through them, he found one that matched his phone. He pulled the phone out of his pocket and noticed the battery had dipped to forty per cent.

"I guess it won't hurt to charge it a bit, if there's power in this place," Trevor noted while finding a socket against the wall and plugging the phone in. To his surprise, the cell bleeped as the charger connected, and the bars showed it was charging.

He went through the rest of the documents only to find reports and notes from the teachers, none of which interested him the least. He moved his search to the walls, hoping for some indication Kathy may have left him a clue as to where she had gone. Beneath the Lunar Nexus on the wall was a large noticeboard with several documents pinned to it.

Prominent among these were four school maps, including the first and second floors, the basement and the roof. He studied it, noticing that the infirmary was just right of the lobby. He took out the street map from his pocket.

"I won't need you right now," Trevor said, packing the street map into a different empty slip on the side of his bag. He then unpinned the maps from the board. "And the school will definitely not need these anytime soon."

He folded three maps together and placed them in his rear pocket, clutching the first-floor map in his left hand. Trevor walked to the office door at the back of the reception room and pushed the dangling door inwards. From the passage, he had perceived that the room looked slightly damaged, but the minimal sight had not done the chaos any justice.

A large portion of the ceiling had collapsed to the floor. It was lying at an angle, with one side still attached to the remainder of the ceiling above and the lower end resting against the floor. Trevor would have been hard put to investigate the room, as the bulk of it was covered by the damage. The light somehow connected and shone from the ceiling against the wall where Trevor stood.

Against the glare of the light, Trevor tried to pierce the darkness of the floor above. He could only make out the far wall that was part of the external structural frame, but none of the room's contents above him. Suspended directly above him on the edge of the broken floor was a desk. Even though it looked as if it was adequately supported, Trevor feared the injury it would do to him should it suddenly fall.

Trevor returned to the safety of the reception area and checked one more time for anything that could help him find Kathy. With nothing glaringly apparent, he decided it was time to move into the school proper.

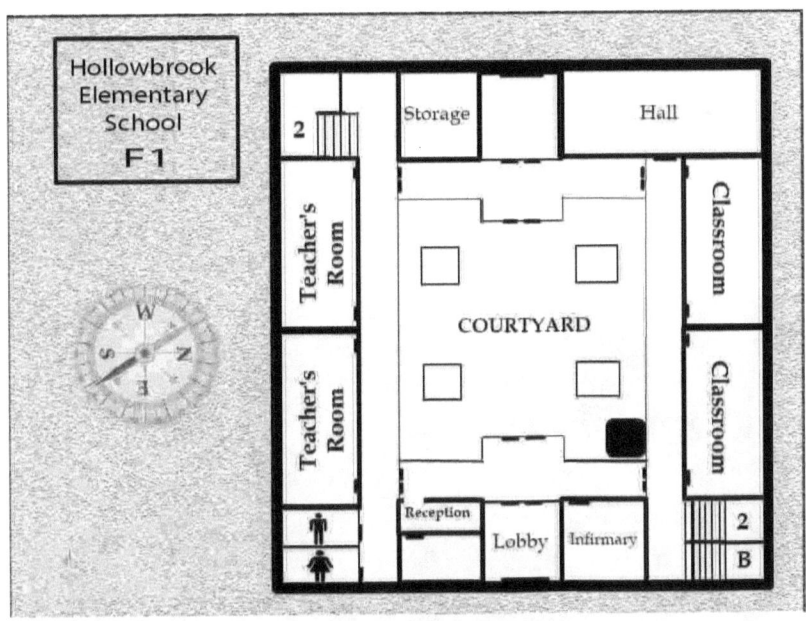

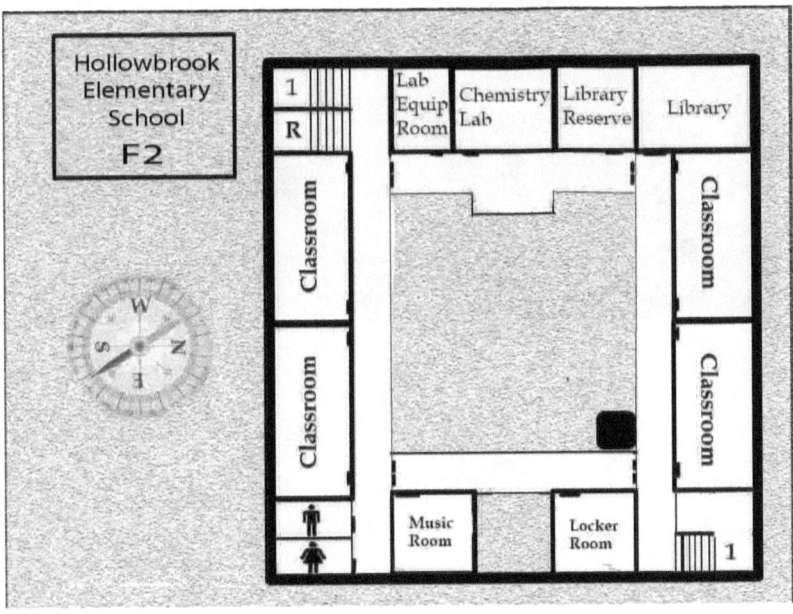

7

THE ART OF TIME

He moved back into the passage and turned left first. The map indicated that the double doors he encountered led to the bathrooms and two teachers' rooms, with stairs at the top end of the map leading to the second floor. Trevor rattled the horizontal bars and shoved his shoulders against the timber doors. It would not give way.

He marked a cross over the doors to remind himself that they were inaccessible. Turning back the way he had come, he passed the double doors on his right that led back to the lobby and another set of doors to his left, which led to a courtyard. Suddenly, he realised he might encounter more creatures if he needed to cross the courtyard or the school itself. And with that revelation, he remembered that his pistol was out of ammunition.

Trevor dropped his duffel bag and searched through his small item compartment, finding the box of ten bullets easily as they were the only items. He clipped the bullets into the magazine, reaching the last one before his radio started crackling softly. It rose in a slow crescendo until he turned the volume down slightly, afraid it might alert the unknown beast to his presence.

It was as soft as he could get it while still hearing it when he heard something moving on the other side of the doors in the courtyard. This was augmented by sniffing by the lower crack of the door. It sounded like a dog smelling the ground, which made him wonder how many Adlets were waiting for him in the courtyard. Deciding not to try the courtyard doors, he threw the bag back on and moved up the passage to the doors ahead of him.

As Trevor went further away from reception, it got harder to see. The light did not penetrate this far, which meant he could not view the map clearly either. Yet, he remembered that the Infirmary had been indicated on the map as right before the next set of double doors.

With what he could see in the stained darkness, he found the double doors ahead of him, just past some lockers to his left. He felt along the wall until he reached the corners and then traced it to the single door of the Infirmary. Trevor tested the knob and almost exclaimed in delight when it opened. Rushing into its interior, he shut the door and found the light on the wall right beside it.

The light flickered momentarily before becoming stable in its soft glow. Trevor blinked, his eyes adjusting as he espied the room he was in. There was a curtain rail ahead of him in line with the door. To his left were a small counter, a wall cabinet, a medicine cupboard and a small whiteboard with a chart. In the far corner to the left was a lonely wheelchair that still looked pristine.

Trevor went to the medical cupboard first. Inside he found two medicine bottles and some torn bandages that were unusable. Once the bottles had been stashed, he checked the lower section of the cabinet. Most of the bottles he found were smashed or had long since dripped to the bottom shelf.

Resigned to having only found two bottles, Trevor stood up again. He knew he needed a weapon, as the pistol would only last so long. He scanned the room quickly for anything that could work. He noticed that the windows had been boarded up with long thick planks. Even though he doubted that the item would do fatal damage, he wondered if it was strong enough to deter the creatures while he made his way through the school.

Trevor moved forward to the window but stopped in his tracks just as he reached the wheelchair. A moaning noise had arisen from that corner. It sounded like a woman in pain as if something was physically ailing her. Trevor stepped forward a bit more, and a scurrying sound like shoes shuffling on the ground swept across the floor to the curtain rail.

The hanging curtain shifted softly as if a breeze had breathed on it before falling still. The moaning continued, although at a higher pitch and rising tempo. It sounded afraid but in torment at the same time. No words could be discerned, as if her mouth had been gagged or taped. The tone elevated to a scream, and the sounds of splattered blood hitting the wall suddenly silenced the anguished spirit.

Against his better judgement, Trevor moved towards the curtain and parted it. Although he could not see any corpse on the bed, the deep blood seated on the gurney's mattress lay in a puddle in the centre. This sight was mild compared to the stained painting on the window's boards. It was not made of any paper or paint. Rather, the words and the image of the wall were drawn in the same blood.

"The Art of Time", Trevor read the words aloud and studied the image of the muscular man with the metal on his head. In his right hand, he wielded a double-sided axe that appeared longer than the man himself. The proportions of his arms and body seemed all wrong. On his sternum, there was a red dot.

Not knowing what to make of the cryptic words, Trevor looked at three hooks on the wall near the end of the stretcher that led to the door. On the first hook was a torch that was strapped around the head. It looked like the ones that Trevor had seen dentists use. Even though it would probably emit only a faint light, he was glad for anything that would provide some illumination and took it. He clipped the back of the torch unit on his shirt pocket and switched it on.

There was nothing on the centre hook, but the last hook had a stethoscope. Although he didn't know if he would have any real use for it, he took it anyway and stashed it in a separate compartment of his bag. Feeling ready to leave, he started to move away when the torchlight glinted off something in the pool of blood on the bed.

Trevor reached forward without thinking and grabbed the drowned object. Seeing a sink by the window, he walked over and cleaned it, revealing a long sharp scalpel. It was pure stainless steel, its cylindrical grip seated quite comfortably in his palm and the curved blade at the end extending two fingers away from his hand.

"This will do," Trevor said, placing it in the same pocket as his map.

Turning around for one last scrutiny, Trevor saw words written on the whiteboard in black ink. It looked like a schedule with times and locations allocated to certain people. As the school had a simple Infirmary and not a hospital, Trevor doubted that these were all doctors or nurses. Schools usually had a medical team of one or two people, yet this board seemed to indicate four.

Then something about their names caught his attention. He turned to the blood-stained wall that portrayed the 'Art of Time', and then back to the names on the board again.

"Raphael, Donatello, Michelangelo and Leonardo," he read aloud in the order that they appeared, which was also the order in which they worked their shifts. He wondered suddenly if it had to do with the words stained on the wall behind him.

Trevor removed his maps and pen and searched for an art room. When the initial examination yielded nothing, he scrutinised it again. No matter how many times he looked, the school did not seem to have an art room.

"Maybe it means nothing," Trevor said, rubbing his forehead.

Something creaked in the direction of the wheelchair, but when he whirled his head to that corner, he saw it was empty. Trevor spun around, looking for any sign of the wheelchair, but it was gone.

His heart was racing again. He wasn't sure if it had been racing that hard since the ghostly incident earlier, and he only just realised it, but the pounding in his chest was very noticeable now. Acting quickly, he scribbled the four names by the Infirmary on the map in the order that they appeared on the board and stashed the pen away.

Trevor took a brisk walk to the door and placed his hand on the knob. As he turned it, the radio awoke with the crackling warning of danger. He reached for the Ruger but then exchanged the map for the scalpel. With his luck and poor aim, he knew he would probably waste all the bullets before they became useful. He had to try his luck with the blade.

He opened the door. The torch shed more light on the white walls and lockers than he had seen before. The noise of the radio did not cease, yet the only strange object that Trevor saw before him was the wheelchair in the passage. It faced him as if someone was watching him while seated within it. Although it did not stir, the clamouring of the radio rose higher and then remained at the same pitch.

Trevor's only conclusion was that something was waiting for him on the other side of the double doors to his right. It was the only route he had left to take, so he knew he would have to risk whichever creature awaited him. Watching the wheelchair carefully for any movement, he stepped to the double doors and pressed on the handlebars.

The object causing the noise was indeed waiting for him. Trevor stepped back a moment, carefully avoiding the chair while raising the scalpel in defence. The Adlet growled at him in that deep horrific groan he had become accustomed to. Trevor waited patiently for two things to happen, firstly for the wheelchair to pass alongside him as he gradually reversed and secondly for the beast to attack.

Both expectations failed him for the time being. He spared a glance to his left and then right to find that the wheelchair had vanished again. He dared not look behind him for fear that the Adlet would choose that moment to attack. And then a second Adlet appeared around the corner from the passage beyond the doors.

Once again, Trevor realised that dying and being resurrected might not be an option. Even if he were to reawaken inside the reception, these beasts were going nowhere. He might have had a second chance with them, but his fate would stay the same. He decided it was time to fight and advanced forward towards them.

The Adlets had been staring at him hungrily, ready to tear him apart only a moment ago. Trevor's unexpected advance caught them off-guard, and their ears dropped as they realised that he was no longer moving away in fear. It took them a few seconds to adjust before regaining their composure, and then both Adlets rushed for him.

The surprise action by Trevor did enough to weaken their initial resolve. He was too close to the first hound for it to gain speed or momentum for a full-on attack, so Trevor gained the upper hand. It had lifted up to attack his face, but Trevor grabbed its forepaw and hand with one arm and slit its neck with the scalpel.

The hound howled and spilt blood on the clean school floor. He hadn't had time to recover from his kill when the second Adlet pounced on him. It bit into his elbow as he stepped back again. Trevor raised the scalpel with the blade facing down and hammered away at the side of its head. He screamed in pain as the Adlet's jaws clamped down further and thrust the blade into the beast's eye.

It wailed in pain, the sound echoing down both passages as it collapsed to the floor and squirmed in agony. Holding his injured arm, he stomped his boots hard on the Adlet's head until it subsided and the radio quietened down. There was still a faint crackle from it on his hip, but not loud enough that he worried about something waiting around the corner.

His elbow was bleeding slowly where the fangs had set in. He lifted his torn shirt to see the indentations the Adlet had left. It didn't look too bad, so Trevor decided to put off tending to it. He knew he could have gone back to the Lunar Nexus to rejuvenate. Yet, he recalled how the pet store's book had lost its shine and didn't want to overuse the reception's sigil in case it did the same.

He would tend to the wound later. Kathy was still his first priority. With renewed determination, he stepped forward to finally cross the threshold into the east passage when the dead Adlets on the floor stopped him again.

Something was happening to them, something that he had not seen happen before. The mottled fur on their bodies started rising up into the air and along the floor. It looked like paint that was falling off an abandoned and spoiled wall. Pretty soon, the flesh of the body melted into the floor, and the stains flowed into the walls and up.

Trevor turned so that the torch could see the left wall more clearly. No longer was it clean white wash plaster, but a sooty pallor had marked it with eeriness. Trevor looked down the passage where he had walked down and saw that the rest was fine. Yet, where he stood on either side, the walls bore evidence of his kills. There was a taint of rusted blood in the black ash that curled up the wall. Upon closer inspection, it looked like the soot was pulsing like a vein waiting to be awakened from a deep sleep.

It made him want to get away as quickly as possible. He ran from the blackened walls into the east passage, not wasting time taking his map out. To the right, he spotted stairs with a sign that indicated that it led down to the boiler room. He also noticed the stairs leading up to the second floor but was not compelled to move up there. He moved away swiftly, fearing what the darkness of the boiler room contained.

The radio crackled slightly again, but not enough that any serious danger was expected. Trevor guessed that it was whatever was in the courtyard and seemed to be following him along the wall. He ignored it and moved to the first classroom he saw on the right.

It was locked. He clasped his hands on a small square pane in the door and peered inside. He could see nothing. Trevor moved to another door further up the passage and found the same thing. The room was as black as the darkest night, with no moon or stars illuminating even the faintest path. He half wondered if the panes had not been blackened out.

He passed several lockers, radiators and a bench along the walls on his way to the next door. The second classroom also had two doors on either end, which Trevor found locked and closed off as the first. Having no further reason to investigate them, he moved to the end of the passage. He tried the door to the Hall, which was also locked. Trevor spared a moment to mark the doors in the passage with a cross, hoping that the double doors to the left of him would open up.

Before he could try, his radio signalled something approaching. At first, he thought it was perhaps the creature in the courtyard, but the sound of nails on the floor alerted him to something behind him in the passage.

"Didn't I kill you?" Trevor said as he brandished his scalpel defensively. He realised that the Adlet before him could have come from the Boiler Room instead of being one of the hounds he had killed.

Learning from his latest experience with them, he rushed forward to catch it off-guard. As before, the Adlet stumbled back in surprise and then tried to recover. Trevor fell upon it before it could move forward, slashed at its neck three times, and then struck the blade's tip down into its skull.

The beast fell, dying instantly, while Trevor pulled the scalpel out. He watched carefully while the corpse's fur, flesh and remains vanished into the floor and then onto the walls, hoping to learn something from it. The walls were stained black with the soot of the hound's soul, the deep streaks pulsing softly as if waiting for some call.

Discovering nothing new, he moved to the double doors and gladly found it open. The only accompaniment he had from the radio was still the soft noise warning him of the courtyard. As he tested the second set of locked doors to the end of the Hall on the right, the noise followed him along, patiently waiting for him to meet it. He ignored it, walking between a bench to his right and a set of lockers to his left.

When he walked to the double doors that would have led him to the rear exit lobby of the school, he could hear the hound in the courtyard sniffing by the base of the courtyard door as if to check that he was still there. Trevor pushed on the bars of the rear doors, but they would not budge. It felt like something was blocking the way behind it as opposed to simply being locked.

Disregarding the courtyard and its mysterious predator, he moved to the last room in the passage. The storage room door was unlocked. Trevor walked in carefully, using the pocket torch to check the interior before advancing and closing the door behind him. He saw a key in the door and decided to lock it, wanting some time to inspect the room in peace. As soon as the door locked, his radio fell silent.

Trevor dropped his back's baggage on the floor. He switched on the light, and by doing so, he noticed the wall opposite the door immediately. Three lights were suspended from a bar on the ceiling and shone directly on the wall. This gave the effect of the rest of the room being darker by comparison. Trevor switched his torch off when he realised it had paled against it.

There were three large notches on the lower end of the wall, with two smaller notches above them. While the two small niches were horizontally aligned, with a small portion of the wall between them like a bulwark, the larger notches were arranged in an upside-down arch. The left and right were aligned, with the centre notch, directly below the smaller niches, being the lowest of all the openings.

The light cast his shadow on the wall while he stood feeling the surface. There was nothing irregular with the plastered brick walls. It was spotless, as if it had recently been cleaned, with no speck of dust resting on the lower edges of the notches. The inner surface of the larger notches felt solid to the touch.

Yet, as Trevor felt the smaller niches, it felt like the inner surface shifted slightly. He pressed firmly against the left and then the right niche and could feel the wall section definitely move backwards. His hands could only push it so hard, though, before it resisted and held him back. It simply slid back into place once he let go.

Deciding to ignore the wall for the time being, Trevor looked around for anything useful. There were wide storage shelves lining both side walls. Vertical wooden slats split the wall-long shelves into three compartments.

He first inspected the shelves to his right, walking to the end by the door by the first section and putting his torch back on. There were some books on architecture, the arts and Renaissance artists. Tracing and sketch pads with drawings on them were piled on the lower shelves, none of which meant anything to him.

He started moving to the second section when the tip of his boot knocked something on the floor. He bent over and saw something gilded peeping out from under the lowest shelf. After failing to inch it out with his fingertips, he knelt down to use both hands to pull out the heavy object. It was a large painting. Trevor looked at the wall and wondered if it belonged there.

When he got to the lit wall, it became clear that the painting belonged in one of the large notches. He held the painting over the first left notch, noticing on the lower part of the gold-plated frame that it was simply labelled 'The Resurrection - Raffaello Sanzio da Urbino (1502)'. Trevor recognised the name easily. He had always admired Kathy's manner in which she pronounced the Renaissance painter Raphael's name while most people just called him by his common name.

Seeing the painting made him miss Kathy tremendously. She had been such a comfort to him, especially after he lost Caroline. He remembered all the nights he had spent with her cuddled on the sofa under a warm blanket on winter nights, sipping hot chocolate while they went through her book collection on artists and their famous paintings.

Trevor shook his head, the memories making his eyes water and bringing a fresh perspective to his mind. He placed Raphael's painting in the left notch. When nothing happened, he put it in the centre and right notches. Still, nothing happened.

Taking the painting out and placing it on the floor against the wall, he wondered where the other pictures were. He set out to the middle section of the shelves on the right wall again, first looking under the lowest shelf with his torch. It was empty, but looking further down, he saw something under the last section.

After pulling out another large painting, he read it was 'The Last Judgement - Michelangelo di Lodovico Buonarroti Simoni (1541)'.

Suddenly, the names on the Infirmary's board came to mind. He looked at the map, looking at the order in which he had written the names: Raphael, Donatello, Michelangelo and Leonardo. There were five slots, though.

Trevor placed Michelangelo's painting to the right of Raphael near the right corner of the wall, wanting to keep them in the same order as his map notes. He quickly went to the shelves on the left wall now, lying flat on the floor and looking under them. He spotted another one under the end shelf by the lit wall. Pulling it out, he moved with excitement to the light.

"The Annunciation," Trevor read aloud, "completed in 1475 by my dear friend Leonardo di ser Piero da Vinci."

Confirming his notes, he placed da Vinci's at the right end of the wall after Michelangelo. He didn't even spare a moment to stare at the gorgeous artwork before him. Trevor was so exhilarated in finding the paintings that he had, for that moment, forgotten the real reason he was at the school.

He dropped to his knees and slid to the left shelves' mid-section, then moved to the end when he found nothing. The final section also had no paintings. Trevor stood up and scratched his head, turning to the lit wall. He had the three large paintings, but the two smaller ones were still missing. Trevor looked to the shelves and then up, realising that there was a higher shelf near the ceiling. With renewed determination, he assumed that it had to be there.

There was no ladder in sight, so he clambered up the sides of the shelves, using the lower ones as footholds, and rose to the top. He unclipped his torch and scanned the highest shelf with it. He could not see a painting, but there was a roughly rectangular shape that looked like it might fit into one of the smaller niches. Shifting along the shelves that creaked under his weight, he reached it and dropped to the floor again.

It was a bronze relief. It might not have been the original, but the detail on the sculpted painting was exquisite and had aged rather well. He cleared the dust off the relief, looking closely at the men standing at the table's right end. The middle of the table was cut off, and that's when Trevor realised the relief was incomplete.

Something about the sculpture came to mind. Trevor remembered Kathy speaking to him in depth about this relief and how so many had debated in which year the artist had completed it. He tried to remember more about it, but it had been so long ago, and all the events in Sacred Valley had jaded his memory a bit.

Placing the relief on the floor by the paintings, he checked the other shelf by climbing to the top again. The first item he saw was a long rectangular wooden box with a lid that appeared to slide off one end. He reached for it, opening the box on the shelf instead of climbing down again. When the top was off, the torch shone dully on the straw yet brightly on the weapon within it.

Trevor grinned hugely as he took the double-barrel shotgun out, moving now down to the light to inspect it further. It looked familiar, although he knew so little about firearms that they may as well all have looked the same. He saw a note tagged to the trigger guard by a thin string and read the label, identifying the shotgun as a Browning Citori 425 Blue Laminate Special Edition.

It brought to mind where he had seen it. He had joined Jay at the shooting range as an observation guest. The Citori was a standard-issue police shotgun where Jay was stationed. Trevor had always admired the weapon's shape and stock. Jay had brought Trevor through a session of identifying the parts of the gun and showed him how to load the shells. That was the most experience he had had in handling it.

This Citori was slightly different, though. Where the standard Citori had a brown stock, receiver and forestock, the special edition in his hand had timber with blue and black knots and bands. There was a chrome plate on the chamber guard with a silver symbol he did not recognise. The standard Citori also had a standard smooth barrel. In contrast, this Citori had ribs along the sight rail and ventilated ribs between the upper and lower barrels. The barrels had a splendid blue sheen to the metal to complement the blue bands on the timber parts.

Trevor ripped the tag off and opened the twelve-gauge chamber. It muted his enthusiasm when he found it was empty. In his opinion, a shotgun without ammo was useless unless he risked using it as a bat.

Nevertheless, it was the best weapon he had at hand, so he took it to his bag at the door. He was about to place it in the slip where the copper pipe had been but decided to reserve that for melee weapons. He looked on the opposite side for the other slip and tucked the Citori in there.

"Now, back to the paintings," Trevor mused.

Climbing back up where he had found the shotgun, he hunted down the length of the shelf until he reached the door's end. Another relief lay there, and he grabbed it and jumped down without hesitating. Once by the light, he saw that it was not a separate relief but rather the second half of the first.

The other end of the table on the relief was now visible. He remembered now why the sculpture had caught his attention originally when Kathy had introduced him to it. It had the image of a man's head on a plate at the end of the table. Trevor quickly turned it over to read an inscription in pencil: 'The Feast of Herod - Donato di Niccolò di Betto Bardi (1425)'.

With Donatello's final piece in hand, he placed it in the left small notch at the top, quickly followed by the other relief in the right. He tried pushing it into the wall further, but it would not budge. Checking his map list from the Infirmary, he placed Raphael's Resurrection, Michelangelo's Judgement and Leonardo's Annunciation from left to right. Taking a breath, he pressed the relief in again.

Still, nothing happened. The right one slid slightly back before returning to position, but the left one had not moved at all. His excitement had turned to frustration. Trevor was tempted to leave the paintings alone and go in search of Kathy elsewhere instead, but he hated giving up so quickly. For all he knew, she was being kept captive behind the wall by whoever was torturing them.

He thought about it a bit longer, trying to find a common element that he could use that might solve the riddle. He noticed that they all had dates on them and tried to sort them chronologically. First was the 1475 Annunciation, next the 1502 Resurrection and finally, the 1541 Judgement. Hoping for the best, he pressed against the reliefs again.

As before, the right one moved in only slightly and returned, while the left one didn't budge. He slammed the side of his fist against a free space on the wall, making the paintings shake. He was so sure there was a reason for the clues towards the paintings. After all, why would everything lead to him solving this riddle if it amounted to nothing?

And then something came to mind. If it had nothing to do with the order of the names or the order of the dates, perhaps it had something to do with the events in the paintings themselves. He stepped back and looked at them from under the light rail on the ceiling. While setting the relief of the beheading as the starting point, he tried to make out which would be the next most likely event.

Out of the three, the Annunciation would have to be first, which was the first announcement of the divine's coming to earth and the woman's role in that destiny. Then it was the Resurrection of the divine Lord to heaven, where the Last Judgment would be performed.

Trevor's heart sank in despair. This was exactly the order it was in now, yet nothing had worked. He turned around, about to head to his bag and leave the room, when he decided to check the last area he had missed. The middle shelves on the left of him had various boxes and canvas sheets over some items. Using his torch to pierce the darkness, he scavenged through it.

Most of the boxes contained more books and items. It seemed like someone had been packing to clear the storage room but had not had the chance to relocate them yet. Trevor felt like he was just wasting further time when his hand brushed over something hard behind one of the boxes.

He pulled it out and saw that it was wrapped in linen. The weight felt like the other reliefs in the wall, and his hopes were aroused again when he uncovered it. It was another relief like the one in the small left niche, appearing like a duplicate at first.

Trevor's inspection under the spotlight revealed something very different about this version, though. Where Donatello's original masterpiece had a head seated on the plate only, the head was complemented by the torso on the table.

The head was not connected to the torso, though. Trevor just began to wonder where the limbs were when he saw two people on either side of the table, each holding an arm and a leg. He tried to get more light on the faces, until he realised who they resembled the most.

"No," Trevor said quietly. "Jay and Philip?"

He then noticed that, where the original loose head on the plate was quite bearded and hairy, this one was clean-shaven with short hair. Trevor turned the relief around and saw the only words scrawled on the back: 'The Feast of Trevor'.

"What the hell?" Trevor breathed hard.

He moved quickly to the relief on the right. He couldn't remember what Herod had looked like in the original painting, but the man at the right end of the table looked eerily like himself.

Not wanting to waste too much time analysing the possible meaning behind the relief, he replaced the original left relief with the new one. He tested both sculptures by pressing them in. This time, both slid in slightly before moving out again.

Motivated by the correct pieces, he had only to find the right placement of the lower paintings. Leaving the Annunciation as the most obvious first placement, he changed the remaining two to have the Last Judgement and the Resurrection in the centre and on the right.

The difference in the sculpted reliefs made him inspect the large paintings more closely while changing them. He had not noticed it before since the detail of the images had seemed irrelevant at the time. Still, he suspected certain elements looked suspiciously wrong and out of place.

Before testing the reliefs, he acquired the Renaissance book on the shelf and brought it back to the lit wall.

He found Raphael's section and shifted through the pages until he found the Annunciation. Nothing at first caught his attention until he saw that the one on the wall was sans Halo. The two figures in the original had bright yellow bands over their heads to represent their sanctity, but the wall paintings had none. Also, the woman on the wall painting resembled Caroline too much for Trevor's liking.

Shifting to da Vinci and his Last Judgement, the initial scrutiny had revealed nothing. Yet now that Trevor knew what he had to look for, he quickly spotted the differences. Instead of the divine Lord standing in the midst of the heavenly orchestra, laying down his judgement on all, Caroline stood over four people amid a crowd of people pointing at them.

The first person on the left had small dogs biting and pulling at her legs while she tried to crawl away in her own blood. The second beside her had ropes tied to his ankles and wrists while four flying beings pulled them apart, his torso and lower body splitting at the waist. The third had a bull digging its horns into his back. And the final victim was standing, raising his hands in supplication towards Caroline, a long axe driven through his back and out the front of his torso.

Almost too afraid to look at the last painting, he inspected it anyway. He knew it was the resurrection and half expected Caroline's face on the body that rose into heaven. Yet, it was not, and neither was it a woman. Instead, it was a man that rose from four dead figures lying on the ground, resembling the four victims in the previous painting. He had a tattoo on his left upper arm.

The main difference was that he recognised the face as someone who definitely was not divine or godly. The more he thought about it, the more he realised that the rising man and the dismembered man on the table of the 'Feast of Trevor' was exactly the same.

"Oh no," Trevor muttered. "It can't be…. no, no, it cannot be!"

Propelled by fear of the potential revelation, he rushed forward and pushed hard on the reliefs. They slid all the way back this time until he could hear a click, followed by a grinding mechanism. The reliefs moved sideways and outwards, revealing a hidden storage unit behind both of them in the wall.

The contents were minute in comparison to the chamber, despite the chamber's own small stature. The one was a key with a tag that read 'Library' on it. The other was a long paintbrush with a fine point. The entire length was made of hard polished oak wood, including the tip.

Trevor grabbed the items and ran for the door. He placed the key in his map pocket and threw the bag onto his shoulders. The bag was gaining weight with the addition of the shotgun, and he made a mental note to empty some of his clothes and unnecessary personal belongings the first proper chance he got.

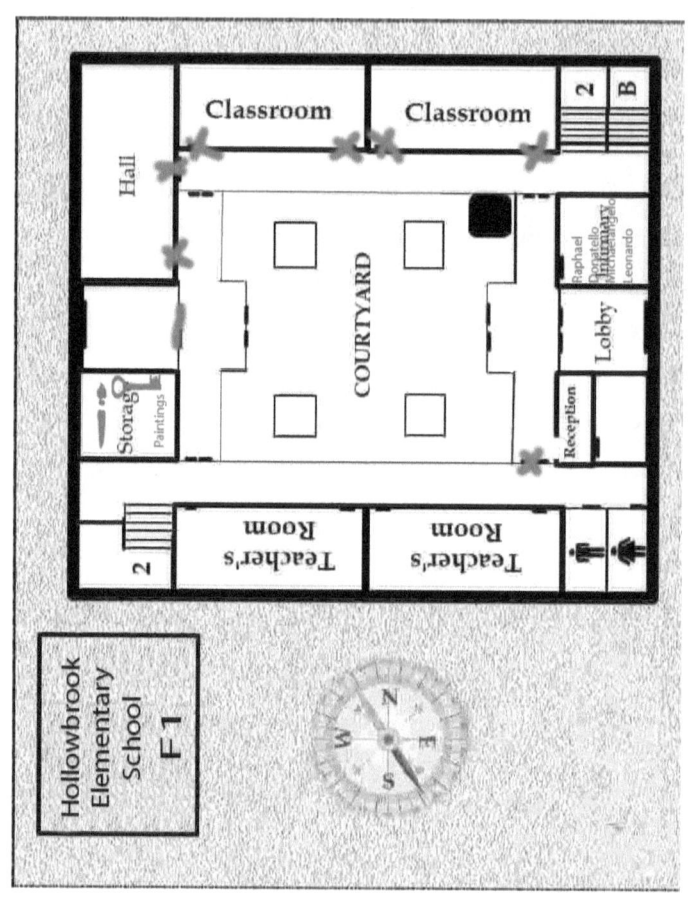

8

THE WORDS OF TIME

Trevor unlocked the door, despite the radio's alarming signal. He felt confident in his ability to deal with another Adlet and wanted to dispatch with it to make his way to the Library. He turned the knob on the door just as the radio grew softer and suddenly went very silent.

He entered the passage softly, realising that a soft light was streaming in through the upper windows from the courtyard, less than before. A large mass of light drew his attention to the centre of the passage. With great anxiety, he discovered that the courtyard doors stood open.

There was a faint smell, like a farm, lingering around him. Trevor sniffed the air more; it smelled like a wet goat's fur. He recalled the creature that had been following him all around the passages and wondered if it was the cause of the smell. Trevor also wondered which school kept goats on their premises, but more fearfully, who had opened the doors.

He checked his map quickly under torchlight and saw that the library was not on the first floor. Scanning the second-floor map, he located it in the passage above him on the other end. The maps revealed two flights of stairs that could take him up, one by the stairs that led down to the Boiler Room and the other just past the doors he stood by.

He moved quickly, pushing on the door handles. It would not budge. He rammed his shoulders against it and kicked it, but it would not open. Trevor had one final option left: making it to the Boiler Room stairs and heading up from there.

Wanting to keep the maps safe from whatever creature had passed the storeroom, he stashed them in his pocket. He decided to take his Ruger out and extended his arms out in front of him. He went to the open courtyard and stepped onto the white lawn.

It looked like it was snowing. It was overcast overhead, either with clouds or deepening mist. The sky was a lot darker than when he entered the school. He still would have been able to see without the torch, thanks to four street lights in each quadrant of the courtyard.

Trevor moved further in, wondering why his radio remained quiet. He saw four trees in the courtyard, each placed within its quarter next to each street light. Standing in the centre of the yard, he noticed a dilapidated clocktower in the corner to his left. Someone had boarded up the front panel that opened up to its inner workings. Clearly, they had not wanted anyone to tamper with it.

He saw something out of place to his right that sent chills up his spine. In the snowy white ash was a large dark brown coffin. It looked like it was made from the same wood type as the tree its side rested against. The bottom of the coffin was well hidden in the snow, while the overhead foliage cast the top lid in shadow.

Keeping his gun in hand, he walked over to the coffin. The body itself had no intricate designs and was quite plain, but the centre of the lid had a gap in it. Trevor peered into the opening, wondering if he could spy on what was inside. Yet, it did not go right through. Instead, it seemed like some item had been removed from it.

It did not have any regular shape. There were four corners that should have made a square, but strange looped shapes extended on the upper and lower ends. And in the centre of the impression was a hole pressing further down.

Trevor momentarily thought about it and retrieved the wooden paintbrush he had acquired from the storeroom. He leaned over the coffin lid and first pushed it down the hole, timber brush tip. It went through smoothly, and the diameter of the brush fit perfectly. When it reached its end, he heard something click into place.

He tried to pull the brush out again, but it was locked in. As much as he yanked up, it would not release. Leaving it in place, he checked for seams of the lid against the body of the coffin, but he could find none. The coffin was one complete body with no apparent means to push the lid off or open it up.

Suddenly, Trevor's head pained. He held his free hand up to his forehead as it spun, and strange words entered his head as if someone was sending a message to it. It was incoherent, though, with some deep grumbling. Once again, Trevor smelled goat fur, and a piercing ringing sounded in his ears. He was unsure if it was from the radio that started clamouring again or if something was wrong with him.

With what senses he had left, he made every effort to turn around. As soon as he faced the doors whereby he had entered the courtyard, the noises and spinning in his head died down, but the radio continued to bleat its warning. Trevor now saw the hound that had followed him along the walls through the passage sniffing at the doors. And it was not an Adlet.

The hound's body was completely covered in dark black fur, darker than any of the Adlets he had seen. The blackness seemed to be from the darkest night, and its eyes were burning red. Not only were the eyes' colour red, but there seemed to be a trail of pure red flame rising from it.

Everything about the beast screamed canine except for two unique features. Where paws should have been, goat hooves stood on the snowy ash. The top of its head sported a heavy black mane that trailed along its neck and back like a stallion's. With rising trepidation, he remembered where he had read about these creatures in his mythology and lore.

It was a black Cadejo. In the lore he had studied, it had been mentioned that these beasts mainly hunted travellers at night, which explained to Trevor why he had not seen them on the streets. Knowing what it was now, he realised where the goat smell had come from and why his mind had gone crazy for a moment. He also decided that he could not turn his back on the Cadejo again, for if he did, his mind would spin out of control again.

They both stood frozen, still staring at one another. Trevor wondered why it had not attacked yet and if it was waiting for him to turn his back on it and run. The clamouring of his radio increased despite the hound not moving. After a few seconds, it was joined from the passage by another black Cadejo by its side.

The Cadejos moved towards him. Trevor raised his gun at them, walking sideways to the centre of the yard. He knew it would prove useless. In the lore, it was said that nothing could kill these beasts. All Trevor could hope for was either to harm them enough to rush past them or be killed and revived by the Lunar Nexus in the reception.

He almost decided on the latter. It would have been far easier to reach the stairs from the reception. Yet, giving into death was not something Trevor desired to do. He wanted to believe that he had more guts than that, even if that meant wasting his bullets on something he couldn't kill and going down with a fight.

The first Cadejo he had seen left the other one's side in a sprint. It growled and lunged for him as he released his first set of three shots. The bullets hit its shoulder and then its ear, making the hound yelp and look up at him angrily.

It ran forward again, Trevor firing three more shots just as it jumped up on him. It missed the beast completely, but just as its body rose above him, he pressed the nozzle against its chest and fired. The hound cried out in pain as he hit it aside into the snow, lying there in agony.

Hoping it would spare him a moment to deal with the next Cadejo, he noticed that the remaining hound watched the injured Cadejo with a blank expression and then ran to attack. While raising and aiming his gun, Trevor missed how the white snow moved to cover the trailing blood of the Cadejo. It rose on the blackest fur, covering the hound that squirmed on the lawn. Only when it had covered the beast completely did the hound lay still in complacence, recovering from the bullet buried in its chest.

Trevor had shot the final four bullets at the black Cadejo racing towards him and jumped out of the way as it attacked. Its claw clutched onto his leg, scraping the pants open and causing his shin to bleed. He exclaimed, holding onto his injured leg as he rolled into the snow. The pain made his head spin again, and each time his back faced the hound, the dark voices sang in his head, making him feel like he was losing his mind.

He rolled to face it again and sat on his knees, waiting for it to kill him. It was the only way out. Realising he still had the pistol in his hand, he holstered it. The Cadejo observed him as if deciding whether to take the bait. And then, with no further ado, he charged in for the kill.

Trevor closed his eyes for the impact when something swift passed before him and knocked the black Cadejo to the ground. He watched as the beasts rolled on the snow, biting and gnashing at each other's necks and heads. Their fangs clashed, and blood dripped over the pure white on the ground.

When the rolling stopped, the new white hound drove its fangs deep into the black Cadejo's neck and ripped it open. The black hound quivered for a moment underneath it and then died. Its corpse slowly dissipated into the snow, becoming one with it under a sheet of blood.

Trevor watched as the white hound made its way over to him and sat before him patiently. It had the same red burning eyes, rolling mane and goat hooves as the black Cadejo, but it was entirely white. He then remembered that one thing was mentioned in another book he had read, indicating the sole way a black Cadejo could be killed. That weapon was now before him in the form of a white Cadejo.

Reaching forward to ensure it was friendly, the Cadejo leaned down and pressed its mane into his hand. He ran his fingers through it and rubbed its head, very happy with how his luck had turned. The Cadejo growled softly in happiness, rolling its head around playfully and enjoying the attention.

The soft growl was the only noise left in the courtyard, causing Trevor to realise that the radio must have gone silent when the black Cadejo had died. Taking this as the final confirmation that the white hound was an ally, he rose up only to fall back to his knees in pain. His shin throbbed from the previous attack and was still bleeding on the lawn.

He dropped his bag and got the only first aid kit he had. He applied the salve to his shin and then rapped the bandage around it. It soothed the pain slightly, and he could rise without too much discomfort. He wondered if he should use one of the two medicine bottles he had found in the Infirmary but decided against it. The kit helped enough that he could walk properly.

Trevor lifted the bag but felt the pressure that the weight pressed on his shin. He unzipped the main compartment of the duffel bag and looked at the clothes he had thrown in there haphazardly. He could think of no reason that he would need a change of clothes in Sacred Valley. If he, Kathy and Jay escaped the town.... No, *when* they escaped, he would get some more.

He removed the clothes from the bag, throwing them on the floor. When it was empty, with only the shotgun, notes, street maps and health bottles, he strapped it onto his back. It felt much lighter, and his shin no longer hurt as much as before. As he moved towards the closed courtyard doors to his left, the white Cadejo left the sniffing of his clothes to join his side.

The courtyard doors opened easily, and he was back in the passage that led to the reception area. Trevor suddenly realised how stupid he had been. Instead of wasting his only first aid kit, he could have just used the Lunar Nexus to rejuvenate all his wounds. He felt angry with himself but then remembered the book's Lunar Nexus that had died. Trevor was still unsure how many times he could use the Lunar Nexus. With that in mind, he realised it may have been best to spare using the Lunar Nexus if he didn't have to.

With the Cadejo faithfully following him, he headed to the classroom passage again and then turned to the stairs. He still feared going down to the Boiler Room, but at least he did not have to just yet. The small torch on his chest lit the area immediately ahead of them as they moved up the stairs.

Where the landing was for the stairs to turn up to the second floor, Trevor spotted rubbish lying in one corner. There were boxes and wooden planks piled on top of one another. He checked the planks and found a lengthy one with long nails at the end of it. With no bullets left and only the scalpel to fight with, he realised that this was his best option for the time being.

Trevor and his Cadejo stepped onto the second floor while checking that he had the right floor plan in his hand and packing the rest away. He saw that the double doors ahead of him led to a locker room and the school's music room. He tested the doors with a hard thrust, but something was blocking the door behind it. It moved slightly back like it was unlocked, but the pressure from behind would not let him proceed further.

Walking down the passage towards the Library at the end of it, he checked the small panes in the doors of the first classroom on the way. As on the first floor, the windows revealed nothing but darkness. Before Trevor reached the second classroom door, the radio announced the presence of something evil near him, along with the stench of goat fur. While he moved further forward, the radio grew louder, but he did not need its increasing squeal to tell that the beast was ahead of him.

The torch would not reach its body in the darkness, but he saw the fiery red eyes. The black Cadejo growled at them as the white one by his side sent a warning back towards it. The white Cadejo dug its feet in, holding its head low in preparation for the attack. The black hound did the same, and Trevor waited for the two to meet. Although the black beast had stopped moving, the radio continued rising in volume.

A clicking sound of nails sounded from behind them. Trevor unclipped his torch and held it up in the air, hoping it would give him more sight ahead. It took a few seconds before the hand and paw of the Adlet became visible on the floor before him.

"Alright," Trevor said in the echoing silence, "You take the bad one; I'll take the easy one."

As if in answer, the white Cadejo bounded forward. Trevor clipped the torch back on and held the long plank in front of him with both hands. He heard the two beasts crash into each other behind him, claws and fangs entwined, as the Adlet leapt for him. He struck it with the wooden plank from side to side, dodging as the front paw claws raked towards his chest.

The Adlet turned and jumped again. Trevor parried another claw attack with the plank and then brought the nails at the end down into its skull as it lunged forward to bite him. He pulled the nails back out as it fell, wailing to the ground, and bashed its head further until it stopped moving.

He watched as the Adlet's remains moved into the floor, and the black stains crept along the walls to pulse to their own beat. The two Cadejos had gone silent, but Trevor was elated when he saw the white hound safely returned to his side with blood trailing the fur around its mouth. As he moved forward to inspect the black Cadejo, the radio fell down to its normal silence.

The black hound also melted into the ground, with the stains moving to the walls like the Adlet had. However, the stains that drove up the wall seemed tainted with fine red lines. The lines connected two red orbs on the wall, with black pupils set within the fiery circles that watched Trevor. As he moved away from it, the eyes watched him leave, following his every movement.

Ignoring the next classroom, he headed straight for the Library at the end. As he expected, he found it locked. He retrieved the key he had recovered in the storeroom and unlocked it. Once he and his Cadejo were inside, he locked the door behind them and dropped his bag on the floor.

Finding the switch to the left of the door, he flicked it. Lights trickled on behind aisles of tall bookracks to the right, faintly illuminating the desk by the left wall. Trevor walked to it and inspected the surface. A few notes were lying on the side, and a large desk calendar was horizontally on the centre of the desk.

He checked through the three drawers on the left side of the desk. Most of it contained more papers and memorandums, but in the last drawer, under some crumpled paper, he found a box of ten 9mm bullets. Hastily in his eagerness, he opened the box and reloaded his Ruger.

Curious to see if the paper had any importance, he opened it up. On it, he read *'RES999.4 – RES999.61'*, written in pencil by a rushed hand. He tucked the paper in his front pocket behind the torch in case it had some relevance.

Moving down short steps to the Library proper and where the ceiling-high bookracks began, he passed a short pedestal and walked among the racks, inspecting the spines. It was the normal assortment of books that one would find in any Library, and nothing seemed out of place. He felt like he was wasting time searching through the books when he saw another parchment on the floor at the end of one of the aisles. He opened it up and widened his eyes when he saw it was addressed to him.

"My dear Trevor," he read out loud. "I really hope you find this and that there is still enough time for you to locate me. I'm not even sure if you're in this creepy town. But if you find this note, someone is hunting me. I haven't been able to see him clearly yet, but it looks like that man that made us crash. You know, the one with the strange head.

"There's something about him, though. He doesn't seem to belong here, and I only catch small glimpses of him, like he's a ghost. I did see a mark on his arm that reminded me of a tattoo I once saw. I think I know who he is.

"Wait… someone's coming", Trevor read, the final part written more hastily. "I love you, Trevor, more than anyone ever did. Please find me. Kathy."

He felt crushed. Now that he knew she was definitely in the school and had been in the Library, the situation felt more real to him than before. Her plea stung his heart, and he felt guilty for taking so long to save her. Folding the paper neatly into the notes part of his bag, he continued his search for her in the Library.

He was about to turn into the row at the back that followed the wall along the sides of all the racks when something on the wall caught his attention. As before, in the Infirmary, words were written in blood on the wall:

The Words of Time

Looking down the back row, he saw a white pedestal in the corner. As he neared it, he noticed a glass box over the top surface of the marble column. Just before the container started, there were six rotation discs with numbers set within the surface. Three of the discs were set to the left of a small bronze plaque and three to the right. The name 'Aristocles' was engraved on the plaque.

As Trevor fiddled with discs, rolling the numbers over and over, he wondered if they were combination locks. He heard a soft whine behind him and turned to see the white Cadejo waiting for him at the other corner of the room. A short jog got him there quickly, and he inspected another marble pedestal with an empty glass box above it too.

The plaque read 'Aristotle' and also had a set of three rotating discs on either side of it. He recalled the pedestal he had passed so briefly on the way down the steps and rushed over to it with the hound behind him. This pedestal did not have a box on it, but rather on the floor beside it, smashed on the steps around the pedestal's base. The thought crossed his mind that someone else had tried to solve this mystery before.

The final plaque read "Socrates" with the same combination locks on either side. He fiddled with the numbers, but with no idea what they meant, he had no hope of unlocking them. He moved up the stairs to the right of the desk, hoping something could help him, when he saw a door in the right corner.

The words on the glass door revealed that it was the reserved section of the Library. Trevor assumed this was where the restricted books were kept for academic purposes only. He took the paper from his front pocket and noticed that both numbers started with 'RES'.

"Catalogue numbers!" Trevor exclaimed in excitement.

He pressed his hand over the circular knob and turned, finding it locked. Frustrated and irritated, he bashed his elbow through the door's glass, sending the shards flying inwards. Reaching in, he turned the knob from the inside, unlocking the lock's central pin.

As soon as he was inside, he flicked the switch on the wall. The light was brighter in the small room compared to the Library. The hound waited inside the actual library, keeping watch on the main door. Trevor saw that each wall had racks reaching the ceiling, but in the centre, there were aisles with racks that only reached his waist.

He walked to the first line along the wall to his left just as the light bulb dangling in the centre of the ceiling blew. The Library Reserve was cast into darkness, except for the minimal light that Trevor's torch shone from his chest. He continued inspecting the books on the rack despite the bulb's sudden termination.

The numbers started at 750, and he realised that the books he sought would not be close to it. He turned around to the smaller rack behind him and checked the numbers. It started at 865. He moved to the small rack closest to the door, which began with 960 and ended with 1005.

Kneeling down, Trevor hunted for 999. He found it quickly enough and then searched specifically for 999.4 and 999.61. The two thick books were next to each other and featured writing on Geology. Frowning at their relevance to the Philosopher plaques found in the Library, he took them out anyway and placed them on his lap.

He paged through the first book quickly, looking for any writing or loose papers within them. Much to his disdain, there was nothing that he considered relevant. He lifted the first book off, changing focus to the second book, when some papers fell off it to the floor beside him.

Trevor picked the paper up gingerly, as it felt fragile. A cursory scan of the document made him realise it was a newsletter published by Dunst University many years ago. He flipped the papers over until he saw an article by Doctor C. George Boeree, a resident professor of the University.

The article was entitled 'Ancient Philosophers: Socrates, Plato and Aristotle'.

His eyes skimmed the information quickly and noticed that by each small note on the philosophers were their birth and death years, each containing three digits. Trevor jumped up with the papers clutched in his hand and raced to the first pedestal by the steps. He confirmed Socrates's name on the plaque and then read the first part of Socrates in the article:

Socrates (470-399) was the son of a sculptor and a midwife, and served with distinction in the Athenian army during Athens' clash with Sparta. He married, but had a tendency to fall in love with handsome young men, in particular a young soldier named Alcibiades. He was, by all accounts, short and stout, not given to good grooming, and a lover of wine and conversation. His famous student, Plato, called him "the wisest, and justest, and best of all men whom I have ever known" (Phaedo).

Spinning the rotating discs, he numbered 470 on the left and 399 on the right. A final click sounded, and then a central portion of the marble top shifted. Dust fell over the sides as something inside the pedestal moved onto the platform. As a head appeared, he realised that it was the bust of Socrates. Once the head was through, the marble top closed underneath it.

Trevor moved towards Aristotle's platform with the Cadejo following hot on his heels. Upon reaching it, he scanned the foremost detail on the philosopher:

Aristotle (384-322) was born in a small Greek colony in Thrace called Stagira. His father was a physician and served the grandfather of Alexander the Great. Presumably, it was his father who taught him to take an interest in the details of natural life. He was Plato's prize student, even though he disagreed with him on many points. When Plato died, Aristotle stayed for a while with another student of Plato, who had made himself a dictator in northern Asia Minor. He married the dictator's daughter, Pythias. They moved to Lesbos, where Pythias died giving birth to their only child, a daughter. Although he married again, his love for Pythias never died, and he requested that they be buried side by side.

As soon as he touched the discs, he flipped them until 384 and 322 were on either side of the plaque. Once again, the platform shifted to lift the head of Aristotle onto it, covered neatly by the glass box.

Making his way to the final platform, Trevor stopped and frowned while staring at the plaque. The only other information the articles contained was on Plato, but the plaque clearly stated Aristocles. He was about to turn to look for a fourth pedestal, but his eyes caught Aristocles's name in the first section of the article:

Plato (437-347) was Socrates' prized student. From a wealthy and powerful family, his actual name was Aristocles -- Plato was a nickname, referring to his broad physique. When he was about twenty, he came under Socrates' spell and decided to devote himself to philosophy. Devastated by Socrates' death, he wandered around Greece and the Mediterranean and was taken by pirates. His friends raised money to ransom him from slavery, but when he was released without it, they bought him a small property called Academus to start a school -- the Academy, founded in 386.

Taking that as his cue, he inserted 437 and 347 on the locks. Plato's head rose into the glass box. Once it had settled, Trevor's exhilaration at solving the locks gave way to confusion. He had no idea what to do with the heads. The blank eyes of Plato simply stared up at him as if laughing at his foolishness.

A sound of turning gears at the front of the Library made Trevor duck behind the racks with the Cadejo sitting beside him. The grinding noise churned for a few more seconds before it ended with a click. Trevor crept along the book rack on his haunches until he reached the end near the Socrates pedestal. He breathed deeply and listened to further noise, only then noticing that the windows he faced were boarded up with planks.

He peeked around the corner to see if anyone had entered. The door was still closed, and for all he could tell, it was still locked. Trevor looked at the desk, not seeing anything out of the ordinary at first until the desk calendar caught his attention. It had been lifted off the tabletop by something underneath it. Still, the light from the main library section was insufficient to reveal what it was.

About to stand and move towards it, he was frozen by the awakening of his radio. It scratched and crackled, not loud enough to cause Trevor great alarm but enough to make him realise something was out in the passages. Then he heard the scraping of something heavy along the passage floor. It sounded like it took great effort to haul the object across the floor. It screeched louder than the radio as it passed the Library door and then faded away into silence again.

When the radio confirmed its absence with its silence, Trevor bolted to the desk. He threw the calendar onto the floor and saw three small platforms on the surface, reminding him of the platforms on which the three busts rested.

The torch on his chest lit up words that a crude object had etched onto the timber surface. It had either been a nail or other sharp metallic object or someone's nails, but he could at least make out what it said:

The wisest of them all, favouring men above women,
Always receives the centre of attention.
His beloved student, his right-hand man,
Desired freedom from slavery by those that loved him.
The Grandson of wisdom, left to his own devices,
Ensuring that his love was buried by his side.

Yet always will the students look upon their master,
Who even in death only looked forward to eternal glory.

Trevor referred to the article for more information on the philosophers. Even though Kathy had sometimes spoken of her knowledge of ancient philosophy, they had not delved as deep into it as her love for art. The little he knew about these specific patrons was enough to baffle him, and he hoped that Professor Boeree would succeed where he failed.

He scanned the notes on Socrates at the top, noting that Plato had been his prized student. Furthermore, Plato had considered Socrates to be the wisest, justest and best of all the men he had known.

Turning around, he ran down the steps to pick up the heavy bust of Socrates. He moved it back up the stairs as quickly as he could, placing it on the centre pedestal and ensuring that he remained 'the centre of attention'.

Trevor sprinted to the left corner from where he stood, hastily collecting Plato as Socrates's prized student. He moved back again to where the Cadejo waited for him, content to let the human do all the running. It wagged its tail at him in greeting as he placed Plato's head on the right pedestal, seeing as how he was his 'right-hand man'. He confirmed with the article that Plato had indeed been imprisoned and noticed that his friends had wanted to pay the ransom that would have freed Plato from pirates' captivity.

Before running to Aristotle, he checked that he was indeed Socrates's grandson. There was no clear indication of any lineage between him and Socrates, but since Aristotle was Plato's prized student, and Plato was Socrates's prized student, Trevor felt he understood the reference well enough. However, the article confirmed that Aristotle loved his wife so much that he wanted to bury her beside her.

He hurried to the final bust and returned, placing it to the left of the other devices. He waited patiently, grinning like an idiot while staring at the three heads that faced him. Trevor waited for a click or gears or some evidence that he had succeeded, but nothing happened. He rechecked the words and saw the final clue that he had forgotten about.

"Of course," Trevor said, turning the outer heads of the students to look at their master. Socrates's bust couldn't get much more attention than that.

The click and gears he had initially expected finally arrived. Something under the desk's top dropped to the floor, and Trevor ran around to investigate it. A hidden cardboard container within the thick desk top was released by the three busts. Trevor pulled out his scalpel and opened it.

Within it, he found two objects, like in the storeroom painting unit. The first was a key to the Music Room. The second was a wooden block which resembled an open book, except for a strange indentation around the pages and the hole through its centre.

Trevor remembered the coffin's lid where he had placed the brush in. He recalled that there had been a square shape, and he wondered if this book was the part he needed to insert into it. The brush would easily pass through the centre of the book.

Knowing that the Music room was the next destination, he understood what the strange shape was in the book and extended into the upper and lower reaches of the coffin's indentation. It resembled the treble clef symbol on a music sheet, the same symbol on Kathy's charm bracelet with the book and brush. Trevor was confident that that was the final item required for the coffin.

Having just packed the key and book block away, Trevor looked up at the door in sudden trepidation. If all the clues were tied to Kathy's passion for art, philosophy and music, then everything led him to believe she was in that coffin. His heart paced at an insane beat again as his head reeled.

If he was right, Trevor's fears that someone avenged Caroline's death by blaming Trevor for it was justified. This person obviously felt that killing his lover was the best retribution they had to offer. With that thought came the sinking feeling that Kathy was already dead in the coffin and this mysterious hunter was trapping Trevor by using her and all these clues as bait.

Be that as it might have been, Trevor had to go along with the sick game. He had to try with every living part of him to free her in case she was still alive. He could not just leave her behind and assume she was dead. He would only leave once he either held her warmly embraced in his arms or lying dead within them.

He could think of only one person who would have wanted to avenge Caroline. It was the same man he had seen in the paintings; it could have been the same man that Kathy had alluded to in her letter. However, Trevor knew that was impossible, and it had to be someone else that had been close to them. After all, the man in the painting was dead... Trevor had made sure of that.

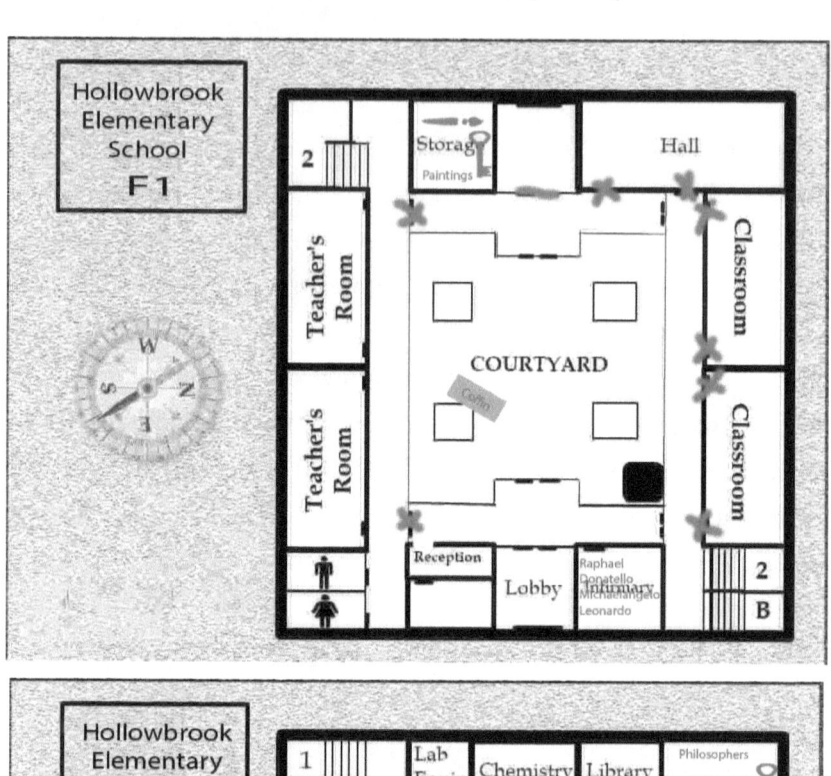

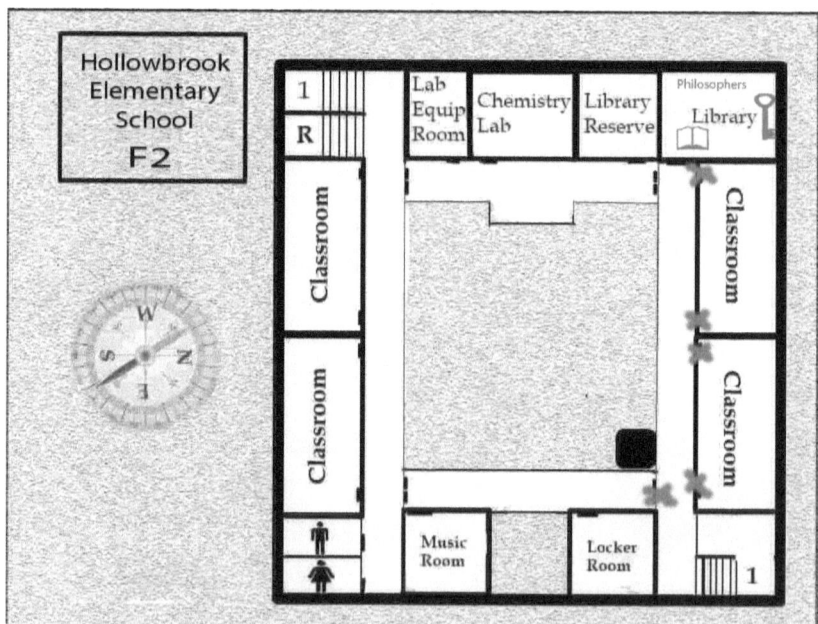

9

THE NOTES OF TIME

The passage outside the Library was quiet. If the doors to the music passage were open at the end, he would have preferred to have gone through them instead. The only option Trevor had for the moment, though, was the doors to his right, and so, with the white Cadejo still walking beside him, he opened the doors and entered.

He saw another door to the right and used the map to identify it as a second door into the Library Reserve. Having no need to go back in, he moved on and checked the Chemistry Lab door, which would not open. The final door in that passage was to the Lab Equipment Room, which was not locked.

Trevor entered, leaving the door open. The Cadejo sat at the entrance and held guard. Hoping to find more ammunition or health items, he went through the drawers, cupboards and equipment units. When he was almost at the end of his search, he found a first aid kit hidden at the back of a cupboard.

Giving up on finding anything else that could be useful, he moved back out into the passage. As soon as he closed the door, the radio greeted him with a small whine. Trevor looked at the Cadejo for a sign that trouble was approaching, but the hound simply looked back up at him.

He grasped his wooden plank and opened the doors that led to the next passage. While walking into it, the radio increased in volume. He checked the map and moved to the stairs that led to the roof, causing the radio to go softer. The stairs were completely blocked off by rubble and building material. It looked like this part of the school had caved in. Trevor hoped he needed nothing on the roof, as there was no other way to get to it.

Heading back down the passage made the radio pitch louder,

confirming that a creature waited for him further down. Still, the Cadejo made no sign of going after it or warning him. Trevor checked the first classroom on his right. Both doors were locked, and he could not see anything within it.

The clicking of nails on the floor finally revealed that the creature was close to them. There was no stench of goat fur, so Trevor assumed it was just another Adlet. Soon enough, his torch established that he was right, but Trevor wondered why the white hound didn't make any motion to attack it. He suspected it would only attack another Cadejo, meaning he would have to deal with the beast alone.

Having become accustomed to killing them now, it only took a moment to eliminate the Adlet. He got it to fall to the floor to be finished off by the nails on his plank, and, as with the others within the school, its remains crept along the floor to find its home in the wall.

Knowing that it was probably pointless, he checked the first door of the last classroom. As before, it was locked, and the darkness within was impenetrable. He moved to the final door, expecting the same thing. The door was certainly locked, and peering through the glass, he saw nothing.

As he moved his head away, a glint from within the classroom caught his eye, and he looked back in again. He still only saw darkness. He frowned, squinting into the light as if that would assist him somehow. Giving up, Trevor turned away once more, only to catch the glint again.

Annoyed, Trevor looked through it one more time. He watched carefully, trying to find the source of the glint, when he heard voices coming from within. It sounded like children shouting and screaming in excitement. Their words rang like a chorus, rallying around someone. Listening more carefully, he finally heard what they were saying.

Kathy! Kathy! Kathy! Kathy!

Raven? Who nicknames themselves after a bird? And such an ugly one too. Well, let's wet this bird and see if she can fly!

The chorus shouted louder in jubilation and then fell silent. Water splashed in the darkness, and then the children laughed at the victim of the assault.

Come on, little Raven, the tormentor called, *are those tears on your face, or are you just unhappy to see me?*

Suddenly, the children exclaimed and fell silent. There was a loud smack and then something falling to the ground. Trevor heard the patter of feet on the floor. Then he fell backwards as the classroom door suddenly opened, slamming shut immediately thereafter.

He quickly caught sight of wet footprints sprinting across the floor and got up to chase them. He exchanged glances with the map to see that they were heading to the toilets at the end of the passage.

He tried to keep up with it, determined not to lose the wet footprints in case it changed direction. He slowed down when they reached the last part of the passage with the doors to the music room passage on his left. Trevor tested the passage doors, ensuring he could reach the music room when he was done investigating the footprints. To his utter dismay, he realised that these doors were also bolted closed, and he could not get through.

Ignoring the footprints for the time being, he shouldered and kicked the doors hard, but they seemed blocked from the other side too. The Cadejo reached his side, but then its ears pricked up. It didn't growl or whine in warning but seemed to be sniffing and looking into the dark passage for something.

The only place left to go to was the toilets that the footprints led to. He followed them and passed the boy's room, which he tested and found locked. Trevor moved to the final door. Procrastinating for a moment, he took his pen out and made last crosses on all the remaining doors he had found locked along the way. He included the objects he had seen in past rooms as well as the wet footprints. With that task done, he knew all that was left was this final room.

Opening the door slowly, he listened to his radio for any sign of trouble. It was dead quiet, without even the slightest static. The Cadejo watched him for a moment before turning around to check the passage for any problems like a sentry. Trevor closed the door behind him and flicked the light switch. Instead of the bulb turning on, the fitting suddenly swayed from side to side on the cables that dangled from the ceiling.

Trevor only had the torch on his chest to guide him. The footsteps led to the middle stall along one end of the wall. There was no threat in his immediate vicinity, so he moved towards the stalls. The other stalls were open, so he checked them first.

The first door creaked softly on its hinges as if a breeze blew against it. Trevor could not feel any wind stirring as he stepped in. The door rattled slightly more, with the broken toilet seat hammering on the bowl as he approached it. He looked into it. There was no water within, the bowl having gone dry a long time ago.

Trevor tugged on the flush lever, ignoring the door and seat that banged incessantly now. Green fluid ran into the bowl from all sides and drained down the pipe. The liquid was thin and drained easily, not leaving a stain behind. He checked the cistern, finding it as dry as a desert. There was no indication of where the liquid had come from.

As he left the stall, the seat and door calmed down and became still as he moved away. The final stall remained silent as he entered it. Investigating the dark cubicle with his torch, he found the bowl also devoid of any water. He flushed it, watching as nothing happened. The cistern was just as dry.

The middle stall was closed, but he noticed it was slightly ajar and, therefore, not locked. He nudged the door forward as it creaked on its hinges. The cubicle had a musty smell, one that he could only associate with the toilet not being cleaned for years. As the door stopped against the partitioned wall of the stall, he saw a puddle of water around the toilet's base.

Within that puddle was a black book. It was a thin large book bound in black leather. Trevor sat down on the toilet and picked it up. He wiped the water off the book and felt a design on the surface that he had not originally seen. An image of a raven was embossed on the cover with the same black leather, barely perceptible and only noticeable if one was looking for it.

Trevor opened it up and saw that it was a diary. The only name provided by the author was Raven. There were drawings and sketches inside. Some were of the girl's favourite animals or landscapes, while others were more dark and sinister. He paged through the pictures, ignoring the images and words at first, until one page in particular caught his attention.

It was the Lunar Nexus. Three of them had been drawn, one under each other in the vertical centre of the page, each in its own colour. The top one was the red that he was familiar with, with the word "Resurrection" written under it. The middle one underneath it was in blue, labelled "Damnation". And at the bottom was one in black, with the caption "Transmigration".

Hoping he didn't anger the spirit, Trevor ripped the page out and put it in his bag's note section. He inspected the diary further until another part caught his attention. It seemed related to the incident in the classroom, so he took a moment to read it.

'I hate her so much. I don't know why she just can't leave me alone. Maybe she is just jealous that my marks are much higher than hers.

Today she took my pens. And everyone just laughed at me. No one wanted to help me. How am I supposed to make notes without them? I stole this pen from the teacher's drawer just so that I could have something to write with.

I thought maybe it's how she gets treated at home and feels she can take it out on the weak, but today she was bragging about how good she had it at home. Especially with her dogs. She can't stop talking about her beloved dogs.

Oooh, I would love to set some dogs on her... I know some of the best kinds.'

Trevor paged over until he found the final page Raven had written, which bore relevance to the exact incident in the classroom:

'*I'm hiding in the toilet, too afraid to leave it, but I think she may just find me. She got what she deserved. Who does she think she is? Tormenting me in front of the whole class, and then dumping water on my head?!*

I couldn't stop myself. Something inside me exploded, something dark, and I reached up and hit her. I wasn't aiming, and my fist went straight into her groin. It felt so good watching her double over. I felt so warm, like I could just raise fire and burn her right in front of me!!

I bet if I was like that other girl I could do that. If I was like Selena, who everyone says is a demon's child or witch, I could summon demonic beings to eat on her while I watch and laugh back at her.

And I'm not afraid to put Kathy's name down in this book anymore. I don't care if anyone finds this and knows who I am talking about. She will no longer have that power over me.

And one day Kathy will get what's coming to her. One day, I won't stop until I see her own dogs devour her.'

Trevor shut the book. Kathy had told him she had come to this school, but that was as much as he knew of her childhood. They had spent more time in bed than actually dredging up the past. There was no reason for them to.

The significance of Kathy's past was very relevant now. All this time, he had suspected that Caroline was involved with the happenings in Sacred Valley, but now it seemed to revolve around this girl who called herself Raven. Suddenly the dark hounds made sense, as well as Kathy's kidnapping.

It also helped him understand how anyone else could have known about Kathy's passions for art and culture. Anyone who had it in for Kathy this badly would surely have followed her academic studies. They would have looked up the worst lore on hounds and used those against her.

As excited as Trevor was to make this discovery, he knew his theories still had too many holes. It still did not explain his suspicions of who the mysterious man in the metallic head was. It did not illuminate the reason behind the riddles or why Trevor and Jay had gotten involved. Perhaps that was why they only took Kathy and left them to wander the streets. Perhaps Raven did not want them to find her.

Trevor's mental considerations were brought to an end. The radio began making a noise on his side just as he heard a click at the main toilet door. Trevor dropped the book to the floor and grabbed his plank. He listened to the sound of clopping hooves on the tile floors and suddenly got the stench of goat fur.

"No, it can't be," Trevor whispered softly to himself. "How did it get past my Cadejo?"

Almost as if in answer, he heard the white hound howl outside the door and clap its hooves against it. It was growling and biting into the door, trying to gain access.

Trevor looked for the latch of the stall's door so that he could lock it, but it had been broken off. He kicked his legs against the door, hoping it would hold the creature out. His radio got louder as he pushed harder, his back pressing the duffel bag against the toilet's cistern.

He knew nothing he had on him would kill the beast if it was the Cadejo. His only hope was that his white hound would break through the door. He could hear timber splintering as the white Cadejo bit into and kicked the door.

The beast within the room finally attacked the door that Trevor held closed. It was immensely strong, hurting Trevor's legs as his knees bent up. He lunged out again, just managing to kick the door closed again. He had caught a glimpse of the black Cadejo just as the door shut against its face. It resembled the one that the white hound had killed earlier, except for a scar over its dead left eye. Only the right eye was burning with determined fury.

It burst against the door again, and Trevor could not hold it back this time. Its force was too strong. His knees gave in, and he exclaimed as the pain shot up his thighs into his lower back. The black Cadejo stared at him triumphantly, grinning wickedly at its prey.

Trevor lifted his plank in vain, being the weapon he could raise the easiest. The Cadejo twisted its head sideways, staring at him almost disbelievingly. It growled deeply and then lunged forward, knocking Trevor's defensive kicks down with its hooves and climbing up on his lap to bite into his neck.

The movement had been fast and effortless. Trevor's arms fell slack by his side, the plank falling to the floor. The Cadejo had its fangs in its neck, the blood trickling down his shoulders and back as he stared blankly at the wall behind the beast. When the bathroom door burst inwards, the hound dug its fangs in further to ensure it had killed its target.

The black Cadejo let go and reversed out of the stall. As it turned to face its enemy, the white hound bounded into it, and they rolled away in battle. It was too late, though. Trevor could feel his life waning away. The sounds of the radio and the hounds fighting it out faded away as he closed his eyes, and his head fell to the side…

…only to be jerked up again. Trevor was lying on the floor, the blood coursing warmly through him again like a torrential river in a rabid ravine. He raised his hand to his neck and felt the fang wounds close. His strength was returning, and his sight was better than ever.

Trevor looked around, realising that he was no longer in the bathroom. The Lunar Nexus gleamed on the reception wall behind him, and a soft light shone off the desk. He stood up and saw that it was his cellphone. Retrieving it, he noticed that it was fully charged.

Trevor unplugged it, about to put it in his pants pocket when he saw a green image on it. Kathy was lying somewhere dark, but the green light illuminated her still figure. He wasn't sure if she was dead or simply unconscious, but then he noticed her diaphragm moving, and she was breathing.

Just above her, he saw a thin cylindrical object suspended from the top. He brought the phone closer and saw that the tip looked very much like the end of the paintbrush he had acquired in the storeroom.

"She's in the coffin!" he exclaimed, finally confirming his suspicion.

Before rushing off to the courtyard, he checked his inventory. The only missing object was the plank he had dropped on the wooden floor. His radio was silent but intact. He made for the reception doors into the passage when an eerie howl echoed from the second floor.

Trevor could only assume that one of the Cadejos had won the battle. The school fell into silence once more. He truly hoped that the white hound had been victorious, as he had grown close to it in their short time together. Also, he would not be able to defeat any further Cadejos without it.

The light streaming in from the office behind him made him turn around. He checked the second-floor map, realising that the music room was right above him. He walked to the lit office and looked up again through the hole in the ceiling. The final artefact for the coffin was above him.

As hasty as he was to release Kathy, he had to take the time to find it. Without it, he would not be able to open the coffin. Trevor placed his feet on the fallen ceiling to test its strength and then used it as a ramp to clamber up to the second floor. He pulled himself up and then stood inside the room.

There was no longer any further doubt that he was in the Music Room. Musical instruments of all sorts were grouped by their types within them. What he had assumed before was a desk lingering over the edge of the floor was, in fact, a grand piano. The piano's lid was propped open, and on the surface of the lid facing Trevor, the words '**The Notes of Time**' were painted in blood.

Due to the ceiling lying at an angle against the lower floor, the light attached to it supplied enough light into the Music Room that he could see everything within it. The main door that led to the outer passage was blocked by heavy wind instruments that he did not feel like getting through. The light switch for the room was also beside the barred door. Still, as the ceiling below provided enough illumination, he thought he did not have to bother getting to the switch.

Trevor walked around the piano and inspected the music rack. There was no music sheet on it. He ran his fingers over the keys and realised five white keys were missing. He quickly checked under and around the piano, ending with the piano's interior by the strings. Although he did not see any keys inside, he discovered a pamphlet.

The pamphlet was an advert for a seminar on five classical guitar players. It described what would be discussed at the workshop, as well as the names of the five guitarists in question, namely Andrés Segovia, John Williams, Christopher Parkening, David Russell, & Julian Bream.

After his experience in the school and the previous two riddles, he didn't think it was a coincidence that there were five keys and five classical guitarists. Trevor decided to focus on the classical guitarists and find anything to do with them.

He started with the books lined on a single wall shelf to the left of the piano. Most of them had to do with musical instruments, but one was titled 'The History of Music Through the Ages'. Trevor worked through it, hoping to find a section on classical guitarists. To his dismay, he realised that it dealt more with the broader history of classical musicians and was not specifically aligned with guitarists.

"What are you doing, Trevor?" he asked himself, shutting the book. "We're not going to find keys hidden in books."

He looked around, focussing specifically on the various stringed instruments behind him. He inspected the guitars, hoping some might have the guitarists' names etched on them. Trevor brought some closer to the ceiling light, thinking that perhaps his torch was simply failing him. He gave up after the fourth guitar had been checked.

As he placed the base of the guitar back on its stand, he stood with his hands on his hips. He sighed heavily and then looked up at the wall behind the guitars. Somehow, he had missed that framed portraits of musicians were lining all four walls. Trevor moved among the guitars until he reached the one closest to him. It was a portrait of Julian Bream.

He unhooked it from the wall and brought it to the fallen ceiling's light. He inspected the front of the portrait, hoping for a clue as to where any of the keys could be. There was nothing remarkable about it, no marking that hinted at where he should look. As he lifted it up again to return it, the back brown paper lit up by the light, he saw a small block at the base against the bottom frame.

Trevor pulled out his scalpel and slit the paper open. In joy, he found the first key. On the top surface, Bach's name was written in black. Leaving the painting on the floor, he ran to the front of the piano and placed the key on the music rack for safekeeping.

He inspected all the paintings on the walls, finding John Williams and Christopher Parkening on the wall to the piano's right. Andrés Segovia was above the bookshelf, and David Russell was on the wall behind the piano at the edge of the hole in the floor.

Once he had them all gathered on the floor around him, he proceeded to open the back covers. As he expected, he found the last four keys with the names Byrd, Beethoven, Brahms, and Bartok inscribed on them. He took them to the piano, ready to set them in place.

Trevor guessed it would have to be set in some order, just like the Renaissance paintings and the sculpted philosophers. Testing his theory, he placed the keys in any order, not knowing much about classical music. This was once again an arena that Kathy was more familiar with and in which Trevor was not interested.

Once the keys were set, Trevor listened and waited for something to happen. Unsurprisingly, the room was silent, only disturbed by a soft crackling that suddenly awoke from the radio. He moved towards the fallen ceiling, but the radio softened its cacophony. Trevor shifted to the wall that the Music Room shared with the bathroom passage, which increased its pitch. He assumed that it was the black Cadejo that had killed him, and therefore supposed that it had won against his white hound.

Annoyed by the radio, he switched it off. If he could not get through the blocked door to the passage, which was also barred by the double doors at the end, then surely he was safe from the beast. The only way in was via the ceiling ramp.

Returning to the piano's keys, he looked the names over again. They were clearly classical musicians. If Trevor was right, they all played the piano as an art form. He remembered seeing Beethoven and Bach's names in the history book, so he returned to the shelf.

He opened the book, scanning through it again, when a page near the front caught his attention. It was a full list of all the classical artists, sorted into various musical groups. Reading through the Renaissance list, he saw Byrd's name listed. He returned to the piano and removed all the keys, placing Byrd's name in the first empty slot on the left.

The next list was Baroque, and Trevor spotted Bach's name within it. He placed Bach's name four keys down to the next empty slot. Beethoven was listed in Classical, Brahms in Romantic and Bartok in Modern. In that same order, he placed the remaining keys in the next available slots.

Trevor waited again for something magical to happen. When nothing did, he slammed the book hard onto the floor beside him, kicking it further until he was sure it could feel his torment. When his frustration had been vented, he pulled the keys out again, looking for further clues.

Deciding to check inside the empty key slots themselves, he finally found what he was looking for. Hoping it would take him one step closer to solving the riddle, he inspected the fine writing inside. From left to right, the letters Cl, Re, Mo, Ro, and Ba were etched in the back panel of the slots.

Taking this new avenue of possibility, he reinserted the keys in the order of the musical eras indicated by the abbreviations in the slots. He started with Beethoven on the left and then placed Byrd, Bartok, Brahms and Bach. Trevor waited again, his previous anger still flowing in his veins, when his impatience was rewarded.

The music rack lit up as a small fire broke along its length. Nine letters were carved by the fiery wisps into the wood of the rack: C, G, E, C, F, E, A, C. The fire died down, leaving Trevor to determine what they meant.

"Notes," he said as it sunk in. "Five notes, five keys. I need to play these in the right order. Just one problem. I have no clue which keys are which notes."

Remembering that there were books on musical instruments on the shelf, he walked over to it, looking for one on pianos. There were books for all the instruments in the music room, except for the grand piano. Trevor went through them one more time to make sure, but it definitely was not there.

"Of course!!" he shouted. "How convenient!"

He was breathing heavily from all the shouting and venting, taking a moment to calm down and check on Kathy. The image on the phone revealed that she had woken up and was feeling around inside the coffin for a way out. The fear in her eyes called out to him, making him panic on her behalf.

"Quick; think, Trevor," he said hastily, his resolve returning.

Suddenly he looked at the guitars. He had an idea. He found a book on guitars and opened it up, looking through it until he found a page with a fret and string chart. Holding the thin book open, he grabbed the closest acoustic guitar, hoping the instruments were tuned correctly.

Sitting on the piano seat with the guitar on his lap, he spread the guitar book open to the left of the keys he needed to play. He pressed the first Beethoven key. As the sound of the piano played through the room, he ran his fingers over the frets, playing the corresponding strings at various frets until he found the sound closest to the piano's note. When the piano died down, he pressed the key again. He played the guitar until he found the exact note that rang harmoniously with Beethoven.

Trevor referenced the guitar's note chart. The note he had just played was G. He took his pen out and marked G just under the music rack above Beethoven. Trevor next played Byrd, Bartok, Brahms and Bach, tracing the guitar notes until he discovered which notes each played on the piano. When he was done, Byrd had C written above it, with Bartok's F, Brahms's A and finally Bach's high E ending it off.

Trevor closed the book and dropped it to the floor, moving the guitar off his lap and against the closest wall. He sat up straight on the piano seat and cracked his fingers in front of him above the keys. Carefully, he played the notes exactly as etched on the music rack: Byrd, Beethoven, Bach, Byrd, Bartok, Bach, Brahms, Byrd.

He got a fright as the seat beneath him lifted up, jumping off. He opened the seat and found a wooden music clef within it. Dropping his bag, he retrieved the wooden block he had seen in the Library and placed the clef into the shape of the book.

Trevor smiled, glad that he had finally worked it out. The clef fit perfectly.

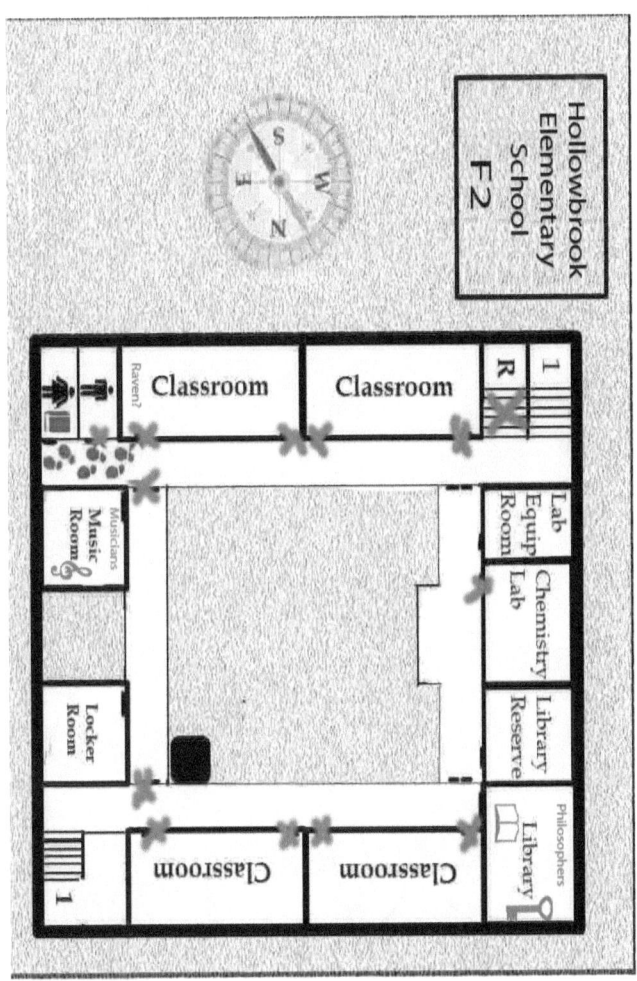

10

BOILING DARKNESS

Sliding back down the ceiling ramp, Trevor made his way through the reception area. His radio returned to silence as he moved away from the Cadejo on the second floor.

The Lunar Nexus still burned brightly on the reception wall, but it was more complete now than before. The final space, which had originally been the only blank area in the outer circles, now had a new name: ⊗↑⋀↑ꓱ .

"Philip," Trevor read out loud, wondering where he had activated the Lunar Nexus.

Deciding to do the same, Trevor ran his hand over the sigil and felt the warmth of life fill him as before. His wounds healed, and his body felt rejuvenated. Pulling his hand away, he saw that the glow of the Lunar Nexus still remained bright and did not die down like the pet store's book.

Trevor made sure the passage leading to the courtyard was empty before proceeding to its doors and opening them. Recalling that this was where he had first encountered the original Cadejos, he moved gingerly across the white lawn towards the coffin on his left. A breeze picked up, swaying the upper foliage of the oak tree above the casket. Trevor stood still for a moment. From everything he had experienced in Sacred Valley so far, he would not have been surprised if the tree suddenly stood up and attacked him.

When the branches continued to simply sway under the dark sky, Trevor shook his head at his foolishness. The paintbrush was still in the centre of the mechanism in the coffin's lid. He placed the book's hole over the brush and lowered it until it fit snugly within the four corners of the square indentation. Finally, he lowered the clef down the brush until it was within the book and coffin's matching shape.

The objects glowed faintly as an earthy sound groaned within the coffin. The lid lifted slightly and then shifted towards Trevor. He stood back and watched as the lid fell to the ash-laden ground. Kathy's hands appeared as they gripped the sides of the coffin, lifting her into a seated position.

It felt like years since they had seen each other. It was evident from the wetness in Kathy's eyes that she had been crying a moment ago, and the redness on her fingertips revealed that she had tried hard to find any way out of her imprisonment. She simply stared at Trevor with mixed fear and jubilation in her eyes.

He bent forward and embraced her, helping her out as she clung to his torso. They stood together for a long while, her long hair hiding her face on his chest. He rubbed her back, feeling how she quivered in his arms. He was unsure whether the tears flowing down his chest were from the joy of seeing him or what she had been through.

"I never thought I'd see you again," Kathy finally said, her voice muffled against his clothes.

"I would never stop looking for you," Trevor replied, receiving a tighter hug in response. Then she pulled back slightly and looked up at him.

"What's going on?" Kathy asked. "Why are we here?"

"I'm still trying to work that out," Trevor said, offering a comfortable smile. "I'm just glad you're alright."

"How did you find me?"

"Oh, that's a long story," Trevor laughed. "Let's just say I recalled you saying that this school felt like home to you, so that was my best bet. After that, I just followed the clues."

"Clues?" Kathy frowned.

"Yeah, don't worry about that for now," Trevor said quickly. "I'm more interested in what happened to you since the car crash."

Kathy let go of him and walked away, staring at the ground. Trevor wondered what she was thinking about and why it made her step out of his arms. Had the occurrences since the accident had such an effect on her?

"Kathy?" Trevor said, encouraging her to speak her thoughts.

"After the crash, I woke up at the front of the school," Kathy said. "I was not sure how I had gotten there until I heard a noise and turned to see someone opening the school."

"Who was it?" Trevor asked.

"I couldn't really make it out," Kathy said. "As soon as I turned, the person grabbed me again and pulled me into the building."

"There must be something; anything?"

"Well, the person didn't feel exceptionally strong," Kathy responded, "just stronger than me. And I thought...."

"Yes?" Trevor asked, wondering why she had fallen silent.

"I thought I saw something metallic on its head," she finally confirmed.

Trevor was the one now to stare at the ground in contemplation. It was not the first sighting of the mysterious being, but something in Kathy's account did not make sense. The man he had seen in the mist on the road before the accident had seemed supernatural and had bulging muscles that looked strong enough to haul a building behind him.

"Did it have clothes on? Trevor suddenly asked.

"Yes," Kathy frowned. "That's a strange que..."

"Do you remember the man we saw on the road?" he interrupted. "The one that had caused us to spin?"

Kathy closed her eyes as she attempted to recall the memory. Trevor waited with patience, but it was running out. The urgency to leave the school and get to Jay arose within him, yet he needed her to describe what she saw. He had to be sure.

"Yes, I do!" Kathy said in excitement. "He was topless, had huge muscles and looked very evil."

"And was this the same person who took you to school?" Trevor pursued.

"No, no. I definitely don't think so. I mean, he could have put clothes on,

I guess, but this person was much smaller."

"Then it's not him," Trevor said in uncertainty. He knew they were guessing and reaching for straws, but they had nothing else to go on.

"So, who do you think it is?"

Trevor looked at her. The small gap she had made between them suddenly felt like a chasm. He was almost too afraid to bring up old ghosts, worried about what it would do to Kathy... or rather, what she would do. Yet, he realised that Kathy may hold more answers than she realised and therefore decided to rather pursue the matter.

"Kathy," he started, swallowing before continuing. "Do you perhaps know someone called Raven?"

She stepped back, her eyes widening. As he feared, the name frightened her so much that it looked like she wanted to escape Trevor as quickly as possible. For a moment, it seemed like she would bolt for the open courtyard doors behind her.

"I found a diary," Trevor continued, walking towards her slightly faster, "where this Raven was bullied in school. She said some hateful things about one of her tormentors."

Kathy stood frozen on the white lawn. Trevor dropped the duffel bag to the ground, the weight of it irritating him with the new tension building between them. He wanted to make sure he could run freely if she decided to escape him. When he reached her, he grasped her shoulders firmly.

"The main instigator was you," he completed. "You drove her mad, to the point where she wanted you killed. All these demonic dogs that are running around the school, it's living up to her dream of you being eaten by them."

"No, it can't be," Kathy said, shaking her head and trying to pull out of his grasp, but he held her still. "That was so long ago. Why would she wait until now?"

"Maybe she waited for the right time," Trevor offered, "when she felt you must have forgotten about her. I don't know. Only you would know."

Trevor could see she was holding something back. He felt she already knew the answers, but she did not want to reveal them to him for some reason. He gripped her shoulders tighter, wanting to wring it from her somehow.

"You need to tell me what's going on," Trevor said. "Jay and I have ended up in this demented town because of someone's determination to pay you back for what you did."

"You don't understand," Kathy said, making a motion to move back into his arms. Trevor acceded, holding her against him again. "I was a wicked child in my youth. I treated everyone with disdain as if the world owed me. No one knew what it was like growing up in my household."

Trevor held her and listened attentively, trying to console her by rubbing her back again. He waited for her to continue, to share the part of her life that he knew almost nothing about. Instead, he felt the Ruger's holster unclip and pulled away just as Kathy grabbed the pistol and aimed the end at his face.

"I tried to escape my past life," Kathy said as Trevor watched her walk back to the courtyard doors. "I thought I had found a new beginning with you. I was so tired of her having everything and taking it for granted."

"Kathy," Trevor said in supplication, "please put the gun down."

"I'm not going to kill you, babe, unless you make me," she replied, fresh tears rolling down her eyes. "I need to deal with this; this is my demon."

"Let me help you," Trevor offered, moving forward again.

"No!!" Kathy shouted, renewing her aim on him to make him stand still. "There's so much you don't know about me… about us."

"What are you talking about?"

"Leave Sacred Valley, Trevor," Kathy warned. "If Raven is after me, then you are safe. Get out of here."

"I'm not going withou…"

"I'm not asking," Kathy finished.

Her heels had reached the threshold back into the school. She stepped back into the passage and stood staring at him one last time.

"I love you," she said, turning to run for the lobby doors.

Kathy had barely moved when a black Cadejo appeared and bit into her ankle. She fell to the ground as the hound pulled her away into the passage towards the Infirmary. Kathy screamed as she was yanked away, the Ruger falling onto the passage floor.

Trevor ran for the courtyard doors. The sky seemed to darken further, and thunderous rumbles began to sound from the thickening clouds. Trevor's torch was insignificant against the darkness that started to build all around him. As he reached the courtyard doors, they slammed shut before him.

He rammed against it, trying to push them back open, but they refused. Deciding not to waste time fighting with them, he turned and raced to the doors on the opposite end of the courtyard. The darkness became suffocating as he reached them, and he threw the doors open with all the force he could muster.

Turning right, he made his way up the passage into the next. He slid into the wall and was about to change direction down the passage leading to the Infirmary at the end, when a growl to his right caught his attention. At the other end of the passage by the Storeroom, he saw a black Cadejo stare at him with burning eyes.

"Shit," Trevor muttered and ran for his life.

His feet pounded on the passage floor as he realised he had left his duffel bag with most items in the courtyard. The only weapon he had on him was the scalpel in his pocket, and he knew that that would do nothing against the Cadejo. The thunder in the sky above grew louder, and Trevor saw red streaks of light cross into the passage from the upper windows.

Trevor spared a moment to look back and saw that the Cadejo had calmly walked into the passage at the end behind him, watching him run. It paced forward slowly before bolting into the hunt.

He reached the doors that would take him to the main passage where

Kathy had been knocked down when he heard a scream rise from the stairs near him, which abruptly died down as if someone had silenced her. Trevor looked at the foreboding staircase, realising that Kathy's screams came from the Boiler Room. He turned his head to see that the Cadejo was halfway down the passage already and so made a last-second decision to follow the screams.

Running as fast as he could without falling, he descended the stairs to the basement floor. There were two doors ahead of him. The door on the left had a sign stating it was the Storeroom, while the right one was the Boiler Room. The Boiler Room's door was wide open and still swaying on its hinges, so Trevor ran into it and closed it behind him.

The lock on the door was broken, but he ignored the danger of the approaching Cadejo. The Boiler Room's generator thrummed loudly while he searched for any sign of Kathy. He saw small blood specks on the ground and followed them around the bulky machinery and overhead pipes. When he turned into the front corner of the room, hidden by the boiler, he saw a large Lunar Nexus painted on the floor.

This Lunar Nexus was not glowing red like all the previous sigils he had encountered before, though. Instead of a burning fire, the Lunar Nexus glowed deep blue. There were also only letters representing Kathy's name in the top right section of the concentric circles. Trevor searched his pockets for the page he had torn from Raven's diary before he recalled placing it with his other notes in his bag.

Trevor couldn't remember what the blue had meant, but he knew it was something bad. Even Jeanette had alluded to it in the café. Checking the rest of the room, he realised that Kathy was nowhere inside. Wherever Raven had taken her, it was not here. The thunder rumbled louder outside the school, sounding very much like it was with him in the room, when a low growl from a dark corner made him look around.

The scarred Cadejo that had killed him in the girl's bathroom walked towards him out of the shadows. It was in no rush since its prey had nowhere else to go and nothing to defend himself with. It grinned maliciously, and Trevor swore that, somewhere among all the thunder, he heard the beast laugh demonically at him.

Trevor remembered that he had touched the Lunar Nexus in the reception. The only way out he could think of was to let the hound kill him and then search the rest of the school for Kathy and Raven. It also meant that he could claim his pistol and bag again, and therefore have a better chance against the hound.

The thought of this evil hound biting into him sent dark chills up his spine. He stepped back from it as it moved forward. It didn't seem intent on killing him just yet. Trevor wondered if it was playing with its food before it ate him. It stepped forward again, still grinning at him while the thunder roared outside. Despite his earlier decision to let it kill him, he stepped back again, his foot landing on the blue Lunar Nexus.

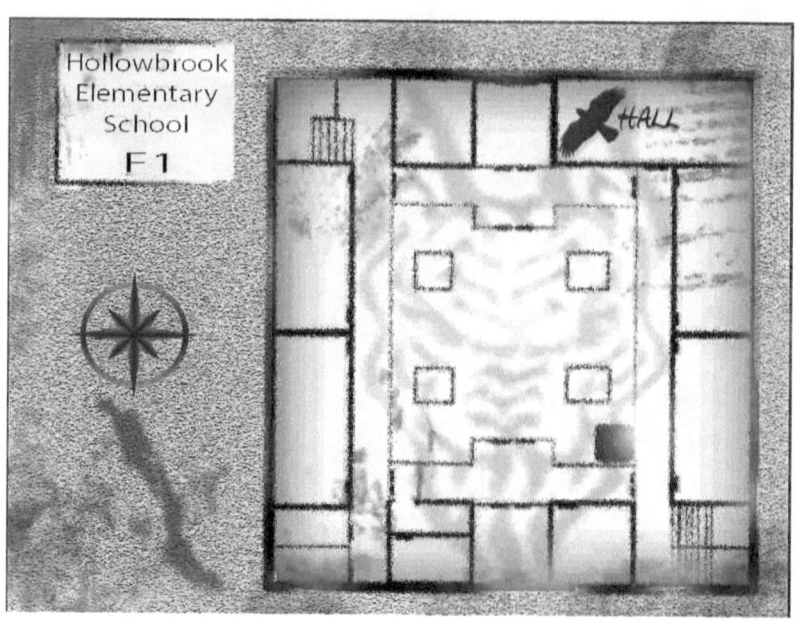

11

RUNES OF CREATIVITY

Trevor froze in place. The thunder died down, replaced by the sound of a siren somewhere outside the school. The siren rang up and down, echoing above the remnants of the storm outside. The Cadejo before him stopped moving forward and simply sat down and watched.

Just like the Adlets that Trevor had killed, its fur rose like falling paint. Instead of trailing along the floor to the walls, it rose up into the air towards the ceiling. Soon, the room around Trevor began to change as well. The paint and plaster broke loose from the walls as the smell of burning fire and sulphur entered the room.

Everything around him was falling apart and tearing to pieces. Portions of the floor collapsed, with only one line of the floor remaining that led to the room's exit. Steel framework replaced the brick masonry that had formed the school's base, while what remained of the walls was rusted and decayed.

The boiler had blood dripping from its sides. It seemed to be fuelled by the red liquid burning within its belly. The Cadejo facing him was gone now, leaving the path out of the room wide open.

Not waiting for the floor below him to collapse, too, Trevor ran for the door. When he reached it, he saw that it was not there. There was simply an exit out of the room through the doorframe. He moved into the passage and noticed the walls were also corroded with rust, dirt and blood.

What was once thunderous roaring in the sky was replaced by the roar of the fire beneath the school. Trevor stepped back to look at the fallen floor in the Boiler Room again. The fire was nowhere near the school but seemed to be very far down into the bowels of the earth. Despite its distance, the fire sounded like it was right beneath him.

Trevor made for the stairs, switching his torch off as the fires burning underneath him were enough to show the way. He noticed quickly that the door to where the storeroom was before was completely gone, simply replaced by an extension of the wall. In the corner, he saw some loose papers on the floor.

It was a set of maps of the school. Unlike the clean white paper of the original maps Trevor had been using before, these were yellow and burnt at the edges. There were black and red smudges of what appeared to be old dirt or blood. And within the background of the maps, there were watercolour images of a demonic hound's head.

"What the hell is going on here?" Trevor asked, inspecting each of the floors.

A mark on the Hall got his attention. Instead of being blank like the rest of the rooms on the map, none of them having names on them, the Hall's name was crystal clear. And above the Hall's name was a small imprint of a black bird.

"Raven," Trevor murmured.

Keeping the first-floor map on him and stashing the others in his pocket, he proceeded up the stairs. He made it to the mezzanine landing between the basement and first floor when a light above caught his attention. It was a female spirit, her bright white hair swaying behind her. She smiled at him once and then ran down the passage.

"Kathy!" he shouted after her, running onto the floor in pursuit.

She was halfway down the passage as he passed the double doors leading to the reception. She was supernaturally fast, flying into the wind as she made for the Hall's doors. Trevor struggled to keep up with the spirit that resembled Kathy and then stopped as she vanished through the doors.

His chest was rasping. Trevor knew he was unfit, but the short sprint should not have made his breathing so bad. He realised then that the acrid smoke smothering the school air was why he struggled to breathe properly.

He took a moment to regain his composure and moved forward again.

The walls on the floor were different than before too. In many places, the steel formwork stood out from the walls, revealing rusted spalling that protruded like mounds of fungi. The spalling and rust glowed with rivers of fire from within, as if the fires fed the walls with its evil. The paint and plaster had peeled off the brickwork on the walls, revealing blood flowing through the stone clay.

Something on the dilapidated wall between him and the Hall moved. It shifted and glowed a dark green, moving like soft smoke off the wall until it materialised before him. The shape formed into a hound, Trevor watching fearfully to see if it was an Adlet or Cadejo.

The new form completed its transformation, and he realised it was neither. It had green fur mottled as the Adlet, but its feet were canine paws. The paws were too large in proportion to its body, though, and as the hound opened its mouth, he saw that it had razor-sharp teeth like knives. Its eyes had green wisps of light that curled up into the air like the Cadejo's red eyes.

Suddenly the hound lifted its head and howled three times in quick succession. Trevor turned to run when he found the beast behind him. Somehow, it had traversed the space between them in a second. The hound jumped onto him and bit at his face just as Trevor grabbed a handful of fur and threw it against a steel frame.

The frame clanged as the heavy body of the hound connected with it, but the beast merely shook it off. It circled before him, Trevor's hand ready to defend himself again from the blades in its mouth. Remembering that he had a blade of his own, he took the scalpel out of his pocket and held it towards the hound. It took offence to the gesture and lunged forward just as Trevor swung at it.

The hound bit the tip of the scalpel and broke it off with its teeth. Trevor dropped the handle as it clanged on the metallic floor. It jumped again, and Trevor raised his arms over his face. The sharp teeth sank into his arms, and he screamed in agony, falling to the floor as the weight of the hound collapsed on him. Trevor lifted his knee into its chest and cracked it hard, making the hound yelp as he lifted it over his head into the floor behind them.

Despite his pain and throbbing arms, Trevor's fear made him rise and run for the Hall. He couldn't hear the beast was following, as his breathing had gotten worse, and his pulse was beating in his head. The doors were right before him, some strange markings etched into the wood as he rammed into them and found them locked shut.

Trevor turned to face the green beast. It growled at him, the sharp fangs glistening in the firelight from the openings in the walls and the red clouds casting their glow from outside. Red lightning streaked across the sky, but no thunderous applause followed. All he heard was the deep demonic drone from the dog before him.

It stopped in its tracks and lifted its head again. The beast howled thrice as Trevor backed into the Hall's door behind him. By the third howl, Trevor closing his eyes for the fatal blow, the beast vanished from the passage.

Trevor slowly opened his eyes again, hoping he had awakened from this nightmare. Yet, the fire and the red clouds remained, and the decaying walls haunted his vision. Still, the foul green beast was nowhere to be seen.

Twisting around, he pounded at the Hall doors, rattling them hard and hoping someone would open them from the inside.

"Kathy!" Trevor exclaimed, muffled by the delayed rumble of thunder. He banged his fist relentlessly against the door. "Kathy, open up!"

On the final slam, he felt a strange groove on the door's surface. In his battle with the green hound, he had forgotten about the image he had glimpsed on the door. He ran his fingers over the grooves of the symbol, recognising what it was.

"A pentacle," he said, noting that the top point of the star was facing upright as opposed to the upside-down triquetra in the pet store. "How ironic; a bad sign in a good world, and a good sign in a bad world."

Each point of the star had impressions on them. Within the impressions were five symbols. In the top point, the symbol was a circle, with a dot in the centre. The top right point had a triangle facing down, while the lower right had a triangle facing up. The lower left had a triangle facing down, and the upper left faced up, both left triangles with a horizontal line through their centres.

"Finally, something I do know," Trevor sighed in relief. He started naming the symbols from the top in a clockwise direction. "Spirit, Water, Fire, Earth and Air."

Trevor stood there stupidly facing the door as if simply naming the elements that the symbols represented would open them. He sighed again, grasping that he would have to find the items that belonged in the impressions. And he had a suspicion that it would relate to the elements.

He turned to his left, only realising at that point that the double doors leading to the next passage were gone. As with the boiler room, only the frames remained, with no indication of what had happened to the doors. He walked through the frame, watching for any sign of the new green hound he had seen.

Trevor hoped that his bag and items were still in the courtyard. Remembering that Kathy had dropped the Ruger in the entrance passage, he wondered if that was still there too. With new hope coursing through him, he ran for the courtyard doors, only to find they were also gone.

The opening in the walls led straight into the courtyard. The red clouds swirled overhead with maroon lightning that streaked within them. There was a low grumble of thunder now and again, which was discordant with the flashes of lightning.

The courtyard itself was a scene of death and decay. There was no ash or snow on the ground. Rather, whatever grass had once been there had long ago been burned to cinder. Trails of rust and decomposition ran along the outer walls, where they were not damaged by vast openings. And the large oak tree ahead of him had no leaves on the withered branches above.

Not sure whether or not he was disappointed, Trevor discovered that his bag and weapons were not lying in the courtyard where he had left them. The coffin still rested against the tree, its wood rotten and falling apart on the mouldy ground. Trevor walked forward to inspect the coffin further, peering over the lid that leaned against the coffin's side.

A small, brown elliptical object lay within it. Trevor reached down and picked it up, inspecting its surface. A Futhark rune was etched into the timber surface, covering the bulk of the space.

"Űruz," Trevor said out loud, identifying the symbol immediately. "Rune of strength and an invitation to creativity. But more importantly, dear rune, you represent the earth element."

Turning the thin object around in his fingers before placing it in his pocket, something began to trouble him. As far as he knew, Kathy had no interest in Futhark runes. The more he thought about it, the more he realised that out of everyone he knew, it was only with Caroline that he had shared this interest.

It made him wonder if the incidents at the school were really merely to deal with Kathy's past. If Raven had only wanted Kathy, surely she could have lured her alone without Trevor and Jay? And Phillip's name appearing on the red Lunar Nexus also contradicted Kathy's earlier theory that Raven was simply out to get her.

He was about to voice his suspicions about the one person they were all involved with, the man he had seen being resurrected in the storeroom's Renaissance painting, when he heard a scraping steel echo from within the school. It was coming from the passage that led back to the Hall and heading towards the courtyard opening Trevor had entered.

He ran for the opposite opening by the entrance lobby. He ducked behind a broken wall, ensuring he was well hidden. The sound grew louder, reverberating through the passages until it shifted into the courtyard. Then the scraping metal stopped, and Trevor could not help but peek around the steel framework into the courtyard.

It was him. He stood there, the metallic distorted, twisted head just reaching over the top frame of the doorway. It looked like his face had been smashed in before being replaced with a broken metallic substance. He stood just inside the courtyard with a huge steel axe behind him.

His muscles bulged out of his chest and arms disgustingly, with rippled black veins running over them. His lower body was covered by a brown robe with red stains all the way down to his black boots.

Besides everything that made him look ghastly, where his neck and arms met the torso were massive red scars. The scars stitched over the joins that kept the body together. Trevor squinted; it looked like the flesh of each limb had been melted like wax with the meat of the torso.

Trevor was unsure whether or not the man was looking at him, with the twisted metal facing him but no sign of how he was seeing out of it. He suddenly swung the double-sided axe he was dragging into the courtyard with absolute strength and power, aiming the end of it in the air towards Trevor.

With the man's right hand raised, pointing the axe head horizontally at him, Trevor saw a mark on his right shoulder. At first, he thought it was a brand, as it looked like red swells rising up on the skin. Yet, as he inspected it from his hiding spot behind the wall, he recognised what had once been a tattoo.

Not waiting to watch just how fast he could run with that blade, Trevor twisted his body to run back to the passage near the boiler room. As soon as he was up and about to sprint, he saw the wall shift and light up to his left, barring his way through as another green hound appeared before him.

Remembering that he still had no weapons, he raised his arms to wrestle with the hound. He heard the blade drop on the courtyard's ground and dragged through it, getting closer. Trevor decided the best tactic would be to get around the hound and avoid confrontation altogether.

The green wolf finished its materialisation and howled into the air three times. Trevor ran for it, ready to dodge it, when it vanished from sight by the last howl. Before he could react, the beast pounded onto him from behind, biting into his shoulders and removing a large chunk of flesh. Trevor screamed, twisting to knock the beast in its face with his elbow.

It fell off to the side, its head knocking against the wall. It took a moment to shake its head and recover and then looked up at Trevor. He slid backwards on the ground towards the Boiler Room passage, his finger crossing the threshold between passages. It growled at him angrily and planted its feet on the ground, raising its head to howl.

As the second howl rang, Trevor saw the metallic twisted head bend under the courtyard door's framework and enter the passage. The green hound howled a third time as Trevor's back hit the wall, and then it vanished. He waited for the final kill, for the fangs to sink deep into his neck or bite his head off, but nothing happened again.

The gigantic man was still making his way down the passage towards him. Trevor was about to get up and dash for the Hall again, when he saw another green hound drift down from the same spot it had the first time. His only free path was the staircase behind him and the stairs up to the second floor.

When he turned to run up the stairs, he realised that that was not an option either. The stairs were broken, and the steps had disintegrated into the fires below a long time ago. The stairs down to the Boiler Room were the final option, but Trevor knew there would be no way out there unless the Lunar Nexus could send him back to the foggy Sacred Valley he had come from.

Taking the chance, he ran back to the basement and into the Boiler Room. He walked carefully on the only path towards the blue Lunar Nexus, glad to see that it was still there and noticing that only Kathy's name was still within it. Trevor hastily jumped onto it, waiting for it to transport him back.

Yet the fires still burned beneath him, and the decayed walls still surrounded him. Trevor moved off it and jumped back on, hoping it would somehow activate if he tried again. He could hear the blade start banging on the steps as the man with the twisted metallic head walked down it. Desperately Trevor jumped off again, bending his knees to jump back on again.

Something glinted from within the fire of the active boiler. Trevor halted his jump and looked into its depths. A small elliptical object shone brighter than the fire it was in. He soon realised it was another rune, possibly linked to the fire symbol in the pentacle.

Trevor looked around for something to rake it out with, seeing the blood pouring out of his shoulder wound. In his anxiety to escape this version of the school, he had forgotten that he had been bitten. He ignored the throbbing pain that came with it, searching the floor and walls for anything to reach the rune.

Above him, he noticed that the steam ducts were loose, and from one of them, there was a steel pipe as long as the copper pipe he had found in the café's kitchen. He lunged for it twice before hovering his hand on it and jerking it down. Some of the duct pipes gave way and collapsed, slamming into the portion of the floor he stood on and then ricocheting into the fiery abyss below.

Trevor shoved the bent end of the pipe into the fire and stoked the flames until he cleared a path for the rune. He manoeuvered the rune around until it finally fell on the floor by his feet. It dawned on him only at that point that he had nothing to cool the object with.

With the rune out of the fire, the brilliant light it had emitted from within the flames died away. Trevor reached down and felt it. It was still warm to the touch, but it did not scorch him. It glowed a beautiful orange as if it contained the essence of the boiler's fire within it. It had another Futhark rune on it.

"Thurisaz; great force or giant," Trevor reflected, shoving it in the same pocket where the earth rune rested. "The fire symbol, usually signifying facing a great challenge or deadly enemy."

With that in mind, Trevor suddenly realised that the basement outside the Boiler Room had gone quiet. The scraping sound had ceased at some point during his excavation in the fire. He looked at the steel pipe, wondering if it would do the demented beast any harm, when he saw that the steel at the end of the tip had gone white with heat. It gave him an idea.

Thrusting the tip of the steel pipe back into the boiler, he let it burn up further until he was satisfied that the heat would remain for some time. With the fiery tip before him, he moved towards the room's exit, watching every second he approached the basement floor for any sign of the metallic head.

Even though he had expected it, seeing the twisted metal head at the bottom of the stairs leading to the first floor made his heart wrench. The metallic top was just below the ceiling, and the man towered above him. His sword was still on the staircase at an angle behind him. He had clearly been waiting for Trevor to return.

He grabbed the handle of his axe with both hands. His biceps expanded as he lifted the heavy weapon and switched the sharp damaged edge sideways. Trevor waited for the blade to slap into the staircase's wall, knowing that might be the only moment he had to attack.

As the blade struck the side walls of the stairwell, it sliced right through the steel frames and remaining brickwork. The edge passed through the air and over Trevor's head as he ducked, not only from the weapon but from the flying debris. The top end of the blade hit the Boiler Room wall beside Trevor, where it finally got stuck in the formwork.

Taking his opportunity, Trevor ran forward and rammed the burning hot pipe end into the man's chest. It sliced through the right pectoral muscles, passing through the flesh and sinews, getting stuck midway through the torso.

A scream erupted within the twisted head. It was not the scream of a normal human being but rather a guttural, tormented howl that made Trevor cover his ears. It caused the room, floor, walls and ceiling around them to shake to the point where he almost lost his footing.

Anxiety getting the better of him, Trevor ran up the stairs despite all the tremors and the horrendous shrieks threatening to burst his ears. The sound softened, and the floor was stable on the first-floor landing, so he bolted towards the Hall. A green glow ahead reminded him that he still had the latest green hound to deal with. He slowed his pace again.

"Ok, I need to find the other runes," Trevor said as the hound noticed his presence. "I just need to avoid you long enough to do that."

Trevor did a quick roll-call of the runes he had left to find. Air was all around him, so there was no clear hint of where that rune could be. There was no time to pull out the map as the hound was halfway down the passage heading towards him. He mentally tried remembering the rooms he had seen in the normal school.

When he recalled the library, something dawned on him. It was the most logical place that the air rune could have been. He remembered studying esoteric lore, where the air element represented not only intelligence and communication but also both those aspects being manifested in the written word.

He was broken out of his reverie by a heavy jolt from below, the sound of the blade being broken free ringing up to him. It made him aware that the hound had stopped proceeding and was starting to howl.

Trevor ran into the passage by the Infirmary and raced for the courtyard. His chest was still tight from the foul air, but sheer determination drove him now. He heard the third and final howl from the green hound and expected it to appear before him. Instead, he looked back and saw it had appeared behind him, teleporting out of thin air.

"Cu Sith," Trevor whispered, suddenly remembering what the beast was.

He didn't have time to dwell on lore now, though. He had run past the courtyard opening, missing it completely. Trevor panicked, remembering that the double doors at the end past the reception were locked in the normal world. The panic immediately changed to elation when he saw that the doors were not there anymore, and he picked up his pace.

Trevor spared a quick moment to look into the office behind the reception, feeling more than hearing the hound running after him. The ceiling ramp to the music room was gone, leaving only a large gap in the floor above where it should have been dangling from. There was no way that he could use the absent ramp as a shortcut. He needed to reach the other set of stairs and hope that they were still in place.

The patter of paws on the ground behind him made him spin around and grasp the hound in a bear hug. He held his neck tight against its jaw as they hurtled to the floor together, ensuring the pressure prevented the Cu Sith's knife fangs from sinking into him. The hound pushed against him as their heads crashed into the next passage's wall, trying its best to break it free from his vice grip.

Trevor was losing stamina, so he bent his leg and kicked it away. The hound slid across the floor and then stood upright, facing him again. Trevor also rose and saw the masked man's head appear on the opposite end of the passage from the Boiler Room. It turned its smashed head to Trevor and then changed directions towards him, dragging the blade behind.

The Cu Sith started howling again. Trevor relaxed slightly, preparing to run down the passage towards the stairs. In the last battles with this hound, it had vanished after the second set of three howls. He waited until the third howl rang and watched gladly as the hound disappeared from his sight. He began sprinting when the Cu Sith suddenly pounced on him from behind.

Knowing that the weight of the hound would keep him down, Trevor rolled as he hit the floor face-first. It made the Cu Sith unstable, and the hound fell to the side and lunged for him again. It bit into his ankle as Trevor kicked at its jaw, making Trevor scream in agony. Without thinking it through, he clutched at one of the wall's steel frames, causing the hound's tug to cause more pain as his leg stretched out.

Something felt loose in his left hand. He looked up and saw a steel pipe broken off from the formwork. He grasped it in his palm and let go of the column, lifting himself up with his elbow and kicking off on his free foot. The

Cu Sith let go of the ankle as Trevor rose, dodging as the pipe came down and clanged on the floor.

Trevor swiped to the left and connected the pipe against the side of the hound's face. The screeching of the huge blade on the floor was closer now, and Trevor looked up and saw the metallic head through broken patches in the wall. He was by the courtyard entrance in the previous passage.

The second's distraction was enough for the hound to catch him off-guard. It bit into the steel pipe, wrestling the weapon in its mouth until the force made Trevor let go. He backed away as it chewed the metal up in front of him, the pieces falling uselessly to the floor. All Trevor had to do now was turn around and run for the stairs.

The Cu Sith began howling again. Trevor twisted around to run, fearing the moment when the hound would teleport and bite him again. Trevor was losing what endurance he had left and stressed that the hound's next attack might be its last.

In testimony to his fading strength, Trevor tripped over his own feet as he made for the stairs. He landed hard on his elbows, causing sheer pain to shoot through his body. Lying prone on the floor, unable to move, he rolled onto his back, waiting for the pain to subside just as the hound uttered its final cry.

Trevor remained still, waiting for the final kill. It was over. He couldn't fight anymore, and he couldn't save Kathy. Raven had ensured he could not reach her and that she could have her way with her old adversary. As he lay still on the warm floor surrounded by the dilapidated walls, he muttered his final goodbye to Kathy.

The death he had expected did not come. Trevor opened his eyes, his chest in pain from breathing the putrid air, and looked around. The Cu Sith was gone. The only sign of impending trouble was the sound of the huge blade dragging on the floor, coming from the corner at the other end of the passage.

Postponing the flood of thoughts that rushed into his head, he jumped up and ran for the stairs despite his pain. His ankle felt swollen, and he limped slightly until he got into a rhythm, trying his best to forget the warm shooting discomfort up his leg. It felt like ages before he finally reached the stairs.

Looking up into the darkness, he was glad to see that the stairs were intact. The man with the metallic head was still heading towards him, but for some reason, the demonic being was in no rush. Trevor came to the same conclusions again about Raven keeping him away from Kathy, the thoughts rushing in again like a flood, but he ignored his calculating brain. Before contemplating anything else, he needed to pass the physical hurdle of making it up the stairs.

He lifted his uninjured leg onto a step, followed by the injured one. He winced as the pain shot through. Grabbing onto the side rail, he used his arm to rather pull him up, but then the hole in his shoulder burned. Resigned to taking it slowly, he crept up the stairwell until he finally reached the second floor.

There was less polluted air. It didn't make breathing easier, as the air was still thick with humidity, but at least it didn't burn his chest anymore. The walls had no holes in them, even though streaks of blood and rust were still running over them. Being back on even ground made it easier to walk, and so Trevor moved faster towards the archway leading to the next passage.

He took out his tattered maps and checked the rooms. Without the names, the map was quite useless. In his current state, it was hard for Trevor to remember the rooms he had passed through before in the fogged world. He tested the first doors on the left but found them locked. Then he checked the next door, which opened up easily enough. Moving in, he shut the door behind him immediately.

Trevor saw the desk before him and moved around it, pushing it against the door. He needed time to recover and to work through his thoughts. If he was going to still save Kathy, if she was even still alive, he needed to work out where the rest of the runes were. And if he was going to do that, he would need to work out how to either fight or evade the Cu Siths.

He made it to the desk's chair and fell down onto it. His body thanked him as he felt a wave of relief pass through him. When he had seen the Cu Sith teleport, he remembered where he had read about the beast before. He should have caught on from the green fur and large paws already, but the teleportation did the trick.

And now he had to recall whatever other parts of the lore came to mind, specifically how to kill it. His mind raced through the knowledge of the beast, his brain battling to ignore the sores that ached through him. His ears also listened for any sign of the large blade being dragged up the stairs.

That train of thought reminded him of everything that had rushed into his brain at once earlier in the passage below. He tried to focus on just one thing at a time and then decided to concentrate on the twisted-head man's slow approach. He knew that it wasn't the large blade keeping him down.

There was a possibility that the twisted man was using the Cu Siths to seriously injure Trevor, but keeping him alive for him to finish him off. That could explain why they first fought with him and waited until he was maimed before leaving. Yet it nagged at him that the first two had teleported after the second howl, and the latest one after the third. Why would they vanish after maiming him, instead of waiting until their master had caught up?

Suddenly, Trevor realised what it was. Thinking of the times they had attacked him and howled caused him to determine the one key element in all situations. None of the lore he had read had said anything about vanishing after three howls. The howls were simply for teleportation and a warning to the victims that they are going to be attacked.

The teleportation was always behind the person's back. There was never one account of it being in front or the sides. There had been one moment on the first floor where it had appeared before Trevor, but that's because Trevor had turned at the last howl to run.

Trevor smiled. It was as clear as day now. Each time the hounds had howled and vanished permanently was when there was no back to vanish to. His back had either been against a wall or the floor when the last howl had sounded, meaning that the Cu Sith had nowhere to shift to.

The realisation of a possible solution made him feel physically and mentally better. If he was right, he could at least search for the runes without being pestered by the hounds and sustaining any further injury. He stood up, ready for the hunt once again. He checked his pockets and felt reassured when he found the two runes still in place.

Trevor surveyed the room he was in to get his bearings. The only light he had was the torch on his chest. He inspected the room's tables and found chemistry sets on them. He remembered that he had been in a Lab Equipment Room before in the foggy world and realised that this must have been the room next to it.

"Surely this room of all the rooms should have a first aid kit," Trevor mumbled, surprised to hear how hoarse his throat was.

He moved to the back of the room with the idea of working his way from the back to the front. Along the back wall was a counter that ran the length of the wall, which also contained chemistry sets. He inspected each glass canister or vial, hoping any one of them would reveal any healing properties, when five Bunsen burners caught his attention.

Above each burner was a stand with a glass container resting on it. Each burner had valves and temperature indicators to show how hot the burners were. Since all the burners were off, all indicators were at zero. Within the glass containers were transparent liquids, and a small elliptical blue object was within each of them.

Trevor used the torch to find a metal stirring bar. When he found one in a tool set fixed to the wall behind the burners, he stirred the liquids until he could see all surfaces of the objects. None of them revealed any runes on them. Trevor suddenly wondered if all the fluids were water, getting a strange smell from two of them.

"I guess there's only one way to find out," Trevor said as he looked for the matches.

Behind the burners, he saw finger-length matches with a strike pad below them. He quickly lit one of the matches while releasing gas into each burner. Lighting them, he turned the valves until each one's thermometer read '100°C'. And then he waited.

Two of the containers started sizzling softly. Another of the containers remained quiet while the fourth boiled very rapidly, making some of the liquid pour out in foam. Trevor quickly switched that burner off and then turned his attention to the second last container from the right.

Not only was the liquid boiling steadily, but the blue object was starting to glow. The blue became crystalline as a rune formed on one of the surfaces. Trevor watched as the Futhark letter was completed and then turned the burner off, grabbing a pincer and removing the object.

"Pertho," Trevor read. "Secrets, or the start of something new. Rune of water."

Stashing the rune with the other two, Trevor continued his search for any items that could heal him but found none. He moved towards the external wall of the school and was about to look along the windows when something in the corner caught his attention.

There was a hole in the wall. It was a vertical aperture that led through to the next room. The hole itself was horrid, though, with triangular teeth set on each side in infected gums that stretched into the walls. Trevor wondered if it was a trap, if the teeth wouldn't immediately close on him and kill him.

Next to the aperture, on the counter in the corner, was a small box of ammunition. It was only a moment of excitement until Trevor realised he could do nothing with it. His Ruger wasn't on him, having been dropped by Kathy before being taken to this demented version of the school. In his rush to save Kathy, he had forgotten to pick it up again.

There was something different about this box. It wasn't the same as the ammunition box he had found before. Trevor picked it up and opened it, gaping wide-mouthed at the six silver bullets in it. They glistened against the glow of his torch. He took one out and inspected it further, wondering if it was pure silver.

The scraping sound that he was becoming used to emerged in the passage. Trevor turned quickly, dropping the bullet in fear. The metalhead man had finally made his way up. Unsure if he knew where he was, Trevor bent down to pick up the fallen bullet. As he pinched it from the ground, he saw another box on the floor beneath the counter.

Not knowing what he would do without a gun, Trevor stashed it in two separate pockets anyway. The beast outside seemed to stall at the Lab's door since the scraping sound had stopped. He realised dreadfully that there was only one way left into the library, and that was through the dental aperture.

Trevor carefully positioned himself sideways by the hole, putting his right arm through first. The gums made a sucking sound as he passed through. His every nerve was taught, waiting for the teeth to snap shut on him. His head passed through the centre, and he had a line of teeth points facing him. Trevor swallowed hard, almost choking on it.

Finally, his left arm passed through and then was in the Library Reserve. He remembered the racks along the walls and in the centre.

Strangely, nothing about this room seemed out of place. The walls had some faint rust marks along the cornices, and where plaster was visible, it had peeled slightly. Other than that, the room was fairly intact.

Where the door to the main library was before was just an open frame through which Trevor passed. The library itself was in a much worse state. The racks had fallen over each other, and the books had been burned. All that was left were their charred remains on the floor.

The three pedestals that held the Philosophers' heads stood in the same positions as before but without the busts. Instead, each one held a large glass jar. The closest jar by the steps was glowing bright yellow with something floating in the middle. From the darkness in the rest of the room, Trevor could tell that the other two jars were unlit.

Trevor investigated the lit object in the first jar. It held a yellow rune inside, with a Futhark letter clearly written on it. As far as he could tell, nothing held it in place, and it was simply floating in the midst of the jar.

"Tiwaz," Trevor translated. "Strength of purpose and justice, or resolution of a conflict. Rune of air."

Excited by the acquisition of another rune, he lifted his right arm and slid his hand into the jar's opening. As he closed his palm over the rune, the glass suddenly smashed, some shards flying into his hip. Trevor tried not to scream, worried it might alert the metallic man more than the smashing glass might have already.

Instead, he hissed through his teeth and removed the three shards that had entered him. The rune was not in his hand, and the light had moved to the left rear corner of the library. Squinting across the distance, Trevor saw the rune now floating in one of the other glass jars.

Trevor navigated a path through the fallen racks, stopping as he approached the glowing jar. On the rear wall between the two remaining jars were large words written in the same rust and dilapidation Trevor had seen throughout the school.

"Beware the Guardian," Trevor read out loud, frowning and wondering who the guardian was. "Why should I beware it?"

Deciding that he would rather not find out, he continued to the glowing jar. He stood there for a moment, wondering what other way he could use to get the rune out. There were no objects around him that he could use to grab the item, and he was not willing to tempt putting his hand in again.

Getting an idea, he pushed the side of the jar until it fell off the pedestal and the glass smashed on the floor. Yelling again in pain, Trevor fell to the ground after some shards struck his left leg. For the low height the glass was placed at, he swore the glass shattered with greater force than it should have. Nursing his leg and removing two more shards, he stood up and saw that the rune was gone.

He turned to the final jar and saw that it was alight. The rune was also visible within it. Sighing with exhaustion, Trevor stepped over racks and scorched books until he was at the jar. He feared this was his last chance to obtain the rune, as there were no other jars visible from where he stood.

"I need to use the air somehow," Trevor thought out loud. "How do I get the rune without the glass being in the way?"

Unsure if it was uttering the words that had stirred his brain into life or the sound of the scraping blade now outside the library, Trevor suddenly got a new idea. He grabbed the sides of the container with both hands and lifted it slightly off the pedestal. He waited a moment to see if the glass shattered.

When nothing happened, he turned the container upside down. He made sure not to let the glass touch the floating rune inside, simply turning the container over until the opening was underneath. Carefully, he lifted it until the rune was freely hovering in the air and then put the jar down on the ground beside him.

The rune twirled and glowed, floating above the pedestal. Trevor reached forward and grasped it in his palm. He looked down at the jar and waited a few seconds, comfortable that the rune was his when nothing happened. He placed it with the other three runes in his pocket.

It was then that he realised that he once again had no idea where else to go. The final item was the spirit rune, and he had no associations to place on that. Forlornly, he took the maps out, knowing full well that without labels, it was pointless. He paged through the basement, first and second floors, trying to remember anything associated with the soul.

"Isn't music supposed to be associated with the soul?" Trevor wondered. He vividly recalled that the music room had been above the reception before, so he quickly checked the quickest route.

As he paged over, he saw the roof map. Trevor stopped for a moment before proceeding to the second-floor map. He hadn't seen whether the stairs he had come up with went further to the roof or if the path had been destroyed. Even though the music room had seemed like a clear choice, he suddenly doubted himself.

The spirit was often seen as the seat of all power. There was the possibility that the rune was on the floor above all. Trevor looked at the library door, wondering why the metalhead man had gone quiet again. He hadn't heard any more scraping, which suggested that the giant beast was waiting outside the library door for him.

The roof was closer if Trevor quietly escaped through the Lab's door. He wanted to at least eliminate it as a possibility, instead of running all the way to the music room for nothing. Having made up his mind, he packed the maps away and headed back through the wall of teeth and into the lab.

Trevor opened the Lab door slowly. As the fires outside and below the school did not penetrate the upper passages, it was harder to see down the length of the passage. He wasn't sure if the shape he saw by the library door was the muscular man or a large stain on the walls. Venturing further into the passage, he kept watch on the spot, but there was no movement.

The passage behind him was quiet too. The eerie silence and emptiness made him more apprehensive. He watched the walls for any signs of a Cu Sith peeling off from them as he inched back towards the stairs. When he reached the junction of the passages, he looked down to the other end and wondered whether he should try the music room anyway.

A soft wisp to the right caught his eye, and he looked quickly. The same ghost form he had seen before that resembled Kathy was moving up the stairs. She watched him for a moment before gliding up and out of sight. Trevor ran after her, ignoring all pain and agony as he sprinted up the steps.

Ghost Kathy passed through the door to the roof with ease. Trevor slowed down as he climbed the final steps, looking at the ominous red door before him. It had intricate trims of arched wood along its surface, looking very ornate for a roof door. The red was deeper than blood and shone with a fine gloss. He had a terrible sensation about entering this door.

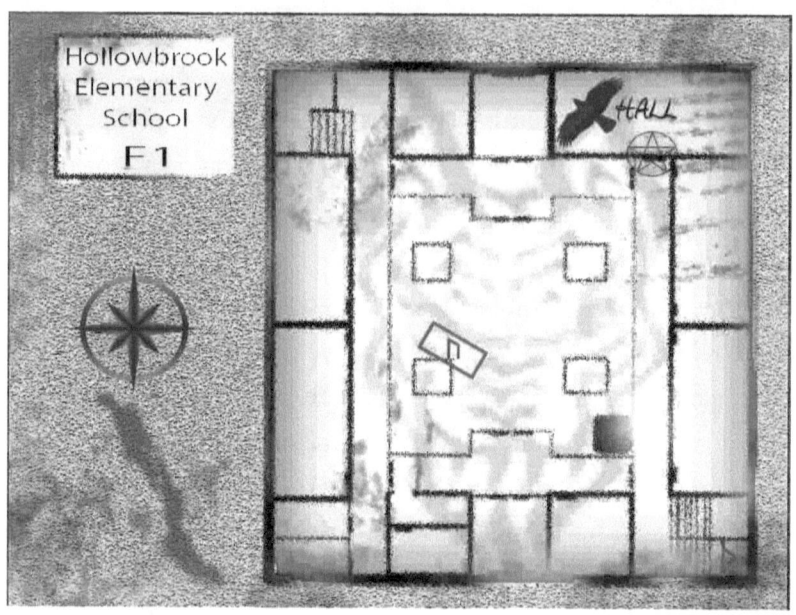

12

HELL HOUNDS

Trevor stepped forward and reached for the handle. As his fingers closed on the ironmongery, it moved down of its own accord. The door creaked as it swung inward towards him, and he waited to see who was waiting on the other side. There was nothing but a dark sky; even the mist had vanished, simply replaced by the deep black clouds with tints of red in the sky.

The huge blade echoed in the background, waking Trevor to action. He stepped over the threshold of the opening and onto the roof. As soon as he was completely through, the door slammed shut with a loud bang behind him. Trevor sighed. He wasn't really surprised. Raven would do everything to keep him from Kathy.

When Trevor refocused his attention on the roof, he wondered if he had mistakenly guessed the spirit rune's location. Instead of a solid concrete structure, there were webs of steel frames and bars all around that served as flooring. He looked through the bars beneath him, expecting to perhaps see the school floors below, but all he saw was more darkness.

On the furthest wall, he saw two spotlights shining down on the centre of the roof. The rest of the roof was faintly lit by these lights, and he could see that the entire floor was made of the bars. And the steel structure was not any version of grey but rather continued in the vein of rusted red that he had seen throughout the school. He bent down to investigate and smelled the slight odour of dry blood.

Nothing gave evidence of any creatures on the roof. If Raven was present, she kept herself well hidden. A soft ticking sound emanated from the far wall, but he could not espy anything that caused it. From where he stood, the only object on the wall was a long downpipe from an upper surface somewhere in the darkness.

Realising that standing there would not help matters much, Trevor moved towards the centre of the flat roof. There was a tiny dip in the steel formwork, with an accent of brighter red around it. As he got closer to the centre, he realised it was a symbol of some kind that had been painted over the steel bars. With the gaps between the bars, he struggled to determine the design, though.

The most he could determine was a triangle within two concentric circles. The symbol appeared to be in disuse, as if it had served some function years back but had faded into distant memory. His feet clanged on the bars as he stepped into the circle and saw something in the very centre of the triangle.

It was a metallic block, fused with the steel formwork below it. Its upper surface was as flush with the roof as it could be, considering there was no even surface to serve as a base. And on the surface was etched an elliptical object with a Futhark rune inscribed on it.

"Ansuz," Trevor read, feeling the bevelled contours of the runic letter. "Unlimited potential or divine power. How apt for the spirit element. Now, how do I get you out?"

There was a strange change to the air. Trevor looked around him, realising that he had forgotten to put his radio on again. A breeze picked up and passed around him towards the far wall with the spotlights. It spread the dust off the wall that seemed to have been there for aeons until a shape began to form on it. It glowed a dark green, fur growing out of the walls like a fungus until Trevor figured out what was emerging.

The Cu Sith materialised further until its full form had drifted down from the wall and stood growling on the steel platform. This one seemed bigger, and from what Trevor could tell, it was more ethereal or ghostly. A more solid core in its centre pulsed with a deeper green than the surrounding body of fur.

Reaching for the scalpel, Trevor suddenly remembered that it had been smashed by the teeth of the first Cu Sith he had fought. Shifting his stance, he got ready to tackle it with his bear fists when he recalled the theory he had developed regarding its teleportation.

The Cu Sith steadily stepped forward and planted its large paws on some bars. Trevor waited patiently, lowering his weight on bended knees as he got ready. His timing had to be impeccable. As anticipated, the green hound lifted its head and started howling.

Trevor waited until the last howl sounded and dropped his back to the floor. He winced for a moment as the thick bars slapped his body, the feeling ringing through his spine. Yet, it was nothing compared to what would have happened if the Cu Sith teleported and bit into him, so he stayed there longer, accepting the pain.

The silence comforted him. After several seconds, he dared look up and saw that the hound was indeed gone. Trevor arose, elated that it had worked but frustrated that the rune was still lodged in the metallic object. He still had no means to release it. The idea to break the metal block off and press the runic surface against the Hall's door occurred to him when the wind shifted again.

To Trevor's horror, two forms emerged before him. The Cu Siths stood against the wall, one to his left and the other to his right. He panicked, unsure whether he would be able to banish both at the same time. They watched him hungrily, staring at him as if waiting for their master's call before moving.

If there was a signal, Trevor did not hear it. They both bolted, fangs like sharpened steel bearing down on him. He swallowed hard as they got equally closer and lunged at him at the same time. Trevor grabbed the right hound's mane and shoved it to the left. He grabbed the next hound within his hands and twisted its head until the point of its one fang caught the inside of his lower arm.

He managed to lift his arm in time before it sank any deeper but let go of the mane simultaneously. The other hound started howling as the closest beast bit into his left upper leg. Trevor screamed as the aching pain raced into his body, trying to wrestle the hound's head off him. Its fangs found meat, forcing Trevor to collapse to the bars as the second howl sounded. With what consciousness he had left, he flattened his back on the bars with the last resounding howl.

He lifted his right leg and kicked at the last hound's face. The teeth lifted out and sank back in again, making him pull its fur and scream louder.

Satisfied that the other hound had not teleported, Trevor fought through the agony and lifted himself off the floor. In combined anger and exhaustion, he knelt with his free knee on the hound's face, making it let go. It whined in pain as he drove his knee harder into the side of its face, distorting it against the bars.

Trevor's knee passed through its face and snapped against the metal beneath it. The Cu Sith had shifted into a ghostly form from beneath him and then moved back to the wall, where it became solid again. His breathing became hoarse and hard with the physical exhaustion and volumes of suffering passing through him. Trevor stood up, his chest visibly heaving as he heard the howls pass through the air. As before, he fell down by the third announcement and covered his back.

He doubted whether he would be able to rise again. Simply lying there, he took a moment to recover as much as possible. His strength had been sapped in the last confrontation. It felt easier to give the darkness his life and be done with it than to continue this endless battle. If he was going to survive, he would need to focus on removing the rune between attacks.

As if suspecting his plan of action, the wind changed again, but this time with more force. Trevor didn't feel like getting up to face more Cu Siths and waited for the wind to subside before he looked up. There were now four hounds along the wall waiting for him, each growling in fury.

Trevor rolled onto his belly and onto his knees before finally standing up. He wondered idly if they were just going to keep doubling every time he defeated them. That would mean that the next quantity was eight. Forlornly, he looked down at the rune by his feet, knowing that the need to release it was more important than ever now.

Something on the floor caught his attention. He didn't have time to inspect it, but there were three faint glows where he had dropped to banish the Cu Siths. It was almost as if their essence had been trapped in the bars, waiting to be released again. He noticed it lit up the faded lines of the unknown triangular symbol. Still, movement ahead pulled his concentration away from it.

As two of the hounds moved, he decided to test a new idea. It had come to him from the glistening of their metallic teeth, reflected by the spotlight overhead. He recalled how those fangs had ripped his scalpel apart. The steel bars supporting the metallic box thinned out in comparison to the rest of the floor's bars. Excited, he got ready for his plan.

When the first hound lunged, he kicked up into its chin, and as it rose up from the impact, he planted his fist into its face. The Cu Sith fell hurtling to the ground as Trevor grabbed onto the next hound's head. It was strong and would not easily be pushed down, so he used his knee again to press its mouth to the bars. When he had it by the metal box, he hopped up and down until the teeth sank through the metal around the box.

Trevor got a fright as he realised one of the hounds at the wall had reached their third howl. He had been so preoccupied with the two facing him that its howling had barely been perceived. He was about to fall to his back when it teleported behind him and attacked.

He twisted as it jumped into his arms, lifting its upper body against his chest. He clutched at its shoulders, keeping its fangs from him as the Cu Sith by his feet gagged and choked. Trevor distinctly heard the other hound by the wall howl as he deliberately stepped on the bottom hound's head, waiting for it to bite loose. The second howl rang, the Cu Sith in his arms reaching forward and yapping with its teeth near his nose. He pushed back against its weight, listening carefully as the third howl sang.

Letting the Sith in his arms fall with him, he kicked the lower hound's head and received a clank as the box ripped off into its mouth. His back hit the bars hard again at the end of the last howl, and he kicked the hound above him in its belly and sent it flying over him. Having forgotten about the fourth hound, he turned to see the lower Cu Sith spit the metallic box out as the fourth beast rammed its body against his abdomen.

Trevor hit the back of his head hard on the bars as he collapsed. His head spun terribly, and he struggled to focus. His hand on the hound's throat above him was all that kept it at bay. It lurched down, forcing his elbow to bend, its teeth just skimming his throat as he pushed it up again.

The ability to push back against the beast gave him the impetus to fight back again. The metallic box was next to him while the hound that had bitten it loose had started howling. Trevor frowned, wondering if the beast knew what would happen by the third howl. To add to the confusion, the last hound joined it in chorus. Apparently, it confounded the Cu Sith above him just as much as it turned its head to watch them vanish.

Not sparing any time for the final beast to turn on him, Trevor grabbed the box and slammed it against the hound's head. Getting up as it rolled to the side, he noticed that the symbol on the bars beneath him was almost completely lit up with one final patch remaining.

The Cu Sith also noticed it as it looked at Trevor with a new light in its eyes. Something about the rejuvenation of the symbol had caused it to find a new purpose. So it growled and steadily walked towards Trevor. He backed away, holding the metal block as a weapon.

Yet, the hound didn't attack. It kept moving slowly towards him as he backed away closer to the spotlight wall. It was only then that Trevor discovered what it was up to. The Cu Sith wanted his back covered so that it could complete the symbol, joining its comrades in the ethereal world. It was time for Trevor to outsmart it.

He placed his back against the wall next to the downpipe and watched carefully as it started to howl. The second howl rang, and Trevor tensed his body. As the Cu Sith lifted its head for the final howl, he dashed forward from the wall and waited for the teleport to happen.

As if the hound had expected it, it closed its maw and lunged forward, the third howl forgotten. With a sudden reflex, Trevor dropped the box and caught the beast under its neck. He yanked at the mane beneath and whirled the hound around him. Its body smashed against the wall hard, cracking bones resounding around the roof. The downpipe broke where the hound had connected with it, and the loose lower part fell to the channel beneath it along the wall.

Despite the horrific noise of the Cu Sith connecting with the wall, it stood up and faced him again. He could feel its intense anger at having been handled like that. Trevor steadily backed away as it proceeded to step towards him, picking up speed until it was rushing headlong at him. When it was a few steps from him, it bent down and then jumped up, Trevor watching helplessly as its weight slammed into him and made him fall onto the caged floor.

He expected it to tear down into his neck. Any moment now, the steel fangs would rip his throat apart. Yet, as he stared at its brown eyes, he could not detect any fatal movement to end his life. Instead, it smiled maliciously before raising its head and sounding its last howl. As with the others, it vanished into the steel frames beneath him. Trevor had a sinking suspicion it had joined its comrades in completing the strange symbol.

Wondering what would happen if he just remained on his back, he got up anyway. True to his assumption, the triangular image within the concentric circles glowed a pale green. It was shimmering along the lines, almost in the air above it. The green changed slightly to sky blue before it became orange. When it was a deep red, flames broke out over the symbol.

Trevor stepped back to the spotlight wall as the fire rose higher and wider. Something was taking form inside of it. The lower end was becoming more solid than the gassy flames that lifted off from the ground. He watched the solid part transform into a huge body with four massive legs. Paws complemented each leg, with the body standing slightly higher than his head. Huge claws bigger than his face sprung out on each paw, clanging hard against the steel cage floor.

While the upper body formed, Trevor noticed that the body had no fur. Instead, it had a scaly appearance, much like a reptile. The scales shone gold and emerald in the fiery light that still rose higher in the air above him. Then his attention was stolen by the seven necks that solidified above the body. The flames trickled up each neck into the dank, humid air where the heads began to form.

Even though the body appeared to belong to a reptile, the seven heads did not. Growling wolf heads growled down at him once the transformation was complete, the flames finally finding homes in their fiery pools of eyes. Black manes trailed down each of their necks into a bush of black fur along the reptilian back towards a pointy, shaggy tail.

The fire in their eyes did not die, though. They burned bright and bigger than the Cadejo's had, and their steel fangs were much larger than the Cu Siths. With that realisation, he grasped that each head belonged to each of the hounds he had killed on the roof, who had joined into the mysterious symbol and become one.

Trevor's back clanked into the part of the downpipe still connected to the wall. He looked down at the piece that had broken off, instinctively thinking of using it to defend himself. As he reached down, he saw something lodged inside of it. He went in and pulled out a silver dagger.

The hounds went silent. They stared at the object in his hand, clearly upset by its presence. Yet, it did not stay them from their objective, which was clearly to either kill him or keep him from stopping Raven from completing her mission. They resumed their growling, the fires burning brighter in their eyes until balls of flame flew down at him from one of the heads. Trevor jumped and rolled out of the way at the last moment, brandishing the dagger before him.

"Teju Jagua," Trevor said out loud, recalling the name from lore. "Now

I wish I had some fruit or honey on me, but I guess silver will have to do. I know how much you lupine monstrosities hate it so much."

The Teju's focus shifted away from Trevor. The seven heads looked to the floor, and he could not help but follow their gaze. There was no doubt in his mind what they were staring at. The metallic box with the spirit rune lay on the caged floor where he had dropped it earlier. With a sinking feeling, he realised that all they had to do to stop him was take the rune away from him.

Hurtling forward, irrespective of the immediate danger the Teju created, he lunged onto the ground and reached for the box. His ribs scraped on the steel formwork beneath him as his fingertips grazed the box. He tried to clasp his hand around it as it suddenly rose into the air and soared towards the beast. Trevor turned and watched the rune break free from the box. As its former container fell to the floor, the rune swirled in the air by the beast's chest where the seven heads were joined.

The rune sank into the reptilian chest. As it locked in, the flames of the Teju's fourteen eyes changed from red to purple. Not only did the colour change, but the heads transformed from solid to fiery gas form, the huge purple balls of flame licking the air above each neck. The fire still resembled the hounds' faces, though, with the eyes a darker shade of purple, bordering on black.

"Ok, I don't know where you learnt that from, but you're not meant to do that," Trevor said, his voice shaking in fear.

Not sure what use it would serve, Trevor got up and held his dagger before him again. The intricate design on the hilt gave him a steady grip on it, but he was unsure what the writing on the blade meant. He just hoped the silver curse held as true with the Teju Jagua as it did with lycanthrope lore.

The Teju gave him his first chance to test it. One of the heads bent down to bite at him as the heavy reptilian body moved forward. Its fiery teeth still seemed to have the steel of knives in them as the maw opened up to bite his head. He raised the dagger and slashed across its face, making the beast wail as the head lashed back up.

Before Trevor had time to recover or move into attack, two heads lashed down simultaneously. One bit into his wrist, making the dagger fall to the ground, while the other bit into his abdomen. The mouth curved around his entire width and lifted him into the air as the other pulled his arm to the side. The hound's head locked onto his wrist was forced to let go as the other head whipped his body from side to side and then threw him into the spotlight wall.

His body cracked into the wall. It reminded him of the Cu Sith he had sent hurtling into the same spot. As Trevor looked up into the hound's face, he imagined seeing the same hound grinning down at him in pleasure and vengeance. Trevor's gaze was distracted by a ghostly figure standing by the entrance to the roof. In his pained state, he made out Kathy's spirit, but he was unsure whether she was there to spur him on or watch him die.

The Teju did not wait for him to rise again. Trevor saw the dagger being trampled underfoot, causing the beast to cry out and move away from it. Three of the heads leered down at it in demonic ire while the remainder returned their gaze to Trevor. The body moved towards him again as three heads barked and bent down to him, just as he rolled out of the way and ran for the dagger.

Trevor jumped and grabbed the hilt as two other heads caught his ankles. The dagger almost slipped out of his grasp as he was pulled upside down into the air and turned around to face the Teju. Trevor bent up towards his legs and cut into the two hounds' necks, forcing them to let him go. Trevor fell towards the floor again as another head attempted to bite into him. He twisted mid-air and slashed, the blade cutting across the hound's nose.

His neck collided with a steel bar, as his body collapsed on the floor. The sting ran through his body in vibrating chimes of agony, and it felt like the impact had paralysed him. The seven heads were above him now, glaring down at him. It looked like they were mocking him with their grins as he pathetically raised the dagger above him. His hand shook uncontrollably above him, the blade swaying from side to side.

Almost as if in pity, the central hound bent down and bit into the dagger. There was a slight whimper as the silver sizzled in its fangs before the beast spat it back on the floor beneath it. Feeling that victory was a moment away, their eyes flared darker than before, and the purple along the neck roared louder. Trevor suddenly wished he had something to attack all heads at the same time with, like a whip.

And then an idea came to him. His hand stopped shaking as he realised there was hope. The thought made him laugh out loud at himself for some reason, but the mirth was enough to recover some of his strength. The hounds above him looked at each other in confusion, becoming frustrated with his new attitude. Deciding to end his life rather quickly, the heads all bore down on him simultaneously.

Trevor reached into his pocket and grabbed the box of silver bullets. As he threw it up in the air, he pinched the box's sides and split it open, causing the bullets to spray out to either side. The heads had been plummeting too fast, and when they realised what was happening, they attempted to pull their heads back up.

A moment sooner would have saved them. One of the bullets struck the central head and exploded on impact. The silver spray made it howl in pain, causing the other heads to swing as the body jerked back. More bullets found fiery homes in necks or heads and also exploded, causing the reptilian body to sway from side to side as it tried to break out of the chaos.

Just as Trevor knew it would not kill the Teju, he also knew he did not have much time before the bullets stopped exploding and the beast recovered. He got up and ran for the beast, sliding on his knees over the caged surface and falling over himself as he reached for the silver dagger. One of the heads noticed what he was doing and ignored the searing pain that coursed through it. It snapped down at Trevor as his fingers locked on the hilt again and then cried out as he drove the dagger into its chest by the spirit rune.

All seven heads cried out in agony. The sound was so terrible and loud that Trevor let go of the blade and blocked his ears. It pierced his hands, driving through his body and making him lie on the floor again. They continued to cry as the silver blade glowed in the fiery darkness, brighter than anything around it.

The body collapsed on the floor as the hounds continued to howl and cry, making Trevor scream in pain. It was a delirium of cacophony and misery that embodied the evil rhythm of Sacred Valley. This pulse was both sick and hideous in form and sound. When it ended, Trevor's scream was the last sound that rang on the roof.

13

THE TORTURED GODS

His ears still rang, and his body retained the lingering vibrations that the Teju Jagua's cries had sent through him. As it subsided, he opened his eyes and looked around. Instead of the large bulk of the beast, he only saw the triangular symbol on the caged floor. It glowed deep black, the design appearing to emanate the fading darkness that was the remnants of the seven-headed hound.

The spirit rune and the silver dagger were in the centre of the symbol. Trevor crawled on the caged floor towards them. As he picked up the rune, he checked his pocket to confirm that the other four were still in place. He took the dagger, the only weapon he had left. The remaining box of silver bullets was useless unless he could find a firearm for them.

Finding the strength to stand, he made his way over the lattice framework to the roof door. To his amazement, he found it unlocked. He descended the stairs, listening for evidence of the metallic-headed man. Trevor switched his radio on as he was in no mood for further surprises.

It made only the faintest of noises. Trevor's feet landed on the second floor, and he looked down both passages ahead of him and to the left. The school was eerily quiet. It was still rusted and encrusted with stains of decayed blood, but there were no signs of Adlets, Cadejos, Cu Siths, or their hulk of a master. Nevertheless, Trevor held the dagger before him, ready to slice into anything that appeared.

He moved down the stairs to the first floor. Crouching at the wall of the passage that would lead him to the Hall, he stared down its length. There was absolutely no movement. The radio sizzled as softly as it did when he switched it on. Trevor gripped the cold steel of the dagger tighter as he bolted down the passage.

As he neared the Hall's entrance, he slowed his pace. Nothing had appeared to attack him. He frowned as he reached the rune door and looked down the next passage. It was just as silent as the rest of the school. If Trevor didn't know any better, he could have sworn all the creatures had left the building. Yet, he was still trapped in this insane version of Sacred Valley without knowing what had happened to Kathy.

Trevor turned to the door, occasionally looking around to ensure he was alone. He shone the torch on the pentacle before him, retrieving the five runes from his pocket. Carefully, he placed the earth rune on the upside-down triangle with the horizontal line in its centre. The rune shrivelled and sank into the pentacle, with the triangular symbol glowing gorgeous green. The Űruz letter shone over the triangle, and the two became one.

Despite his exhaustion, he could not contain his excitement. He placed the other three natural elements in their slots. First, he pressed in water, then air and thereafter fire. The Pertho letter became one with the upside-down triangle on the top right point, flowing a beautiful blue. The Teiwaz joined the upright triangle with the centre line in the top left and yielded a yeasty yellow. In the bottom left, the Thurisaz united with the upright triangle and burned a radiant red.

Trevor stood there with the final Ansuz spirit rune. He looked around one more time. Usually, he would have found comfort in the fact that no creatures were trying to stop him. Yet this time, it caused him concern. He had to save Kathy, though, so he ignored his fears and placed the final rune at the top point within the circle. The letter joined it as the image pulsed a purging purple.

Stepping back, Trevor heard a creak in the door's timber. The pentacle suddenly broke forward from the wood and turned in an anti-clockwise direction. It continued to turn until the spirit rune was pointing down. The block of wood settled back into the door as he heard the doors unlock from the inside.

"A pentagram," he whispered, afraid more than ever to enter now.

Where the pentacle had resembled good and the almighty forces that guarded it, the pentagram was pure evil and represented the complete opposite. It made him recall the upside-down triquetra in the pet shop again.

He stepped back further, his previous resolve wavering. He was not sure it was such a good idea to go through there anymore. It felt more like a trap than an entryway towards Kathy. Everything inside him told him to turn, run, and leave Sacred Valley by any means possible. He lacked the courage to proceed any further.

Something to his left caught his attention. It was the same blue ghostly Kathy he had seen before. She was wearing the same nightdress and smiling at him as she walked towards the door. As she pushed it open, a bright white light from within hid her from view as she passed into it.

Bound by curiosity, Trevor walked forward without realising he was doing so. The white light called to him... literally. He could hear his name being spoken softly by a female voice that sounded very much like Kathy's. It lured him in, his hand rising up to meet the white mist lit by something hidden inside. And then, he stepped through....

...waking up in a soft, warm bed. He opened his sleepy eyes to Kathy beside him, calling his name softly. She smiled down at him and gave him a gentle kiss on the lips.

"You slept through the night," she warned him, but did not seem to be concerned about it.

"Oh no!" Trevor made to jump up, but she pushed his chest down.

"It doesn't really matter anymore, does it?" Kathy asked. "You said you were leaving her anyway. And it's not like going back home now is going to save you."

"I know, Kathy," he replied, "but I want to talk to her about it first. I don't want Caroline finding out about us like this."

"Why? You're cheating on her anyway. What does it matter how she finds out?"

"Don't say that."

"Say what?"

"Cheating," Trevor repeated, throwing the sheet off his naked body. "I don't like that word."

"Well, whether you like it or not, that's what you're doing," Kathy replied, ending it with a giggle. "But it doesn't have to be this way. We can be happy like this forever."

Trevor stood up, pulling her hands off his chest. She stood up, too, the sunlight from the windows glinting against her nude form. He was distracted by her body for a moment, wondering if it could be as easy as just remaining there and not returning home.

As if reading his mind, she moved closer to him and wrapped her hands behind his neck, bringing his head down for a soft passionate kiss. His hands automatically moved onto the lower curves of her back, bringing the skin of her body against his. The fever took over all rational thought as he continued to kiss her, his hands surfing her back as she rubbed her lower body against his.

Suddenly the apartment door crashed in. Trevor let go of her as he looked down the passage to see a man rushing down to meet them. As the man entered the bedroom, he looked Trevor and Kathy up and down, a wide smirk forming on his face.

"I thought so," he said, spinning around and walking out.

"Bishop!" Trevor shouted after him as Kathy grabbed her clothes and started dressing. "No, wait!"

The whiteness washed away. Trevor stood at the entrance of the Hall. He shook his head and wiped his eyes clean. Had he really seen that? It felt like he had watched as an outsider at the events that had happened before in his past. Why was he remembering this now? Did it mean something?

Any further questions he had were cleaned away by the sight in front of him. The Hall was predominately empty, and its only occupant was Kathy lying on a gurney. She was strapped down by her ankles and wrists, and she was unconscious as far as he could tell. He ran towards her, gripping the dagger tight again.

"Kathy!" he shouted, hoping it would wake her. He lightly tapped her cheeks and then set to cutting the leather straps. "Kathy! Wake up!"

She stirred and moaned, opening her eyes softly. Trevor helped her sit up, but then she moved forward into his arms as she embraced him. He held her tighter than he could ever remember holding her until she sighed with relief and sagged against his chest. For a moment, he thought she had died.

"Where are we?" Kathy asked, looking around the Hall. She noticed how rotten some timber finishes looked and the rusty, blood stains on the tiled floor.

"I don't know," Trevor said, joining her observation of the room. "It seems to be Hollowbrook Elementary, but there's something wrong with it."

"How did we get here?"

"You don't remember?"

"I remember a black dog grabbing my ankles. It had a scar on its eye. It pulled me to the basement, but my head knocked onto the floor. I must have passed out."

Trevor studied her momentarily, but it seemed like she was telling the truth. It made him want to broach the topic that had upset her in the courtyard before, but he was worried she would turn on him again and try to escape. She didn't look like she had the energy to run from him a second time, though, so he took the chance.

"Kathy," he said softly, "I think it's time you told me about Raven."

She looked up into his eyes, and for a moment, he thought she might run. However, she peered down at her hands and paced away from him and around the gurney as if to put something between them.

"Alright," she said, "I'll tell you. But you're not going to like it. You may leave me once I tell you the truth."

"Strangely enough, I leave people who lie to me above those who are honest. Consider it a pet peeve of mine."

"I had a terrible time growing up," she confessed. "My parents were never good to me. Especially not my father."

"Did he abuse you?"

"No," she replied. "But how he treated and spoke to me was abuse enough, I guess. The worst part was feeling that I was unloved or unwanted.

"A child doesn't understand things as much as they do when they are adults. I didn't realise that my father's treatment of me was showing through at school. I was very envious of children with loving parents; so envious that I bullied and hurt them."

"I take it Raven was your favourite victim?" Trevor asked, noticing that she had become relaxed while regaling him with her past.

"She was always the nicest girl in school and treated everyone with respect," she continued. "Something about that made me detest her. It was easy for her to make friends. The only way I could make friends was by making them fear me. The only ones that truly loved me and were faithful were my dogs.

"Looking back now, I cannot believe I behaved that way. It's shameful and disgusting. Only later in life did I start changing my ways; at least, I thought I had."

"What do you mean?"

"Did you know that Caroline grew up in Sacred Valley?" Kathy asked him.

"She mentioned she grew up in a small rural town but never really gave me specifics," Trevor acknowledged and then looked into her eyes. "Why?"

"She lived around the corner from here, down an alley off Langley Street," Kathy replied, walking away and pacing some more. Trevor followed. "Her brother had just finished schooling at Hollowbrook Elementary when she started. His parents sent him to a high school in

Dunst."

"Caroline came to Hollowbrook?" Trevor said, pointing back at the school.

Suddenly, the realisation dawned on him. He looked at the floor, his mind drawing some conclusions. Kathy remained silent while she watched his mind at work, wondering how long it would take before he said it. He looked up at her again, the words stuck in his throat.

"Yes, my dear love," she finally said to him. "Caroline was Raven."

Trevor stepped back and leaned against the gurney, which shifted slightly under his weight.

"So… you knew her before I met either of you?" Trevor asked.

"Yes," she replied.

"And you knew I was with her when I met you?" he pursued.

"Well….yes," Kathy said, walking slowly back into the light. He saw now that her eyes were moist. "I had seen her one day at the shopping mall in Ashbourne. Some of the old envy and anger had risen again, but I held it at bay. And then I saw you.

"I saw how happy you two were. Because of my upbringing, I had a hard time keeping stable relationships. You two made it look easy."

"So you decided to destroy our relationship for your own happiness?"

"Not at first," she replied, rushing forward to hold his arms. "I bumped into you at the Ashbourne Town Library. That was an accident."

"Oh yes, I remember," Trevor said, a slight smile rising at the memory.

"I could see why Caroline was so in love with you. You have a certain charm about you that drew me in."

"Yet you could have stopped it," Trevor said. "You knew Caroline and could have told me."

"You were the married one!" Kathy retorted. "If you really didn't want it, you could have stopped it. My past with Caroline was irrelevant."

"Maybe to you," he said, stepping away from her and waving his arms around, "but clearly not to whoever is doing this. And now I am wondering if you ever loved me or if it was simply getting what Caroline had."

"I did love you!" Kathy shouted, rushing forward to his arms again. Trevor stayed her with a palm against her chest. "Despite what happened between me and her, I meant everything I said and did in our time together."

"It's hard to believe that now," he commented but lowered his palm.

"Let me put it this way then," she said, moving against his chest and looking up at him. "If there was no past, if I never knew her, I would still have pursued you….pursued us."

He considered her words for a moment. He had been too naïve with others in his life, and it was hard to trust someone who kept things from him. This was a tremendous truth that was hard to ignore. He decided to rather focus on immediate questions that needed to be answered than matters of forgiveness.

"It still leaves the mystery of who is behind all this," he finally said. He noticed in her eyes that she incorrectly assumed the change of topic meant he would take her back. He would deal with that later. "Caroline committed suicide, and probably because of us. So if Raven is gone, who is doing this?"

Kathy stepped back slightly and looked down, her right hand reaching her temple.

"Are you ok?" he asked.

"Yes; it's just, there are some other things I remember after being brought here."

"Like what?"

"I had moments where I woke up for a bit," she said, then shook her head. "Well, I don't really know if I was awake. I thought I saw myself... I mean, a ghost like me. And, there was a man, a massive man."

"Did he have a large twister metal head by any chance?"

"Yes," she replied, looking down at her feet again. "And that's not all. He had a mark on his arm….. no, wait, a tattoo…"

It was Trevor's chance to step back slightly, remembering the tattoo he had seen on the man in the Storage Room painting. He waited for her to work through what she recalled, waiting in abated breath for what she would say.

"Oh shit, Trevor," Kathy looked up suddenly, her eyes wide. "There was someone else there that I could not see. She said his name. I know who he is."

"Who, Kathy?!" he shouted, grasping her upper arms firmly. "Who is he?!"

Her revelation was cut short. Somewhere behind them, they heard a slight yapping. This was exchanged with a soft growl and then yapping again. Kathy walked towards it first, shortly followed by Trevor. His torch lit the mesh floor ahead of them as they followed the sound to a dark corner.

Trevor stopped, almost throwing up. The stench was horrid, but the sight was even more terrifying. A small dog's head was trapped in the floor's steel mesh, its neck swollen and cut open by the fine steel around its neck. The rest of its body was trapped under the floor. He could tell by the broken steel floor and the open neck wounds that it had been struggling to get out for some time. It had only recently woken up for another attempt.

A ball of meat was just out of reach of the dog's mouth. He realised that this was the source of its anguish. As much as it tried to grab the food with its teeth, the steel held it back, biting further into its flesh. Kathy raised her palm to her mouth in astonishment.

The dog didn't have much left to give, though. As much as it strained to get to the food, it was obviously using its last energy. Trevor noticed on the steel floor how much blood had been lost; it would soon die.

Suddenly Trevor understood what was going to happen. He looked up and saw hanging hound corpses with nooses around their necks, set on the walls within large picture frames. It all made sense to him now. This was what everything was building up to. And, as Kathy's sympathetic hand reached down to feed the stressed dog, it gave up its last breath.

"No!" Trevor shouted, reaching down to grab Kathy's arm. "Kathy, step away!"

It was too late. As his fingers graced her skin, some force hit him in the belly, sending him flying across the room. His back slammed into the meshed floor, but he looked up quickly while ignoring the renewed pain shooting through him.

Kathy had risen into the air. From the dead dog, a spirit of various colours and shades of light had picked her up and began entering her. Her arms were spread to either side with her legs wide open. It looked like she was screaming, yet the only sound was the howling movement of the essence that opened her mouth and eyes.

The essence ripped her clothes off, but her nudity was quickly concealed by fur that grew from her skin. Her body became bulkier as her arms, legs and chest became more muscular. Not only did she increase in bulk, but she grew taller. Her feet touched the ground as soon as she was twice his height, the last of the essence entering her. As soon as the transformation was complete, he knew nothing of Kathy remained.

He should have realised that an Inugami was being summoned sooner. With the canine lore that had abounded at the school, the presence of the trapped dog should have alerted him earlier. Now the souls of a thousand godlike spirits were inside her, doing the bidding of whoever had invoked the being.

The Inugami stood before him as its life force settled into the new body. Its head was that of a large wolf, its eyes the fiery red of the Cadejo. It stood tall on its hind legs, its entire body covered by fur. As it growled at him, he saw the same knife-fangs of the Cu Sith, which were complemented by sets of knife claws on its forepaws. Its huge breasts were both feminine and muscular, with huge dark nipples protruding out from the fur.

Trevor got up and ran for the Hall doors. He grasped the knobs and pulled, but the doors refused to open. Looking for any locks to release, he saw that it had none. Suddenly, the handlebars of the doors sizzled into the wood of the door itself, and he faced two wooden boards with no fittings.

He turned back to the Inugami, pulling out his silver dagger. He hoped it worked as well on this being as it did on the Teju Jagua. As he stepped forward, the framed corpses along the walls suddenly erupted with a chorus of laughter and yapping, howls and barks. It felt like he was in an amphitheatre, a gladiator facing his greatest enemy with an audience hungry for bloodshed and death.

As the Inugami walked forward to face him, he attempted to recall any lore on how to kill it. Although he could not remember any such account, he knew that whatever could be summoned could be banished. The only problem was that he did not know how to banish a thousand godly spirits.

Trevor's eyes opened wide as the Inugami turned its right palm to the ceiling and called fire to it. The flames sizzled as a ball in its hand without singeing the outer fur. The reflection burned in its eyes as it lifted the ball and threw it at Trevor.

Taking him by surprise, he jumped out of the way at the last minute. The ball exploded on the wall behind him, sending him stumbling towards the beast just as he had regained his feet. He fell down to the floor, and his face connected with the mesh. A clang resounded over the roar of the Inugami as the dagger hit a steel frame, stinging his hand.

He felt more than saw the beast approaching. Trevor rose up again, wielding the dagger in his hand and hoping for some form of fear to appear in his opponent. Yet, it simply ignored it as if it never existed. Instead, it brought down a hulky foot to stomp him into the mesh.

Trevor rolled to the side, carefully not to roll too far. As soon as the foot shuddered the floor beneath them, he bolted for the foot and stabbed the blade into it. The Inugami screamed with the voices of a thousand feminine and masculine beings, causing Trevor to release the blade and close his ears.

With the unearthly screams stopped, he looked up and saw a fist moving down to slam him. Trevor rolled again, but the fist opened up, and the claws struck his chest as he stood up. It sent him through the air again, his chest spraying blood in the air before him as his back connected with a wall beneath one of the framed hounds.

Trevor was dazed, but he could hear the Inugami walking towards him. He opened his eyes and saw flames in its hand again. Not knowing where he got the energy from, he rose up and jumped as the ball of flame crashed with the wall he had been leaning on, sending him falling to the side.

The dagger was still lodged in its foot. Trevor noticed smoke rising from it as the fur started falling to the floor. The skin was boiling and bubbling where it was lodged, but the Inugami seemed to ignore it as it raised its left hand this time. It aimed it at Trevor as if it would strangle him from afar.

Trevor shouted in alarm as his body rose in the air, much like Kathy's had. Before he could fathom what was happening, he crossed the gap between them at lightning speed. The Inugami's hand closed around him in a vice grip, causing him to splatter blood from his mouth onto its upper finger. It squeezed harder, causing something in his rear pocket to crack and bend uncomfortably.

The knife fangs glistened in the eerie light of the Hall as his torch snapped and broke on his chest. Trevor used his hands to push against the fingers holding him as the fangs bore down at him, slipping down within the fist just as the maw closed where his head had been. The teeth bit into the beast's hand, causing him to release Trevor in agony.

As he landed on the mesh ground, he reached for the dagger in the foot nearby him. His hand grasped the hilt and pulled out, but a backhand struck his body and sent him flying through the air again, spinning around before he hit the ground with his left side. He felt a rib crack, which caused him to spit out more blood as he coughed to get his breath back.

The dagger had been slapped out of his hand. Trevor looked around and saw it lying against the wall near the Inugami. The beast raised its right hand and threw a fireball at him again. With what strength he had left, he rolled out of the way as the ball exploded on the ground. He simply let his body lift off the ground and connect with the mesh again, not having much impetus to stop it.

The grinding of metal and steel made him look up. The Inugami was using the force of his left hand to pull one of the corpse frames off the wall. The bottom of it had pulled loose, but the upper half kept the frame connected to the wall. The beast increased its power, and it snapped loose.

Before it could reach the Inugami, it swirled its wrists and aimed at Trevor. The frame changed direction in mid-flight and soared towards him. He stood up, clutching his injured side and ran out of the way. The cage collided with the wall and broke into several pieces. Trevor stood breathless as he watched the Inugami, wondering how he would survive this beast.

He knew the answer was clearly silver. The dagger had shown as much. Yet, the task of first getting to the dagger and then using it in a way that could kill the beast appeared insurmountable. And then, he remembered what he had done to the Teju Jagua and realised he still had one box of silver bullets left. That gave him a new idea.

He had been so caught up in his thoughts that he had not realised that the beast was throwing another ball of flame towards him. Empowered by his new objective, he ran and jumped just as the ball hit the floor. The explosion lifted him up into the air, but he landed on his feet and ran in an arc around the beast.

When he saw the Inugami lift his left arm, he reached into his pocket for the box. The box had broken in his pocket, and the bullets were lying loose. He felt the air shift as the force from the hand began pulling at him. He took a bullet out and threw it into the air before him just as the force clutched at him and pulled him at lightning speed. He kept his eye focused on the bullet despite the jolt and saw it enter the hand that was about to grab him.

The Inugami screamed again. The force evaporated, and Trevor fell to the ground, holding his ears closed as he landed on the mesh between the beasts' feet. He ran for the dagger nearby, but the Inugami kicked him in the chest and sent him to the opposite wall. Trevor righted himself before the collision and made sure the impact was minimal.

Another flame ball came his way, but he was fast enough to move away this time. He had seen the right hand lift and had started running already. The blast didn't affect him, and he ran in an arc again. The Inugami lifted its left hand, causing Trevor to grab another bullet, but it reached for a cage again. He watched the frame being torn from the wall and then thrown at him, making sure to run from the point of impact again.

Trevor tried to shake the feeling that it was getting easier to avoid being injured. Now that he knew the Inugami's attacks and methods, all he had to do was figure out a plan of action that he could incorporate with it. He would run out of bullets eventually, so everything he did from this point forward had to be aimed at getting the dagger.

With that in mind, he waited for the Inugami to pull him in again. As predicted, it lifted its left hand, and the force tugged at him. He had the bullet ready but waited for the last minute. He rose in the air and, just before being propelled at lightning speed, he released it before him. They both soared towards the hand that was ready to grip the life out of him.

As the fingers closed around him, the bullet bit in and the Inugami howled again. Trevor held onto the upper fingers and kicked against the palm, making sure he was angled towards the right place. He saw the dagger beneath him as he fell towards it but had misjudged the Inugami's recovery. It snatched at him with the other hand and brought Trevor up towards its face again.

As Trevor was lifted up, he noticed something while struggling against the grip. Beneath the fur on the right breast of the beast was a symbol. He stopped squirming long enough to see that it was the Lunar Nexus but in black. He thought back to Raven's book, remembering that there were three versions of the insignia, but he could not remember what the black version meant.

Whatever it was, it gave him new hope. His distraction had given the Inugami enough time to bring its teeth down on him again, but he found space to push himself down again. The teeth bit into the fingers again, and he dropped down.

This time Trevor watched for any attacks while falling. He clutched a bullet as a foot came towards him and threw it as hard as possible. In any normal circumstance, the bullet would have just bounced off harmlessly, but since the Inugami seemed allergic to silver, it caused the beast to howl again and drop the foot. Trevor connected with the mesh ground.

Ignoring the impact, he ran for the dagger and picked it up. He heard a sizzle behind him and saw the metal before him light up. He jumped immediately to the side as the fireball collided with the wall, but he was too close. It threw him into the air again, some of the fire burning into his leg's skin, and his back snapped hard against a frame high up against the wall.

He fell down on all fours. Trevor found it so much harder to breathe now, but he was elated to see the dagger was still in his grasp. He stood up, his chest out and his fists gripped tight. His body wanted to give in, but his spirit refused. He knew what he had to do and watched as the Inugami raised its left hand. He smiled despite trying not to.

The Inugami lifted him into the air while walking towards him. Trevor hid the dagger behind his back for the moment, afraid that the beast would change its mind if it saw what he wanted to do. He allowed it to pull him into its grip, waiting for the final moment when the fingers began to close around him, and then brought the dagger up in a vertical strike against the palm.

The fingers opened out, and he grabbed to hold onto one of them. He pulled himself onto it and saw the other hand coming down to swat him. He swiped the blade horizontally, causing the beast to howl in pain and pull the hand away. As its head bent back in the howl, Trevor jumped up into the air. With both hands, he gripped the dagger above his head, watching the Lunar Nexus beneath him as he soared down towards it.

As the Inugami's head came back up, the dagger sank into the Lunar Nexus. Its eyes went wide, but it made no sound. Trevor was dangling on the breast, his foot pressed on the nipple as he wedged the dagger in further. The Inugami swallowed softly and then closed its eyes.

The explosion that followed was unexpected. Trevor was hanging by the dagger one moment, and the next, he was on the ground across the Hall, clutching at his head at the severe pain coursing through it. He could hardly hear anything above the thrumming that suddenly filled the room like a very loud generator.

When Trevor found the strength to look, he saw that the spirits of the Inugami were leaving the body. Its head was tilted back, and its arms were spread out on either side. It reminded him of how Kathy had looked before the possession. The spirits flew out from its maw and shifted through the ceiling, vanishing from sight.

After several seconds, he realised that the Inugami was getting smaller. It transformed back into Kathy's nude form until nothing was left of it, her former pale skin now etched with patches of scars. Her body drifted towards the floor, dropping and slumping onto the steel mesh.

Trevor had already reached her side by the time her body settled down. He fell to his knees, picked her upper body into his arms, and rested her on his legs. He pressed his chest against hers.

"Kathy!" he shouted over the dying noises of the departing spirits. "Kathy, stay with me!"

Trevor looked up. The school was shaking. He first thought it was part of the chaos surrounding them after the Inugami's slaying, but realised now it was something more. A bell sounded somewhere in Sacred Valley, and the walls and floors were changing around him. The plaster and tiles returned to the school, shifting from the hellish version he had just traversed back to the foggy school he had entered.

"My love," Kathy whispered to him, drawing his attention away from the school. "I'm not going to make it."

Trevor saw the black Lunar Nexus on her breast glowing softly under the collecting rivers of blood, the dagger mysteriously gone from sight. He ran his hands through her hair, oblivious to the tears falling from his eyes onto her cheeks.

"We can make it," he replied. "I just need to get you to the red Lunar Nexus."

"No," she coughed, blood trailing out of her mouth. "I'm not going to make it."

Trevor hugged her tight, his face hidden in her neck. He pressed her body against his as if that would save her. He rocked her back and forth, her mouth by his ear. She was moaning softly now, whispering words he could neither hear nor make out. In the end, when the noise of the school's transformation fell to absolute silence, she spoke her final words with absolute clarity.

"The man with the metallic head... it's Bishop."

Trevor lifted his head to look at her and then became frightened when he noticed the surroundings. They were in the middle of the courtyard, and the storm was gone. Grass as white as snow was beneath them, and the mist rolled over them like a white blanket. There was a tremendous amount of light beyond the mist again as if the sun had risen from a long slumber.

Turning to look at Kathy again, he saw movement by the courtyard doors ahead. A black Cadejo was standing there staring at them, white steam rising from its breath. Trevor recognised it by the scar over its fiery eyes.

It started moving forward but then looked behind it. Its face reflected alarm, and then its body was smashed by a white form. The two rolled out of view, and a loud growl was cut short by a whine and then silence. Trevor waited, staring at the courtyard entrance for the creature to appear.

The white Cadejo limped onto the white lawn. It was the same one he had assumed had been killed by the black hound on the second floor by the bathrooms. Its neck showed signs of gaping neck wounds, and its front leg had recently been freshly injured.

When it reached him, it collapsed beside Kathy's legs. It gave one last puff of breath that sent a plume of snow into the air and then closed its eyes.

Trevor looked down at Kathy, felt her neck for a pulse, and realised she was gone too.

ACT TWO

BLOOD OF A SERIAL KILLER

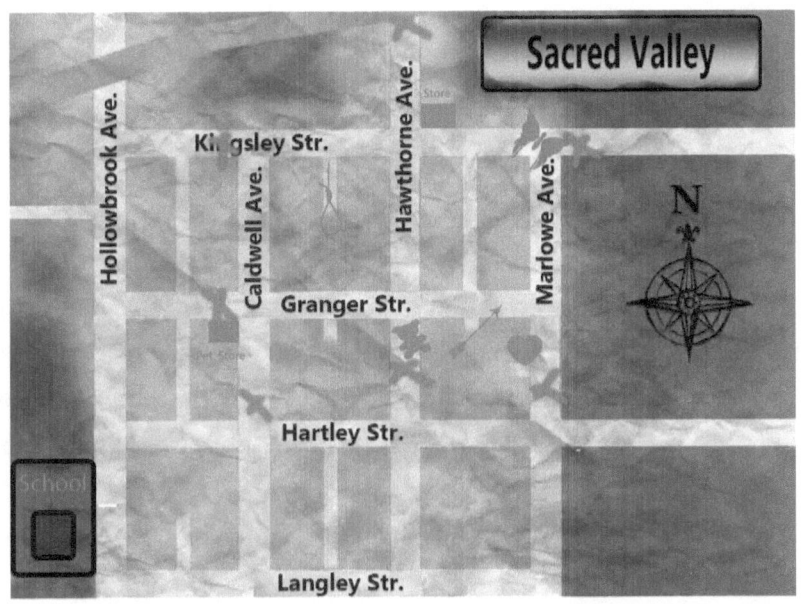

14

RAVEN'S GUARDIAN

Trevor stood by the courtyard coffin. He stared down at Kathy's pale form in the coffin, her body now covered by ashen snow he had piled on her. Her expression gave him the impression that she had finally found some peace. He brushed some of her hair out of her eyes before closing the coffin lid.

The Lunar Nexus had rejuvenated him completely, healing all his wounds and closing the gaping hole on his shoulder. He had winced as his ribs had shifted back into place. After that, he sighed as the energy returned, and he no longer felt so tired. No matter how much he had tried, the Lunar Nexus could not bring Kathy back from the dead.

The Lunar Nexus's insignia on the reception wall further demonstrated that she could not be brought back. Her name was no longer glowing red like the rest of the symbol but was written in dull black. It made her death feel real; there was no way to bring her back.

Now he stared down at the coffin he had found her in and to which she had been returned. His duffel bag and shotgun had been found in the courtyard where he had left them. The Ruger had also been found where Kathy had dropped it. Trevor checked it immediately and found the bullets still in place.

"May you rest in peace now, Kathy," Trevor said softly. "I'm sure you are in a much better place than this."

Trevor waited a moment longer, struggling to pull himself away, before proceeding to the Boiler Room stairs. Moving up to the second floor, he reached the Library without interference. Ever since he had killed the Inugami, the school was empty. Nothing jumped out of the walls, nor was there any scraping of a metal blade being dragged on the floor. It was very silent.

The Library also provided him with easy access. Instead of ashen mist, the light that broke into the room revealed a soft cloud of dust in the air. The pedestals that had held the philosophers' heads were still in place, but the busts were gone. Trevor continued, eagerly moving along the bookracks that were again in place, scanning their spines for the relevant subject matters.

He slowed down when he reached books that covered mythology and ancient lore. There were at least two rows covering a variety of topics and specific myths, but one book in particular caught his attention. It was a thick, large hardcover book bound with red leather.

"'An Omnibus of Magical and Mythological Creatures'," Trevor read aloud, taking the book down and wiping the dust off the front cover with his palm. He opened it carefully, fearing any sudden action might damage the book.

Even though the pages seemed stiff and aged, they felt anything but fragile. He toyed with one of the pages between his fingers, wondering how old the book was. Turning to the contents page, he tried to see how relevant the information was.

The sections were categorised by the types of monsters or creatures found in mythology. Running his fingers over the headings, he found one that read 'Canines and Their Kin.' In eagerness, he paged through to the relevant section and skimmed through the various beasts quickly until he found what he was looking for.

Among all the various lore on hounds and canine beasts, he found all of the ones he had faced so far in Sacred Valley. Each had different accounts for the tales transferred and translated through centuries of generations. There was very little that Trevor could gain from the knowledge that he did not already know.

Specifically, his lack of knowledge on how to kill them more efficiently was not supplemented by anything within the tome. He read through each of the creatures he had faced more carefully, but the only one that had a clear indication of killing them was the black Cadejo. He already knew that it could only be killed by a white Cadejo.

Trevor slammed the book shut, causing dust to rise and making him sneeze. Despite the tome not revealing much he didn't already know, he feared he might cross a creature he was ignorant of. With that in mind, he slipped the tome into his bag instead of placing the book back on the rack.

Surveying the remaining books on mythology revealed that the other books had even less on the topics and almost nothing on the beasts he had already faced. Trevor turned to move back to the library door when his foot hit something underneath the lowest rack. He bent down to see what it was, having to reach in to grab it. When he pulled it out, he couldn't contain his laughter.

"Really?" he said, more in mirth than for anything else. "I could have used this much sooner."

It was a box of 10 shotgun shells. Loading the Citori with two shells and then putting the remaining ones in his pocket, he decided that he would need to be more thorough in searching areas. There seemed to be a wealth of valuable items, weapons and ammunition lying around, and he appeared to have missed them in his haste.

When he reached the school's main doors, he placed all his school maps in his bag and took out the street map. Trevor looked back through the roads he had been before, remembering there had been no way through to the bridge at the end of Hartley Street. He was also unsure whether Hollowbrook Street was safe back the way he had come before, remembering the large-scale attack on his way to the school.

His only safest bet was travelling down to Langley and making his way to the bridge from there. He hoped Jay was still waiting for him by the Police Station. As much as seeing Kathy's name faded out on the Lunar Nexus distressed him, it suddenly relieved him. Jay's name had still been glowing red, which had to mean that he was still alive.

Closing the map, he headed out. He walked out into the mist again, looking back at the school and hoping he wouldn't have to ever go in there again. In the same measure, he suddenly missed Kathy terribly. It was almost overwhelming. His heart ached, but he knew he could not stay there. Turning back to the streets, he headed for the pavement and turned south.

Feeling the need to be ready for an attack by any of the hounds that he had encountered, he checked if he had any melee weapons available. Suddenly he realised just how much bad luck he had had with keeping them on him. The copper pipe had been dropped in the streets, Jay had taken the kitchen knife with him, a Cadejo had knocked the plank out of his hand before killing him, and a Cu Sith had chewed up the scalpel.

So besides the determination to search areas more thoroughly, Trevor was now also determined to preserve his weapons as much as possible. With Kathy gone, his only objective was to find Jay and escape Sacred Valley. If there was a way in, there had to be a way out. And if he was to find a way out, he would probably need to find more history on the town.

He took the Citori shotgun in hand and walked towards Langley. He ensured his radio was on and saw it had suffered superficial damage on the sides and face. The radio was silent, and Trevor hoped it was more from a lack of creatures than actual internal damage. He had come to rely on the noise it emitted to warn him beforehand of trouble and would hate to have lost that too.

Before he reached the turn into Langley, Trevor saw an overturned bus. It was lying on its right side, with all the windows shattered long ago. This allowed him easy access through the front window. He walked inside and searched it for any valuable items.

Fortunately, his new determination had paid off. He found two medicinal bottles at the back of the bus and a box of bullets for his Ruger. Trevor made sure he was meticulous while searching for anything else, but that was all he could find. He returned to the exit when his radio sang its old song again.

Trevor raised the shotgun chest high, unsure how to handle the weapon. The radio increased in pitch as the creature approached the vehicle. He waited for claw, fur or fang to appear. His finger itched along the trigger of the blue Citori, his sight staring down the blue steel of the upper barrel's fins. When the creature appeared, the radio's siren was complemented by the patting of feet on the street.

"What the hell?" Trevor said, lowering his shotgun.

It was definitely not a hound of any kind. It walked on two legs but had no arms at all. It had some fur on its body, but in the centre of the body was a childlike face that peered out from it. It resembled the baby face of the Tiyanaks he had faced before, except it seemed slightly older, like a toddler.

He began to wonder if it actually meant him any harm. The baby's face was serene and sweet, and he doubted its baby teeth could actually do him any damage. Trevor also had reservations about planting shotgun shells in its face. Surely he couldn't kill something that seemed so innocent.

Then the creature started gargling. It spat on the ground and twisted in front of him, the fur mangling on its body. The baby face pushed out and was replaced by a cold, grey face with no eyes. The milk teeth twisted into two rows of razor-sharp teeth on each jawline. Where there was a flat face before, there was now a long mouth that pushed out.

The human feet had been replaced by big feet with three large toes each that reminded him of a velociraptor, except that the skin was more like a pachyderm's instead of reptilian. The fur on its back had been replaced with a hard grey shell that seemed part of the body instead of just a protective cover.

Yet, it still had no arms. Trevor saw a forked tongue flick out from within its maw as they watched each other. He wondered if it could actually see him, or was it just sensing where he was? It flicked its tongue out again and then twisted its head more in his direction. Like a snake, it was using its tongue to detect where its prey was.

The creature jumped towards him, and Trevor reacted instinctively. He pulled the trigger and shouted as the shotgun jerked wildly in his arm. Unused to its power, his arm had pulled to the side, and the ammo had ripped through the bus's roof. Sensing danger, the creature hopped onto one of the seat bars and proceeded to jump along the others to him.

Knowing what he was in store for this time, he grasped the shotgun more firmly and aimed at the centre of the beast's face. He pressed the trigger again, the recoil pad on the gun's stock jolting into his shoulder. Trevor held it firm, ignoring the initial pain as the ammunition shredded into the creature's face and sent it hurtling back towards the front of the bus.

Lowering the Citori and ejecting the spent shells, he reloaded two more. He walked towards the creature that was writhing in pain. He could tell by the deforming of its body that it was trying to return to its original furry shape but was struggling. It was a mess of flesh, blood, fur and grey skin, its face hardly discernible. Trevor unholstered his Ruger and let two bullets fly into its head.

The creature lay still, and the radio fell to silence again. He noticed in passing that it had a tail behind it, which was also covered in fur. Massaging his shoulder, he holstered the Ruger but kept the Citori at hand. Mentally he calculated that he should have six shells left in his pocket and two in the Citori's chamber. He hoped that he found more along the way to the Police Station.

As he entered Langley Street, he made a mental note to check for Gryllus in the mythology tome when it was safer. He recalled lore on a beast with no arms and a head set in the body. Once again though, the town seemed to have twisted the mythology for its own purposes. He could not remember the second version of the monster being recorded anywhere.

Another soft whine on his radio brought him out of his thoughts. Forgetting that it would do no good, he squinted into the dense mist for any sign of what it could be. The radio sounded louder, and as the creature came closer, he could tell by its shadowy bulk in the mist that it was another

Gryllus.

Trevor lifted the shotgun to his shoulder, wincing as the previous jolt pained slightly. He waited for it to get closer but then thought better about it. It felt like such a waste of shells, which he might have needed later on. Lowering the weapon, he decided to run further down Langley and away from the creature.

He could tell from the radio that the gap between them was increasing. It was almost down to silence when Trevor slowed his pace. The road broke ahead of him, falling into that dark abyss that he had forgotten about. Trevor ran up and down to either side, finding no way past it. He marked a cross on the map.

As he did so, he noticed that there was an alley down Langley. He squinted, wondering if there was something else he had forgotten. Hadn't Kathy said something about an alley down Langley?

"Of course," Trevor murmured in the mist. "Caroline's home; I think she said it was down there."

His study of the streets was interrupted by another cry from the radio, causing him to stash the map in his pocket again. It was interweaving between soft and rising waves of pitch, making Trevor wonder if a creature was moving back and forth or if there were scores of them heading his way. He shouldered the Citori again, moving forward along the pavement towards the general direction of the alley.

A Gryllus appeared ahead of him in furry form, spying the shotgun in his hands. It began to transform into its more demonic form when Trevor let a shell loose. The beast fell to the ground, twisting in pain and stuck in its transformation. He moved up towards it, about to unholster his Ruger, when something slammed into him from the side.

Its four rows of teeth bit into his hip, spilling blood over him, the beast and the street as they both fell. Trevor bit his tongue, trying not to scream. He swung the butt of the stock into the Gryllus's eyeless face. It released its jaws, stepping back in pain momentarily before striking again. Trevor twirled on the street until he was on his back and raised the barrel. As the beast fell upon him, he shot its face, sending it arcing into the air and onto a building's wall nearby.

Holding his bleeding side, he stood up. He saw that the initial beast he had shot was recovering and completing its transformation. Not wanting to wait for it to do so, he ran for the alley again. His left ear was blocked as if he was getting a cold, and he could hear his breathing better than his feet stamping on the floor.

He made the alley entrance and ran between buildings and residential property. Too afraid to slow down, he checked each side for any sign of Caroline's previous house or some form of safety. The radio had gone towards a softer tone, but as he neared the end of the alley, it picked up again. Trevor twisted his head back and forth, unsure if it was behind or ahead of him…. or both.

The answer became clear. A Gryllus was standing on the lawn of the last homes on the right. This one was exceptionally huge, though. Where the other Grylli had only been about waist high, this one towered at half his height above him.

"What are you, some sort of Super-Gryllus?" Trevor mocked, in too much pain now to be frightened anymore.

Trevor lifted the shotgun with haughtiness and shot. The Citori sang back with a click, but nothing else happened. Suddenly realising that he had not reloaded the weapon, he scrambled in his pockets for the shells. The giant ahead of him lurched forward, transforming into its more demonic form. As it did so, its body gave off green smog that rose into the mist and intoxicated the air.

Its massive jaws opened and roared, sounding very much to Trevor how he imagined a Tyrannosaurus would. As he completed the reloading, he held his arm to his nose and stumbled backwards from the stench. It was smothering him, causing him to gag and cough. His eyes watered from the sting, but he lifted the shotgun nonetheless. The beast was almost upon him.

He shot up at it but forgot to keep his shoulder firm. It propelled him backwards onto the alley floor just as the Gryllus cried out in pain. Trevor looked up and noticed the attack had smashed some of its teeth. Encouraged by this, he shot into its mouth again just as it wanted to roar. The shot blasted into its lower jaws, making the beast recoil and twist its head to the side.

Instead of dying, it chose a more evasive manoeuvre. The Gryllus ran down the alley in the direction that Trevor had come from. He watched it disappear into the mist, and the radio slowly died down to silence again. Reassured that it was gone, he stood up and walked to the house it had guarded.

Trevor tested the door. It was locked. He kicked and shouldered it with his uninjured side, but it would not budge. Moving down to the lawn, he started to head back to the other houses when something near his feet glinted. He bent down, at first only noticing the teeth he had shot out of the Gryllus. When one of them glistened more than the others, he inspected it.

It was a key. The ring it was attached to was stuck around the tooth. He tried to pull it off, but it had been there so long that it had somehow become welded to the tooth's enamel.

"' McKenzie Home'," Trevor read out loud, getting excited. It was Caroline's home, after all.

He suddenly wondered if he would find her inside. After everything he had seen in Sacred Valley, the thought was no longer strange. There was a genuine possibility that she was waiting for him in there. And Trevor was not sure if he was ready to face her yet.

Then another thought occurred to him. There was also the chance that Bishop was inside, waiting for him with his twisted metallic head and the massive axe. He knew, at least, that he was not willing to face him again. Yet, Trevor knew there was no real alternative. Every road so far had led him to this, and there was no other way to the Police Station.

He unlocked the door and opened it slowly, the door creaking as it moved inwards. Locking it again, he found himself in a small kitchen area. The walls were covered with white cupboards, and the floor had grey tiles. There were no items that stood out, so Trevor took to checking the hidden storage areas for anything useful.

Coming up empty, he moved to the lounge area through an open arch in the wall. It was a medium-sized lounge that permitted a lounge suite on the left wall and a wall unit on the right. There was a rug on the tiles in the centre of the room, and ahead was a door that led to the front yard.

The radio remained silent, and the mist obscured the view through the windows. The light that passed through was enough for him to investigate the wall unit, but he tested the light switch anyway. It confirmed that there was no power to the house. Since he no longer had a torch, having lost it to the Inugami, he had to rely on the little light he had available.

It was enough to draw his attention to photo frames in one wall-unit section. There were various images of Caroline and her parents. Trevor reached out and grabbed one of Caroline in her teens. She looked like she had been very excited about something in it.

He noticed another photo that had been vertically torn in half. Caroline was on the left, someone's arm around her shoulder. The mysterious person on her side had been removed, so he could not determine who it was. It looked too young to belong to any of her parents. It was then that Trevor realised that there were several frames with no photos in them. He wondered why they had been removed.

Deciding to move on, he walked down the passage between the lounge and the kitchen. It was darker there as all the doors were closed. He tried the first door to the right, opening it up to light again. It was the bathroom. It had a shower in one corner, a bath along one wall and a mirror cabinet along another. Checking the cabinet, he found a first aid kit and an ampoule.

Trevor remembered wasting a medicine bottle outside the school and then finding a Lunar Nexus symbol within it. Learning from his mistake, he chose to finish searching the house first before applying any medicine to his injuries. The blood on his side had soaked into his shirt, but it seemed to have stopped for the moment.

The door opposite the bathroom led to the toilet. There was nothing special in the room, so he moved on. Three doors were remaining, one straight ahead at the end of the passage and one on either side. Trevor guessed that the central one led to the main bedroom and tried it first. It was locked, but he tried harder anyway.

When he was convinced it would not open, he moved to try the door on the right. Turning the knob, he thought he heard a cough from the main bedroom. He pressed his ear against it, listening closely. Holding his breath, he closed his eyes, waiting for the repeat of the sound. Trevor was unsure if he heard right, but it sounded like someone was just on the other side of the door, breathing against it.

He tried the door again but with no success. If someone was in there, they would not let him in. His radio remained silent, so he was confident there was no threat. He tried the right door again, but it was also locked. Forlornly he tried the final door, finding it open to his surprise.

Trevor closed the door behind him, as he didn't want someone creeping up quietly and catching him off-guard. As the door closed, he saw the burning red insignia of the Lunar Nexus on it. He pressed his palm on it eagerly, ignoring the light that passed over his eyes and enjoying the warmth and rejuvenation that passed through him instead. When it was done, he noticed that Kathy's name was also blackened on this one, with Phillip, Jay and Trevor's names still unblemished and glowing warmly.

He lifted his shirt up. The teeth marks and blood were gone. Twirling his shoulder around, he felt the shotgun injury was gone too. He shifted his focus to the room, dropping his equipment to the floor.

"This must be Caroline's room," Trevor said, his voice sounding so strange.

His words were accompanied by the giggle of a young girl. It came from under the bed. Trevor dropped down and investigated, not seeing anyone underneath it by the dampened light emitted through the mist. Instead, he saw a small bag and brought it out onto the bed.

It was a pink satchel with small black birds printed on it. Trevor unclipped the front and opened the flap, peering inside. There was a litter of paper materials inside, which he overturned onto the light red duvet. It was an assortment of notes and photos, with some sketches in between.

Trevor trailed his fingers lazily through the items when one of the photos caught his attention. It was the other half of the ripped photo. The boy, a few years older than her, smiled broadly. Scanning the other images, he realised they must have been taken from the photo frames in the lounge.

Trevor lifted one where he was holding a medallion. Underneath the image was a caption. There were specks of dust and dirt over the words, so he cleared it with his thumb.

"Hollowbrook Elementary, Athletics Day," he read out loud. "First place, Bishop McKenzie."

Dropping the photo, he looked through the others. It became apparent just how close Caroline had been to her brother. During Trevor's time with her, she had mentioned him on a few occasions, but there had always been a sense of tension between them. Trevor had met him a few times too. He had always felt uneasy with Bishop.

Judging from the images, their youth had had happier times. The sketches were also about them together. If it weren't for the knowledge that they were siblings, Trevor would have guessed that the two were a loving couple. He took one of the notes and read Caroline's words:

'Bishop showed me today just how much he cared. He came to walk with me from school today. He said they had an early day off, so he came around to see me. I'm so glad he did. That girl was making fun of me again as I left, and Bishop saw it. He wanted to go sort them out, but I asked him not to. I'm wondering now what he would have done if I let him go.'

Trevor turned the page around and saw a sketch of a man. She had drawn Bishop with large muscles on his arms, chest and belly, which seemed out of proportion or abnormal. Underneath it was scribbled *'My Guardian'*.

"More like a twisted guardian at this point," Trevor said, sneering. "It looks like he's still trying to protect you."

Shifting through more of the papers, the first line of another note caught his attention. The page was smudged on certain spots as if the writer had been crying. The page was also quite wrinkled. Trevor wondered idly if she had thrown the note away before retrieving it again.

'Bishop's leaving today. Officially. Not because of school this time. He especially came around to say goodbye to me. Told me he needed to go away for a while, but he would not explain why. He just said it had to do with some group... no wait, I think he said it was a religious association of some kind.

'Mum also says we may need to leave. The municipality told us that the fire that broke out a few weeks ago and killed all those people is spreading further. What happened to Selena is just...devastating. They've been evacuating residents since then. There's a chance that it may take the whole town. I hope it burns Kathy before she gets the chance to leave.'

Trevor looked up in astonishment. It was hard for him to believe that she could have had such animosity within her. He was done with the notes and images, momentarily wondering who Selena was. Remembering that Kathy had told her that the man with the metallic head was Bishop, things started making a little more sense now.

The Twisted Guardian was indeed after him, not for what they had done to him, but rather for what they had done to her. He was, after all, her protector.

15

THE SHADOW GRAVE

After having searched the remainder of the house, Trevor decided it was time to continue heading to the police station. He took one last look at the house's interior before moving out the front door onto the lawn. The mist seemed denser than before he had entered Caroline's house, but there was no evidence of any trouble nearby.

Checking the map as he stepped onto Caldwell's pavement, he saw that the road had broken into an abyss on his left. Making sure to mark it, he turned right towards Langley again, hoping that Hawthorne would grant him access to Hartley Street and thereby prevent going up another alley.

The streets were quiet again, accompanied by a harmoniously silent radio. The mist passed through his hair with a slight breeze that howled softly against his right ear. He suddenly wondered if the Citori was loaded and checked the chamber, noticing that the shells were spent from the last fight with the Super-Gryllus.

Emptying and reloading the chamber, he realised that he had two shells left in his pocket. The Police Station was a long way off still, and his fear of encountering another large creature made him cautious. He reached up and slotted the shotgun on the duffel bag's side, returning the Ruger to his hand.

The shortage of ammunition reminded him to look for anything he could use as a melee weapon. He entered Langley and turned left, noting the abyssal gap he had marked to his right. The radio was still quiet, strangely making him more on edge this time instead of comforting him. Trevor moved to the middle of the street in an effort to bypass the alley.

It was pointless. He reached another break in the road. He marked it on his map with a heavy sigh and noted that the only way to Hartley was through the long alley he had passed.

"They should call this place 'Sacred Alleys'," Trevor said, more in irritation than in humour. "I'm more in them than the actual streets."

Making sure there was no way past the gaping hole over the edge of the street, he headed back towards the alley with the Ruger held at the ready. As his feet cut through the threshold into the alley, his radio immediately picked up its whining salutation. Trevor stepped back out, causing the radio to cut out. Moving back in, it stepped up again, proving that danger awaited him inside the pathway.

"Well, I guess there's no other way," he said, moving further in. "Keep talking to yourself, Trevor. I'm sure someone's listening."

Not satisfied with just having the pistol at the ready, he lifted it within line of sight. He moved it from side to side, ready to shower anything that moved with bullets. The radio was getting louder the more he moved in until he finally found a Gryllus in furry form.

The creature had not seen him yet and was padding back up the alley. It stopped moving the closer Trevor got to it and began to turn. He moved swiftly, making sure to get to it before it could change, and kicked it down onto the ground. He offloaded two bullets into its head and watched as it bled out.

The radio had not gone back to silence again, only reverting to a softer tone. Trevor tried not to laugh at himself, but he felt like he was in a secret agent movie. He clutched the pistol at his side and moved with his back against the alley wall, waiting for the beast that was making his radio go louder.

The next Gryllus appeared. Trevor assumed it must have reacted to the gunshots, as this one had just finished transforming into its demonic state. The grey-blue pachyderm body ran towards him on its reptilian feet, the sets of teeth hungrily wanting to eat at him. Trevor shot one bullet into its head, causing it to fall onto its back and then another to finish it off.

And still, the radio kept singing. The enjoyment and thrill of winning turned to annoyance. Trevor wondered if the entire alley was filled with them. Determined not to be swayed, he continued his skulking espionage down the alley, almost forming a bond with it, as the radio rose up to its shrilling climax.

There were two more demonic Grylli before him, both at running speed already. In a panic, Trevor shot the closest one on the left first, causing it to fall down. The second was almost on him when he let his Ruger hit it, making it fall at his feet. He dispatched them quickly, giving them one more bullet each to finish the job.

Worried about his ammunition, he checked the loading indicator while the radio continued to cackle softly. He was so glad that he had, as he had spent the entire magazine. Trevor rushed to open one of the two remaining boxes and clipped the ten bullets into the mag. As he hit it back into the Ruger's butt, he raised and fired two bullets into a Gryllus that had suddenly jumped out of the shadows.

"Finally!" Trevor exclaimed as the radio went silent again.

Keeping his Ruger at hand, he moved as quickly as he could without running up the alley. When he reached the end, he saw that the shop on the left corner had a smashed window. Trevor looked up and saw "Cut-Str8 Chainsaws" on the building's signboard.

"Ooooh yeeeaaah," Trevor smirked, not wasting time entering through the opening.

Holstering the pistol, he went to work looking for a chainsaw. He had expected them to be lining the walls but then realised he was mistaken. The racks and shelves that once held the products were empty. He shook his head; he couldn't believe he had been so naïve.

He searched the shop anyway for any other items. There was nothing near the vicinity, but looking for the till, he noticed something small on the counter. He made his way to it, also observing a piece of paper under it.

When he reached it, he saw a box of bullets and a box of shells. Stashing them in his bag, he read the note.

'Hey Trev. Sorry man, there was only one chainsaw, and I couldn't resist. I've left you some goodies in exchange. See you at the Station.'

"Jay, you asshole," Trevor said, smiling anyway. He had some slim hope that Jay had gotten over Trevor pulling the gun on him before. It also relieved him to have some sign of life other than the inscription on the Lunar Nexus.

Trevor looked around the store one more time, ensuring that nothing was hidden away that could assist him. When he was sure there was nothing else, he walked onto the foggy streets again. He checked the map and headed east along Hartley towards the bridge.

Just as he hoped nothing further would get in the way of his current objective, a Gryllus appeared before him. It seemed to move faster than the others and was in his immediate radius just as he had his pistol at hand again. He kicked out at the beast first, sending it falling to the ground, before offloading two bullets into its face.

As Trevor began to cross over Hawthorne Avenue, he marvelled at how good he had become at using the Ruger. He could only assume that it came with the practice. It put a stride in his walk, and his previous sense of foreboding and tension on the streets had faded away. Eager to find the bridge and reach Jay, the only thing that slowed his pace was a large building that loomed to the right.

On the corner of Hawthorne and Hartley was a large building. Signs on either side of the main entrance doors on its northern façade identified it as Sacred Grove Church. Trevor stared at it, listening to the radio for any trouble. His enthusiasm to find Jay was momentarily numbed by the recollection of Jeanette's goal to reach the church. Wondering if she had ever made it through the haunted streets, he allowed his curiosity to get the better of him.

While walking towards the steps leading up to the main doors, Trevor admired the church's appearance. On either side of the central section of the northern façade, the red face-brick walls protruded further out until they met with the last step on the ground. The central section contained a rectangular portal within which the two entrance doors were set. There was a semi-circular arch over the top length of both doors.

Trevor looked up and tried to see how high the church was, but the mist blocked the view. He could just make out the shape of a wheel window near the top of the central section of the wall before the rest faded from sight.

When he reached the two wooden doors, he politely knocked on them before attempting to enter. Despite becoming accustomed to finding doors locked in Sacred Valley, he was somewhat surprised to discover the church inaccessible. Jeanette had been clear that she had been hiding out at the church, so he assumed that entry would not pose a problem.

"Hello!" he shouted, looking around to see if it had caught any attention, whether good or bad. The mist continued to roll over the streets towards the east, and his radio remained quiet. He banged the door with the side of his fist, making sure the sound that erupted was loud enough to echo down the streets.

Waiting a few seconds yielded nothing except a sense of concern. Trevor returned to the pavement and walked towards the next building to the left of the church. As he moved closer to it, he noticed a small pathway along the side of the church, fenced off by a wire gate. He tested the catch and found that it opened easily.

The steel hinges creaked and then screeched. Trevor walked slowly down the path towards what looked like the church's backyard. Once he was in the open again, he saw a fenced-off section further back. When he reached it, he discovered that it was a small graveyard.

Opening another metal fence gate, he entered. Small tombstones littered the floor. A few were still upright, while others had toppled over into ruins. He walked calmly among the graves, looking in particular for two names. There was nothing that caught his eye immediately once he had reached the western end, so he turned back.

His foot caught a patch of dirt slightly higher than the rest of the ground's level. Regaining his balance, he looked down at an unmarked grave. There was nothing remarkable about the mound of earth except that it was the only one without any form of identifying who had been buried there.

Trevor kneeled down to investigate the dirt when something glinted on the ground at the rear of the graveyard. He trained his eyes on the location, but his sight could not pierce the mist. Leaving the grave for the moment, he headed away from the church towards the object.

He got a fright when he reached a brick wall. The initial shock of finding the wall was supplemented by the disappearance of the mist. Trevor turned around and saw that the mist was still behind him. He stepped back into it, observed that he was completely surrounded by it again, and then stepped to the wall again. As before, he was no longer inside the mist.

Trevor looked down the length of the wall and saw that the mist didn't touch the wall at all. Unlike within the mist, he could actually see across the distance to a footpath at the centre of the wall's length. Wondering why it was still so dark, he looked up. The mist rolled over the property beyond the wall like clouds in the sky, as if some barrier existed to prevent it from penetrating.

Deciding to move along the wall to the footpath, he first looked down to find the glistening object. At his feet was a pistol. Excited to inspect it, Trevor bent down and picked it up. It felt and looked very different to the Ruger he had become so accustomed to. As if to convince himself, he unholstered the Ruger and looked at both of them.

The new pistol had a longer barrel than the Ruger that now looked rather stub-nosed in comparison. The muzzle of the new gun also extended out, whereas the Ruger's was flush with the end of the barrel. The grip was longer, which made Trevor unclip the magazine. Where the Ruger only had place for ten bullets, the new pistol had fifteen. The bullets looked precisely the same as the 9mm Luger ammunition Trevor had been using for the LC9.

The immediate major advantage of the new pistol over the Ruger was that it had a torch attachment underneath the barrel in front of the trigger guard. Trevor tested it and saw the light switch on immediately. Switching it off again, he got excited about having a new means of lighting dark areas. His enthusiasm was only slightly tainted when he realised that the chamber did not have a loading indicator like the Ruger, but not enough to stop him from switching pistols.

Trevor studied the handgun further, looking around its surface for any label until he finally found one on the frame under the barrel. It was a Beretta 92fs. He also noticed that it had a prominent hammer at the rear, whereas he could not easily spot one on the Ruger.

"Well, let's try you out for a bit," Trevor said, feeling strange to hear the sound of his voice again.

As the Beretta was already loaded to capacity, he put the Ruger in his bag with the bullets still in the magazine. The Beretta fit awkwardly in the holster, but he clipped it in anyway. With new life in his step, he walked towards the footpath ahead.

When he reached it, he found two large black swing gates. At the top right of the left gate near the opening end was a huge decorative 'S' made from the same metal as the gate and set within the upper frame. Similarly, a 'D' was on the right gate in the upper left corner close to the 'S'.

Trevor peered into the yard within the walls. There was a massive building to the rear of the yard with an ornamental external structure. The yard had various fruit trees and rose bushes, which appeared to have been tended to recently. While he studied the rest of the property, something moved near the entrance of the building. He could not be sure due to the limited light, but it looked like a wolf with white mottled fur.

"If you look any further, you might just fall through," someone said behind him, making him jump in fright. He turned around to see a woman grinning at him.

"Jeanette!" Trevor exclaimed, embracing her quickly. "I wondered what had happened to you."

"Don't lie," she toyed with him, moving closer to the gate and away from the mist. "You thought one of those demons killed me."

"Well, I really hoped not," he replied sincerely. "It's good to see you."

"Ahhh, did you miss me?" she continued to tease and then stroked his arm.

"Uhm," Trevor swallowed hard. "Yeah, I guess you could say that."

"You don't sound too convincing there, Trev," she replied, causing him to frown. Only a select few he knew called him 'Trev', and he wondered how she felt so comfortable doing it so soon.

"Do you know what this place is?" he asked, snapping back to some sense of normality and pointing to the enclosed yard.

"I don't really, no," Jeanette sighed, moving to the gate and stroking the bars, leering at him through the corners of her eyes. "No one does. This yard was always empty before.

"And then one day, that mausoleum appeared. The strange thing is, a man has been seen sometimes walking around the yard. I'm not sure I believe what gets said about him, though."

"What do they say?" he asked, instantly intrigued.

"Some of the former church attendees mention seeing him practising some form of combat."

"Like martial arts?"

"In a way," Jeanette replied. "Except he seemed to be using the elements."

"What do you mean 'using the elements'?"

"It's hard to explain. Some have said they've seen him summon weapons made of fire or wind, and others say he raised creatures made of stone from the earth to practise against."

"You know, from what I've seen in Sacred Valley so far, that's not really too hard to believe," Trevor said, looking through the gates at the mausoleum. "But, if he's alive, then I wonder if someone he loves is buried there."

Jeanette joined him in surveying the ground before stroking her fingertips over the back of his hand on the gate. He could feel how tense his nerves were. As he watched her trace his hand, he wondered why she acted so strangely and seductively. Suddenly, he could not help but notice how pronounced the shape of her breasts was in the yellow jersey.

"You mentioned to me in that café that you studied this town?" he said to distract himself.

"Yes," she replied, smirking at his awkwardness. "I'm not a guru, but I know enough."

"How did all this happen?" he asked, pointing at the mist. "What happened to this town?"

"Hmmm. When I met you in the café, you didn't seem all that interested in the history." Jeanette took a moment of silence as she walked around him, leaving him between her and the gate.

"Humour me," he said evasively.

"Alright, but you may not like what I tell you."

"I doubt it's worse than what I've already witnessed."

Jeanette looked at him carefully as if calculating how much she should reveal to him. Trevor waited patiently, shifting the bag on his shoulders to ease the weight slightly.

"There are different views on what Sacred Valley is," Jeanette finally said, "or rather, has become. Sacred Valley has many tales since its fall, each an epic story on its own. It's hard to tell whether each story takes part in the same Sacred Valley, or in a version on its own.

"What Sacred Valley was before is easier to explain. That you can find in any old articles or historical books in the libraries. In the late 1600s, settlers arrived and established their settlement in this area. The town grew in size until the 1700s, when an epidemic broke out and killed many. It was decided to rather abandon the town for the safety of the survivors since they could not contain it.

"In 1810, there was a need to establish a penal colony, and so, with the town deserted, they could not think of a better place. Due to it being so abandoned and being on what they considered holy ground, it was at this time that they decided to name the town 'Sacred Valley'. At the same time, Ravenscroft Sanitarium and the Sacred Valley prison were constructed."

"I've heard of Ashenfall Hospital, but not Ravenscroft," Trevor interjected.

"There are various districts in Sacred Valley," Jeanette confirmed. "You are in the northern area known as North Vale, which consists of this Old Sacred Valley area, Central Sacred Valley over the bridge and the SV Resort by Silvercrest Lake. Then there is the South Vale, just south of Silvercrest Lake where Ravenscroft Sanitarium and the Observatory Overview are situated. Finally, there is the South-Eastern district near Devil's Abyss mines. There was also a small colony to the west in what came to be creatively called West Vale."

"Alright, so the town is bigger than I imagined," Trevor sighed. "So what happened after they established Sacred Valley?"

"A second epidemic hit the town, but luckily Ravenscroft Sanitarium was able to deal with it that time. Shortly after, the Devil's Abyss mine was opened, just before Maine became a state in 1820. In 1840, the prison was closed, and people started losing interest in the quiet town.

"It was only in the 1850s that Sacred Valley became popular. The miners had found a vast coalfield beneath the ground, which led to the opening of the Donald Coal Mine. Four families left Sacred Valley in 1853 to establish the neighbouring town of Birchfield Hollow to the east.

"When the civil war broke out in 1861, Silvercrest Prison was constructed for prisoners of war. When the war ended, this was turned into a correctional facility."

"You really seem to know about this town's history," Trevor remarked.

"You won't believe how much I've invested in learning about Sacred

Valley," Jeanette commented and then seemed to regret saying it. "Anyway, in the 1900s, things went downhill. The prison was closed, and the Sacred Valley Historical Society took its place. The coal mine was running dry, so that was closed too.

"In the end, another source of revenue was needed. This led to the creation of the Sacred Valley Resort. As you can imagine, this caused an influx of tourists and thereafter, Sacred Valley was seen as a tourist attraction as opposed to a prison or mining colony."

"Listen," Trevor interjected again. "Not that I'm not enjoying learning the history of how Sacred Valley came to exist, but none of this explains what has happened to make it turn into…. this.

"I've just given you the formal, official history of the town," Jeanette explained. "There is another history that is less popular and not shared as much as the original. No one really wants to talk about what really happened."

"Well, here's your opportunity," he said, opening his arms in invitation. "Give it your all."

"The part that most are too ashamed to tell is that natives were living in the area when the settlers arrived," Jeanette said, lowering her head as if she was ashamed. "It had been called *The Place of Sacred Spirits* by them and was considered sacred ground. Hence the name Sacred Valley by the early settlers.

"When the settlers moved in, they not only attempted to move the natives but had many of them executed. They ignored the warnings that the spirits would take their vengeance. The rituals they had in place were the only things that kept the spirits at bay and prevented disaster and chaos from entering the world."

"Seems a bit far-fetched to me," Trevor commented.

"That's exactly how the settlers felt when they had them killed. They worshipped a specific deity that was the most terrifying, called Kwekwaxawe."

"What does that mean?"

"I'm not sure, but the tribe that worshipped it called this area Kwekwaxawe Kanesda, which means *Nest of the Raven*." Trevor's eyes went wide, but Jeanette went on regardless. "It was believed that this deity granted a special gift to fallen souls whereby they could rewrite their personal history, allowing them to defeat those who had defeated or betrayed them before."

Jeanette went quiet as Trevor swallowed hard again, taking in her words. He was unsure, but it almost seemed she had personally addressed him in that last sentence. Yet, he knew he was just being paranoid. Jeanette did not know Caroline or Bishop, so he simply considered it to be guilt playing on his mind.

"What happened next?" he asked, hoping to move away from his immediate feelings.

"Remember I mentioned that in the 1700s an epidemic broke out?" Jeanette asked to which Trevor nodded. "Just before that, when the Salem witch trials happened in Massachusetts, a woman named Emma Bennett was accused of witchcraft. She was burned alive here in Sacred Valley."

"Oh no," Trevor gasped, getting a feeling of where this was going.

"Yes. There is a tomb dedicated to her in Ravenshade Memorial, and Bennett Street by Ravenscroft Sanitarium was named after her."

"Was she the cause of the epidemic?"

"That can only be surmised. No one knows for sure, but it isn't a huge leap to believe that she was given a chance to avenge her justice. And with the epidemic causing the settlers to leave the town, the spirits got their sacred ground back too."

"Alright, so what caused the second epidemic?"

"Well, as you now know, they then established the prison and hospital just before that happened. There are no records of what really occurred or caused it, but it is believed that the spirits had tried again to rid the land of people. Yet, with no one around to worship them anymore, their strength had waned, and they could no longer overpower the people or those in Ravenscroft Sanitarium who were doing their best to fight the epidemic.

"At the same time that the spirits faded, Sacred Valley flourished. The Resort and Silverview Hotel were built. Tourists flourished in the thousands. It seemed like the inhabitants had won their battles against the sacred spirits."

"So what changed?" Trevor asked, wrapped up in her story.

"A cult that many have referred to as The Order," Jeanette replied. "Following the death of Emma Bennett, a secret sect called Twilight Covenant had formed. From the notes I've gathered on the Order, it seems that their beliefs and principles incorporated the traditions and rituals of the original natives."

"In other words, they woke up the ancient spirits," he completed for her.

"Indeed." Jeanette smiled in approval. "In the 1900s, after the Resort was established and Sacred Valley became a tourist attraction, strange things started to happen. Whole ships with tourists on them would vanish in fog. Families that supported the Resort or who worked for Resort-funding companies ended up dead or gone.

"No one could work out who was behind these incidents, as the Order was so well hidden and secretive that no one really knew about them. It was only through relatively recent events that the Order became known, and the Twilight Covenant members were investigated and hunted down."

"What happened?" Trevor asked.

"The Order believed that they could bring their chief deity or god into this world to repay the citizens for the desecration of the sacred land. The incident that sparked the initiation of this event was the birth of Selena through Seraphina Nightshade."

"Hold on," Trevor stopped her suddenly. "I read that name somewhere recently."

"Can you recall where?."

"Not really," he remembered, half-lying but not wanting to share too much information about Caroline. "I think it was somewhere in Hollowbrook Elementary."

"Alright. Well, I can spend hours relating what happened next, but let me summarise," Jeanette continued. "Since Seraphina claimed that Selena was born without a human father, the citizens feared the worst: that Seraphina had used witchcraft to fall pregnant through one of the spirits and thereby gave birth to Selena. This led to the kids at the Hollowbrook Elementary torturing her for being a witch too."

"I remember reading about a witch being bullied in one of Caroline's journals I found at the school," Trevor finally remarked.

"It went further than being bullied. With the townspeople terrified of Selena and what it meant for the town, they took the only solution they knew; the same answer they had for Emma Bennett."

"They burned her?"

"Yes, when she was twelve at the end of 1977. The tale you will read in history books is that the fire burned into the earth and found a vent that entered the abandoned coal mines underneath. This woke the old gasses, and the town erupted with fire and ash. To this day, it's believed that the fires still burn beneath Sacred Valley and that that is the cause for the constant mist and ash around the town."

"And the unofficial version?" Trevor pursued.

"Well, they are not far wrong," Jeanette replied, turning from him to face the mist. "The Sacred Valley you see before you in the mist is indeed from the coal fires burning beneath the ground. Some of the streets have collapsed over the years from vents and passages caving in.

"Do you believe in other dimensions, Trevor?" she asked suddenly.

"Before I came to Sacred Valley, I would have said no," he answered truthfully. "This town has somehow managed to convince me otherwise."

"Some say that this fog is not the real world, that we are trapped here until we account for our sins. There is also another version of Sacred Valley," she continued, still looking into the mist, "where the sacred spirits live. This town is on a nexus of power, forgotten by the world. The last ones to have felt its true power were the natives executed by the settlers.

"Even though the Order tried to revive it, they could not raise it to its true power. But, where the spirits live, the power is at its real potential. Selena was the first to try and bring that to our world by using her body as a vessel."

"But Sacred Valley is abandoned," Trevor said, walking up to her at the veil of mist. "There's no reason for it to be protected anymore."

"Mankind will not stop until they have taken everything for themselves," Jeanette said. "It won't be long before someone else tries to populate the town again. If the deity were to pass through…"

"Then it could keep everyone away for all time," Trevor acknowledged.

"Or take the entire world for its own," Jeanette concluded.

Trevor took a step back. The tone in her voice suggested that she supported that movement. Suddenly he wondered whether her studies of Sacred Valley and the Order were idle curiosity, truly academic, or for some deeper, darker reason that she kept hidden from him.

"I don't understand what any of this has to do with me, though," Trevor said, testing her for a response.

"Sacred Valley has more than one canvas, painted by the taint of your sins. Consider this your personal hell."

Before Trevor could stop her or remark on her tone and attitude change, she walked into the mist. He grabbed towards her, but once she had passed through the veil, she was gone.

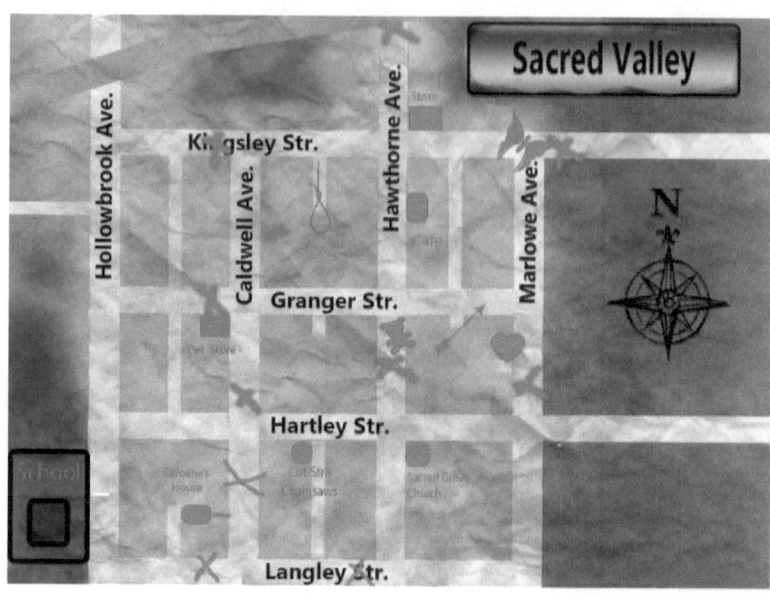

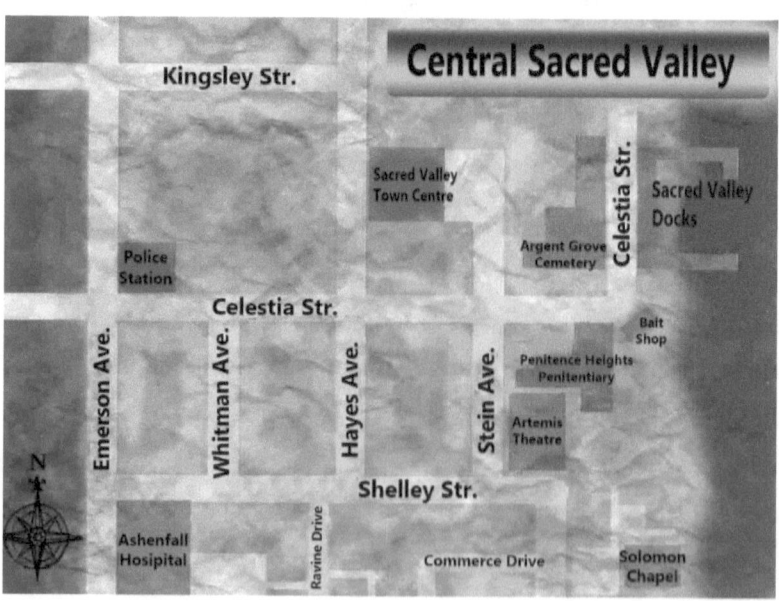

16

ASHENFALL HOSPITAL

Trevor ran into the mist after her. Everything turned a deeper shade of grey again as the ashen drops fell before him onto the graveyard. The slight warmth he had taken for granted by the mausoleum's gates changed to a cold breeze he had gotten used to before.

Jeanette was nowhere to be seen. He frowned as he ran for the street before Sacred Grove Church. It had only been a few seconds before he had followed her in, yet he could not spot her in the backyard, down the alley or on Hartley Street. He ran up the steps to test the church doors, but they were still locked.

For the first time, he realised that Jeanette possibly knew more about why he was in Sacred Valley than she let on. Her last words ran through his head as he walked back to the street and looked down both lengths.

"Canvas painted by my sins? My own personal hell? What did she mean?"

Taking out the street map, he looked at the right edge where the bridge led over the river from Silvercrest Lake towards the other side of Sacred Valley, or Central Sacred Valley as Jeanette had called it. He suddenly realised that once he reached the bridge, he would be going blind; he had no idea what Central Sacred Valley's layout was like and where the Police Station was.

Trevor headed towards the bridge, securing the Beretta in his hands with the torch lit underneath the barrel. It only lit the road immediately ahead of him, but he felt safer with it on. He checked the radio's volume knob to make sure it was actually on, as it was as silent as the streets.

Just before he reached Marlowe Avenue, a faint light caught his attention to the right. Moving towards it, he saw a light fixture lit above a garage door. The garage door was secure, so he moved further up. He saw two gas pumps and discovered he was at a gas station.

There were yellow banners above on the wall, but the writing was so old and faded that he could not make out what it said. Falling back on the vow he had made to check out as much of the town as he could, he tested the door into the commercial side of the station and found it unlocked.

"Finally," Trevor commented, glad to find another building accessible en route to the Police Station.

It was quiet inside, and the lights were off. He tested the switch on the wall, but it produced no results.

"How the hell does the garage light have power but not the shop?" Trevor said out loud to give himself a chance to air his frustration.

Fortunately, nothing in the shop responded to his query. Using the pistol's torch, he inspected the shelves for any food or liquid that he could find. His appetite was returning, and he was unsure where he would find a Lunar Nexus sigil again.

He found some bars of chocolate, but he did not need to see any expiration dates to know that they had long gone off. A cursory glance showed him that every other consumable product was in the same state. He also found some old magazines but felt no need to read any of them.

In the far back corner, he discovered a door and opened it. Trevor moved down a small passage that passed by disused toilets until he reached another door. He smiled as it opened, hoping it was a sign of his luck changing. He entered a softly lit room and saw that it was the inside of the garage.

There was also the soft hum of a generator at the back of the garage. Trevor inspected it and wondered how long it had been running. He knew generators could run on a supply of gas for only so long, and the gas station looked like it had been abandoned for years. He checked the fuel gauge and observed that the needle was empty.

"What the hell?" Trevor commented but decided to leave it alone.

There were steel racks along the side walls. He quickly inspected them and smiled in jubilation. There was a crowbar he could use as a melee weapon. Holstering the Beretta, he took the crowbar in hand and felt the weight of it. He was confident that it would do sufficient damage. He was also glad to be able to save the ammunition he had at hand.

On another rack, he found an adjustable wrench. It also packed some weight behind it, so Trevor stashed it in his bag in case he needed it. There were three cans of gasoline that Trevor stowed as well for when he found Jay.

With nothing else being useful, he left the garage and headed to the front of the dark shop. He inspected the till area and the shelves under the counter, using the torch of the Beretta to reveal the interior. At the far back, he saw a hand torch with a belt clip on the side. Even though it meant he would have to hold the torch every time he used it instead of it being attached to his shirt, it was better than taking out the Beretta just for light.

There was also a key in one of the drawers that had the letters 'D.B.' on them.

"D.B? Distribution Board?" he wondered out loud. Despite his uncertainty, he pocketed the key anyway.

Feeling that there was sufficient light on the streets for the time being, he clipped the torch to his pants and holstered the Beretta again. He gripped the crowbar as he headed out to the streets, which met with a soft singing from his radio.

"Well, at least I get to test how well this crowbar works," Trevor said, marvelling at how confident he felt in battle lately.

Walking in different directions to test where the creature was coming from by the rising radio pitch, he realised it was near the bridge. He ran towards it with the weapon held at shoulder height, waiting for the beast to appear before him. When he did, he saw that it was another Gryllus.

As the beast ran to him bearing fangs, Trevor smacked down at it. It howled out in pain, and then he brought the weapon up again in a backhand uppercut. The forked tip of the crowbar smashed into its face, sending it flying up into the air and crashing down onto the pavement.

It writhed in pain for a moment before Trevor brought the weapon down three more times. When the beast stopped crying out and the radio died, he looked down at the dead creature. He was suddenly filled with a new feeling, much darker than before. Gripping the crowbar tighter, he remembered the one and only time he had felt like that before.

His thoughts were ripped away from the memory he was forcing down. His radio came to life again, but not with the usual serenade that was soon followed by the approach of a beast. There was a voice in between the crackles and white noise.

"Jay?" Trevor asked, lifting the radio from his belt and listening carefully.

"Trevo….trouble at the Pol… injured," Jay's voice said. "Make your way…Ashe…Hospital. I found… can't believe it. Bishop…."

His voice faded, and the crackle died down.

"Jay?" Trevor said, shaking the radio as if the simple act would bring his voice back. He pressed the radio's button. "Jay?! Are you there? I'm coming, buddy."

No one answered, and the radio fell back to silence. Trevor ran for the bridge, clipping his radio back on and gripping the crowbar tight. He had entered the part of Hartley that formed the bridge and charged onto it.

His radio sang again as he passed a small two-storey building to his right, but he ignored it. The radio went silent again as he ran beyond it towards the bridge's centre when he realised he could go no further. His pace slowed down until he arrived at his new obstacle.

The central portion of the bridge was up. It was only at this point that he realised that the bridge was a drawbridge. For a moment, he toyed with the idea of scaling the side of the bridge but knew it was ridiculous. The gap between the two parts of the bridge would be huge.

Trevor looked back at the building he had passed. He guessed that it was the bridge's control room. Clutching his weapon for reassurance, he headed back towards it to be met by the rising wail of the radio again.

When he reached it, he saw stairs along the outer wall leading to the upper room. The room was visible through windows that provided a panoramic view all around. As he climbed the steel steps, the radio sang louder. Trevor held the weapon tighter as he reached for the doorknob and then thrust it open quickly.

The Gryllus had been waiting for him. It leaped into him and sent them flying over the upper rail behind him. They toppled over, the beast falling to the ground first. Trevor fell on top of it, the crowbar dropping out of his hands.

Rolling on the floor from the impact with the beast, Trevor crawled away from it towards the crowbar. He tasted dirt on his face and felt a wound burning on his left jaw. He got on his knees to crawl faster, hearing the Gryllus moving behind him as his hand snatched at the weapon.

Large hands grabbed his ankles and yanked him back away from it. He felt the course cement beneath him scrape at his belly as he yelled. He spun his back onto his duffel bag and saw the Gryllus pulling at him, licking its teeth in anticipation.

Remembering he had other weapons, Trevor whipped out the Beretta and offloaded five bullets. It had been so careless that the first three ripped through the air above it. The final two hit the centre of its forehead, sending it soaring off his leg onto the concrete behind it. Trevor hopped onto his feet, grabbed the crowbar and smashed its face in.

Even though the radio had stopped wailing, Trevor kept smashing until nothing was left of its face. He stood there heaving heavily over it, blood soaking the bar's steel down to his hand. The warmth of the liquid brought him back from his murderous stupor.

Trevor moved up the stairs again, clipping the crowbar in the slot on the opposite side of the shotgun. When he reached the room, he saw the controls at the window facing the bridge. The room was lit with a red glow but not from any bulb or natural light source.

"Yes!" Trevor exclaimed, making his way to a small Lunar Nexus burning on the immediate left wall just beneath the run of windows.

Falling to his knees, out of sight from anyone on the streets, he wasted no time touching the sigil. The usual blinding light broke into his vision, and the nurturing health and rejuvenation bled into his veins and muscles. He could feel every wound and ounce of exhaustion fade away just as his appetite vanished.

When his sight returned, he removed his hand and examined the Lunar Nexus. Kathy's name was still scratched out, but Philip, Jay and Trevor's names burned brilliantly as they had the last time he had seen them. It made him wonder if Jay had met with Philip at the Hospital.

With renewed strength, Trevor got up and went to the console. He saw the switch to move the bridge down and pressed it. Nothing happened. Examining the console further, he saw a slot that turned the power to the console on. Above it were the words "Drawbridge Control".

"Drawbridge Control," Trevor read aloud and then pulled out the key he had obtained from the gas station. "D.B. stood for Draw-Bridge."

Testing his theory, he inserted the key into the slot and turned it. Small lights flickered and came alive, but he only focused on the one by the switch. He pressed it again, then held his hands on the console to stabilise himself against the sudden shuddering.

He watched with delight as the bridge moved down. It was slow and took some time, but eventually, the two parts of the bridge sank into place. There was a huge cranking noise as the two parts slotted into one another. When nothing further happened, Trevor turned the console off, retrieved the key, and pocketed it again.

Turning around to run out of the room, the Lunar Nexus's glow lit something on the floor against the console. He bent down to pick the paper object up, unfolding it to reveal another street map. Trevor used the torch to study it and observed the words "Central Sacred Valley" written at the top of the map.

"Nice," he remarked, stashing away the original map he had been using in his bag and keeping the new one on him.

Studying it, Trevor saw that the route to the hospital was over the bridge onto Celestia Street and then a right into Emerson Avenue. Stashing the map in his pocket and running back to the bridge, he hoped it would be as easy as that.

His feet padding onto the concrete bridge was the only sound that accompanied him until he passed over the connection point halfway across. A soft sizzle rang from the radio as if danger was far ahead of him. Using the torch, he surveyed the road ahead and noticed small insects moving away from him towards Central Sacred Valley.

On closer inspection, he noticed they were tiny black spiders, not insects. Not one of them was larger than his fingertips. Wondering why he had not seen them before, he turned back and saw them clambering up from under the second part of the bridge he stood on.

"I must have disturbed them when I moved the bridge," Trevor said out loud. "How the hell did you get to the hospital, Jay?"

He continued on his path, hugging the right side of the bridge so that he could cut into Emerson at the first opportunity. The spiders led the way before him as he stepped onto Celestia Street properly, leaving the bridge behind him. He had barely moved further forward when the sizzle from the radio grew louder.

Trevor kept the crowbar at the ready, wondering why it was not crackling like it usually did when he approached a beast. Testing a theory forming in his mind, he moved off the line of spiders until there was space between them and him. The sizzle died down softly but did not vanish entirely.

Maintaining the distance between them, he walked to the intersection with Emerson. He turned right, noting that the arachnids were also charging in the hospital's direction. It filled Trevor with a sense of unease. The last thing he wanted to face now was a spider monster. Proceeding further down the road despite his foreboding, he kept a lookout for any beast that might be waiting for him.

Shelley Street broke away to the left of him, and he realised he would have to cross the street to get to the hospital. The map did not reveal the entrance's side, so he tried the Emerson side first. When he reached the opposite pavement, he saw a boundary wall that belonged to the hospital grounds.

The radio changed from a sizzle to a soft crackle, and he realised no spiderlings were underneath his feet or anywhere near him. As he moved along the wall further down Emerson, the radio fell silent. The wall gained him no entry to the hospital, and soon, he encountered a part of the road that broke off into an abyss.

Marking the break on the map, he moved back towards Shelley. The crackle returned to the radio and increased in pitch as he turned the corner. Before him, to the right, set in the boundary wall, was a sliding gate. The spiders he thought he had lost were crawling under the gate into the property.

Trevor looked over the gate and saw a sign identifying the building as Ashenfall Hospital. He pushed the gate, using a bit more strength to get it to budge before it rolled on its worn wheels. He only opened enough of it to let him through and then closed it again. The radio was wailing now, causing Trevor to spin around and survey the area.

The main entrance to the building was to his right in the form of two doors. As he moved closer, he saw that they had a metal chain around each handlebar, with a padlock connecting the two ends and effectively barring him from entry. A light fixture above the doors glowed eerily in the surrounding mist.

He was about to look for another entrance when a shuffle on the ground further in caught his hearing. Silencing the radio's rising wailing, he saw a woman stepping out of the dense mist into view.

"Please, mister," she said to him as she approached him at a slow pace, "Can you please help us?"

It was only then that he realised she had something in her arms. It was wrapped in a baby's blanket and covered so completely that he could not see what it was. He heard a soft cry from within and could only assume it was her child.

The woman was in a seductive red dress that ran just below her waist. It had no sleeves, ending just below the shoulders on her arms. It made Trevor feel cold, wondering how she could walk around so exposed in the mist. There was a certain beauty about her in her pale face and green eyes, and her thin, curvy form could have persuaded him to do anything at that point.

"What seems to be the problem?" Trevor asked, attempting to clear his dirty mind.

"Can you look after my boy?" she responded as she stopped immediately before him. "I just need to pop over to the shop across the road for some milk. I'd rather not take him with me."

"Uhm...," he frowned. "Have you seen the state of the food in this place? I don't think anything is edible."

"Please, it's only for a moment," she persevered, looking into his eyes imploringly.

"Alright," he agreed, finding it hard to deny her such an easy request.

She passed the child into his arms, thanking him with a kiss on his cheek as she moved past him. Trevor smiled and watched as she ran for the property's gate and onto the street. He looked down at the baby and saw just how much she had covered him. His face was not visible under the wrappings, so he pulled it aside.

Trevor's breath caught in his throat as it momentarily went taught from fright. Instead of the baby's face he was expecting, he saw a bundle of shiny white oval objects, each the size of chicken eggs. Inspecting the body of the wrappings, he saw that the entire parcel was filled with them.

Hearing a sound similar to a chorus of crickets, he noticed how the spiderlings had collected at his feet. The moment his attention had been drawn away, the eggs shook and cracked open. He dropped the parcel to the ground without realising it, causing some eggs to break and the green yolk to roll onto the tarred ground.

Of the eggs that had hatched, large spiders emerged. When they first crawled out, they were barely the size of his feet. As Trevor watched in trepidation, the spiders grew in size with each passing second. When the growth stopped, seven arachnids reaching his waist stood before him.

"Hell and damnation," he said, clutching his crowbar in defence.

The first two spotted him and rushed towards him. Further panic set in when he saw that they each had eight eyes on their heads: four small eyes in a line at the bottom, two large eyes in the centre line and two medium eyes at the upper end. They also had auburn hair compared to the black spiderlings.

"Wolf spider!" Trevor shouted, bringing the forked end of the crowbar down on one of them.

The beast screeched in a bitter serenade as he swept the weapon sideways in an attempt to hit the next one aside. It thudded against the side of its face, making minimal impact. The arachnid hit his wrist, sending the crowbar flying towards the entrance doors.

Instinctively, Trevor reached up and pulled his shotgun out. Just as he aimed it at the one that had hit his wrist, it jumped up to bite into him, the barrel stretching between its saliva-covered fangs into its mouth. He pulled the trigger and sent it soaring back into the mist, its guts falling over the others in a shower of flesh and green blood.

The shot had caused the other five to run away into the mist towards the hospital's walls while the first spider he had smacked turned to disarm him. He prepared the weapon, aiming straight at its eyes and fired. The beast cried out again before falling down in a lump before him.

Trevor quickly ejected the spent shells and reloaded with the two spare shells in his pocket, realising that the one box he had left was in his bag. Two wolf spiders had crept onto the walls to the right and were running towards him. As they neared the entrance doors, he discovered they weren't as normal as he had first supposed.

Their backs had mounds on them that protruded up into the air. The more Trevor studied them, the more he noticed how they looked like faces grimacing in pain and mouths open in anger and fury. Their necks stretched out of the arachnid bodies as if they wanted to break free.

It gave him an idea. While they were still on the wall bearing down towards him, he slipped the shotgun back onto his bag and pulled the Beretta out in one movement. He shot the mound head of one and then the other, watching with pleasure as the spiders fell off the wall and onto their backs.

Their legs twirled the mist above them as the beasts cried out. He ran for the entrance doors and grabbed the crowbar, returning to drive the chiselled end through the closest spider's belly. He twisted it until he heard a crack from within the flesh, and the spider died down.

Before he could reach the fourth fallen beast, only just pulling the crowbar back out, a fifth spider attacked him from the side. It trapped him against the hospital wall as he lifted the bar horizontally in both hands, his right hand struggling to keep the Beretta in his grasp.

Using what strength he had, he slowly lifted the beast up higher, the crowbar just keeping the fangs off his face. He supported the weapon with his left hand and pointed the pistol between its fangs into its mouth. He pulled the trigger and then gagged as green blood spilt over his face. The spider fell to the ground before him, shuddering in its final moments as another clambered over it and jumped onto him.

Its fangs bit into his left shoulder as he collapsed to the floor. His shout rang against the hospital walls. Barely maintaining a grip on the two weapons, he pressed the Beretta against the beast's belly and fired, crying out again as it pulled off him.

When he got up, he realised the shot had not killed it but simply wounded it. It ran away, allowing the last two spiders to attack him. The intense pain in his shoulder made him look at it. One of the fangs had remained in his flesh, yanked out when the spider had jerked off him.

As he prepared the pistol in his right hand and the crowbar in the left, his eyes fluttered as he suddenly became drowsy. The venom burned into his veins as he stuttered back. The two attacking spiders slowed down and watched as he swayed from side to side, trying to maintain his focus on them.

Suddenly, his left arm went numb, and the crowbar fell out of his grip to the floor. As much as he tried to move it, the arm was limp at his side. He shook his head while trying to regain his focus. Deciding to use the best weapon he had at hand, he grabbed the shotgun from his bag, aimed it at the closer of the two and pulled the trigger.

The effect of the shot pushed his wrist to the right, and it missed. The sound of the shot made the spiders run away to the dark corners of the hospital's walls. It offered Trevor a moment of respite as he dropped the duffel bag and dug around for one of the medicinal bottles.

As he downed the contents, he felt only slight relief from the pain and restoration of his senses. The venom's impact was dulled, but it did not restore the feeling to his left arm. Seeing the ampoule he had found at Caroline's house, he grabbed it and smashed open the upper end. The liquid was warm as it ran down his throat.

A wave of health and regeneration similar to that which the Lunar Nexus provided coursed through his body. He could feel his strength returning as the sensation in his left arm brought pins and needles to his flesh. He tested his fingers, his wrist and then the muscles in his arm. It appeared as if the venom had been cleared from his system.

The sound of movement came from the direction where the spiders had run. Trevor placed the crowbar on his bag and slung it on his back. He held the shotgun up as he moved towards them, hoping to be rid of them so that he could find a way into the hospital.

In one corner between two wings of the hospital, he found all three remaining spiders. The one whose fang was still lodged in his shoulder had died during its attempt to escape. The two others watched him carefully before deciding to scamper up the walls towards the roof.

Trevor stared down the barrel and shot one of them in a mounded head on its back. The beast cried out as it fell to the ground. He immediately thrust the crowbar into its belly, cranking it sideways again until he heard the snap inside.

The other spider had vanished onto the roof. He carefully ejected the spent shells, realising that the next box was still in his bag. Slotting the shotgun away, he took out the Beretta instead. He could not tell whether the spider was coming back or not. He switched on the radio, listening as the crackle died and faded into silence.

Holstering the pistol, he moved along the walls to find another way in. The windows were all boarded up from the inside. He found a single door on the wing opposite the main doors, but it was locked. He returned to the main entrance, wondering if he could use the crowbar to break the lock open.

On the way to the doors, he recalled the woman he had met who had handed him the spider parcel. It reminded him of a Joro-Gumo. He decided to look up the lore in the mythological library book when he had more time, but from what he could recall, the Joro-Gumo also seduced strangers with a spider-egg parcel.

He also remembered that, in some circles, it was believed that the Joro-Gumo could transform her lower body into a spider. Once the transformation was complete, she would then spin the men she seduced into a web and eat them.

"I need to get into this hospital now," Trevor said as if to urge himself on.

Adding to his suspense, the radio began to crackle again. There was a new whine, like a soft siren ringing between the white noise. Fearing what was approaching, he took the crowbar and jammed it into the links next to the padlock. With a quick jerk, he broke the connection, and the chain fell. Trevor pushed onto the entrance doors and found that they opened easily.

With one last look outside at the sliding gate, he saw the woman's beautiful face appear before he shut the doors.

17

ALCHEMIST'S POUCH

As soon as Trevor turned around to study his dark surroundings, he heard a click from the main doors. He checked it quickly and found that it was locked. Ramming his shoulder against or kicking them yielded no results other than adding to his frustration. He had fought so hard to enter the hospital, only to be locked inside it.

Turning the torch and radio back on and placing the crowbar on his bag, he decided to contact Jay.

"Alright, Jay," Trevor said into the radio, "I'm here at the hospital. Where are you?."

No one replied. There was no static from the presence of demonic creatures or any response from Jay. He tried again, speaking clearly into it and ensuring he was holding the button down properly. There was still no response.

"I hope you're just taking a nap," Trevor said as he placed the radio back on his hip, leaving the volume high.

To his left, he spotted a reception desk with a door behind it. The only way to the door was over the reception counter itself. A passage broke away to the right of the reception and the room behind it, but Trevor busied himself with the glowing object on the counter first.

The Lunar Nexus burned brightly, etched into the wood of the counter. Jay's name in mirrored Hungarian hieroglyphs still glowed, along with Philip and Trevor's. He placed his right palm on it, welcoming the warmth that reset his body to its full health.

Once the blinding light was gone, he moved towards the passage to the right when a noise in the reception area made him stop. It sounded like scratching and, as he waited, the frequency of the sound increased until it finally died away.

"I need something for these bites," a male voice said, echoing down the passage. "I can't take this itching anymore."

Trevor stood dead still. The voice had not appeared to come from anywhere specifically near him. Rather, it had been rather omnipresent in that it felt like the room itself had spoken. Treading carefully, he walked around the corner edge of the counter and peered down the passage, shining the torch down its length.

Realising the passage was empty, he proceeded into it. He passed a door to his left mid-way through. As far as Trevor could tell, it led to the same area that the door behind the reception did. The sign on the door marked it as the Examination Room. He tried the door, only to find that it was locked. Jogging further down, he found another door at the end that was also locked.

"Damnit, man," Trevor cursed. "Where do I go now?"

He trailed back to the reception with an idea in mind. As soon as he stepped into the waiting room again, he heard the same scratching sound as before. Once again, the frequency of the scratching increased until it faded away.

"Ooooh, ahhh," the voice said. "This is too much. It's going to kill me."

Ignoring it, he removed his duffel bag and placed it over the countertop onto the desk behind it. He followed shortly after that, leaving the bag on the desk for the moment. It was such a relief to be rid of it for the time being.

When he tried the door and it opened, he almost jumped in the air in relief. He pulled the bag in with him and closed the door behind him. Flipping the switch did nothing to light the room. Trevor shone the torch onto the desk near him and saw a desk lamp. Clicking the button along the wire made it come on.

"Ok, so the plugs have power, but not the light circuit," Trevor mused out loud, making a mental note to find the distribution board at some point.

"This is definitely not the Examination Room."

Hoping to find a map of the hospital, he took to searching the desk's drawers. The top drawer only revealed some old stationery, but the second drawer contained a box of 9mm bullets. Stashing them in the bag, he inspected the lowest drawer. It had some papers stacked haphazardly in them, and he found a notebook underneath them.

Trevor sat down and opened it up. For the most part, it was filled with medical notes and procedures. However, he found a picture of a crudely drawn man at the end. Its upper body was naked, but it had the same type of apron as he had seen on the Twisted Guardian. The face had no eyes or ears, and where its mouth should have been was a slit with scars that seemed to seal it shut.

"The Zephyrite Conclave?" Trevor read the caption underneath the drawing.

Further down, Bishop's name had been written with several question marks behind it. He tore the page out and placed it with his other notes. As he packed the book back in the drawer, he saw a letter on the desk before him. It would not have interested him usually, but the greeting at the top caught his attention. Bringing it closer to the lamp, he read through it:

You used me!

I should have realised sooner who you are, but the state of trauma you displayed had fooled me into believing that your fear was very real. Perhaps the person you fear most is yourself.

With the knowledge I now have, I cannot pretend to ignore the situation any longer. Count the days of freedom you have left!

Dr. E.K.

Trevor remembered the drawing of the faceless man and Bishop's name at the bottom and wondered if the letter had some strange connection. He placed the letter with his notes, hoping he could make more sense of it after he found Jay.

Inspecting the office further produced no positive results, so he moved on. At the very least, he had thought the office would have a hospital map, but it appeared his assumption was wrong.

Opposite the door he had entered, in the right corner, was another door. Carrying the bag's straps in his right hand, he tested the door and found it opened freely. He stepped through and placed the bag in the corner to his right, leaving the office door open.

"Geez, it's warm in here," Trevor observed.

"I'm burning up," a male voice said, filling the room like the one in the reception had. There was a sound like a pot of water boiling in the background. After a moment, it faded away. The radio remained silent on his side. "Isn't there anything that can bring the temperature down?"

It felt like several radiators were on at the same time. The room had more light than the office, as three gurneys to the left had lights attached to stands plugged into the wall's lower part. The lights shone down on the beds. Trevor realised he was in the Examination Room, seeing the door to the right that he had tried to open from the passage.

Further study of the room was paused when a door on the left wall, past the gurneys, suddenly opened. He jumped for his bag and pulled the crowbar out, wielding it before him. And, just as quickly, he slowly lowered the weapon when he recognised who it was.

"Philip?" Trevor said, his emotions alternating between jubilation at seeing someone he knew and confusion. "What are you doing here?"

Philip closed the door and walked closer into the light. He wore a white overall with blood smeared over the chest section as if he had just cleaned his hands on it. His short hair was untidy, and the bridge of his glasses cropped the tip of his nose like a crow perched on a cliff. He had an open brown folder in his hands.

"Such a precarious question could be levied at you," Philip replied in the same haughty tone and manner that Trevor had become accustomed to. That sense of familiarity made him feel at home. "I mean, how peculiar is it to find a doctor at a hospital? You, on the other hand..."

"I'm looking for Jay," Trevor responded.

"Ah yes, that police fellow of yours," Philip said, placing the folder on the gurney closest to him and pinching the glasses off his face. "Why would you be searching for him here? Wouldn't he be at Ashbourne Police Station?"

"We're in a bit of trouble," Trevor replied, moving closer to him. "Remember when we brought Bishop to you?"

Philip's face lost some colour. He looked down without shifting his head and then back up at him. Moving passed him and closer to the office, Philip turned around and seemed to be considering something.

"Of course, I remember," he said finally. "You mostly killed him."

"What do you mean 'mostly?'" Trevor asked, frowning heavily.

"Why are you asking me about Bishop?" Philip asked, changing the course of questioning.

"It's the reason we're here," Trevor responded. "I got a call from Jay that the police had found some evidence implicating us. We needed to escape and then ended up here in Sacred Valley."

"Of all the places in the world, why on earth would you come here?" Philip asked, almost sounding angry.

"It was the best we had at the time," Trevor said, deciding not to explain too much to him. For all he knew, Philip was involved in letting the police know. Yet, his mannerisms so far had not betrayed any such indication.

"Wait, if you're here, then where is Kathy?"

Trevor had hoped to avoid that topic altogether. He sunk his head, unsure how to explain what had happened. Deciding to take the easy way out, he quickly formulated a response.

"She was with me when we escaped," he replied.

"Are you out of your mind!?" Philip exclaimed, moving up and shaking his fist at Trevor's face. "You brought my sister to this place?!"

"Hey man, I didn't know that demons and monsters were running around on the streets!" he shouted back.

"What?" Philip said, stepping back. "You've seen them too?"

"Of course, I've seen them," Trevor said, frowning again. "Why wouldn't I?"

"I thought it was just me," Philip replied, visibly calming down. "Well, I thought I was alone here. Everything seemed fine until that fog covered the town, and I heard those strange noises outside. Like demons calling out to their kind."

"Are you saying you were here before the fog?"

"Oh, Trevor," Philip said in a condescending tone. "Do you think you're still awake, or even alive for that matter?"

Trevor was too afraid to even question what he had meant. After his discussion with Jeanette at the graveyard, he had been wondering the same thing. She had mentioned different versions of Sacred Valley, and he had been considering just which version he had found himself in.

"Tell me, did you have some sort of accident when you entered Sacred Valley?"

"We spun on the road and smashed our vehicles," Trevor confirmed.

"And when you came to, everything was different?"

"Yes."

"Since I've been here, I've gathered some notes on this town and its past. This 'fog' state seems to be a place for travellers; an in-between place. I don't think we are in the real world we were born into."

"And the other place? The version where everything is demonic and evil and burnt?" Trevor asked.

"What are you talking about?" Philip asked carefully.

"There's another version of Sacred Valley, much darker than this. Whatever power is bringing up these beasts seems to reside there, trying to bring its power here."

"The Darcwurld?" Philip asked quickly. "You've been there?"

"Yes," Trevor asked, trying to avoid saying why he had gone there.

"Wait, hold on," Philip said, causing Trevor to swallow hard. "Why isn't Kathy with you?"

"When I woke up from the crash, she was gone," Trevor told him. "I finally found her in Hollowbrook Elementary, but she was taken into the Darcwurld by Bishop."

"Bishop? I thought he was dead."

"I thought so too," Trevor replied. "We didn't know at first because of that twisted metal he wears on his head, but Kathy had seen him in the Darcwurld and confirmed it was him."

"Twisted metal on his head?" Philip questioned but turned to the side as if it was directed at someone else. "Zephyranth..."

"Hey, Philip, you better start sharing some insight here."

"You never finished telling me what happened to Kathy," Philip said, ignoring him.

"I was too late," Trevor lied. "Bishop killed her."

Philip clenched his hands into fists by his side. Trevor waited for him to explode or show some sign of bitterness and anger, but it seemed like his self-control was better than expected. He sensed that Philip was keeping something from him, that there was some secret reason he could maintain his calm manner.

"Does Kathy know what happened to Bishop?" Philip finally asked.

"No," Trevor answered, trying to remember if it slipped out. "I made her believe it had to do with Caroline's suicide."

Philip simply nodded, turned around and walked into the office, closing the door behind him. Trevor heard a key entering the lock, but he could not believe the sound. He ran to the door and pressed on the handle. He had indeed locked himself in the office.

"Philip!" Trevor shouted, banging on the door. "What the hell are you doing?"

"You came here for Jay, so I suggest you go look for him," Philip's muffled voice said. "I have more important things to worry about than someone who let my sister get killed."

Trevor let go of the handle and realised Philip was right. He did go to the hospital to look for Jay. Their tense conversation had made him forget about it. He was about to move away from the door, determined to leave Philip behind when Jay and he left the hospital to find a way out of the town, when he heard a shuffle under the door.

"You might need this," Philip said.

He bent down and picked up the papers that slid through. Opening the folds up, he saw plans for the hospital floors. There were four of them, from the basement up to the third floor.

"Thanks," Trevor responded, slightly grateful for the show of kindness.

Putting the street map away in his bag, he stashed all but the first floor's plan in his rear pants pocket. Before looking at the map, he studied the Examination Room properly. The only things that really stood out were the gurneys. The one to the left was empty, with nothing unusual about it.

The middle one had a medical manikin lying on it with a blue sheet covering it. Trevor pulled the sheet down, wondering why it would be covered. The manikin was not clothed, but small words were written on certain parts of the body.

On the left arm was written *'Pruritus'* with *'Laceration'* on the right arm. On the left leg, it read *'Myositis'* while the right leg indicated *'Scorpionism'*. Finally, the chest revealed the inscription *'Pyrexia',* and the forehead had the word *'Hyperthymesia'.*

"It looks like Philip's been keeping busy," Trevor said, frowning at the medical terms. "What is he up to?"

He moved to the final bed. It also lacked anything on it, but the bed was not as smooth as the first. On closer inspection, he noticed indentations on the mattress, almost as if something invisible was lying on it. It followed the pattern of the manikin perfectly.

Running his hand over the mattress yielded no results. There was nothing on the bed to show what had caused the indentation.

"Philip must have moved this one," Trevor assumed.

A single note and a small brown pouch on a mobile chest of drawers beside the final bed caught his attention.

"Alchemical Remedies," he read the cursive writing on the note softly. "Sweet Basil, Catnip, Sunflower, Rosemary, Lemon Thyme, Lavender."

Trevor suspected that Philip had written the note. He inspected the pouch, but it was empty.

"You're going to need to come out for this," he muttered softly, watching the office door as he placed the note in the pouch and stashed both in his left pocket.

Positioning his bag onto his back again, he walked to the door at the end, passed the gurneys. As he placed his hand on the handle, he saw a scribble of words on the door before his eyes in black ink:

Did I not say to you that if you would believe you would see the glory
of God?
Lazarus, come forth!
Loose him and let him go!

"What the hell?" Trevor said, wondering why scripture had been written on the door. With one last look back at the indented mattress, he proceeded into the next room.

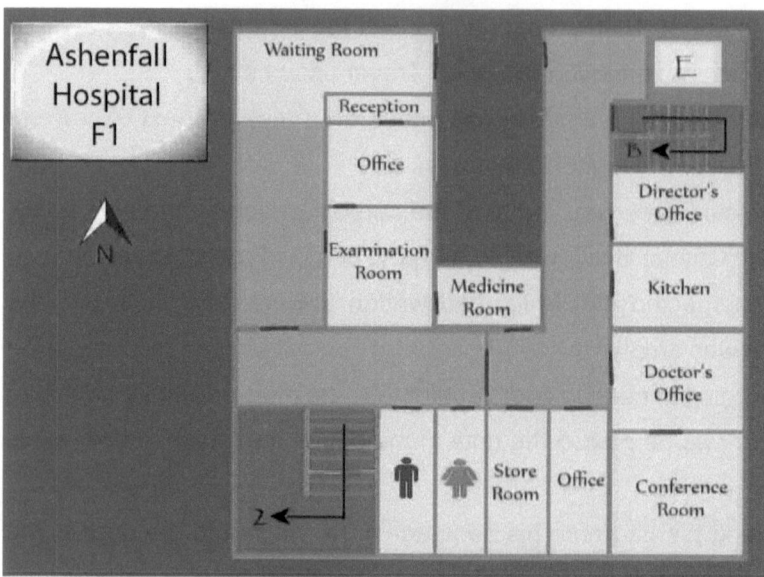

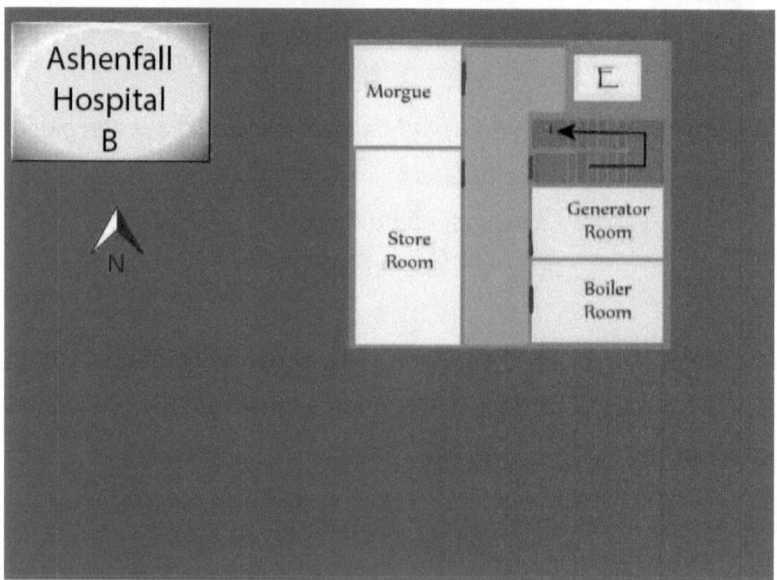

18

DARK CORRIDORS

The Medicine Room he entered was dark, lit only by the secondary light emitted from the Examination Room. The radio was still silent, so Trevor used his torch to look through the room. Some notes were lying on a table and drawers for him to check through, but there was nothing that he considered useful.

He proceeded to the next door that opened up to a passage. It was utterly dark, having no assistance from the light in the Examination Room this time. He found and tested the light switch behind him next to the door to the Medicine Room, hoping these lights were on a different circuit. The passage remained dark. Trevor left the switch on in case he could restore the power later.

He checked the map with his torch to get himself orientated with the rooms in that part of the hospital. As the double doors to his right led to the toilets and stairs, he checked it first. The doors were both barred, and there seemed to be no way to open them.

He walked ahead and tested the storage room's door, finding it open easily. The room was not as tidy as he expected from a hospital, and he wondered if Philip had been going through it. In terms of usefulness, the room only provided him with one medicine bottle. A box of ampoules was in a cabinet, but each glass container had been smashed.

Exiting the room back into the dark passage, he checked the office beside it. It opened slightly, but something on the other side stopped him from pushing it further in. He could barely fit his finger in the gap between the door and the frame. He rammed his shoulder to move whatever was blocking it, but it would not give way.

"Jay?!" Trevor shouted, waiting for the echo to die down as he listened for a response.

The passage turned left into the east wing. The yard where he fought the wolf spiders was just past the left wall. To his right were all the rooms that filled that part of the wing. He checked the Doctor's Office, which was locked. He noted on the map that this room had the only access to the Conference Room. He could see that there had once been a plaque on the door to identify the room or the person it was allocated to, but from the strip, he could tell it had either been removed or fallen off.

Next up the passage was the Kitchen, which was also locked. As he moved further down the passage, it seemed to get darker. Trevor considered that his mind was playing tricks on him since the wing had no light. Yet, as he approached the east wing's final room, the torch seemed to get dimmer. Trying the door, he also found it locked with a strip indicating the lack of another plaque.

"Oh man, don't tell me I have to go down to the basement again," Trevor muttered, rechecking his map.

He passed the stairs after the Director's Office, hoping to avoid it altogether. To the left, he spotted a door and assumed it was the locked one he had found after fighting the spiders. He checked it again and still found it locked.

He saw an elevator on the opposite wall behind him, next to the stairs. The doors were open, but he did not see any lights from any of the buttons or panels. Too afraid to step in completely, he simply leaned in and pressed one of the buttons. When nothing happened, he walked into it to inspect the inner panel.

Suddenly, he heard a groan. He spun around and inspected the floor, walls and ceiling. There was no one with him, but someone was definitely moaning as if in pain. He was paralyzed with the fear that it had been the elevator groaning, ready to collapse or fall down.

"It's so big," a male voice said, different from the others he had heard.

"Isn't there anything that can bring the swelling down?"

As if given momentum by the sound of the voice, Trevor found the strength to leave the elevator. He stood there momentarily, catching his breath and reaching to clutch the crowbar from his bag. While recovering from the fright, he studied the weapon and torch in his hands and decided on a more efficient idea. He put both away and took out the Beretta, switching its light on.

With nowhere else to go, he gave in to going down the stairs. He packed the map away and checked the basement floor plan first. He observed that besides the elevator, there were also four rooms. Making a mental note of which they were, he stashed the map away and held the pistol before him.

Trevor walked steadily down the stairs, listening more than ever for the slightest noise of anyone in the basement or the crackle from his radio. All he could hear was how deep his breathing had become. The air seemed heavier down there, and the torch on his Beretta was getting dimmer.

When he reached the basement floor, he turned left to the Generator Room, ignoring all the others. The torch flickered slightly as if it struggled against some invisible force to stay lit. Trevor stifled an urge to cough to clear his throat and lungs. The door opened, and he stepped in.

The massive generator before him was off, causing Trevor to wonder what was powering the plugs in the hospital. Assuming the electrical provision to the building was still fine, he searched along the walls until he found the distribution board. He opened the cover and inspected the switches, realising the problem.

Some of the switches had tripped, but the plugs were still on. He read the labels for the switches and found those that powered the lights to various parts of the hospital. He tested the first one, getting a slight shock from a momentary electrical discharge when it tripped again. Each of the successive light switches did the same.

Leaving the lights, he examined the labels until he found the elevator switch. Flipping it up, the switch remained on. Success was further confirmed when he heard a thrum of power from outside the room and felt the floor vibrate slightly before it faded away.

He closed the panel and moved back out of the room. He did not want to check the other rooms and prayed that Jay was not in any of them. He walked straight towards the elevator and saw in joy that the up button was lit. He heard a sound behind him as he leaned forward to press it.

There was a metallic door opposite the elevator. Trevor listened carefully for any further sound, shining the torch on the door. A wide slit at head height ran horizontally across it for three-quarters of its length. Deciding to rather move on, he halted when he heard someone call out and scream from within.

"Jay!" Trevor shouted, running towards the metallic door and peering in through the slit. The door was flushly embedded into the surrounding walls, with no means to open it from the outside.

It was so dark that he could barely make out who was inside. Using the pistol, he shone the light into the room. The opposite wall was lined with mortuary chambers where corpses were usually stored. The torch passed over a chamber that had been slid out. As far as he could tell, there was no corpse on the bed.

"Jay!" he shouted again. "Are you in there?"

He felt stupid suddenly. If he was in one of the chambers, then either Jay or Trevor would not hear the other shout. And if Jay was dead already…

"Kill it!" a male voice shouted, echoing from within the room. "It stung me! Use your heel!"

He waited a moment longer, listening for any further reply. He could feel his heart pounding against the metallic door, not realising how hard he had pressed his chest against it.

"It's too late," the voice said again. "I can't feel my leg… the venom's deep in there."

"Jay!" Trevor tried one more time, but not even the voice replied.

He turned around and moved to the elevator. The doors were closed, so he pressed the button to call the lift down. He wasn't in the mood to run up the stairs in case something was waiting up there for him. When it arrived, it pinged as the doors opened, and he entered it.

He pressed the second-floor button. The lift jerked slightly but did not close the doors or move up. The light on the button fizzled and died out, leaving only the first and third floors lit.

"Stupid technology," Trevor said, pressing the third-floor button.

The doors closed. The lift rose slowly, and he watched the floor number change as the digits ticked from one to the other.... 1, 2, 4, 3. Trevor blinked and looked at the numbers again. It was steady on 3 when the doors opened to the third floor, but he wondered if he had imagined it. Had the lift indicated a fourth floor?

Lifting the pistol up again for both the light and in preparation for any trouble, he stepped out of the lift. He was in an enclosed room with a door ahead of him. Exchanging the first and third-floor maps, he saw he was in a lift foyer and beyond the door was a passage with rooms along the east side.

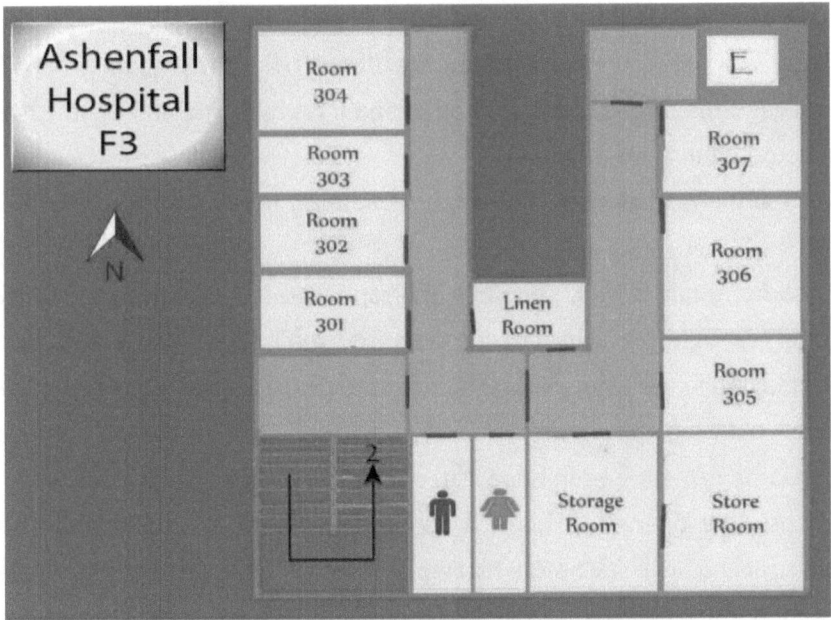

He opened the door and stepped into the passage. The torch lit the area directly ahead of him, with the passage stretching into the darkness. The radio was still quiet, surprisingly not making Trevor feel at ease. He had become so accustomed to its constant whining that he wondered if he had broken it during the spider battle.

Trevor found Room 307 and tried the handle. The door was locked. He knocked on the door anyway to make sure no one was in it, but there was no response. As he proceeded down the passage, he tested Rooms 306 and 305, but none opened. Finally, he reached the final room before the double doors that led to the west wing. The storage room was locked, too.

"Note to self," Trevor said in frustration. "When entering an abandoned hospital, look for the master keys."

He considered the thought further and realised the locked doors were in his favour. The fewer the rooms he had to search, the quicker he could eliminate them from his investigation. With that in mind, he took out his pen and crossed all the doors he could not access.

Trevor pushed his hands on the double-door handles, expecting them to give way. He hurt his wrist as the doors held back against him. He scrutinised the edges of the frames to see if barrel bolts held them closed, but he could not see anything.

"Hell man, what now?" he said, wondering if that was the end of his search.

As he turned around, another door opposite the storeroom's entrance caught his sight. He checked the map and realised he had not seen the door that led to the Linen Room. It appeared the room also provided access to the west wing.

"Come on," he said in hope, "let me in."

The door opened to his soft command. Trevor only let it open a bit before raising his pistol before him again. The radio began to sizzle, causing him to inspect the interior before proceeding. Someone was sitting by a solitary desk in the centre of the small room. Unfortunately, he could not make out who, as the person had their head slumped on the desk with linen over it.

"Hello?" he called. "Wakey, wakey."

The person did not respond, but the radio died down. He stepped into the room and closed the door behind him. The torchlight shone directly onto the person's head, waiting for any movement. He tread lightly, moving closer to the table until he could lift the linen off the head.

Her face stared to the side towards Trevor, revealing her long blond hair under a nurse's hat. Her eyes were open, but there was no life left in her. Further uncovering showed her sitting in her nurse uniform. When the torch returned to her face, he noticed something in her mouth.

"What have we here?"

He pried his fingers into her mouth and pulled out a ball of linen. From what he could deduce, someone had suffocated her with the linen. He checked her neck for a pulse just to be sure, but he was surprised when he felt how warm she still was.

"As far as I know, corpses are supposed to be cold."

Checking for anything else noteworthy in the room, he left it behind into the west wing. Ahead of him was Room 301, and to the left were the toilets and stairs. He decided to go down to the end of the passage and return to the stairs. That would give him a chance to search the second floor for Jay.

He took a light jog to Room 304, ensuring the torch lit his path. Just as he suspected, the door was locked. He knocked before moving down the passage to each of the other rooms, each barring him from access. Room 301 was no different, and he moved toward the toilets, wondering if Jay could be hiding in there.

19

PSYCHIATRIC THERAPY

As he stepped away from Room 301, he heard a click and the door creak on its hinges. Trevor swung his pistol around immediately and aimed it at the door.

"Jay?" he said softly, too afraid to call out initially, but then tried a bit louder. "Jay?!"

No one answered. He walked closer until the butt of the Beretta was in the gap and then pushed it open. A candle was burning on a coffee table in the far corner beside a bed. From the light of the candle, he could make out someone lying very still in the bed.

At the foot of the bed was a wheelchair. It faced Trevor as if someone was sitting in it and looking at him. He wondered if his mind was playing tricks on him, as the wheelchair looked much like the one he had seen at the school.

Ignoring it momentarily, Trevor closed the door and examined the body. It was another manikin, covered by the white sheets of the bed. He pulled the sheets off and immediately saw a hole in the sternum where the heart was meant to be. Looking down at the body, he saw it was also missing the right leg.

Where the shoulders, neck and leg joined the torso were black lines with minute measurements and indicators. Trevor didn't know much about medical procedures. Still, he had seen similar lines in a documentary once when a body part would be cut for an operation.

"Are these incision lines?" he wondered out loud, inspecting them a moment further before moving back to search the room.

When he looked around, the wheelchair was missing. The end of the bed was vacant, and a dark trail led from where it had been standing to the room's door. Shining the Beretta's light at the door revealed it was still closed. Trevor chose to focus on his search before following the trail.

He didn't need to look far. Next to the candle on the table was a tape player that fit in the palm of his hand. Inside the player was a tape labelled 'Patient XV007 – Session 1'. Not able to contain his curiosity, he sat down at a nearby chair and played the tape.

"This is Dr. Hoffman. This is the first psychiatric session with Patient XV007," a female voice said. "The patient was not referred to me but personally asked to consult with me. He is a surgeon who deals with extreme medical cases that may be fatal. This interview is being held in a boardroom of the hospital he practices in.

"For the sake of confidentiality, I will not use actual names of persons or locations, specifically not where you work. If you should choose to do so, then you may. Is there anything you want me to call you, or should I just use your name?"

"Well," an older man said in a shaky voice, "I guess since my code ends in 007, you can just call me James."

"Very well, James," the psychiatrist said, giggling as she did. "You requested to have a session with me. I will let you take the lead on how I can help you."

"No problem, doc. It has to do with a certain case I have had to deal with recently."

"At the hospital?"

"Yes, at the hospital. It concerns one of the patients that was brought to my attention. I was called out of bed in the morning and told about a man brought in for a scorpion sting to his leg."

"Is that unusual in your line of work?"

"No, not really. We've had a few cases like that in the last two months, specifically where tourists hike in places where scorpions are prevalent. I only get called in when the venom has done too much damage, and the leg needs to be amputated."

"Alright, I see. And I take it this was such a case?"

"That's correct."

"Ok. So why don't you tell me what made this situation so different from the others? You wouldn't be here unless it really traumatised you, I assume?"

"When I arrived at the hospital, the man was already too far gone. They had called me in too late, and the venom had done most of the damage. I did what I could to remove the leg, but the loss of blood just compounded the problem. Unfortunately, he didn't make it."

"Oh dear," she replied. There was a creak of a chair as one of them moved. "But James... surely you've lost patients before?"

"Well, it's more what happened later that bothers me," the patient continued. "After the body had been taken to the morgue, I left to get some sleep in one of the hospital's staff quarters before my official shift began. A few hours later, they woke me up again, asking me to meet them at the morgue.

"When I got there... I'd never seen anything like it before."

There was a moment of silence. Trevor pressed the tape closer to his ear, wondering if something was wrong with the cassette.

"It's ok, James. Take your time. When you're ready, tell me what you saw."

"It's not really the scene that disturbed me. I'm used to blood and flesh. It was more the act that bothered me. Someone had severed the man's limbs and head from his torso and taken the infected leg.

"Taken? Like stole it?"

"Yes. I stayed long enough to hear the investigating profiler mention that the culprit could have taken it as a trophy. They're still searching the hospital in case someone discarded it. They are also interviewing staff in case someone has witnessed anything peculiar.

"The heart had also been removed from the chest. And it was quite messy, like someone with untrained hands."

"So someone entered the hospital and then the morgue, slayed the body, and walked out without being noticed."

"That's right."

"That sounds quite unbelievable."

Trevor waited for the conversation to continue, but the cassette player stopped. Confused, he rewound it to the last part he had heard and waited again. The tape clipped off. It appeared to be the end of the recording.

"Wow, ok," he said as he stood and placed the player and tape in a side pocket of his bag.

Scanning the rest of the room revealed nothing further, so he moved out and closed the door, using the Beretta's light to follow the wheelchair's trail on the floor. As soon as the door closed against the frame, he heard another lock click and a door creak open.

The wheelchair's trail led to Room 302. Trevor carefully followed it, exchanging glances between it and the room ahead. When he got there, he saw that it was marginally open. As before, he nudged it further with the pistol and stepped in.

The wheelchair was at the foot of another bed. A similar scene was before him, as in Room 301. A manikin was lying under a sheet with a candle in the corner. When he pulled the sheet off, it also had a hole in the sternum, with the left arm missing this time. Trevor looked at the corner table and saw a cassette beside the candle.

Stepping back to walk around the bed, he saw that the wheelchair was gone again. There was a double set of wheel tracks, one leading in and the other out. He walked around the bed and claimed the cassette labelled 'Patient XV007 – Session 2'. Exchanging the tapes in the player, Trevor sat by the window chair and listened to the new recording.

"This is Doctor E. Hoffman, and it is the second session with Patient XV007, referred to as James as per the previous session," the female voice introduced. "Welcome back, James."

"Thank you, doc," the man replied, his voice less shaky than in the first recording.

"Well, it's been two weeks since I last saw you," the psychiatrist continued. "I know I told you to feel free to schedule when you are ready to see again, but the request seemed rather urgent."

"Yes, sorry about that. The killer struck again. And unfortunately, it was another call that I was on."

"Hold on," she stopped him. "Slow down a bit and give me some more details."

"Sorry, I'm just anxious," he replied, some of the nervousness rising in his voice again. "It was another patient that was brought in. This one had had a chronic allergic reaction to a mosquito bite. We initially thought it might have been malaria, but his entire left arm was engulfed with rashes.

"It was like nothing I have ever seen before. The patient was delirious, but he still claimed only one had bitten him. Yet, his arm looked like it had been attacked by an entire hive!"

"Could you save him?" she asked.

"We gave him a sedative at first, hoping it would soothe the itching and pain while we went to work on testing his blood. He didn't last five minutes after that."

"I'm sorry to hear that," she said, the sympathy clear in her tone. "So tell me about the killer. Did he abuse the body in the morgue again?"

"I went to inspect the body later, not suspecting that an attack would happen so soon again or even in the same hospital," he replied. "When I arrived, the mortician asked me what body we were talking about, as none had reached him."

"It was gone?"

"Indeed," he confirmed. "We thoroughly searched the hospital, but after several hours, we decided to leave it to the police. When I arrived for the next shift the next morning, I did not need to be told that the body had been found."

"How so?"

"The limbs and torso were scattered in a bloody mess in the centre of the reception portal."

"The same M.O?"

"Yes. The parts had been severed as before, with a messy hole where the heart should be and the infected arm missing."

"Alright," she said, sighing. "I will let the police worry about how that happened and why no one saw it happen. For now, I want to know how you are. Honestly... are you coping?"

"Well, I wouldn't be here, doc, if I was," he replied, a sign of irritation in his sarcasm.

"I know you're upset, James," she said comfortingly, "but..."

"No, no. I'm sorry. I should have better control of my emotions. You're only trying to help."

Trevor looked down as the recorder went silent, and the tape stopped playing. Checking that there was nothing more to it, he followed the trail out of the room into the dark passage. As he expected, he heard another click and creak and moved towards Room 303. The wheelchair's path led into the room, and opening the door revealed it was indeed waiting for him at the foot of the bed.

He checked the manikin on the bed, flipping the sheet and inspecting the body immediately. The hole in the chest was replicated; this time, the left leg was absent. Becoming used to the wheelchair vanishing, he ran around the bed to obtain the next tape.

"This is Doctor E. Hoffman," the psychiatrist started as usual. "We are about to begin the third session of Patient XV007, also known by the codename James from the initial session. Welcome, James."

"Thanks, doc," he replied.

"So James, it's been little over a week. Are you well?"

"No, not really."

"I know you mentioned on the phone that your trauma seems to be getting worse."

"That's right. I'm starting to have nightmares now. I'm seeing the victims in front of me, watching their limbs get severed individually."

"It's to be expected. You've seen the victims first-hand. This type of thing has a psychological effect on people and will still affect you for time to come."

"The dreams change, though. At first, I was watching the victims. I become the victims towards the end, watching a faceless person cut me apart. I wake up in a cold sweat."

"How many nightmares have you had since I last saw you?"

"There was one just after our last visit, and then another after yesterday's killing."

"There was another one? So soon?"

"That's right. A man whose leg was swollen from some kind of muscular injury. He could barely walk; it seemed like it would burst. Like with the others, we gave him a sedative, but he died. We found him in the middle of the night, dismembered in the elevator."

"Heart and leg gone?"

"Correct."

"Hmmm," she said. "Besides the M.O., he seems to be going after men only. Surely these aren't the only cases of these kinds of injuries?"

"No, not at all. We had another scorpion infection two days ago, but it was mild, and he made it through."

"That's another trend, going for those that have died already," she remarked. "We can't really call him a serial killer if he isn't killing anyone. Simply disfiguring their corpses."

"Yeah," he said thoughtfully. "I hadn't thought of it like that. That does put a fresh look on things, I guess."

"Let's get the focus back on you since that's why we're here," she said in a more positive tone. "Did you always work at the hospital?"

"Well, not originally. Before I was placed there, I worked at Ashenfall

Hospital in Sac…

"No names, James," she interrupted him.

"Oh yes. Sorry."

"What was it like there?"

"It was so pleasant before the coal mine explosion, and the town was abandoned. I remember the nurses. I so loved their smiles."

The tape stopped. Trevor frowned at the last comment. His tone seemed insidious, almost like he had been leering when he said it. Anxious to see if there was more, he ran out of the room and followed the wheelchair's trail to the sound of the next door unlocking and opening.

Room 304's manikin's entire torso was gone, leaving the legs, arms and head on the bed. He greedily grabbed the next tape and sat down to listen to it.

"This is Doctor Hoffman, with the fourth session of Patient XV007, also called James for the sake of confidentiality," she started. There was a brief pause before she continued. "Ok, let's leave the formality behind. Are you ok? I saw what happened in the papers."

"Yeah, I guess I'm ok," he replied, sounding exhausted. "I mean, the nightmares are getting worse."

"The same as before? Switching between watching the victim and being the victim?"

"Yes, but it includes looking down like I'm the killer."

"That's not so strange as you think. You'd be surprised what tricks the mind plays on you."

"You don't understand. The police are looking into me now as a suspect."

"What? How can that be?"

"This was one of my patients again. He was brought in for an intense fever. His chest felt like it was on fire. No matter what we did, the temperature would not come down, so we placed him in the examination room where we could run some tests.

"We had left him there alone for half an hour. The security had been increased around the hospital since the last slaughter. We thought he would be alright in there.

"When I came back, the guards at the door were dead. Their necks had been slit by a scalpel. And when I entered the room, the body parts had been cut and placed in the different corners, with the torso gone."

"None of that explains why they would blame you for it."

"No one was with me when I had found him, so there were no witnesses to attest that I discovered him like that. Also, every victim had been under my care before they were…. butchered. Unfortunately, the hospital director could not understand why the victim had been placed in my hands since surgery was unnecessary."

"Was there a valid reason?"

"You believe them?" he asked, followed by a moment of silence.

"No, of course not, James," she said quickly. "Yet, I understand their thinking. They need to investigate every avenue, and now, unfortunately, that is the most likely to… Wait! Where are you going?"

There was the bang of a door before silence ended the recording. Trevor had already removed the tape and placed it with the others by his notes in his bag by the time he reached the room door and left. The door closed behind him, and the lock clicked.

He tested the door and found it locked. He was breathing quickly now, wondering if that was the end of the recordings. As if in answer to his curiosity, he heard another click and door creak open, but it sounded like an echo from the other end of the passage.

Checking the floor with the light, he saw the wheelchair's trail on the left side of the passage leading down. He ran after it, checking each room he had been in. All of them were locked again. When he reached the end of the passage, he saw that the trail turned left and ran under the double doors to the east wing.

Before he continued, he checked the doors that led to the stairs and found them locked. Trying hard not to curse and wondering how he could get to the second floor, he tested the toilet doors and found them locked, too. His only option was to follow the trail and see where it took him.

The double doors were still locked. He returned to the Linen Room's door and entered, slipping on the floor and falling on his back. The door slammed shut behind him, and he crept backwards against it.

Someone was standing in the middle of the room by the table where the dead nurse had been. Trevor tried to control his breathing, realising only then that the radio was sizzling softly again. As the sound died down, he reached for the Beretta that had fallen out of his hand by his side.

The back of his head hurt. When he had fallen, it had slapped the door before he had recovered from the fright of the person standing before him. He ignored the pain as much as he could, wondering why his gun was sticky and covered his nose at a sudden smell that had reached him.

Lifting the light up to the stationary person first, he gaped in horror. The same nurse that had been seated before was now standing at his side of the desk, bent over. Her face was flat on its side on the table, staring with wide eyes at Trevor. As before, there was a ball of linen shoved in her mouth.

Where her hips bent, her uniform had been pulled up over her back. It revealed her buttocks, with blood spattered on the inside of her cheeks. The blood ran down her inner thighs to the panty wrapped around her ankles. It flowed like a river onto the floor towards where Trevor had tripped.

Her vagina was not completely visible, though. The same linen that had been shoved in her mouth hung from the opening between her legs down towards the floor between her heels. The cloth had been pressed in deep, leaving nothing to the imagination.

The stench was unbearable. It was a mixture of death, blood and sex. Fighting the urge to throw up, he steadily got to his feet and walked past the bending corpse. His pants and bag dripped with blood as he reached for the door and hastily passed into the east wing.

He found the other part of the wheelchair's trail and followed it to Room 305 ahead of him. The open door was waiting patiently for him. Checking the inside first to make sure there were no more surprises, he ventured in, eyeing the wheelchair carefully.

The heart and right arm were missing. Walking over to the spot where the wheelchair had been a moment ago, he found the next tape and played the recording.

"Doctor Emily Hoffman," she said briefly. "Patient XV007, fifth session."

There was some ruffling of paper near the recorder and then silence before she proceeded.

"I honestly did not think I would see you again."

"Yes, I am sorry for my last outburst," he said, the regret heavy in his throat. "I did not mean to cut off the only person I could talk to about this. With everyone still suspecting my involvement, no one else will believe me."

"I read in the paper about another victim," she said to the ruffling of paper again.

"Yes, he has struck again. Thankfully, though, I had no involvement in it this time."

"They say a call came in, phoning for an ambulance. His right arm had been heavily cut with a kitchen knife, so they ran him through to emergencies. And then there was some mishap…"

"Mishap!" he retorted, and then snorted. "They have no idea what happened to the body! One moment, they were delivering him to the emergency unit; the next, no one could work out where it had gone."

"What about the guys that received him?"

"The nurses? Gone. All five of them, vanished as if they never existed."

"That's strange. The paper says nothing about that."

"They wouldn't. This is the biggest blunder since the Boatman Inquiry."

"Boatman? Doctor Harry Boatman?"

"That's right," he responded in haste. "I've been saying since the third killing that I think someone is either trying to live up to that reputation or outdo him."

"That's quite a peculiar insight to have, James," she said.

"What do you mean?"

"Did they find the body eventually?" she responded, ignoring him.

"Yes, in the men's toilet on the second floor. Same as the rest, blood spattered everywhere, each part of his body in a separate cubicle. Heart and injured arm were missing."

"I noticed this gentleman was quite senior," she remarked. "Just like the others, he was in his early forties. Not that I can find anyone in the paper remarking on it, but it's a trend I picked up. Isn't that about your age, James?"

There was a light tapping sound that filled the silence. Trevor couldn't work out what it was, but from the change in pitch, it seemed to be coming from the patient.

"I don't like where you're going with this," he finally said. "Don't you think I have enough people trying to accuse me? If he is after men my age, wouldn't that suggest I would be a potential victim?"

"Yes, of course, it could mean that," she said, sounding unconvinced.

"This wasn't one of my patients," he defended himself.

"Which means you had free time to do it," she continued.

"I've had enough of this," he said. The chair made a rough noise on the floor. "I came here for counselling, not for further interrogation."

The door slammed again. Instead of the tape ending, Trevor heard a phone being picked up.

"Darla, can you please try again to find any record of our patient's past?"

This time, the tape ended, leaving Trevor wondering if she had found anything. Moving out, he followed the new trail up the passage to Room 306 that had just opened up for him.

The manikin in the room caught Trevor off-guard. The heart was displaced, but instead of missing limbs, they were all accounted for. The head, however, had a face crumpled in as if someone had taken a hammer and smashed it in.

Trevor located the next tape and sat down. Instead of the usual label, this one stated *'Unofficial recording – Patient XV007'*. Barely unable to contain himself, he popped it in and played it.

He immediately detected a vast difference in the surroundings where it was being recorded. There was a noise as if she was in a place where others were talking quietly among themselves. A car hooted in the background, and then he heard the sound of cutlery on plates.

"Good morning, Emily," the male voice Trevor had come to know as James said. "I can't speak long; I must be off. I have some important business to attend to."

"You know, just because we aren't in my office doesn't mean you can't call me Doctor Hoffman."

"You called me, Emily," he said. "Get on with it. I don't have time for pleasantries."

"I heard about the killing that happened last night," she replied. "I wanted to check on you, see if you're ok."

"You mean, see if I was involved?"

"Please, James," she responded quickly. "I'm here for you."

There was silence before she continued.

"I heard that when they found his severed body parts in the Intensive Care ward, they all were accounted for. Only his face was unrecognisable due to some bashing it had taken."

"Yes, it is an extreme deviation from the killer's normal patterns," he said as if teaching a lecture on the matter.

"They also say that there was no record of the man being received by the hospital and don't know how he got in there or who he is yet," she pursued.

"That's right," he replied, not offering any more.

"Do you think it was personal, or he is trying to send a message?"

There was silence again, and Trevor wondered what he would say.

When he did speak, it was not what he had expected.

"This will be our last session together, Emily. I'm leaving Ashbourne."

"Why? Where are you going?"

"It doesn't matter where I'm going. I need a new start, away from all of these accusations."

"Do you really think running away during an investigation is a good idea?" she asked.

"Thank you so much for your time," he said softly. Then the leer returned to his voice. "You don't know how valuable the sessions have been."

There was nothing more to the recording. Trevor wondered if there was anything in the final room since it sounded like the end of the sessions. He followed the trail to Room 307 and walked into the open door. The wheelchair waited by the final bed, but this one had no corpse.

By the corner table was another tape. Trevor walked around the bed, surprised that the wheelchair remained. He made himself comfortable by the window chair and listened intently.

"This is Doctor Emily Hoffman," the psychiatrist said, sounding alert and sad at the same time. "This recording pertains to Patient XV007, unofficially known as James.

"My personal assistant had been tasked with discovering more information about the patient's past. I can only assume the cops are doing the same with regard to their investigation into the recent spate of murders and their suspicion that James is involved.

"I am not so sure they have detected the same link between James and the murders, though. When looking at his family history, nothing really stands out that would connect him, except maybe the indication of violence between him and his father.

"But looking into the victims that had been found, one had to be so careful not to miss the fact that most of them had been in high school with him. I contacted the former principal of the school to find out if he remembers the boys, and after a long discussion, I was able to discover that the boys had physically and emotionally bullied James throughout his first three years there.

"His parents moved to Ashbourne after that, and the final two years were completed at a different school. On inquiry, the principal said James had excelled there, shining above the others. There were no incidents reported whereby he had been bullied, though.

"There was only one recorded violent event, and it was James who had inflicted it. In his final year, someone had made fun of him in what the others thought was a light-hearted manner. The other children had explained that he lost it for some reason and attacked the boy. When he was done beating the boy's face in, he had to be taken to a hospital.

"The police are still investigating the latest victim whose face was also beaten in. I've asked for more information on the victim so I can see if it was tied to James's past too, but they said they cannot share any details now. They may have nothing they can give me, since the latest news from the media is that the killer had either burned off or removed all physical identification of the victim.

"It is strange for a killer to suddenly change his technique. The previous victims were left on display with a clear indication of who they were. He wanted the world to know who he had killed. Yet, the final one's identity had been stripped. Had James made a mistake? Was the final kill unintentional? Or was he simply toying with the police?

"If it is as I suspect, and James is the killer, then making a mistake would explain why he had to leave so suddenly. I only have one option: to break my oath of confidentiality and tell the police what I know.

"Thinking back now," she said, taking a moment to think before continuing, "I wonder why he came to me, pretending to be traumatised if he was in fact the killer. Does he have a split personality, which makes him unaware that he is killing? Or was he simply using me, hoping therapy would exclude him from suspicion?

"Either way, he…"

The tape went silent. Trevor thought maybe the recording had ended, but then he heard heavy breathing.

"James? How long have you been standing there? How did you get in?"

"I've been waiting for you, doc," the voice said menacingly, "hiding in the shadows. I rather like your conclusions there. Tell me, when did you become a detective. Now, now!"

His voice had become louder while he had spoken, and at the last moment, there was a shuffle as something was knocked over. Trevor could hear their struggle, her screams muffled by something held over her mouth.

"We're going for a ride," he finally said as the struggle began to calm down, "back to my old office in Sacred Valley. I can't have you spoiling my little game just yet."

From the bang that sounded it seemed as though the recorder had hit the floor. Something dragged across the floor until the door creaked open and then was softly closed again.

The player clicked to indicate the end of the recording.

20

SILENT VICTIMS

Trevor arose from the chair, chills running down his spine from the experience recorded on the tape player. In the time he had focussed on the recording, the wheelchair had vanished again.

He sighed heavily. As much as he had enjoyed the sessions found on the recordings, it did not seem he was any closer to finding Jay. Only the second floor was left to explore, but he could not access it.

"Maybe I should just go on without him," he muttered. "There must be a way out of Sacred Valley."

He noticed that there was still a trail of the wheelchair leading out. Following it, he found the wheelchair in the passage right outside the room. It was facing down the path back towards the Linen Room.

Trevor aimed for the door that led to the lift foyer behind the wheelchair. Just before his hand reached the handle, he heard a lock click and a door open down the passage. It was too dark to see which door it had been, even with him aiming the Beretta's light down its length.

Suddenly, the radio came to life. It started with a slow sizzle that rose to a soft crackle. He watched carefully down the passage, waiting for anything to show its face. The radio wove back down to a sizzle as if the creature was moving away.

He moved down the passage, the pistol kept high. The sound of a rusty wheelchair rolled past him, and Trevor swept the light over the floor around him. He could not spot anything and so moved the light to the back of the passage. The wheelchair was still in the place where he had seen it, unmoved.

The radio rose again as the wheels moved past him back towards the

Linen Room. He followed it, keeping an eye on both walls of the passage to see if he could spot the object passing him. It rolled next to him again, and the sound of the creaking wheels echoed back to the lift foyer.

The old sound of the radio came back. It crackled and whined like it usually did on the streets when a creature was nearby. Trevor kept his eye down the top of the pistol's barrel, spotting something white emerging from around the corner at the end of the passage.

He could not believe his eyes. It was the nurse from the Linen Room. She was limping slightly and swaying from side to side as she moved towards him, causing his radio to get more static. Something glinted in her hand. He shifted the light down to see a scalpel in it.

"Stay back!" he shouted, aiming back at her chest. "I don't want to hurt you."

The nurse continued in her sickly gait, her eyes not quite looking straight at him. He saw that the ball of linen was still in her mouth, muffling any noises she tried to make.

Without warning, she raised the scalpel and shrieked. Despite her previous inability to walk correctly, she now rushed towards him. In panic, he pulled the trigger and released two shots to her chest. One hit her right breast while the other hit the shoulder just above it. Her shoulder jerked back, causing her to stop running.

She looked at him in anger and ran again. He shot again. The bullet hit her belly, but she kept going as if it had simply missed her. Trevor reached up at the last moment and pulled down the crowbar. Her hand swiped and cut his left shoulder, making him wince in pain.

The nurse brought the scalpel down from above her head, but he brought the crowbar up horizontally to block it. He couldn't believe her strength. She was pushing down against him, her eyes pure white in the light from the pistol in his right hand.

Remembering that he had other limbs, he kicked forward into her belly. She fell back as he moved forward, slapping the forked edge across her cheek. She spun around just as he kicked the back of her knee so that she could fall on it. When she was in a kneeling position, he brought the crowbar over and down.

The forked edge bit into her skull. The nurse wavered for a moment as the sickening crack filled the passage. Looking down at the radio, Trevor frowned when he realised it had not gone silent yet. To attest that it was not over, she slowly tried to rise again.

"Will you just die!!" he said, aiming at the back of her head and offloading three bullets into it.

Finally, she fell down onto the floor. The radio quietened down to a sizzle, only rising and falling to the sound of the invisible wheelchair rolling up and down the passage. After reclaiming and placing the crowbar on his bag, he quickly did an ammo check in the Beretta's clip. Six bullets were left of the fifteen he had initially found in it.

He shone the light up in the direction the nurse had come from. Ahead of him, one of the doors had opened. He quickly checked the floor map, seeing it was a storage room. He moved forward to investigate it, closing it behind him.

The storage room was bigger than he had expected. It was filled with boxes and steel cabinets with little space to walk among them. By investigating the folders by his feet, he realised they contained patient records and cases.

"These must be the archives," Trevor said, throwing them back down.

He inspected the cabinets first, being the easiest to work through. It took several minutes to work through them all, but nothing helpful turned up. In frustration, he kicked up a box that sent files and folders flying through the air. Something clunked on the floor, and he bent down to pick up a box of shells.

The light of the Beretta caught something metallic next to it on the floor. Brushing the dust off it, he saw a solid bronze key. Attached to the elliptical bow of the key was a yellow nametag.

"Transporter Key," he read out loud, turning the tag around to read the text on the rear. *"Use this key to be brought down to earth.* What the hell does that mean?*"*

He tossed the key up and down, looking at the door and wondering if it would take him to the real world. Anxious to try it, he moved to the door and placed the key in it. He turned it slowly and felt the key tug a bit first before it locked the door. Unlocking it again, he opened it.

It was still dark ahead of him. He used the light to scan the area around him, noticing suddenly that the nurse's body had disappeared. Everything else seemed the same, but something told him it was not. There appeared to be extra doors on the wall to his right than he remembered.

The double doors to his left suddenly rattled and then opened. Trevor swung the light around and aimed the pistol at the doors. It opened quickly, revealing someone behind it. Philip lifted his hand to his eyes to block the light from shining into it.

"Trevor?" he asked, squinting to make him out behind the light. "What are you doing? And how did you get in the store room? I made sure it was locked."

Trevor moved the torch down Philip's body, noting how the overall had more blood on it now. There was a blade in his right hand with blood dripping from the tip.

"Philip; what have you done?"

Philip looked down and saw all the blood. His facial expression displayed shock momentarily before it took on a more sinister look.

"It's the nurses," he said, his lips curling into an evil smirk. "I told them I liked their smiles. All I ever wanted was their smiles. So beautiful.... So stunning."

With that, Philip stepped to the side and entered the room opposite Trevor. He passed through it, opening another door at the other end. Trevor heard the door close.

"Philip, wait!" he shouted, running after him.

He entered the room, expecting it to be the Linen Room, but stopped in shock when he realised it wasn't. He inspected the room and then the next door. It clearly stated *Examination Room* on it.

"I'm in the medicine room," he muttered, looking around again. "How the hell did I end up on the first floor?"

Trevor looked at the Transporter Key again. The only conclusion he could draw was that it had brought him down there. Tucking it away safely in his rear pocket, he moved back to the passage when he realised Philip had left the double doors open.

He swapped maps with the first floor again, inspecting the next passage on it. The stairs to the second floor were at the end of it, just past the toilets. Wondering if Jay could be in either of them, he moved to the closer of the two.

The door to the female toilets opened up. The Beretta's light reflected off the broken mirror before him. The mirror also revealed just how untidy he looked. Leaving his appearance, he turned left to the cubicles. The two side doors were broken and hanging on single hinges while the central cubicle was closed.

The two open cubicles revealed nothing, so Trevor pushed on the central one. It was locked from the inside.

"Jay?" he called and then heard feet shuffle on the floor.

He dropped down and looked under the cubicle door. Shining the light to the base of the toilet he saw feet in slippers pop up from the floor out of his view. Determined to see who was hiding in the cubicle, Trevor moved into the right one. He stepped over the hanging door's side and climbed onto the toilet. Pressing his weight carefully on it, he peered over the dividing partition and looked down.

"Hello?" he called.

The cubicle was empty. Making sure he wasn't just seeing things, he shone the gun's light down. There was murky blood in the toilet's water, but no one was sitting on it. Making sure one last time there was no one in it or the other cubicle, he left the room.

The male toilets were locked, leaving him free to venture up the stairs to the second floor. He exchanged maps halfway up, making sure to keep his torch shining the way ahead of him. When he reached the landing, he studied the map before proceeding through the door.

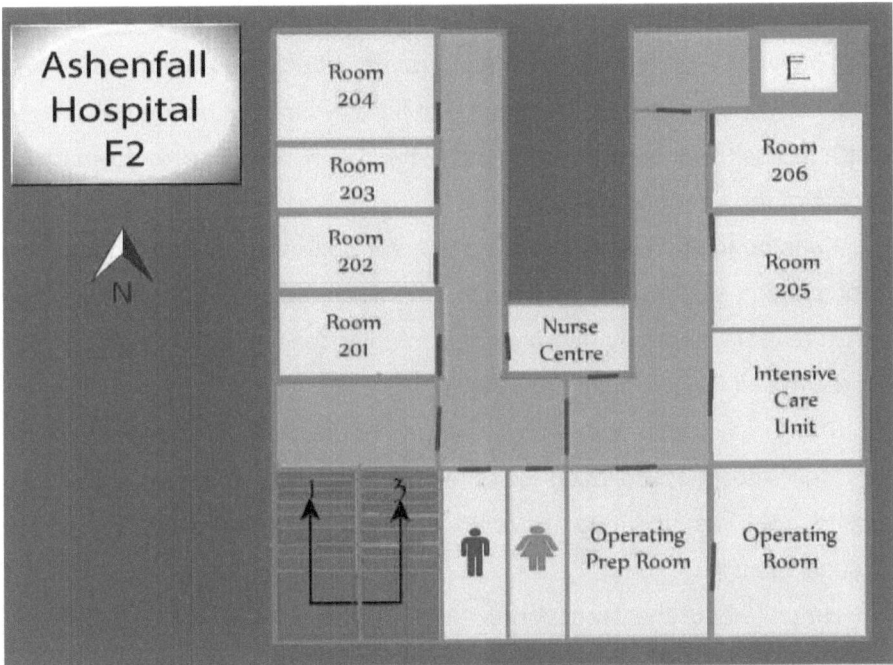

The west wing consisted mostly of rooms again like the third floor. In the centre below the Linen Room was a Nurse Centre. He clutched the Beretta's grip, wondering if he would encounter any more nurses. The highlights of the east wing were the Operating Rooms and the Intensive Care Unit. It made him recall the recordings and Emily's discussion on the final victim.

Deciding not to waste any more time, Trevor stepped through the door and into the west wing. He checked the male toilets to the right and found it open. Unlike the toilets above, the mirror on the wall was missing. All the cubicles were accessible, allowing him to inspect them all.

"Ahhh! Hmmmmm!" a male voice suddenly screamed into the room.

Trevor jumped out of the cubicle he was checking, pistol aimed at the door. He choked on his spit from the fright and coughed to clear it, his eyes watering. He studied the main part of the toilets, but he couldn't see anyone.

"Please, I need some salve for these cuts. They burn so deep! Any aid will help!"

The words gave him an idea. Trevor dropped the bag down and searched for a first aid kit. He noted that he only had two but decided it was worth the risk. Not sure where to put it, he simply threw the kit down in the middle of the floor and waited.

Keeping the gun level with his chest, he waited for anything to happen. Time passed slowly while he hoped something would happen or some sign would reveal where Jay had gone. Eventually, feeling really stupid, Trevor picked the kit up and put it back in his bag.

The female toilet door was locked, so he proceeded to the end of the passage and checked each room, working his way up. Every door was locked. He was about to move to the Nurse Centre when something occurred to him.

He pulled out the Transporter Key and tried it on Room 201. It turned after a slight jag within it, and the door opened up. Instead of a room in front of him, he encountered a passage leading to the right. He kept the door open, almost too afraid to close it.

Moving down the passage, he noticed that there were no other doors. At the end, he entered a large area he instantly recognised as the first floor's Waiting Room. The Lunar Nexus was burning on the reception counter still.

"I need something for these bites," a male voice said, echoing down the passage. "I can't take this itching anymore."

Trevor stood still for a moment. He remembered the voice saying the same thing when he had entered the hospital. Yet, now that he had heard Emily's recordings, he recalled the victim that had died after the mosquito bites that had afflicted him.

Taking out the first-floor map, he wrote '*itching bites*' on the Waiting Room block. He closed his eyes, casting his memory back to when he had heard words in certain rooms. The morgue was the first to be recalled, as the screams from within had had such an impact on him. Pulling out the basement floor plan, he wrote '*scorpion sting*' on the morgue's space.

He recalled that someone had said something in the elevator on the first floor, but not what had been said. His last encounter had been in the second-floor male toilets, so he wrote '*cuts*' on it. Then he suddenly remembered how hot it had been in the examination room and wrote '*heat / fever*' on the first-floor plan.

Following his impression that the voices were related to the murders indicated in Emily's recordings, he thought back on the remaining victims. The only two that remained were the smashed face and the inflammation. This line of thought caused him to recall that the elevator voice had complained about swelling, so he wrote '*inflammation*' by the elevator.

Impressed with himself, he stashed all but the second floor's plan into his rear pocket. He touched the Lunar Nexus to reinvigorate himself again and then moved back towards the passage when a new thought hit him.

He jumped over the reception counter again, turning the office door's handle. It started to open, and he began to move in.

"Who's there!?!" Philip's voice shouted from the other side before he pressed the door closed again. "Stay out!"

"Philip!" Trevor shouted as he heard the door lock.

He pulled the Transporter Key out and tried to insert it into the slot. Philip had left his key in it on the other side, so he could not push it in any further. Angry that Philip had closed him off, he banged his fist on the door and then kicked it.

Trevor headed back to the open door at the end of the passage and walked through into the second floor's west wing. He closed the door behind him and moved towards the Nurse Centre. When he touched the door and opened it slowly, the radio sizzled softly on his hip.

Raising the Beretta up, he entered and passed the light over the room. There was nothing that initially alerted him to any danger until his foot knocked something on the floor. Shifting the light down, he saw four bodies ahead of him towards the door on the other end of the room.

The uniforms identified them as nurses under the pools of blood that covered them. They were lying haphazardly on the floor as if someone had just killed them and moved on. Trevor had to step carefully over them, between legs and arms, to reach the other side.

The most frightening features were their mouths and cheeks. Someone had used a blade to cut into their mouths. The corners had been extended into elongated smiles into their cheeks, revealing gum and teeth where blood splatters allowed.

What bothered Trevor more was that the blood looked very liquid and fresh. Despite his sense of foreboding, he leaned down over one of them to feel the neck with his fingertips and then the rest of his hand.

"You're still warm, sweet cheeks," he remarked, remembering the blood smeared on Philip's medical overcoat. "What did he say about wanting the nurses to smile?"

The radio was still sizzling softly as if there was danger close by, but further scanning of the room by torchlight revealed nothing. Too worried about what awaited him, he left the room without further investigating its contents.

When he stepped into the east wing and closed the door behind him, the radio fell silent again. Trevor frowned and opened the door again. The radio sang the same song, sizzling softly until he closed the door. Not sure what he had missed, he decided to move on.

He went to the door in front of him that the map indicated was the Operating Preparation Room. It opened freely, much to Trevor's surprise. Even more astonishing was that there was light in the room. Closing the door, he noticed the lights were on stands similar to the ones in the

Examination Room. The lights were plugged in via extension leads to the closest sockets.

Next to each of the three light stands were beds with manikins. They were not covered like the ones on the third floor had been, and Trevor immediately picked up what was different about them. Where the manikins on the third floor had body parts missing, these had limbs replaced with actual human parts.

Investigating the one on the right, he saw that the right leg's veins were clearly showing through the skin. There was a large bump on the lower leg beneath the knee, which was red and swollen.

The middle manikin had a human torso that looked normal enough. Trevor moved his hand over the bare chest and immediately retracted it. The heat from the body was overwhelming. It made him remember the fever victim and the voice in the Examination Room that complained it was too warm.

The final bed had a manikin whose left leg was very swollen. It looked like the upper leg muscles were about to burst out of the flesh and skin. He was too afraid even to touch it in case it popped. He recalled the victim who had been inflamed and the voice in the elevator who had complained about how swollen he felt.

Searching the room revealed broken tools and chemical liquids long past their usefulness. As he walked to the door that led to the Operating Room, he wondered why Philip kept the bodies there.

"Are these the original parts taken from the victims?" he asked out loud. His voice helped soothe his tense nerves. "What is Philip planning to do with them? Is he trying to re-enact the killings? And if so, why?"

Annoyed with having too many unanswered questions, he entered the Operating Room. This time, there were two uncovered manikins. The one on the right had a human right arm, with slashes covering it from shoulder to wrist. The other had rashes and bites on the human left arm.

"These are all related to the killings," he said. "It must be. All the afflictions are the same."

As Trevor searched the room, he looked for anything that would give him a clue of what Philip was up to. He was so engrossed in the mystery that he completely forgot what his main objective in the hospital had been. All the room could provide him were medical charts of past patients attended to before Sacred Valley had been abandoned.

He rubbed his eyes. Searching in the dark with only the Beretta's torch made him tired and his eyes ache. He also couldn't remember when last he had slept. With the Lunar Nexus constantly rejuvenating him, he hadn't felt the need to. He also didn't know how much time had passed since he entered the lonely town.

"Let's move on," he finally said, having lost his patience.

When he entered the passage again, it suddenly occurred to him that there was still one victim's body unaccounted for. He hadn't heard any voices complaining about a face being smashed in, nor had he found a manikin with a human head.

He pulled out the tape player and thought back to the recordings. He remembered that the face victim had been the last since it had deviated from the other killings. He played the final tape but then realised it had been Emily's last considerations recorded on it. Playing the second last recording, he sifted through it until he found what he sought.

"I heard that when they found his severed body parts in the Intensive Care ward that all were accounted for. Only his face was unrecognisable due to some bashing it had taken."

Trevor inspected the map and then looked ahead of him in the corridor. The Intensive Care Unit was before him. He moved forward without wasting another moment and clutched the handle, pushing down hard in haste. Without warning, the handle snapped off the door, hurting his wrist in the process.

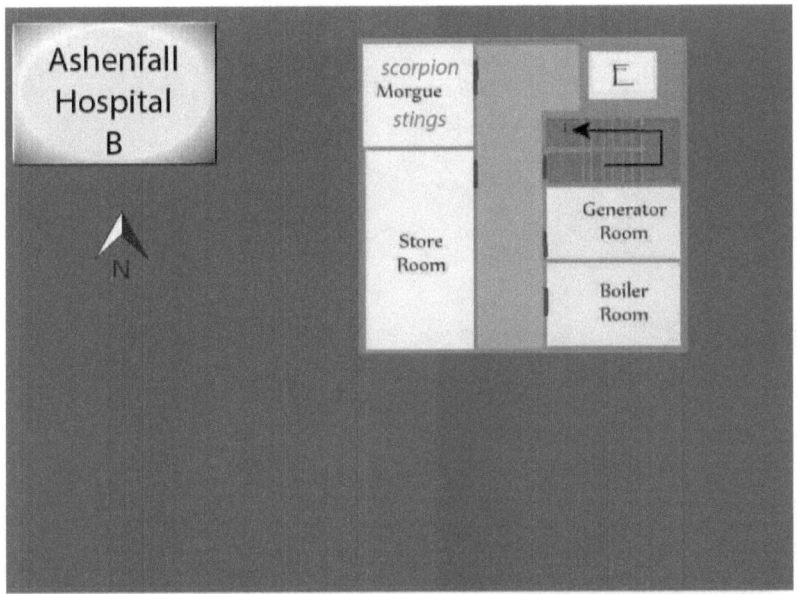

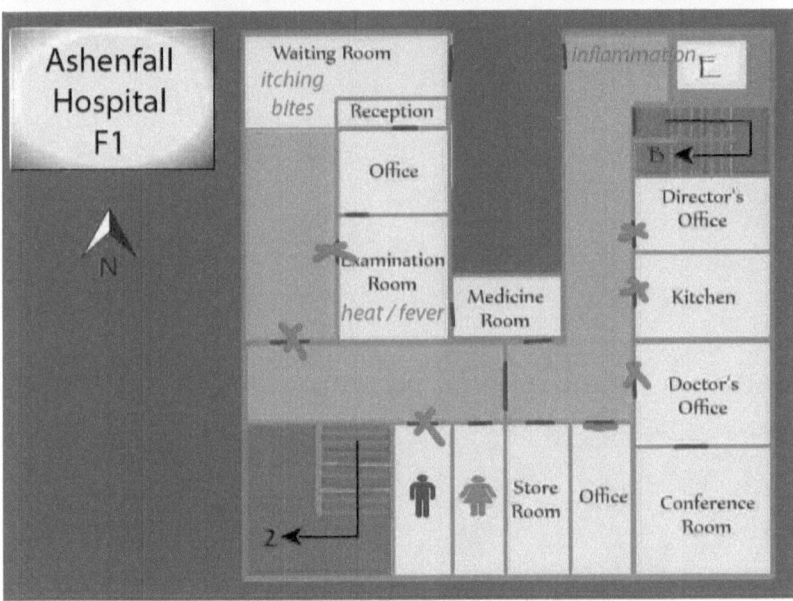

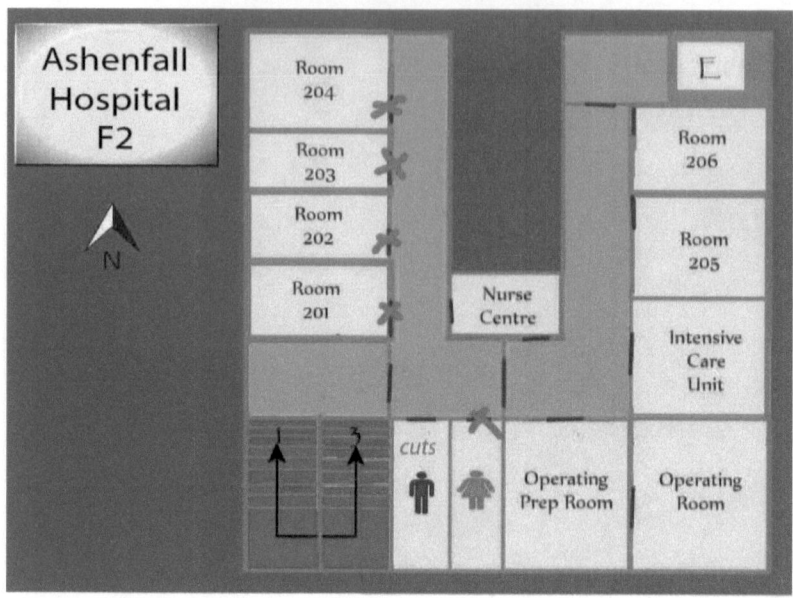

21

HEALING HERBS

"Dammit!" Trevor cursed loudly, rubbing his wrist as the cry echoed down the passage. In frustration, he threw the handle on the floor and kicked at the door.

Other than anger him further, his lash at the door did nothing. Like a kid denied a toy, he stomped towards the remaining two rooms in the passage, finding it locked. As if joining in the litany of forbidden access, the foyer door to the elevator was also locked.

"Ok, so what now?" he asked.

He pulled out the various maps to see if he had missed anything. There was only one section left that he had not been able to access: the east passage offices on the first floor. Remembering how the Transporter Key had taken him to the first-floor foyer passage, he turned to Room 206.

"Ok, so if I put you in here and unlock you...."

The door opened before him. Trevor aimed the Beretta forward and stepped in, leaving the door open behind him. It was definitely more of an office than a room. He walked to the desk before him and scanned the documents.

"Doctor Edward Hoffman?" he said in shock, reading from one of the medical reports. "Director of Ashenfall Hospital."

He picked up the report to make sure he had read it right. Taking out the tape player again, he listened to the start of the recording.

"This is Doctor Emily Hoffman."

Trevor wondered if and how they were related. He reviewed some further documents and papers, which only confirmed that he was in the Director's Office on the first floor.

When he passed the window sill, he saw a potted plant on it. It made him step back and look at it again.

"How is it that out of everything else that has gone bad in this place, you still look fresh and alive?" he said, noting how green the leaves looked.

He studied the pot and found a label at the bottom identifying the plant as basil. Trevor pulled out the note he had found with the pouch in the Examination Room and saw the herb's name on the list.

"That's strange," he remarked. "Philip must have needed you for some reason. Let's find out why."

Leaning forward, he snipped off some leaves by pinching his fingers on the petioles. When his fingers brushed over the leaves, he got the distinct smell of the basil in the air. It was a welcome change from the mustiness he had gotten used to.

He bunched the pieces of basil together and carefully pulled the sticky label off the pot. Wrapping the label over the petioles to keep them together, he placed the basil leaves in the pouch and closed it.

Not finding anything further of use in the office, he moved back out to the second floor and closed the door behind him. When he opened 205 with the Transporter Key, there was no doubt that he was in the Kitchen. The forlorn fridge and stove stood in the dank darkness before him.

Trevor inspected everything else first before he approached the fridge. He was almost too afraid to open it. There was blood dripping out the bottom of the refrigerator that looked as fresh as a recent cut. His fingers lingered on the handle while his other hand held the Beretta at the ready.

"Stop being stupid, Trevor," he said to himself. "With that much blood, surely whatever is inside here is dead already."

Encouraging himself didn't go very well. He still stood there with taut nerves, fearing that something would jump out at him. He readied his aim and jerked the door open, letting three bullets fly in anticipation and dread. The bullets ricocheted off the fridge's inside, one embedding itself deep into his shin.

"Ahhh shit!" he shouted, dropping down on his buttocks as he held the leg in pain. His eyes were moist from the agony that throbbed inside of it. "That was idiotic."

When the pain had subsided, he shone the light inside the fridge. There was no body inside of it or any evidence of what had caused the bleeding. Instead, there were three bushes tied by thin pieces of rope lying beside each other. The labels attached to them indicated that they were thyme, lavender and rosemary.

Trevor stashed them in the pouch and tried to stand, but it hurt too much. He realised that the leg needed medical attention if he was going to go any further, but he was in no mind to ask Philip for that help. He dug around in his bag and found a first aid kit.

After tending to and bandaging his wound, he tried to stand again. It felt better, and it was a lot easier to walk on. He returned to the second floor and then tried the key on the Intensive Care Unit's lock. The broken handle was still lying on the floor, but with the door unlocked, he simply pushed on it and entered the Doctor's Office.

The office appeared darker than any of the other rooms. The air pressed on Trevor and slowed him down. It felt like he would drop to his knees if the pressure increased by even a drop. He moved on regardless, shining the light on the desk ahead of him.

Going through some papers, he realised that the office had belonged to Philip at one point many years back. He had not been the only occupant, as some other files belonging to other doctors were stacked in one of the corners. Yet it was Philip's that lay across the desk as if he had been working on them the day before. The only testament to time and the untouched documents were the layers of dust that had collected on them.

He went through the titles of the books in the glass cabinet behind the desk. His eyes skimmed the spines, not expecting to find anything valuable when one of them suddenly proved him wrong. His fingers pulled it out before lying '*Medicinal Herbs of the Ages*' on the desk.

The content page listed the various herbs and medicinal plants under multiple categories. Pulling out the alchemical note, he looked for the section containing sweet basil and paged to it. He read through the text, wishing he had more light to enable him to work through it faster.

Near the end, he found a sub-heading indicating possible remedies. He read that among the afflictions it healed were poison and scorpion stings. He noted it on the paper. He worked through the remaining herbs in the same manner until he had written insect *repellent* by catnip, *fever* by sunflower, *remembrance* by rosemary, *wounds* by lemon thyme, and *anti-inflammatory* by lavender.

Happy with his findings and some semblance of success, he slammed the book shut and searched the room. Trevor's tension had not been relieved by discovering the list of herbal remedies. It bothered him extensively that he had not found Jay yet. After seeing the dead nurses and assuming Philip's role in them, he feared what Philip may have done to Jay on his arrival at the hospital.

He hastened his pace. In a corner by the door to the Conference Room, he found a potted plant with as much life as the basil. Finding the label identified as catnip, he broke off some leaves and tied the tag around the stalks before placing it in the pouch.

Trevor was busy calculating how he would enter the Conference Room from the second floor if he was barred from access when he found that it opened easily. Inside, he found a long meeting table with a device at the far end that he could not make out with the dim torch light.

As soon as he had entered the room, the heaviness from the Doctor's Office left him. It was easier to breathe and walk, alleviating the throbbing from his injured shin. He saw a lively sunflower in a tray bedded with soil on a table by the structural wall to the left.

The sunflower was huge. It was almost the same size as Trevor's head, and when he stood before it, he could look straight at it without looking up or down. Worried that something would try and stop him from taking the final item on the list, he quickly stripped the leaves off the stem.

While he tied the leaves together with the label, he saw the sunflower head dip down. He shone the torch on it to ensure his mind was not playing tricks on him. The flower continued to wilt, the petals falling to the soil beneath it. For a moment, he thought it was crying the seeds that fell, but closer inspection revealed that blood was raining down.

Not wanting to see it die further, he returned his focus to the room. He moved to the device at the other end of the table, watching for any items he could salvage. When he reached the device, he saw that it was a projector. Studying its sides, he discovered no power cord or audio-visual cables attached.

What he did find was a flash drive in the rear. Removing it from the port, he turned the drive around in his hand. He noticed a name etched on the underside and dropped it immediately, stepping away.

"Caroline," Trevor said, repeating the name he had seen.

Looking at the drive on the floor, he mustered some courage and picked it up. Torn between fear and desire to know what the drive would reveal, he placed it back in the port. He moved away to find a means to power the device when suddenly a blue light shone on the top surface of the projector.

Leaning over it, he saw that it was the power button. He pressed it, stepping back in fright as it switched on. The bulb shone the light on the wall ahead of it. It revealed two files that the drive contained: simply Session 1 and Session 2.

Trevor read the controls on the top surface and found the arrows and selection buttons. He selected the first file and activated it. The screen turned white and then revealed an office. Trevor sat down on a nearby chair, wishing for a moment that he had popcorn to accompany the movie.

That desire died immediately after that. He gaped silently as Caroline entered the room through the door to the side. She sat on a long, three-seater sofa and placed her hands on her lap.

"Welcome," a female voice said to the side of the device that was recording the footage. "I hope you don't mind the camera. I'm trying a new way to record my sessions. You know what they say about keeping with the times."

"That's alright," Caroline said. The smile that accompanied the words sent a sting of emotional pain through Trevor. He recalled how fond he had been of her. "We all need to evolve eventually."

"Indeed, yes," the voice replied. "So let's begin. I usually don't use real names for my sessions, but I guess the camera defies the reason for further confidentiality."

"It's ok; I'm happy with you calling me Caroline. These recordings are kept safe, aren't they?"

"Yes, of course," the voice assured. "So, why did you want to see me? I usually only see to those in the medical profession."

"Yes, I know," Caroline replied, looking down. "It's just…well, I know it's been a few years, but we grew up together. When I heard you were living nearby, I thought maybe you wouldn't mind."

"No, not at all," the voice confirmed. "So, what's troubling you, Caroline?"

"Well… it's my relationship."

"Ok," the voice said slowly. "Not really my strong suit, but let's see what I can do. What's wrong with your relationship?"

"I don't suppose you remember Kathy, the one that I told you about in high school?"

"Mmmm, yes, I do. Those were some painful memories. She was with you in Hollowbrook Elementary, if I recall?"

"Yes," Caroline responded, her voice a bit shaky. "I thought I was rid of her, and I thought the days of feeling like Raven were passed, but it looks like I am wrong."

"How so?"

"I've been seeing her around Ashbourne. At first, I thought maybe she was just passing through, but the sightings have become more regular."

"Ok. Do you fear she has moved to Ashbourne?"

"It's more than that," Caroline said, wringing her hands together. "If she had just moved into the neighbourhood, then maybe I could have gotten over it. Given time. But I've seen her with Trevor."

"Your boyfriend?"

"My husband," Caroline corrected. "We've been married two years now."

Her eyes got wet. The person next to the camera shifted in her seat and leaned forward to offer a tissue. Trevor hoped to see more of her, but her arm blocked most of the view. When she sat back, Caroline cleared her eyes.

"When I first saw them chatting in the shopping centre together during one of my breaks from work, I thought maybe they had just bumped into one another. You know, an unhappy coincidence.

"Yet, a week later, I saw them at a diner as I walked past it on the way to the bank. They were laughing together, waiting for their meals to arrive, most probably."

"So they became friends?" the voice asked.

"If it could only have been that," Caroline replied. "Their hands looked cosy together, and the only sign of agitation was from him looking around in fear of me seeing them."

"And did he spot you?"

"No, I was watching them from behind a wall," Caroline said, sounding embarrassed for having spied on them.

"Was there more? The hand gesture could have been him comforting her."

"I tried to convince myself in the same way, making several excuses for him."

"Did you ask him about it?"

"No," Caroline replied. "When you confront Trevor with such things, he.... Well, he doesn't become violent, but there's danger in his eyes. He turns it into a play of insecurities. I'm so afraid of losing him that I really don't want to bring it up."

"Ok. In my limited capacity on emotional matters, though, I think it would be a good idea if you spoke to him about it. It may be innocent. You won't know…"

"He's been coming home late at night," Caroline interrupted. "Says he has been hanging out with his friend, Jason. As much as I want to believe that, I doubt that a male police officer uses feminine perfume."

"Did you at least confront him about the scent?"

"I commented on it, but he waved it away with an explanation that Jay had some friends over who excessively applied their perfumes."

"Ok, I see why you would start questioning his fidelity," the voice said gently. "Unfortunately, as a therapist, I need to look at both sides of the story and see some benefit of a doubt."

"Come on, Emily," Caroline said. "Be reasonable. I know he's screwing her."

"That's your emotions speaking, Caroline," Emily said quickly. "You need solid proof."

"And until then? I just stand by and wait every night while she lies in his arms?"

"That's not what I was saying," Emily responded.

"I followed him one day," Caroline said, looking down at her hands in shame. "Kept my distance and all that. He entered a jewellery store that we used to visit regularly in the past.

"I waited until he left and then went to visit the teller. I explained that I was his wife and was too impatient to know what he had bought me. She told me it was a charm bracelet. Even told me which charms he had placed on it."

"And it wasn't meant for you?" Emily asked, to which Caroline lifted the sleeve of her jersey and revealed a charm bracelet around her wrist.

"I already have one," she explained. "It's been several days now, and I am sure it was meant for her."

"I don't know what to tell you, Caroline," Emily said, sighing. "Other than having a private investigator look into it, you don't have adequate evidence that he is actually having an affair."

"Well, Bishop offered to look into it."

"Your brother? I thought he left the family when you were still in Sacred Valley? Didn't he join the army or something?"

"Originally, yes," Caroline said. "But he was dismissed for being involved with a cult group that had formed. Something called The Zeph... well, I forgot what he called it."

Although Trevor could not see Emily, he heard the chair shift as her elbows pressed on the table beside her.

"The Zephyrite Conclave?" Emily asked, her voice seeping tension.

"Yes," Caroline frowned. "Do you know them?"

"I've heard of them," Emily said, her tone changing in warning. "Whatever you do, don't let Bishop get involved in this matter with Trevor."

Trevor had been hanging on every word near the end, also leaning forward like Emily did to make sure he didn't miss anything. As her last words ushered towards Caroline, the video ended. The screen returned to the file selection window.

He rushed over to the device and quickly pressed the down arrow to the next file. As he pressed play, a cross with red words appeared on the screen:

File is corrupted and cannot be opened

22

RAISING LAZARUS

Trevor took out the flash drive, hoping to look at it again once he left Sacred Valley. He wasn't sure what bothered him more: that Caroline had confided in a therapist regarding their relationship or that she had known Dr. Emily Hoffman. Before the call from Jay warning of the police report and his journey through Ashenfall Hospital, he did not even know that she existed.

It came to his mind that Philip may also have personally known Emily. Edward Hoffman was the former director of the hospital where Philip had worked, meaning he may have bumped into Emily or heard about her. And then there was the mysterious Patient XV007, or James, whom Trevor already had some assumptions about.

With all the listed ingredients in the pouch, he returned to the Conference Room door. As the torch was aimed directly ahead of him on the wall beside the door, he noticed a cabinet on it. He pressed his fingers on the side and pulled it open.

It was a key register. Trevor would have been happier to have found it had it contained more than one key. He pulled it down from its hook anyway, identifying it on the tag as the Intensive Care Unit's key. He placed it in the same pocket as the pouch and left the room.

He passed back through the Doctor's Office door to the second-floor passage and closed the door behind him. He pressed on the door of the Intensive Care Unit and found it locked again. Reaching into his pocket for the key he had discovered, he paused and looked down towards the Operating Preparation Room's door.

"Wait, there's something I want to see first," Trevor mused out loud.

He headed into the room and then into the main Operating Room. The two bodies with the afflicted arms were still lying there, lit by the overhead lights. Trevor walked slowly towards them, looking at the walls of the room. He shook his head and rubbed his eyes.

"I must be tired," he said, adding the torch's light to the walls to see if he was losing his mind.

The room looked dirtier. It was not so much as being untidy; the walls looked like they were slightly stained by the same blood and rust he had seen in the demonic version of the school. The walls and floors were intact, though, leading him to assume that perhaps he just had not seen it before.

Ignoring his potentially lapsing observation skills, he focussed on the manikins before him. He turned to the one on the left with the bitten left arm and rash marks all over. Retrieving the pouch, he worked through the note and took out the catnip meant to be used as an insect repellent.

Taking the leaves and rubbing them together in his hands, he pressed it against the human arm and moved it up and down the length. As he did so, he noticed the rashes sinking into the skin and fading away. After a moment, all that was left was a spotless manikin arm.

"Ok, not what I was expecting," Trevor said.

To further astonish him, the arm split off from the rest of the body. Trevor picked it up, looking for any sign of what he was meant to do with it. At a loss for the time being, he placed the arm in his bag.

Moving to the right arm, he looked up which item could heal lash wounds and retrieved the lemon thyme. In the same fashion as before, he rubbed the leaves together and pressed them up and down the fleshy arm. The lashes healed and closed up nicely, followed shortly by the human pores and skin turning into the PVC plastic of a manikin arm.

Once the arm had fallen off, Trevor placed it with the other one in the bag. He hastened now to the Operation Preparation Room, feeling like he was getting some form of finality with the body parts. There was a climax of anticipation building up inside of him, yet at the same time, he hoped the clues were not indicative of Jay's body being severed like the six victims.

He started with the first body on the left. Noting the swollen left leg, he pulled out the lavender and used it as an antiseptic. Trevor watched casually as the swelling went down until the leg was back to normal. The human skin transformed into plastic. As he claimed it and placed it in his bag, his radio began to sizzle.

He pulled the Beretta up and aimed it at the passage door to the room. The door was silent and stationary. The sizzle neither went louder nor softer, staying at the same pitch and frequency while he watched the door. When nothing appeared to be coming through it, he lowered his weapon.

Continuing with the manikins, he went to the middle one's human chest. He checked the list and then applied the sunflower leaves meant to remedy fevers. After rubbing it all over, he felt the skin as the temperature dropped to a deathly cold before turning into a manikin's chest and breaking loose from the rest of the body.

The radio's noise turned into a crackle and rose in volume. He turned around again, watching the door and waiting to see if anything would enter this time. With the Beretta aimed at the door, he had his finger at the ready. Once again, no one entered, but he felt something was waiting for him on the other side.

He approached the final body in the room. Its right leg had blue veins and swollen bumps. Trevor assumed it was the scorpion sting, and the blue veins represented the venom inside. He pressed the crushed sweet basil leaves over the leg, being rewarded with the vanishing of the veins and reduced swelling. Within moments, the manikin leg joined the other parts in his bag.

"Alright," he said as the radio heightened to a whining wail. "Let's go see what's bothering you so much."

He kept the radio on, wanting to gauge if the object causing the noise was moving at all. It stayed constant as he moved closer to the door, which caused Trevor some confusion. Reaching the door, he leaned down to open it carefully without lowering his aim.

The light shone into the passage. Nothing was immediately ahead of him, but the Nurse Centre door was open. He shone the light into the room as far as it could penetrate, but the dead nurses were still lying there as he had found them.

He suddenly heard a shuffle to his right and shifted the torch to face it. Standing by the Intensive Care Unit's door was a nurse. Her back was to him, but as the light hit her and the wall behind her, she turned around slowly to face him.

Unlike the other nurses, her face was clean. Her body showed no indication of any injuries, but her expression seemed blank. She lifted her hand up slowly, as if being controlled like a puppet, and then pointed at Trevor.

"You think I'm pretty, right?" she asked, moving an inch forward as if she really struggled with effort to do so. "Tell me, do you think I am pretty?"

He looked her up and down. There was a certain beauty in what he could see in the dark, lit only by the pistol's light. Her small, pursed lips were straight, with not even an indication of a smile. Her medium-length brown hair fell on her shoulders, tied in a neat bun at the back.

"Am I pretty?" she asked, reaching down to a pocket on the side of her uniform, pulling something small out of it.

It was a scalpel. The stainless steel item gleamed in the light as she brought the blade to her mouth in a flash without warning. Trevor gasped and held his hand over his mouth as she cut into one corner of her mouth and dragged the blade across. He recoiled into the wall behind him, wanting to close his eyes from the horrifying scene but afraid she would attack him while he did so.

"How about now?" she said, cutting the smile into the other side of her mouth. "They always say a smile makes you look beautiful. Do I look pretty now?"

He couldn't respond. The blood trickled down her neck as the flesh covering her gums split apart. She didn't show any sign that the injury was causing any pain.

An evil laugh erupted from her. It was a deep sound, like a demon who was quietly enjoying the visual torment Trevor was going through. It made him focus more on the nurse's body than face, just as she raised her scalpel and ran towards him.

"I ASKED YOU IF I LOOK PRETTY!" the demonic voice shouted, making the passage floor quake slightly under his feet.

He lifted his gun up and shot reflexively. The bullet went over her body, and then he shot twice again. The first of the two hit her in her left shoulder, causing her to stumble as the second hit her sternum. She wavered momentarily with the scalpel still raised high as Trevor pulled the trigger again.

The Beretta simply clicked. The magazine was empty. The nurse moved forward again, causing him to simply drop the Beretta to the floor and pull the Citori down. The torch's light played on her feet as she dragged them closer towards him. He pulled the trigger, receiving a click from the shotgun, too.

"What the hell, man?!" he shouted, dropping the Citori too and reaching for his crowbar.

The nurse swiped the blade sideways just as he brought the metal down on her arm. A loud crack of bone resounded down the passage, but the scalpel remained in her hand. It was as if she was impervious to pain. She swiped towards his belly this time, making him swerve the crowbar back to block it.

Taking the offensive, he brought the forked end down towards her head. She shifted to the left, and the crowbar connected with her shoulder. She buckled down from the impact, falling on one knee. Trevor moved forward just as she looked up and sliced at his right inner thigh.

He collapsed onto his back, holding the leg in agony. His eyes were brimming with tears as he tried to keep one eye on her while clutching the injury. She stood up over him and wielded the blade menacingly as if foreshadowing his approaching death.

In anger, he rolled off the bag on his back and swung the crowbar backhanded towards her knees. It caught behind one of them and made her sink again onto it. Without waiting for her to make a move, he brought the chiselled end up into her neck just behind the chin. The crowbar stretched through her head until it broke through the cranium. Pieces of bone flew up into the air, and blood splattered on Trevor's face. The radio's sound died away.

"How's that for beautiful, bitch?" he said as she fell to the floor on her side.

He stood up slowly, every injury screaming at him as he did so. He checked his bag for medical supplies and saw that he had one first aid kit and four medicinal bottles left. He considered heading down to the Lunar Nexus again, but the thought of doing so clashed with his impatience and the required effort to do so.

Not wanting to use the final kit yet, he decided to use one of the bottles. He slugged it down and enjoyed the bit of warmth that filled his body. It did not heal his wounds, but it gave him the strength to continue while he investigated the Intensive Care Unit.

Before proceeding, he dealt with his firearms. Three boxes of 9mm bullets left him with thirty of them. He filled the Beretta's magazine with one complete box and the half of another. From one of the two boxes of shells, he took out two and placed it in the Citori.

With the guns locked and loaded, the crowbar and shotgun back in place, and the bag returned to his back, he shone the pistol's torch ahead of him again. It was definitely easier to walk if one ignored the sharp pain that shot through his legs every now and again.

He used the key he had found in the Conference Room on the Intensive Care Unit's door. Walking in, he took a moment to view his immediate surroundings before approaching the manikin in the very centre of the room. There was an oval light fixture attached to the room's ceiling with four round lights fitted within it. It shone down directly on the sole manikin.

There was no doubt in Trevor's mind that it represented the final victim. The human head had been bashed in badly. It was beyond the point of recognition. His face looked like it had actually caved in. It was surreal standing there staring at the faceless man. It could have been anyone, even someone he might have passed in the streets.

Wanting to be rid of the scene before him, he pulled out the rosemary. He stared at it first, wondering how the herb's properties of remembrance could possibly heal the damage the head had sustained. Having no other recourse or possible solution at hand, he applied the herb to the head anyway.

As with the others, the head began to heal. He had hoped that the face would reveal the person's identity once the healing was done and before it transformed, but the manikin did the complete opposite. The head first turned into plastic before the indentation pushed out like a car being panel beaten. The head popped off the torso, waiting to be collected.

At a loss of what to do next, Trevor studied his maps again. He had almost been to every room. There was no sign of Jay being in the hospital yet. The only choice he had left was to face Philip with the parts he had collected and find out what was going on. Clearly, Philip had been keeping some things from him, which meant that he might have lied about Jay's whereabouts, too.

Remembering that Philip had locked the access to the Examination Room, he moved towards the Nurse Centre. The dead nurses still littered the floor. He made sure both doors were securely closed on either side of him before pulling out the Transporter Key.

He inserted the key into the door leading to the west passage and locked the door first. Then he unlocked it and opened it carefully. As expected, it opened up to the Examination Room. Not knowing what to expect or what Philip's response would be, he lifted the Beretta up again. When he was in the room completely, he closed the door behind him since he had no further plans to head to the second floor. Rechecking the door after that, he found it still locked.

Trevor placed the bag on the floor near the closest gurney with the indented mattress and wiped his brow. He was exhausted from everything that had happened in Sacred Valley. The more he tried to escape the town, the more it seemed to pull him in.

The sound of a door opening to his left that led to the waiting room passage brought him back to attention. The Beretta was up so quickly that Billy the Kid would have been proud. The dovetail three-dot sight at the end of the barrel was positioned to shoot the head off anything threatening that entered the room. He pressed his finger lightly against the trigger as the door opened further.

"Holy shit, Trevor!" Jeanette shouted, ducking down when she caught sight of the pistol.

"Sorry!" he shouted back, moving the gun down and then deciding to holster it. "I wasn't expecting you."

"That's alright," she replied, standing back up and moving closer to him. "I'm just as tense."

"Wait, what are you doing here?" he asked her and then looked at the door. "Was that door unlocked when you got here?"

"Yes, I only opened it now," she replied, frowning. "And I thought you'd be happy to see me."

"I am," he said, rubbing his brow again. He was developing a headache. "I just thought you were staying by the church where it was safe."

"Safe?" she looked at him and scoffed at him sarcastically. "Have you seen what it looks like out there?"

"Well, I haven't been on the streets in a while," he confessed. "Wait, how did you get in the hospital? Wasn't there a woman with spiders at the door?"

"Oh, honey," she said with a sympathetic look on her face. "You must have knocked your head real hard. What on earth are you talking about?"

Jeanette moved forward to inspect him. She looked into his eyes and felt his forehead. Her fingers gingerly trailed down his cheek as she moved it away. Suddenly, he felt awkward with the way she was looking into his eyes.

"You still haven't told me what you're doing here," he pursued, swallowing hard against her touch.

"I'm just looking for some safety," she said, moving closer to him, "and maybe some warmth."

Her fingers tugged at the collar of his shirt before moving down to the top's neckline underneath it. She teased his chest, and his muscles responded by heaving out towards her.

"Tell me, Trevor," she whispered as she moved towards his ear, her body pressed firmly against him as his arms enclosed around her waist. "Can your arms keep me safe? Can you keep me warm?"

The desire overpowered him. He could feel every curve of her body; the rise of her buttocks under her jeans, the firm shape of her breasts against his ribs, the tease of her lips on his cheek as she withdrew from his ear.

When her mouth passed his, he succumbed to her. Their lips pressed against each other and parted open until their tongues caressed the moisture inside. His hand clenched her lower cheeks, massaging them open and closed. She groaned against him as she pushed him onto a vacant gurney and climbed on top of him without a breath to spare in between.

Straddling his hips with her knees, she continued to kiss him passionately. She felt his hardness between her legs and rubbed herself slightly against it. Now it was his turn to moan as he felt the pressure against him, his hands running up to feel her breasts.

He moved his hands down her sides in an attempt to take her clothes off, when they both jumped at the sound of a door opening.

Jeanette looked over her back towards the reception office, followed shortly by Trevor looking to his side.

"Philip?" Trevor said, seeing the look of shock on his face.

"You know her?" he asked Trevor, moving away from the office door around them towards the Medicine Room. He was fiddling with something in his side pocket.

"Yes," Trevor replied, sitting up with Jeanette still warm against his groin. "The question is, do you?"

"Don't do this, Philip," Jeanette said, raising her palm to caution him.

As if her words had prompted him, he pulled a revolver out of his jacket and aimed it at her. Jeanette hid her head in Trevor's arms that pulled around her protectively.

"Don't you mean James, Emily?" Philip asked as he reached the Medicine Room door. With a free hand, he pulled out a ring of keys and worked through them.

"Emily?" Trevor looked down at her as she looked up into his eyes. "Doctor Emily Hoffman?"

"Of course, Trevor," Philip replied on her behalf. "You don't think she really means to sleep with you, do you? Who do you think informed the police of what happened to Bishop?"

"Wait, what?" Trevor said, letting go of her and rubbing his forehead again. Philip had found the key and unlocked the door. "How does she know about Bishop?"

"That's irrelevant now," Philip responded, opening the door and aiming the gun at Emily again.

"So it was you?" Trevor pursued. "You're the serial killer that murdered all those victims."

Philip's body seemed to relax. His stare became emotionless as he looked at Trevor. There was a resolution in his eyes that Trevor could not read, but it appeared fatal.

"So," he finally uttered, "you now know about those. Well done, Trevor. I honestly thought you would get done looking for Jay and then be on your way. But now it seems you two are working together."

"No, Philip, it's not like that," Trevor corrected him.

"Don't lie to me!" Philip yelled, emphasising his aim at them. "You two were about to fornicate on that gurney, and not long after you lost my sister!"

"Philip, please calm down," Emily said, gesturing with her hands.

"Don't tell me to calm down," he said. "There's only one thing left to do."

"Philip, no," Trevor begged, but Philip's eyes were as determined as ever.

When Trevor saw the revolver move up to shoot at them, Trevor grabbed the sidebar of the gurney and rolled to his side, using his other hand to hold onto Emily. The bed rolled with them as they fell over to the floor, and shots sounded within the room.

The impact with the tiled floor was harder than he had expected, and he wondered if one of the bullets hadn't hit him. Then his legs reminded him of his earlier injuries, but he held onto Emily, who was curled like an infant in his arms.

Trevor tried to reach his Beretta, but it was lying under his right hip. He shifted slightly when two more rounds went off. Emily was lying too tightly against him for him to get to the pistol.

Suddenly, he heard footsteps move towards them and looked up. Philip stood in the middle of the room with the revolver pointing down at them. Trevor feared more for the woman in his arms than himself. He knew he could get resurrected by the Lunar Nexus and just deal with Philip afterwards, but he was unsure if she had touched it at all.

Philip pulled the trigger, and a click resounded in the room. Without wasting a moment, Trevor pushed Emily off him and pulled out his pistol. He was about to shoot when Philip threw the revolver towards him, making him swerve his head down. When Trevor looked up again, Philip had run into the Medicine Room.

"Emily," Trevor said, looking towards her. "Are you ok?"

"Yes, I will be fine," she said, moving into his arms again. He held her firmly as she hid her face in his chest.

"Wait, hold on," he said, pulling her out of his comfort. "There are some things I need to know."

"Of course," she said, running her hands down his arms until it was by his fingers. She held them lovingly.

"How on earth do you know about Bishop?" he asked. "It couldn't have been in a session with Caroline. She never knew."

She smiled. It wasn't the soft, loving smile to accompany the touch of her hands. The more Trevor looked down at it, the more it resembled the smile from the graveyard. Wondering what had caused the transition, he got a fright when she suddenly twisted the Beretta out of his hand and aimed it at him.

"Ah, not again," Trevor said, his hands raised. "What are you doing?"

"Getting out of here before it's too late," she replied with the same maliciousness on her face.

Trevor turned his head as a siren sounded from somewhere outside on the streets. Emily opened the door to the reception passage, her eyes on him with every step. The siren bleated for a second time.

"There's something more powerful at work than you can ever imagine," Emily said, looking down at his duffel bag beside the gurney. "You should have just left Jay and found your own way out."

Trevor prepared himself for the right moment. She gave him one last leer as she banged the door closed and ran. He sped to the right, running through the open office doorway Philip had forgotten to close. He sprinted to the door that led to the reception and turned the round knob, releasing the latch and unlocking it.

With haste, he jumped over the reception counter into the waiting room. He glanced around in the dark, having left his torch in the duffel bag. With the little he could see from the glowing Lunar Nexus, he peered down the passage for any sign of her movement.

Confounded, he tried the main entrance doors, which were still locked. He clenched his fists, wondering how she had moved that quickly. He stepped towards the Lunar Nexus and placed his palm on it. The warmth healed his wounds and even made his ire dissipate with it.

He walked back slowly to the Examination Room, remembering how she had looked at his bag and made a reference to Jay. He stood there, looking down at the bag for a long while.

"Jay, I really hope it's not you," he said, finally opening the bag and taking the manikin parts out.

The gurney in front of him was the one with the indentations in the mattress. One by one, he placed the body parts down. He started with the chest, followed shortly by the left leg. He watched nonchalantly as the joint of the leg melded and merged with the waist of the torso. He then added the right leg in its place in the indentation and saw that it did the same.

He placed both arms beside the torso and leaned down to retrieve the head as the arms joined the body. The head was the final piece of the puzzle, but Trevor was too afraid to attach it. The siren was still sounding on the streets, but the haste he should have felt by its foreshadowing was numbed by the fear of completing the manikin.

Deciding to get it over with, he placed the head in its place. It slotted in, the manikin lying there in one piece and looking up at the ceiling. Trevor waited for something to happen, bending down to close his bag when a soft glow on the floor beneath the gurney caught his attention.

The light wasn't coming from the floor, but rather from something underneath the gurney itself. He bent further down to look up at it. His eyes went wide. It was the same triangular design that he had seen on the school's roof, which had turned the seven Cu Siths into the fierce, fiery seven-headed Teju Jagua.

"No!" he shouted and jumped up. Not trusting the symbol and not wanting to wait to see if it was Jay or not anymore, he reached forward to rip the manikin apart again.

The manikin responded by suddenly grabbing his arm to stop him. Trevor tried to release the grip, but the manikin had unusual strength. Human eyes flashed on its face, followed shortly by a mouth and nose. Hair proceeded to grow out of its forming human skin, its fingers refusing to loosen its grip.

The need to be released evolved into desperation. The body was almost near complete transformation, the man lying nude and shaking as the power of the symbol beneath him transferred into him. Trevor not only realised that it was not Jay but instantly knew who it was once the face was complete and the tattoo on his right arm appeared.

He banged his fist on the arm that held him, making Bishop shout out as he let go. Trevor ran for the closest door behind him, frantic to escape from him as quickly as possible. A scorching sound made him look back; everywhere around Bishop's immediate vicinity, the walls, floor and ceiling were starting to tear apart. The rest of the room seemed fine; only the parts in his close radius were affected.

Trevor ran through the Medicine Room and into the east wing passages, feeling his pocket to ensure he still had the Transporter Key. He grabbed the handles of the double doors and pulled. It was locked again.

"Dammit, Philip!!" Trevor shouted, bolting around down the dark passage towards the elevator.

When he reached it, he pressed the button to call it back down from the third floor. Nothing happened. The buttons were not lit, and there seemed to be no electricity again.

"Shit, the power must have tripped again," Trevor muttered.

He was about to head down the stairs to the Generator Room when he heard movement at the end of the passage. Soon, a red eerie light lit the walls, floor and ceiling as Bishop turned into view with the bed sheet wrapped around his waist like a frock. His very essence seemed to exude evil and was tearing the hospital apart around him, turning it into the same metallic, rusty, and bloody version Trevor had seen at the school.

He saw that, as soon as Bishop had moved well enough ahead from the area he had been standing in, the former area returned to its normal state. It was like he was walking in his own cloud of devastation.

The siren rang louder through the streets as if to announce his approach. Trevor remained where he was, simply watching him come closer. He knew that even if he made it down to the generator, he would never get past Bishop back to the elevator.

He welcomed the death about to be handed to him, safe in the knowledge that he would simply resurrect at the Lunar Nexus. That would also give him a chance to get to the Examination Room, claim his bag and thereby retrieve his shotgun to use against the foe before him.

Bishop stopped when he reached him. Trevor expected him to leer at him or give some expression other than a blank one. Yet something shifted in the façade before him. A portion of the manikin's face shifted back before Bishop regained control of it.

Yet even that control came at a cost. The deformation of reality around Bishop waned slightly and closed to some extent. It was then that Trevor realised that the power Bishop had received to have an effect in the foggy world was limited and temporary.

It gave him hope. He jumped to the side to bypass Bishop when Bishop's hand stretched like a harpoon and clutched Trevor by the throat. Despite the drop of power a moment before, his strength was unbelievable. Trevor gasped for air and struck weakly at Bishop's wrist.

His power faded slightly further. The corruption around him decreased in radius. Trevor also felt his grip lessen. Bishop lifted his free hand and looked at his palm. Trevor joined his gaze and looked at it, too. In the very centre, painted in blue, was the Lunar Nexus with just Philip's name. As Trevor shouted out in defiance, Bishop slapped the symbol onto his forehead.

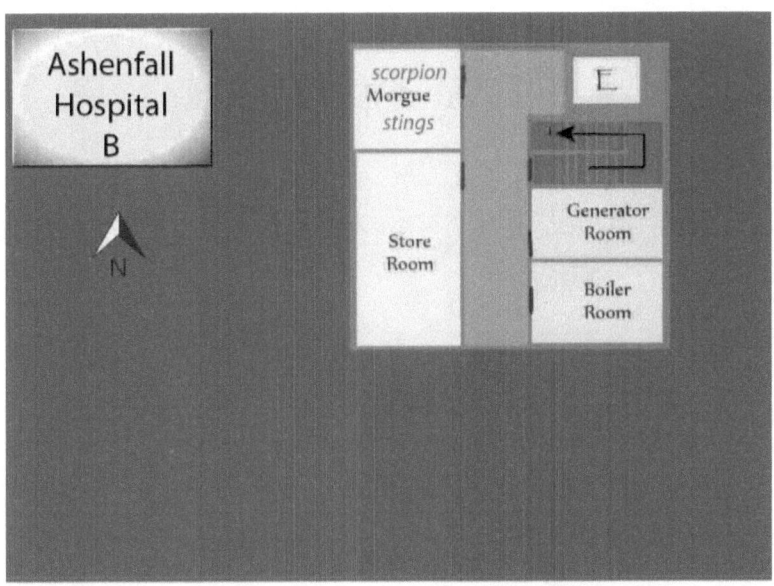

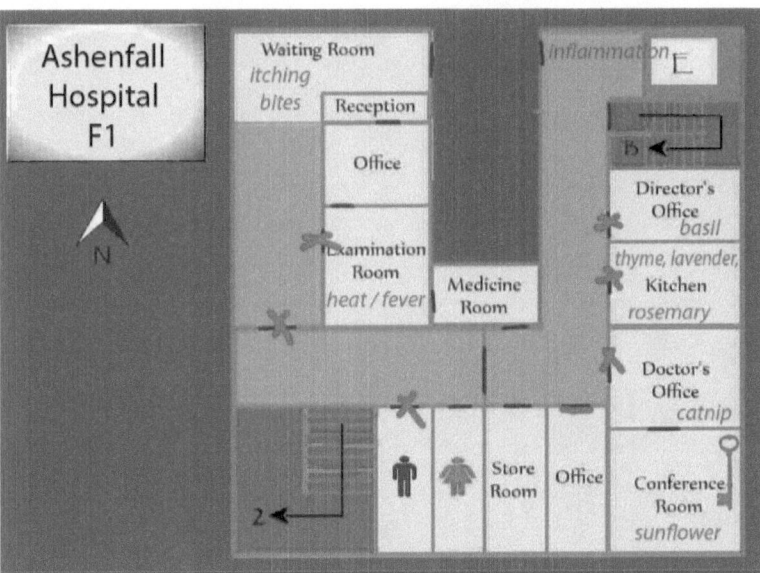

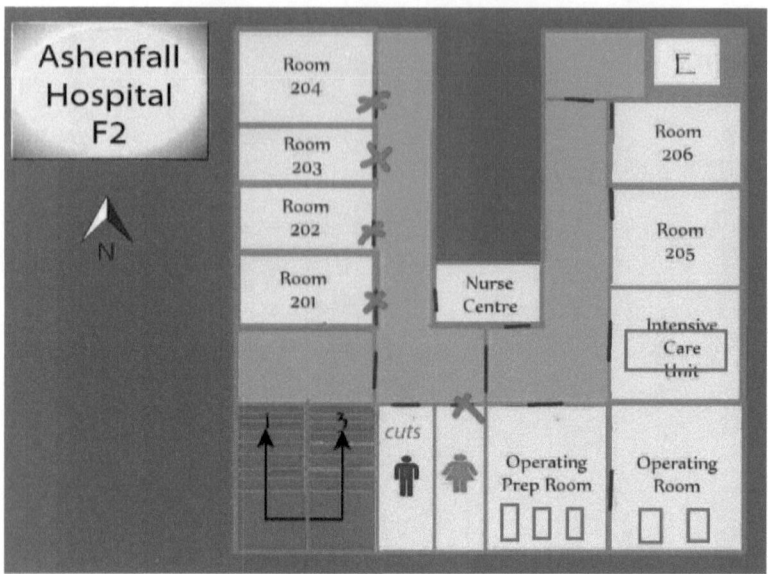

23

THE SEVERED PATIENTS

The impact of the hand on his head made him fall down with his back to the wall. Everything around him was shaking, with floors, ceilings and walls stripping away like the school had done before. The siren was louder now than the radio's crackling sound, bringing decay, corrosion and spalling in the formwork.

Trevor looked up slowly. Bishop was vanishing before him like a spirit moving on to another dimension. This time, he had a massive grin on his face as he turned around, walked away from Trevor and vanished entirely from sight.

With his focus on the space Bishop had occupied, he realised that the passage ahead of him was blocked just past the stairs leading down to the basement. The elevator doors were closed to his left, as was the exit door to his right. Trevor stood up, using the wire mesh on the wall behind him as support. Once he was able to stand freely, the siren came to an end.

The walls had fallen away to his left. He could see that the lift shaft's mechanisms and steel were surrounded by sharp spikes and barbed wire. On some of the barbs, there were pieces of clothing and rotten flesh. The elevator doors were rusted, some spots showing large holes where the decay had really taken its toll.

There was a red light coming from beneath the floors. It glowed under the mesh, steel formwork, and cages he walked on. The door to his right had blood dripping down the sides of the frame itself.

Trevor broke his study of the hellish hospital to check his inventory. The hospital maps were still in one pocket, while the Transporter Key and flash drive were in another. The alchemical pouch was in a fore pocket. He had no weapons or medicine on him. The radio whined on his side, but he was unsure if it indicated creatures being near him or just the demonic state of the world around him.

He tested the steel bars up and around him to see if he could break them off as a crude weapon. They were stuck on tight, and no amount of force on his part would separate them. He treaded carefully to the elevator and pressed the button that was also burning a maroon red instead of its usual yellow.

The doors budged slightly but would not release. He kept pressing it in case it would break loose, but it refused to open. Trevor peeped through some of the holes in the doors to see if he could spot anything inside of it. By one of the lower apertures, he saw a leg. It was lying against the opposite elevator wall. Who it belonged to and whether the person was alive still could not be determined.

Testing the exit door also failed to provide positive results, so he moved towards the rubble ahead of him. He wanted to do as much as he could to avoid the basement. The radio's whine continued at the same frequency and pitch, never relenting or reducing. He began to pull on the large slabs and rebars that had collapsed from the floor above, but it was pointless. They were too heavy.

Sighing in resignation, he walked down the steps. Some of them were broken, the fiery red light burning underneath it. Looking down, it seemed as if it would be a long fall. He could not detect what was causing the light. From the heat, he wondered if it was from some source of fire.

The basement floor was very open. All the inner walls were gone, with only the outer structural walls still in place. The walls were covered with square wooden frames that housed large sheets within them. And on the sheets were splashes and drabs of blood, as if someone had taken to abstract wall painting.

Even though the inner walls were gone, the steel formwork filling the supporting columns was still in place. As Trevor's feet landed on the floor from the last step, he saw the corpse refrigerators on the wall ahead of him where the morgue's room had been. Most of the trays were open and broken, either having collapsed with one side on the floor and the other in their respective cabinet or completely destroyed and lying in a smouldering metallic heap.

Turning to the left, he could see the rest of the other rooms' contents between rows of spalling columns. To his right, next to the morgue, was the former Storeroom. Broken cabinets and filing systems were strewn all over the floor. To the left was the generator, somehow rumbling with power and vibrating the caged floors underneath him.

Walking down the open passage, he saw the burners of the Boiling Room at the end. It was fired up, fuelled by something that Trevor could not see. Its noise joined that of the generator and his radio, making Trevor wish he could find something to cover his ears and dampen the sound.

He reached the end of the passage. Behind the final column by the burners, he saw an axe embedded in the steel. Wondering how the axe could have penetrated the metal, he gripped the handle and pulled on it. With a metallic zing, the cutting edge slipped out of its slot. The weight of it caused Trevor to drop it slightly before he lifted it up again.

It looked more like a fireman's axe than a lumber axe or splitting mall. It had a black leathery grip covering the lower end of a red handle. The pick and mid part of the head were also painted red, but it was smudged with rust along the upper edges of the head. The blade was sharp and clean, as if it had recently been maintained.

While Trevor felt the weight and balance in his hands, he heard a loud crash coming from the morgue' area. It was shortly followed by one of the fridge trays flying across the passage into the stairs. He gripped the axe, diving behind the column he had found it in and standing up as straight as he could.

He dared to look at what was causing the commotion. Peering around the side of the column, he saw a beast moving along the far wall towards the stairs. It stood and walked like a human, but the top where its shoulders met held no neck or chin. Instead, the deformed forehead bulged forward on its chest like a reverse hunchback.

The forehead held no eyes, but the mats of hair were stringed like chest hair on a torso. Two slits underneath the hair represented the nostrils, and a large deep hole on the belly served as its mouth. The upper and lower ends held huge fangs that were buckled and skewed. The chin replaced the groin area on a body that was uncovered and nude.

Despite the creature moving towards the stairs, there was still a noise emanating from the morgue's fridges. Trevor shifted his gaze to the morgue just as the creature transformed into a trail of black smoke and blew up the stairs like a wisp.

The object causing the upheaval finally made an appearance. He was slightly taller and bulkier than Trevor. To all appearances, he was human, except for the large scorpion tail that hung from his rear to over his head. He was also completely nude, but his groin and hips were covered with green arachnid plates or segments.

Besides the fleshy hole by the heart chamber, the most significant feature of the monster to Trevor was his right leg. It had the same blue veins and swollen spot that the manikin leg with the scorpion sting had had. Humouring himself by wondering if the herbs would help, he quickly jumped back behind the column when the man looked his way.

Trevor could hear him coming closer, remembering only then that his radio was still on. It had been drowned out by the burner and generator, but as the scorpion victim approached, it got louder.

"Shut up!" Trevor shouted softly, reaching down and switching it off quickly.

He was breathing heavily while trying to calm down. The wall sheets offered no reflection to help him see if it was still heading towards him. He kept his head to the right side and angled to anticipate an attack. The axe felt secure against his chest.

A shuffle to his left made him jump out of his hiding spot. He had tried to catch Trevor from the other side of the column, but his feet had clanged on the cage floor, giving away the element of surprise. Trevor was back in the passage when the scorpion man jumped back in front of him to block him off the stairs.

The tail lashed out at him, and Trevor dodged to the left, knocking it down like an amateur with the side of the axe. Bunching up a fist, the man hit at Trevor's face. Trevor ducked into a kick towards his belly. His back slapped into the sheeted wall behind him, and he recovered in time to miss another sting lash.

Taking this as his opportunity, he swung the axe into the man's ribs. The weapon bit in nicely, but the beast simply stared down at him as if he had been pinched. No blood dripped out of him. Pulling the axe out again, he lost his breath as he was kicked into the storeroom section and fell over the fallen cabinets.

He stood up slowly, feeling like an old man whose joints refused to move. Hefting the axe into attack position again, he saw something glint on the wall beside him. There was a small key locker with the door open, and the object that had caught his attention was a key within it.

The beast quickly recalled his focus as it charged through the rubble at him. The sting flew out at his head this time, making Trevor duck again. The sting made contact with a broken column behind him, becoming lodged within it. It grunted and growled as it tried to pull the tail out.

Striking again, Trevor brought the axe down on the tail. There was a rush of joy as the axe fell, hoping it would help put the victim down. Much to his consternation, the axe bounced back off the hard shell of the tail.

"What the hell?!" Trevor shouted as it managed to break the tail free from the steel. A fist caught him in the right cheek and then in his chest, making him fall back again.

The beast loomed over him on the floor as it stepped forward. The leer on its face spelled out Trevor's defeat. Quietly, he shifted the axe in his hand on the floor until the pick was facing forward. He watched the tail carefully, knowing it was the beast's best arsenal.

As predicted, the tail struck. Trevor rolled forward and brought the axe before him, slashing into the infected leg. The beast howled in pain as the pick dug into the injured limb. It seethed through its teeth as it tried to regain its composure, but Trevor had already removed the axe and brought the sharp blade edge down on it again.

This time, it sank down on its knee. Trevor gripped the axe harder and brought it down again. The scream rose above the grinding of the burners and generator, shaking the rooms around them like a quake. Not intimidated by its roar, he brought the axe down from over his shoulder to slice through the upper part of the leg.

The blade bit right through it. The beast fell to the ground, writhing in pain. The cry began to soften in volume, with the tail washed out like acid onto the steel underneath them. Its body decomposed into the cages, its meat and flesh sliding over the mesh until it fell into the fiery depths below.

Yet, the single leg remained. As with the manikin in the Operating Rooms before, the infected leg turned into plastic. Trevor picked it up, frowning heavily.

"No ways, man!" he said in anger. "I'm not collecting dummy parts again!"

To affirm his stance, he took the leg and slammed it against the closest column. The PVC shattered, sending the pieces showering around him onto the floor. Trevor held the foot and ankle portion that was still intact in his hand, regaining his breath.

Something slipped out from inside the foot. Trevor bent down and picked up a white disc the size of a large coin. On the one side of it was imprinted the image of a plant, while the other side had the letter B embedded on it. Too worried that the information was important, he pulled out the basement map. Where he had indicated the scorpion victim's ailment before, he scribbled the same letter underneath it. He placed the coin in the alchemical pouch.

Trevor moved to the key cabinet and claimed the key within it. There was no label to indicate what it opened, but he kept it in his pocket anyway. The other hand brought the axe up as he headed back to the stairs.

When he reached the first floor again, he saw the creature with its head hunching out its chest. Its great maw gaped at him as it turned to the elevator. It transformed again into black smoke as it travelled through one of the door's gaps. After a moment, the elevator shook violently before simmering down again.

The black smoke flew back into the passage and over Trevor's head. He ducked, but it passed by him without harming him. Instead, it flew into a space it found in the rubble to the other side of the passage. He was about to inspect the space when the elevator creaked. Suddenly, the doors began to open. Trevor saw two hands grab the insides of the doors and jerk it wide open.

Like Bishop had done, another nude man emerged from the elevator with a bed sheet wrapped around his waist. He wasn't as muscular as Bishop and was slightly shorter than Trevor. Two things caught his immediate attention about the man, though. First was the crude steel bar he had in his hand as a weapon, and second was the swollen left leg that made the man limp. The only thing it did share with the previous victim was the hole by its sternum.

"Anthropophage," Trevor muttered, recalling the creature whose head was seated in its chest above the large mouth. He remembered that it was known for herding its cattle of souls that it collected from the dead. It also had the ability to raise those souls back into animation.

His recollection of mythology was cut short when he was reminded of the victim ahead of him. It charged forward at a sickly gait on its swollen leg, the steel bar raised for the attack. Trevor swung the axe up to hit the bar away and then brought the pick down in a reverse motion.

The pick got stuck in the man's shoulder, but it simply looked at him and grinned. It struck Trevor in the chest with a fist, sending him stumbling back and losing his grip on the axe. With his weapon standing out of its shoulder like a flagpole, the beast struck again with the steel bar.

Trevor dodged under it until he was behind the victim. When it turned around to face him, he pulled the axe out. It struck again with the bar, striking Trevor's left ulna. The impact made him drop the axe and hold his forearm against his chest as the pain passed through him. He hardly had time to recover before it attacked again.

This time, he dodged to the right and swung the axe into its left leg. It screamed and dropped the steel bar, falling to the ground as it held its leg in agony. Trevor yanked the blade out and swung down again. In a fit of adrenaline, he pummelled the axe down thrice until the leg finally split from the hip.

The final screams died down. He watched as the man looked up at him in its final moments. The skin flaked off the body, much like the paint and plaster of the hospital did when it had transformed. The flesh melted away onto the caged floor below and passed through it. In the end, only the plastic leg remained.

Trevor swung the axe down and smashed it. He picked up the lower end of the foot and looked inside. There was a violet disc inside of it. Retrieving it, he inspected the sides. On the one was the insignia of another plant, while the other had the letter L.

After storing it in the pouch, Trevor looked around and jumped back in fright. A red ghostly figure that looked like Philip was staring at him. After a brief smirk, ghost Philip turned to the single door behind him and walked through it.

Trevor pulled out the key he had found in the basement. This was the only door available to use it in. Hoping for the best, he moved towards it and placed the key into it. He heard a click as the door unlocked.

Keeping the key on him, he opened up the door. He had expected to be taken outside to the yard in front of the hospital. He brought the axe up immediately, wondering if he would see the spider woman again. Once the door swung open completely, he brought the axe down again.

He walked forward into the reception area. Frowning, he closed the door behind him and opened it again. It definitely opened up to the east wing again. Somehow, the yard was gone, and the exit and entrance doors were connected. He closed the door again and locked it, ensuring anything he missed couldn't follow him through.

Trevor first stared at the reception counter, hoping to see the Lunar Nexus. The counter was torn to shreds and lying in a splinters pile. He looked down at the radio and switched it back on. It was still crackling but not wailing loudly in warning.

The waiting room was just as disastrous as the basement. The same caged floor was beneath him, but several sections had fallen away at some point, leaving gaps in some corners and other areas of the floor. Fearing what would happen if he dropped into the fiery depths below, he made a mental note to steer clear of the edges.

The walls were not covered in sheets this time. Here, the plaster on the walls drooped down from them like broken flags. Trevor saw a red tinge to them and looked closer at the wall beside him.

"That's not plaster!" he said quickly, stepping away. "That's flesh!"

He was about to step forward when movement from the side passage caught his attention. It was the anthropophage again. It watched him with an eyeless face as it moved behind the splintered counter and bent down behind it. Its arm reached down towards something Trevor could not see. When it was done, it floated into the air like smoke and returned down the passage.

The radio cried out in warning. A nude man arose from behind the splinters, his waist also covered by a bed sheet. This one was Trevor's height with a bit more meat on him than the last victim. In his hand, he had a thin, two-edged sword that reminded Trevor of a Chinese sword he had once seen.

He was inspecting the hole in its sternum when movement on its back brought his eyes up. Four large transparent wings flapped and spread out behind it, two on either side. As it rose into the air over the gaps in the floor, Trevor raised the axe in preparation. He spotted the mosquito-bitten left arm.

It flew straight for him and swung the sword at his head. He ducked and brought the axe up at its belly, but it swerved away and flew around. It aimed for him and swung again. He blocked the sword with a swipe of the axe, hoping to hit the weapon out of its hand, but it was too challenging from below.

With the need to ground the beast, he ran after it as it turned away for another swoop around the waiting room. Trevor lifted the axe and hacked at one of the lower wings. It didn't break the wing off but dented it enough that the man fell from the air and connected hard with a cage below.

Taking the opportunity, Trevor swung the axe over his shoulder to slice at the arm underneath him but missed sight of the sword that cut into his right side. He hissed in pain, stepping back to inspect the wound. Only the tip had entered his flesh. Bolstered by the successful attack, the man stood up before using its remaining three wings to lift him up again.

Trevor bent down to miss another stab at him and twisted around. He didn't want to give it a chance to turn away from him. He attacked the upper wing on the same side, making sure to hit it hard enough. It dented in, too, causing the beast to fall down again.

Instead of touching down on one of the cage tops, it just missed the edge and fell into a gap in the floor. It caught the ledge just in time but had to let the sword go. The weapon fell to the depths below it as he brought the infected left arm up to grab the metallic edge for further support.

It started to pull itself up when it screamed from a biting pain in the left shoulder. Trevor had started hacking away at it already. The axe bit in deep, one swipe at a time, cutting through the flesh and meat until the arm was completely severed.

Its cries broke through the waiting room and washed down the passage. Trevor kicked at the fingers of the right hand until the beast let go. The scream joined it down towards the fires below. When it finally died out, and the radio dropped to a soft crackle again, the fingers that still clung to the steel grid turned into plastic.

He picked it up quickly, afraid the coin inside would fall out. Inspecting it, he saw that the shoulder joint was sealed. He smashed it on the floor beneath him and shook the remainder of the arm until the item dropped onto his palm. It was a red coin with a different plant on one side and the letter C on the other.

Progressing down the passage, he noticed fewer holes and damage to the walls and floors. The sense of evil, rust and grime was still evident along sections of the wall, but the peeling flesh and steel grids were minimal.

In contrast to the stark, hellish state of the hospital were six portraits that hung on the right wall of the passage. He first encountered a nurse in her uniform standing beside a chair. She had her apron raised seductively to reveal her right leg, the foot resting on the seat of the chair and her hand trailing the revealing skin of the leg. Her lips were closed, blood trailing off the corners into an elongated smile.

The following portrait also had a nurse with a bloody smile under a gaze that begged the viewer to touch her. She was closer in the picture, running her hands up her right arm. Where her fingers had passed, there were small rivulets of blood in the wake of her nails.

The third portrait had a nude nurse sitting on a chair placed backwards. The chair's back blocked her abdomen and groin from view, but her breasts were placed over the top of the chair. The nurse clutched her breasts provocatively with fingers wide open, the curves held firmly like a basketball in a wide grip. Her head was tilted back slightly, the torn smile leering at him with the promise of passion.

The next two nurses replicated the first two but in a mirrored fashion. Where the right leg and arm had been displayed before, it was done with the left arm and leg facing the other way. This left Trevor with the final portrait opposite the Examination Room door at the end of the passage.

The background of the portrait was black with shades of red mist. It only revealed a nurse's head and neck with the shoulder line. The nurse had a white mask over her mouth. Her beautiful amber eyes complemented faultless skin on her gorgeous face. Cursive words were eerily written in thin blood across the mask:

Am I pretty now?

Feeling uneasy from how the nurse stared at him, he entered the Examination Room. The floor was solid here, and the walls were completely enclosed. The floor tiles had blood-red grouting, while the red walls were tainted with scratches of black. The room was so darkly enclosed that he felt claustrophobic within it.

The three gurneys were the only items in the room, enhanced by the light fixtures on their stands that provided the only light in the room. The lights were flickering, adding to the scary atmosphere. Only the middle gurney was occupied with a man lying under the covers.

Trevor felt a dark presence move in the room. Even by the dim light provided by the stuttering lights, he could see a plume of smoke move over the man. Instead of becoming solid, it simply hovered over its face and breathed an air of darkness into the corpse's open mouth and nostrils.

The man gasped for air as he sat up. The anthropophage's spirit moved out of the room into the Medicine Room. Trevor wielded the axe protectively again as the radio rose into a piercing whine. The man threw the covers off, revealing his nudity and absent heart. He waited for it to grab a weapon, but it just stood there staring at him.

Then fire broke from its chest. The flames engulfed the torso, but the man showed no sign of being burned. He raised his right hand in a manner that looked like an invisible ball was held within its fingers. A ball of fire formed within it, which was thrown towards Trevor.

It hit his shoulder just as he jumped to the side. His shirt caught alight, and he continued to roll in an effort to kill it. The shirt was badly torn and ripped. When he rose from the floor Trevor pulled the shirt off and threw it to the floor, satisfied with just having his top on.

Another ball of fire arced towards him, but he dodged it just in time. Facing the victim, Trevor realised the predicament he was in. To dislodge the torso, he would have to sever all of the other parts first. He had no further time to contemplate how enormous the task felt as more flames were hurled at him.

He ran forward and slashed the blade of the axe across its cheek. It left a line of blood, but there was no indication that the attack had actually hurt it. With a fiery hand, it punched at Trevor's face. Dropping down, he brought the pick end up into its chin. The beast staggered back, but its flames increased in heat and density.

Instead of throwing more flames, it charged forward in an effort to burn him. As it threw its arm out to tackle him, Trevor swung up and connected with the left armpit. The beast toppled on its side as he placed his foot on its left elbow. With the shoulder joint exposed, he hacked down on it until the arm was off.

He was about to do the same with the other arm when it kicked him in his groin. Trevor doubled over, his belly meeting with another kick from below. He flew through the air and slammed into one of the walls. He ignored the impact, trying to avoid losing his grip on the handle.

He rolled over as fire lit up his face. The flames hit the wall behind him and died out. The inferno beast was running towards him again. Changing tactic, Trevor decided to end this quickly and disable his ability to move around. When the victim was almost right on him, he jumped out of its path and kicked it down onto its belly.

He wanted to hold it down with his foot, but the flames on its back were too hot. Pressing down on the side of its face rather, he sliced into the joint where the right leg and hip met. He chopped away at it furiously, realising just how violent he looked. The thought passed away like light through thin clouds as he continued to hack the leg off.

The man beneath him tried to move around or get back up, but it was too weak and powerless to do so. Even the flames began to die down. Ending the task at hand, Trevor continued to bite the axe into the other joints until only the head remained.

Somehow, it was still moving. The torso was wiggling as the head squirmed under his foot. There was a sensation of domination rising inside Trevor that he really enjoyed. He held the axe in both hands, realising just how powerful he felt at that point. It was joined by a sense of wickedness that made him grin down, teeth and all, at the man beneath him.

With one fast, hard swoop, he sliced the head clean off. It rolled off to the side before sizzling with the other limbs into the tiles beneath them. The torso's flames faded away until only a plastic body was on the floor. The radio's wailing also died down. With the same energy, Trevor smashed it open.

Inside, he found an orange disc. On the one side, he saw a plant with a sunflower head, while on the other, he saw the letter S. Placing it with the other coins, he looked around the room for anything else that could be useful. Only then did he realise there was no door to the office. He checked the first-floor map to make sure he remembered it being there correctly. It confirmed his suspicions but did not reveal why there was no door to it.

In retrospect, he realised he had not seen any entrance from the reception area either. Realising that he was wasting time standing around and thinking, he shoved the maps back into his pocket and moved on.

24

INTENSIVE CARE

He moved into the Medicine Room. Treading carefully, he stepped onto a singular grid in the centre of the room. Both sides of the floor fell away into the red light below. The grid led to the opposite wall, with a t-section that broke away to the other door on the right.

Walking on the grid caused a noise from above, making him look up. He saw a similar grid above him where the Nurse Centre should have been. A creature was crouching on the grid above. It was hard to tell if it was actually looking at him, as it had no face to speak of. It looked like the head was wrapped in its own flesh and skin, with a thin slit that should have been its mouth. The mouth looked scarred and stitched shut.

Its muscular torso was naked but had the same blood-stained apron Trevor had seen on Twisted Bishop. At the angle it was crouched, he could see a marking on its right arm that was more like a branding than a tattoo. It was the same marking he had seen on Bishop when he had first met him.

Strangely, the radio did not whine any louder than before. Taking it as a sign that it meant him no harm, Trevor moved forward towards the next door. The creature crept along the grid like a spider until Trevor stopped again. He stepped back, and the creature crawled back. He stepped forward, and the beast moved in unison with him.

"Ok then," Trevor said, making his way to the door and entering the next passage.

Where the east passage had been separated from the west by large double doors before, it was now wide open with no division. He could see down both ends of the sickly corridor and the stairs to the right that led up to the second floor. He could see very well without a torch, as the floor was exposed in certain areas again and therefore lit by the light underneath.

He walked forward on the cagey floor, causing it to creak. There was also an unnatural whine and grinding of metal that his passing should not have caused. As he moved to the Storeroom door ahead, he tested it. It was locked, but the walls moaned in chorus around him. He turned the knob again; the walls groaned again as if it was in some emotional agony.

He checked the standard Office and Doctor's Office next, both locked and causing the same moans from the adjoining walls. He walked down to the end of the passage where the rubble had blocked him before. All the doors were locked.

He ran back to the stairs, ensuring the toilets were also unavailable. He ascended to the second floor, greeted by the radio's rising volume. It was not a steep rise, so he assumed that the danger was not immediate.

The floor was more solid where he stood. The walls were covered with the same wooden frames and sheets as the basement. Even though no light penetrated from the floor below, a reddish glow emanated from the sheets that dimly lit the passages. It revealed to him that the stairway to the third floor was broken midway up.

"Ok, so I guess I won't be going to the third floor," Trevor said, hoping there was nothing up there he needed.

He checked the second-floor map to orientate himself.

He saw the marking in the men's toilets he had made to indicate the wounded man with the cuts on his arm. He wondered if that was causing the radio to be louder than usual. Stashing the map away and preparing his axe, he turned right and entered the toilets.

The inner brick walls that had separated the male and female toilets were gone. It was replaced by a metal mesh grid all the way, except for an opening that led from one toilet section to the other. In the urinal section where Trevor stood, he looked into the mirror on the wall opposite him, jumping away from the door suddenly.

He had seen the anthropophage behind him. He swung like mad into a space occupied by black smoke. The smoke moved away from him towards the cubicles, floating over the middle one that was closed. The radio screamed at its peak as something inside the booth rattled. Trevor breathed deeply, waiting in anticipation.

When the smoke flew over again, and out towards the female section of the toilets, the cubicle door suddenly blasted out against the wall. A man towering over Trevor emerged, more obese than any others he had seen. On stock strong legs, it walked out from the cubicle, its right arm covered in cuts.

In its left hand was a kitchen knife. Its waist was covered with the usual bed sheet, and its chest had the same hearty hole as the others. Struggling with its weight, it moved as quickly as it could towards him with the knife raised above its shoulders.

Trevor moved forward to meet it. The knife slashed down, but he avoided it with a sidestep. The knife returned for another swipe, but Trevor stepped back and bent his chest as the blade passed over it. He drew the axe head up and knocked the hand with the knife back, circling the handle over again to drive the axe blade into the injured arm.

The man gurgled in pain. It slumped down to one knee as its face grimaced from the agony. Trevor pulled the axe out and brought it down again. He struggled to slice through its layers of fat, but each drive into the flesh caused the beast to drop down further until the arm popped off. The radio quietened down again.

Grease, flesh and modules of fat were all that was left as a puddle on the floor. He took the manikin arm and smashed it open. Inside, he found a green disc with leaves and flowers on one side and a T on the other.

He inspected the male toilets and then walked through the gap into the female area, making sure nothing was lying around that would be helpful to him. When he walked past the cubicles, he saw the cursive words written on each of their tattered wooden doors: Am I pretty now?

Once confident there were no items around, he stepped back out to the passage. As with the first floor, the doors that had blocked access to the east wing were gone. He moved towards the rooms of the west wing first, making a hundred per cent sure he wasn't missing anything.

The radio rose in volume. Room 201 was inaccessible. It wasn't that it was locked, but rather that the handle mechanism was faulty. It felt very loose as if it was broken. Moving towards 202 helped him realise what was causing the radio to cry out. A nurse stood with her back to him between 202 and 203, her upper body slightly slumped over.

His foot creaked on the floor, and the nurse jerked her head over. It was then that he realised that her face was covered with burnt skin. Pieces of flesh spotted the face like a bad rash, but her face had nothing but a mouth like the creature he had seen crawling in the nurse centre.

The main difference was that her mouth was cut wide open into a smile where the others had been scarred closed. She moved in his direction, her head twitching and jerking to each side as if trying to listen to where he was.

Trevor switched his radio off. The nurse stopped. Her head leaned forward as if smelling the air, but she didn't move at all. Her upraised hand revealed a scalpel within it. He could see her legs beneath the knee-high uniform; the skin would have been spotless were it not for the dark red veins that could be seen through it.

He quietly leaned down and turned the knob. It squealed as he turned it, but it was also faulty. The nurse budged forward again, waiting for another sound. He gripped the axe and ran towards her, his feet clanging on the floor underneath. She jerked awake and walked very quickly and awkwardly towards the sound.

Before she could strike, he brought the axe across her throat. She stood there for a moment wavering, the scalpel still held high, before dropping dead to the floor. A movement rushing towards him revealed another nurse approaching past 203 before him.

Her speed was unnatural, and she was on him before he could prepare himself. He brought the axe up to hold her arm up, the scalpel gleaming before his face. He got ready to kick her shin when he screamed.

A blade had cut down his back. He shoved the nurse forward with the force of the handle and looked back. Another nurse had attacked him from behind. She attacked again, but Trevor sliced into her kneecap and then brought the pick up into her burnt face.

She fell down, wiggling and writhing on the floor. He brought the blade down on her face, crushing it until she stopped moving. He heard a muffled cry as the nurse behind him charged, but he twisted and bit the axe into her shin. She toppled over him, the scalpel in her hand driving into his left rib.

He was breathless from the pain, his head spinning. She pulled it out and drove it onto his face. He pulled his head to the right just in time as he kicked her off to the side. Standing again, he dispensed with her before she could rise.

Deciding to put the radio back on rather, he listened as it simmered down to the normal crackle. Walking over to the final nurse, he saw that her face had been covered with bandages at one point, but the burns had melded it with her flesh and skin. The bloody smile seeped through it.

Rooms 203 and 204 could not be accessed, so he made his way back. Almost too afraid to open the Nurse Centre and face the crawling creature he had seen before, he soon discovered he could not access the room from the east passage. The walls were solid steel and mesh at the spot where the door should have been, with the sheeted walls surrounding it.

He passed the corner and tried the west wing. The door on that side was still there. He opened it, expecting to see the grid with the creature on it. What he found was indeed the central grip overlooking the first floor and the fires below, but not the creature.

Instead, he found a nurse with a mask over her mouth and nose. It was the same gorgeous face he had seen on the ground floor portrait. Her hands were devoid of any weapons as she turned to look at him seductively.

"What are you staring at?" she said in a beautiful, angelic voice. "Do you think I am pretty?"

He chose not to answer. He pulled his axe up into the offensive but did not proceed into the room.

"Stunned into silence by my beauty?" she asked, urging him to answer.

When he did not, she raised her fingers to her right ear and released the mask from her face. There was a deep cut across her cheeks on either side, but hers were not as bloody as the others. It seemed to have scarred over the years, with the blood remaining to stain the seam.

Once the mask was completely removed, she opened her mouth into an unnaturally wide smile, cracking the seam open afresh. The skin and tissue tore, causing blood to trickle down her cheeks and onto her neck. He could see her teeth and gums through the sides.

"And now?" she asked again. "Am I pretty now?"

Trevor backed away out of the room into the passage. His radio cried out louder, causing him to look back to the west passage. Three nurses were stumbling their way towards him.

"Wait!" Trevor shouted. "Didn't I kill you already?!"

Behind them, he saw black smoke collect into a cloud before it solidified into the Anthropophage. The primary nurse before him pulled a large butcher's knife out from behind her belt and moved towards him.

Trevor ran. The Operating Preparation Room was blocked by something on the inside, so he moved further into the passage. He could see two more nurses heading his way from down the other end. Following them was a rusted, bloody wheelchair. He was blocked in with only one option left.

Knowing he would regret it, he opened the Intensive Care Unit's door and entered. He closed his eyes, and he pressed his back firmly against it. He was out of breath from the rush and fright. He tried to calm down, waiting for the nurses to start bashing at the door…

"You slept through the night," a voice said.

Trevor opened his eyes. He was back in the apartment. He watched a scene before him as if he were simply an observer. It was the same scene he had seen at Hollowbrook Elementary with the two of them lying in her bed.

"Oh no!" Trevor made to jump up, but she pushed his chest down.

"It doesn't really matter anymore, does it?" Kathy asked. "You said you were leaving her anyway. And it's not like going back home now will save you."

"I know, Kathy," he replied, "but I want to talk to her about it first. I don't want Caroline finding out about us like this."

"Why? You're cheating on her anyway. What does it matter how she finds out?"

"Don't say that."

"Say what?"

"Cheating," Trevor repeated, throwing the sheet off his naked body. "I don't like that word."

"Well, whether you like it or not, that's what you're doing," Kathy replied, ending it with a giggle. "But it doesn't have to be this way. We can be happy like this forever."

The past Trevor before him stood up, pulling her hands off his chest. She stood up, too, the sunlight from the windows glinting against her nude form. She moved closer to him and wrapped her hands behind his neck, bringing his head down for a soft, passionate kiss. His hands moved onto the lower curves of her back, bringing the skin of her body against his.

Suddenly, the apartment door crashed in. Trevor let go of her as he looked down the passage to see a man rushing down to meet him. As the man entered the room, he looked Trevor and Kathy up and down, a wide smirk forming on his face.

"I thought so," he said, spinning around and walking out.

"Bishop!" Trevor shouted after him as Kathy grabbed her clothes and started dressing. "No, wait!"

Trevor ran after him. Bishop was almost by the apartment door. The door's lock was broken from the impact of him breaking into it. He had been walking at a fast pace, but Trevor sprinted to pull him back in.

"Hold on, Bishop, please," he said urgently.

"Why?" Bishop asked, his eyebrows raised. Trevor wanted to smash the smile off his face. "So you can formulate a lie quickly?"

"No, you don't understand, Bishop!"

Kathy rushed past them quickly into the passage and ran towards the stairs.

"Wait, Kathy!" Trevor walked past Bishop and watched her run from the apartment. "Where are you going?!"

Trevor looked back at Bishop, who had taken his phone out of his pocket and was dialling.

"What are you doing?" he asked as Bishop placed the phone by his ear.

"I'm calling Caroline," he replied, moving the phone from his ear. "My sister needs to know what you've been up to, Trevor. I mean, she always suspected you were fucking around with that slut."

"Excuse me?" Trevor said, feeling the anger rise inside him. He closed the door behind him, sliding the latch in.

"You heard me," Bishop repeated, clenching his free hand into a fist. Trevor noticed his biceps bunch up. "While you've been cavorting around with that bitch, Caroline's been wondering what she's done wrong. As if she is the one responsible for you fucking around."

"So she sent you here to spy on me?" Trevor asked, losing control of his thoughts as the swearing angered him further. He moved closer.

"She didn't need to," Bishop said. "I wanted to find out for myself, so she could get rid of your ass for once and for all."

"You never liked me, did you?" Trevor said, the words barely escaping through his clenched teeth.

"No," he confirmed, moving closer until their faces were right by each other. "I always thought you were never good enough for her. And now you and that slut have proved me right."

Trevor lost all control. His fist slammed into Bishop's face before he could say the next word, causing the phone to fall and bounce across the floor. As he recovered, Trevor slipped his leg behind Bishop's and used his shoulder to slam him into the floor. Bishop retaliated by kicking him into the wall and rolling to his feet again.

Bishop delivered two shots to Trevor's ribs, but he shifted by the third blow. Bishop's hand hit the wall just as Trevor grabbed the back of his shirt and slammed his face into the kitchen counter behind him.

"Ah fuck!" Bishop shouted.

He tried to twist to knock Trevor with his elbow, but Trevor was faster. He turned Bishop to face him, pushed his head down and brought his knee into it. Bishop's head bolted up, his eyes hazy. Trevor kicked his knee inwards, making Bishop kneel before delivering a powerful blow to his face.

Bishop collapsed to the floor. Trevor turned him on his back and straddled his chest. His fists dropped like hammers one after another, causing Bishop's face to crack open and bleed.

"Stop calling Kathy a slut!!!" he yelled over the sound of his pounding. "And you're not telling Caroline anything!!"

When he ran out of strength and his arms felt numb, he stopped. He could barely recognise the man in front of him. His eyes were swollen, and his nose had snapped to the side. There was almost nothing to recognise his mouth anymore, and there were red bulges everywhere.

"Shit," Trevor said, looking down at his hands as his senses came back to him. "Bishop? Bishop, can you hear me?"

He reached down to turn his face up, hoping to see if he was breathing or if his eyes moved. Yet, his chest was still beneath him, and there was no movement on his face at all.

"Bishop!? Stay with me, Bishop," Trevor said, standing up and walking back to Kathy's room for his phone so that he could call Jay.

As he turned around the counter, he stepped on something that cracked beneath his feet. He looked down and saw Bishop's phone. His heel had cracked the screen…

Trevor opened his eyes. He was back in the Intensive Care Unit. The floor was one solid grid of steel interlocking bars. The walls were pure concrete, clean and smooth, other than recurring words written in blood along the walls that read "Beware the Guardian".

The steel bars were red, lit by the ceiling oval lights that shone down on the figure in the centre of the room. He realised they were red because the entire grid and the bars were soaked in blood.

The single figure in the centre of the room was lying on a gurney. There were plugs attached to his huge, bulky arms and chest that fell down on either side towards the floor. Instead of being plugged into a machine, it passed through the bars of the floor to an unknown place underneath.

Trevor moved forward, holding his axe at the ready. When he was at the side, he saw cords plugged into the side of the huge metallic twisted head, too. His chest was still, making Trevor wonder if he was even alive. On the floor on the other side of the gurney was the gigantic axe Bishop had carried around at the school.

The floor around him suddenly quaked. Trevor tried to keep his balance, but it inevitably caused him to fall off his feet. His fingers interlocked with the bars beneath him. Despite his bouncing vision, he clearly saw that Twisted Bishop was moving.

His right hand ripped up into the air first, breaking free of the plugs, followed shortly by the left. He reached up to the container on his head and jerked the cords out one at a time. Finally, he sat up, moved onto the floor on the other side of the gurney, and turned to look at Trevor.

The quaking stopped. The red light shimmered on the scars over each joint connected to the torso. The Twisted Guardian bent down and picked up his humongous blade with both hands, his biceps and pectoral muscles bulging out more than it was naturally possible. A demonic groan emerged from underneath the floor, filling the room with a sense of abstract darkness.

Trevor stood up, realising that Bishop was closer to the door than he was. Bishop swung the huge blade sideways and onto the gurney. The edge sliced through it cleanly, splitting it in two. He stepped over it towards Trevor, the blade dragging behind him.

Unsure what he could do to escape the situation, he simply backed away to the wall behind him. Twisted Bishop approached him slowly, the blade slowing him down. Trevor watched as Bishop lifted it up again, the muscles bulging again as he held it beside him, ready to strike.

As strong as he was, Trevor saw that the blade was hefty to pick up. He noted how long it took before Bishop could actually strike with it. He knew immediately that he had an advantage over the monster before him. As Bishop swiped the blade horizontally to cut across Trevor's neck, he slipped down the wall and crawled across the floor as quickly as he could.

It made him remember the creature he had seen crawling above him in the Medicine Room. He looked back to see the metallic head stare down at the spot Trevor had been. He was on the door side of Bishop now and could escape.

The thought of escaping paused in his head. He stopped crawling as the light from the oval fittings caught something on the back of the head just before Bishop turned to face him again. A large bolt just above the bottom lip joined two halves together.

Within a central indentation of that bolt was a blue coin. Trevor was torn between running out of the room and retrieving the coin. It was the last one out of the set, and he did not want to face Bishop again in case he needed it. Taking a deep breath, he decided to at least get the coin if killing Bishop failed.

Standing up, he waited for Twisted Bishop to reach him. The blade swung up, cutting through the ceiling boards and metal and striking overhead at Trevor. He dodged to the side and slammed the axe into Bishop's ribs. The sharp metal cut into the flesh, but Bishop simply turned his waist and slapped Trevor across the room into the broken gurney.

Trevor groaned. Besides the pain that shot through his lower back from the impact, the axe was still wedged in Bishop's side. The giant moved towards him again as Trevor slithered backwards. He met the wall shared with the Operating Room, pinned against it with nowhere else to go.

Bishop was upon him, raising the blade behind him in preparation. His muscles bulged again as he pulled it overhead to strike down at the man before him on the ground. The edge cut through the ceiling again, breaking free and descending on Trevor.

At the last moment, Trevor jumped forward and to the side with the axe, pulling it out. Bishop's blade sliced into the bars on the floor and got stuck. The Twisted Guardian tugged and pulled at the handle, but it would not wedge free.

Trevor took his chance. He jumped up to give himself some momentum and dropped down with the pick on the upper rim of the bolt. Bishop dropped down to his knee as the metallic head split slightly apart. The coin dangled loosely in the slot before Bishop tilted his head back to shout in demonic anger.

The coin fell out of the bolt. Trevor panicked, dropping his axe to dive for the coin before it could fall through the bars. His belly slammed on the steel floor beneath him, knocking him in the solar plexus as the coin dropped on the tip of his fingers and bounced off it. He watched helplessly as it clanged against a bar and spun over into the darkness below.

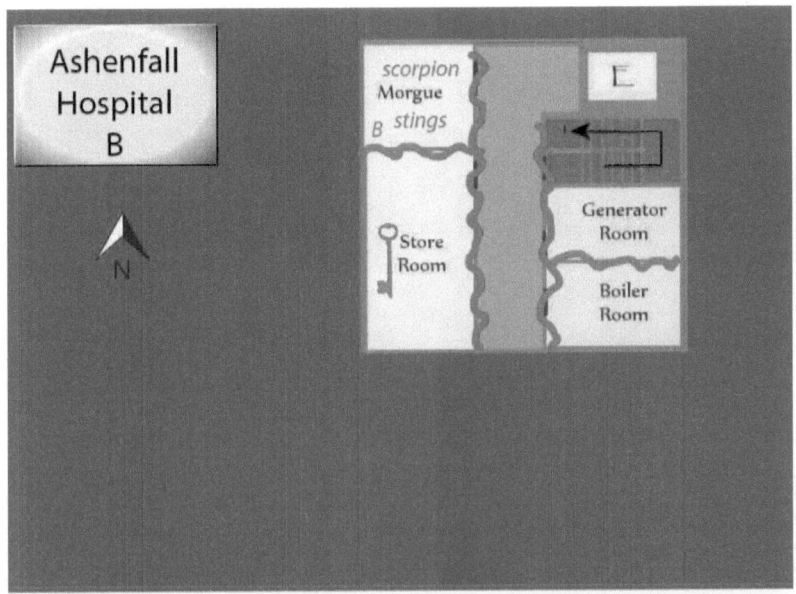

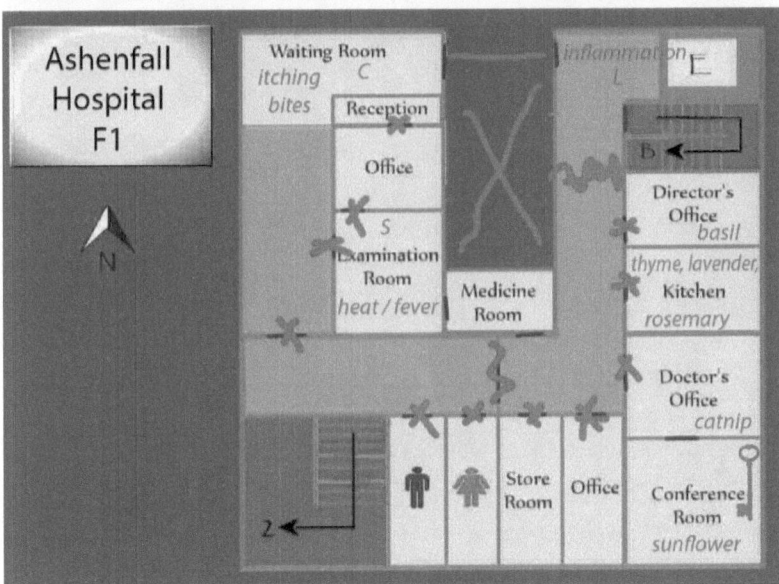

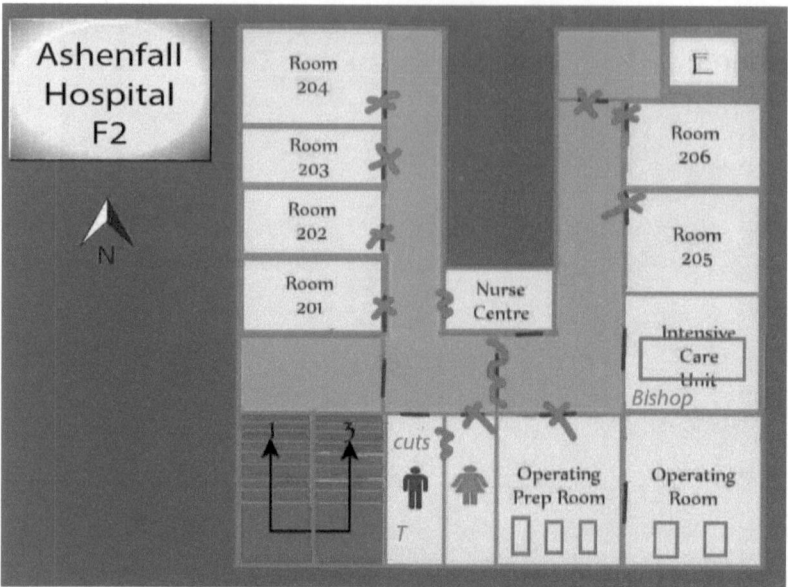

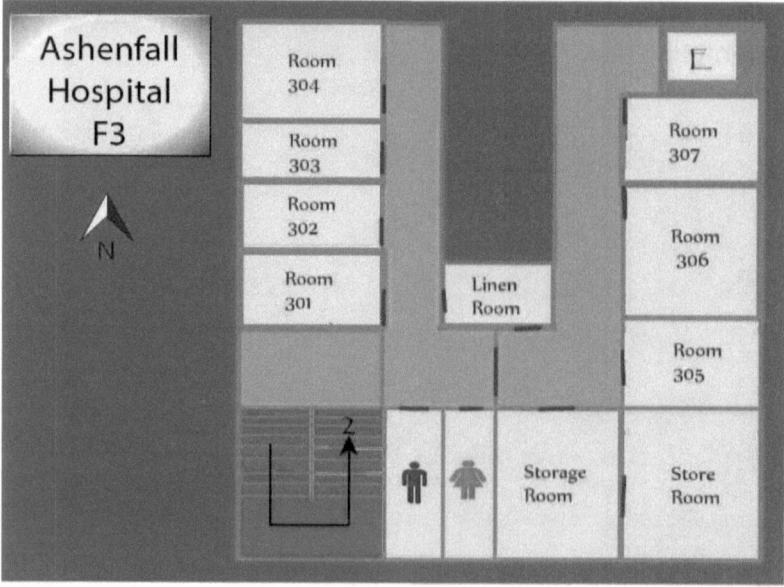

25

CONFESSIONS OF A SERIAL KILLER

There was no time for remorse. The sinking feeling that tried to overcome him needed to wait until he could cope with it. Twisted Bishop had finally managed to break his blade loose from the floor. With no reason left to fight him, Trevor ran for the door and into the passage.

He closed the door and turned. He had forgotten entirely about the nurses. A scalpel cut across his chest from the closest one. It burned, but he ignored it. They surrounded him, and he needed to fight before Bishop attacked him from behind. The path of least obstruction was to his right, so he kicked the nurse back that had attacked him and drove the axe's edge through the neck of one to his right.

As she fell, he ran. He dodged the bloody wheelchair that nicked the side of his knee as it turned around and headed back down the passage. Three nurses started moving at their sickly pace towards him. Trevor looked ahead and saw that the path to the elevator was also blocked by rubble. To his jubilation, though, the walls past the Intensive Care Unit to his right were utterly gone, as were the rooms they once contained.

It was a straight drop down into the Director's Office and kitchen beneath him, which were completely open. The walls that had separated all the rooms from each other in the first floor's east wing were gone. The only wall was the one shared with the passage that had blocked Trevor from entering the rooms earlier.

A blast and crash behind him made him look back. Twisted Bishop had kicked the door off its hinges, causing it to slam into the nurses behind it and into the wall. The nurses that had chased after him stopped, alerted by this new commotion. The nurses right by Bishop lifted their scalpels and slashed at his arms and chest, unable to see who they were assailing.

Trevor realised that the primary nurse with the white mask was not with them. Bishop couldn't bring the blade out with him through the doorway, as it was too long to bring around or gain momentum to break it through. He simply dropped it at the entrance and grabbed the closest nurse by her neck while the others uselessly sliced at his body.

Trevor stepped out of the way of the passing wheelchair, watching the scene at the end of the passage. Twisted Bishop used his free hand to rip the uniform off the nurse in one motion. She dangled nude in the air before him, scalpels flashing beneath her at his ribs and arms. Blood splashed on their bodies as he approached the wall behind her.

Raising a huge fist, he slammed it into the cleavage of her breasts. The sternum cracked as his fist passed right through her body and out her back. Her body crumpled over as he threw her down onto one of the nurses below.

They continued to hack at him as he grabbed his next victim. Not waiting to watch the next slaughter, Trevor looked down again. The floor had grated grids, too, with several sections missing, resembling the waiting room floor. Choosing a spot, he bent his knees and jumped down, landing safely in the kitchen area.

When he passed into the area that should have been Philip's old office, he looked up. He could see the grid formwork the Intensive Care Unit's floor had been made of. He looked down at the grating around him. A lonely square grid was attached to the passage wall with no other flooring around it.

Caught in the steel web of that grating was the blue disc. Trevor could only think of getting to it by jumping across the gap towards it. If he managed to reach it, he only hoped the coin didn't slip further and fall to the fires below.

Taking his chance, he placed the axe down on the floor and jumped over. He landed neatly near the closest edge of it and bent his body forward to prevent falling back. The coin moved slightly, but was too large to fall through the closely knit web around it. He secured the final coin and placed it in his pouch.

Jumping back, he claimed his axe again and moved to the door ahead of him. He opened it into darkness and then closed the door behind him. For the first time since he entered this version of the hospital, he felt safe and at peace. The entire room was enclosed, with no openings anywhere.

And there was only one minute red light in the room. It twinkled on and off, but he could not see what it was due to the surrounding darkness. He walked forward, stumping his knee on the table in the centre and then feeling his way ahead. When he reached it, he pressed the button that emitted the light.

A bright white light shone on the wall. It was the projector's power button that had been blinking, set on an oval boardroom table. He realised that he was in the Conference Room again.

Looking around, he saw colossal birdcages hanging from the ceiling. Each one coincided with a chair at the table underneath it. And within them were skeletons sitting on their haunches with age-old blood staining their bones. On the wall where the projector shone, to the left in the corner, was a thick vertical slit.

Trevor retrieved the flash drive from his pocket and inserted it into the projector. The same two files as before were displayed on the screen. He pressed the Enter key on Session 1. A message appeared on the screen:

File is not corrupted and cannot be opened

He moved it down to Session 2 and activated the file. A recording started to play. Caroline was seated in the chair to the right, and Emily sat behind the desk to the left. The camera had been positioned to film both of them this time.

"Are you ok?" Emily asked.

"Not really, Emily," Caroline replied, tears rolling down her eyes.

"What's wrong?" Emily asked further, leaning forward. "Did you get confirmation that Trevor is cheating on you?"

"Yeah," she said, blowing her nose into a tissue. "Bishop knew I suspected Trevor was sleeping with Kathy."

"I remember you telling me that," Emily said. "I also remember telling you not to get him involved."

"I know. But it's not like he listened to me."

"Oh no. What did he do?"

"I'm not sure," Caroline said. "He came to my place and saw I was crying. He left in anger. The next thing I know, he's phoning me."

"What did he say?"

"Nothing to me specifically. When I picked up, he was talking to Trevor. I don't think he realised I had answered."

"What were they talking about?"

"Trevor sleeping with Kathy. It sounded like Bishop was calling me to tell me what he had discovered. But then a fight broke out between the two."

"Are you sure?" Emily asked, leaning further forward on the desk.

"Well, there was a lot of slamming and crashing. I heard Bishop cry out. And then…."

Caroline's words broke off. Emily waited patiently while she cried some more and cleared her nose and eyes again.

"What happened then?" Emily asked.

"I heard Trevor inform Bishop that he will never tell me anything," she replied. "When the fighting was done, there was silence until Trevor asked Bishop if he was alright."

Emily had raised her hand to her mouth. There was another moment of silence before Caroline continued.

"I think he hurt him really bad. I haven't heard from either of them, and Trevor isn't answering my calls."

"Caroline, you need to inform the police!" Emily burst out saying. "You should have gone there before coming to me."

"I can't!" Caroline objected. "I still love him so much. I don't know if I can have him sent to prison. I told Bishop not to do an…"

"What Bishop decided to do is irrelevant," Emily interjected. "You do realise that he may have killed Bishop?"

"I don't want to think of that!" Caroline shouted as she jumped up.

"You need to," Emily said, standing too. "Caroline, you need to go to the police. Right now."

Caroline looked at Emily with blank eyes. She seemed to be judging the situation before making a decision. Without replying, Caroline walked out of the room. Emily sat down hard and drummed her fingers on the desk.

The recording ended. As he pulled the flash drive out, a thud erupted from one of the rooms he had passed through before. It was followed shortly by the dragging of metal on metal. Twisted Bishop had finally fought free of the nurses.

Hoping it was a way out, he headed for the slit in the wall. Peering through, he saw that each side of the hole was covered in large teeth attached to fleshy gums within the wall itself. He reconsidered the decision to pass through it when the door's opening spurred him on.

He turned sideways with the axe against his chest. He stretched his left shoulder in first and walked through. The teeth pressed against his back as he wormed his way in. Bishop stepped into the Conference Room and looked across it at his prey escaping.

The teeth suddenly closed in on Trevor. It bit into his body all around, making him scream in agony. With slow motions, it began to chew on him, grinding the teeth against him. He tried to push against it with the axe, but he was in an awkward position, and the gums were too strong.

Twisted Bishop had reached the aperture. He brought the blade up to feel its weight in his hands and then brought it down on the wall. Chaos splintered all around Trevor as the supporting wall crashed inwards and wood splinters dusted his face.

The blade bit into the gum before it reached Trevor. The teeth retracted immediately, with a shrill rising from the walls. Trevor fell into the dark office, trying to crawl away but in too much pain to do so. It was easier just to stand up and make for the office door.

It was locked. Trevor kicked it several times while Twisted Bishop smashed away at the wall. The blade collapsed a large portion of it where the projector had been shining on. The light spilled into the office onto the wall next to Trevor. Large words were scrawled onto it.

"What was once down is now up," he read out loud, frowning in confusion and anxiety. "What the hell is that supposed to mean?"

Bishop broke through. There was some rubble dangling from the ceiling in his path, but the hole in the wall was large enough for him to pass through. Trevor looked at the wall again and then felt in his pocket for the Transporter Key.

"It's worth a try," he said, hastily inserting the key.

He opened it up and saw darkness on the other side. Having no choice, he ran through the doorway and closed the door behind him, locking it. A loud, demonic cry resounded from underneath the floor he stood on. A moment later, it died away, and there was nothing but silence.

Trevor couldn't see anything around him. He had no idea where he was or what was around him. The axe was a cold comfort in his hand, so he switched on his radio. It was just as useless; it was so quiet that he wondered again if it had broken.

The passage lit up before him with a soft red glow. Ghost Philip was before him again with the same smirk on his face. He turned around as before and walked through the door behind him, casting the passage back into darkness.

Trevor stepped forward, feeling for anything in front of him. Even his footsteps created no sound. Soon, his anxiety rose to the extent that he could feel his heart pounding heavily in his head. He kept creeping forward one step at a time until he found a wall, and then the door ghost Philip had passed through.

He opened it quietly and looked inside. There were candles on the opposite wall on either side of another door. He entered and looked around. There were piles of linen on the floor. He took out the hospital maps until he found those belonging to the third floor where the Linen Room was indicated.

"That's strange," Trevor commented. "This room is on the map, but there shouldn't be a door there."

According to the map, the area behind the door should have been above the front yard of the hospital, between the two wings. Packing the maps away, he looked for the door that should have led him to the western passage. The wall was solid, with no means of passing through.

Before he could turn back to the new door, something wrapped around his face and pulled him down. It closed over his lips and tried to worm into his mouth. He bit his teeth closed, looking down to see that the linen had come to life. It had been shredded into long strips that were trying to wrap around his arms to bind him.

Trevor kicked and flailed with his arms against it. It simply floated in the air before him and then slapped him across the face with one end. Other linen strips were now trying to bind his ankles together. He lifted his feet up one at a time, kicking down on it in an effort to stop it.

And all the while, the linen in his mouth tried to get in and down his throat. A piece slipped between his teeth, but he bit down, and it retracted. He stepped back and was tripped by linen behind him, falling to the floor. As he landed with a thud, some of it began to wrap around his head and over his eyes.

He grasped at it and pulled it off, yanking at the bits in his mouth until it was out. He wielded the axe and slashed down at the closest linen. The cloth tore in two and fell to the floor. He went to hacking at more pieces around his feet, watching as the linen was shredded and became dormant.

Just when the feeling of victory washed over him, he discovered that it was short-lived. The pieces he had split rose up again, each with its own life. Realising that he would not survive this battle, he made for the door. Some linen reached for his wrists, but he swung the axe's edge to cut it away. Another attached his ankle, but he stepped down on it before it could loop around. Reaching the door, he pulled down on the handle and made it through.

He turned around in fright. This side of the door had red pulsating meat all over the surface. The ceiling and walls had the same fleshy substance but had white cancerous sections bulging out of them in some places. And before him was a long flight of stairs leading up.

As he walked up the steps, he examined the white cancerous bulges. It looked like faces trying to push through the wall from the other side. Their mouths cried out in silence, their eyes shut against some kind of pain that was invisible to him. It terrified him to watch it further, afraid they might try to reach out and hit him, so he moved on at a faster pace.

As he continued up the stairs, the light dimmed and became darker. He put on his radio, wanting to see how much danger he was heading to. It weaved between sizzling and crackling, rising at each growth on the wall and dipping in the space between them. Deciding that the radio was useless at this point, he switched it off again.

And still, he continued to walk up, the stairs simply getting darker and darker. It felt like he had walked three storeys already. He remembered that one of the elevators had shown a fourth floor for a moment, but there was no way that it could be this high. Yet, he kept going, no sign of any door or landing before him.

His legs were also getting heavier, like they refused to go further. There was a supernatural weight on his shoulders, as if someone was sitting on them. Deciding to return to the linen room, he turned around and fell back in fright, his heart running like a racehorse in his chest.

The fleshy door was before him. It was like he had never left it or walked up the stairs at all. When he got up and looked around, the stairs were gone. He was in a small room with just a singular door as the exit. Even the cancerous heads were gone.

Trying the door, it opened easily. The hinges were silent, even though he expected them to creak. As he entered through the door, he heard a baby whimper. It was not a harsh cry but rather a sound indicating discontent.

The room was slightly larger than the linen room had been. It was lit by an orange light, the source of which was not visible. The ceiling had no light fixtures or fittings and was as smooth and empty as the floor. Yet, the orange light lit the room dimly, indicating another door in the wall ahead of him.

The only other item in the room was a small opening on the right wall. It was a thin, wide strip with old iron bars set at regular vertical intervals within it. Trevor walked over to the opening and looked inside. His eyes could just make out the cradle on the other side of the wall.

Whether it was a room or just an open space, he could not tell. The same type of orange glow revealed the cradle rocking back and forth, with baby hands reaching up into the air above it. It also reflected off a wall behind it, but that was the only wall he could see.

A movement on that wall made him look away from the baby. The same faceless creature he had seen crawling on the grating above him in the Medicine Room was creeping down the wall. It reached the floor and made its way to the cradle's side, using it to stand up and inspect the baby.

Hey, leave it alone! Trevor tried to shout. His mouth opened, but no sound emerged. He could only hear the baby's whimpering sounds die down to a soft giggle as it reached up to the creature. With only the apron around its waist, it pulled the baby up onto its naked chest and rocked it back and forth.

And then it looked around at Trevor. Observing that he was there, the creature raised a hand toward him, palms open and fingers apart. It said words in an arcane language that Trevor couldn't understand. Fire and purple light emerged from the palm. Before he knew what happened, Trevor was cast away from the wall and slammed against the opposite wall in the enclosed room.

When he looked up, the hole was gone. The wall was solid again, just like all the other walls. What scared him further was that only one door in the room was left. The door he had come in by was missing, leaving just a hard wall in its place.

Gripping his axe, he arose. He grabbed the handle of the sole door and opened it. He entered a vast room with a ceiling two floors high. He examined the floors, walls and ceiling and noticed that they were all of the same cage material he had seen on the school roof. It took him a moment to discover that he was actually in one, large cage like a trapped animal.

The metal itself was rusty with blood like he had seen in the hospital. The same eerie glow seemed to emanate from it, providing him with light to see, but at the far end of the cage, there was movement. Someone had his back turned on Trevor and was working on a mesh bench that he seemed to have made himself.

"Philip?" Trevor asked as he moved closer.

The man turned around, and he could see that it was indeed Philip. The overall he still wore was in the worst condition he had seen. Not only was it wholly stained with blood, but it was torn in several places. Trevor brought his hand to his mouth when he saw Philip's face. The corners of his mouth had been cut into a smile.

"Oh, I thought it was that spirit I've been seeing that looks just like me", Philip said calmly as Trevor stopped before him. "Do you like what they've done to me?"

"Who?" he asked. "Those nurses?"

"Yes. Specifically the one with the white mask over her mouth."

"Kuchisake-Onna," Trevor informed him.

"What?" Philip asked, frowning as he stepped forward. It was then that Trevor noticed a white cooler box on the crude mesh table that he had constructed.

"Kuchisake-Onna," he said again. "There's an old legend about a nurse with a mask on who is exquisitely beautiful. She asks you if she is pretty while seducing you with her looks and charm. And then, she takes her mask off and reveals a terrifying cut in her mouth and asks you again. If you say no, or are too scared to reply, she either kills you or kidnaps you to torture you further."

"That sounds about right," Philip commented. "At first, I thought she had killed me. She had used this dagger with a blue symbol to cut these lines into my mouth first, then thrust it into my heart. When I regained consciousness, I was here."

"Philip, I need to know something," Trevor said, switching to a more pressing matter that popped into his mind. "Did you really kill all those patients?"

"Strange that you should ask me that now," Philip frowned. "I thought you and Emily were so close. It looked like it."

"Who you call Emily, I only knew as Jeanette."

"Ahh, so it seems she tricked us both."

"Listen, Philip, you've got to help me out here, man," Trevor pleaded, grasping his hands before him like a man begging for his life to be spared. "What the hell is going on?"

Philip moved away to his makeshift table. He tapped the cooler box but did not open it. It took a moment to work things through in his mind before he finally replied, his hand still on the cooler box.

"I had a lonely childhood," Philip started. "Our parents weren't the best there were, and most of the time, they neglected us. I guess that would have been alright if I hadn't needed them so much.

"You see, while Kathy was in Hollowbrook Elementary, I was in a private high school in Dunst. My loneliness allowed me to focus my quality time on more intellectual pursuits. I was reaching the highest scores of anyone at that school.

"Unfortunately, it also gave me unwarranted attention. I was constantly abused; verbally at first and then physically. I've never been one for violence, so I was unable to defend myself.

"There were originally six tormentors. One day, on the way home, I passed through an alley I used to get home safely and out of sight. One of my abusers met me in there, having noticed me going through there before. As usual, he tormented me and insulted my intelligence.

"Something snapped. Using a rusty knife I found in the litter on the ground before me, I turned around and stabbed him straight in the heart. There was a sense of power, exhilaration, as I watched his wide eyes look up at me while he knelt down. I smiled as I wrenched the blade to the side, and he collapsed."

"Hectic," Trevor said, enraptured by his tale.

"That was my first taste of power, taking someone's life. I suddenly realised that my life could turn around. However, the boy's disappearance was noticed, and they began searching for him. I had packed him in one of the black bags I had found and stashed him away in a waste bin in the alley.

"But I was too afraid that I had contaminated the body with any evidence that I had killed him. So I left the house at midnight that night, found the bag and searched for a proper place to dispose of it. It was an abandoned warehouse that became the home of my first killing."

"What did you do?"

"There was an old furnace there that still worked. I simply burned him up, waited to ensure nothing remained of him, and left two days later."

"Weren't your parents worried?"

"Well, they showed a modicum of concern, I guess, but once I told them I had been sleeping by a friend, they just accepted it without confirming my story. And then life returned to normal."

"Why didn't you go after the others?"

"I was too afraid," Philip said. "The first one had been too easy. The other five became closer than ever after losing one of their own. It would have taken some skill and stealth that I was not accustomed to.

"And then we moved. I went to a new school where my talents and intellect were appreciated by my peers. We were above the rest, and no one could touch us. We were respected so much that crowds split apart when we walked through. And then the Boatman murders happened."

"Doctor Boatman? The one that supposedly killed all those patients but whom they struggled to convict?"

"Yes, that's right. I followed that story very carefully while I was doing my internship at Brahm's Medical. There was such a fascination with how he killed his patients slowly with medicine and then claimed inheritance through their wills that made him become my hero."

"You admired him?" Trevor asked, unable to contain the look of shock on his face.

"That first killing had never really left my system," Philip said, taking out an old newspaper clipping revealing Boatman's bearded face and showing it to Trevor. "Boatman helped me realise that, as much as the medical practice was there to save, it was also there to take lives in a way that could not be traced.

"Of course, at first, it was simply a mere admiration for the guy. And then, they got him. They found enough evidence to have him locked away for life. They arrested him and kept him in a cell until he could get bail. The next morning, they found him hanging from the bars by his own bed sheets."

"Wow," Trevor said, realising he had never heard what had happened to him in the end. "So, after all that, he just took his own life?"

"Yes," Philip replied, "but it didn't stop my admiration for the guy. He had simply made a mistake."

"So when did you decide to follow in his footsteps?"

"The first opportunity was by accident, actually. Jerry had gone on a trip in the desert and was bitten by a scorpion. When they brought him to me to amputate him, he had already passed out. I doubt he would have recognised me anyway.

"And that's when the Boatman murders came to mind. When I was meant to give him an anaesthetic and an IV line before the operation, I gave him an extreme sedative that made him go under. I made sure to start the surgery soon so that it could look like he didn't make it during the operation.

"Of course, I knew the autopsy would reveal the drug in his system, so I made a plan to get rid of the body. And that's when I decided to have some fun with it. I managed to sneak into the morgue when no one was around and severed his limbs. It really was as easy as that."

"And no one caught you?"

"Nope," Philip smiled, the pride glinting in his eyes. "Of course, it was just my luck that not long after that, Benjamin was brought in for those mosquito bites. I followed the same procedure to put him down, but I knew cutting him up in the morgue again would be no good. Security had already been increased there.

"While one of the scrubs was taking him down, I knocked him out with chloroform and took the body. I knew there was an old abandoned basement in the hospital that had long been forsaken, so I started using that as the base for my special work. And with security mainly primed for the morgue, it was easy enough to litter the parts at the reception area when they switched patrols."

"That's crazy," Trevor said, some things coming to mind.

"I got addicted to the killings and the reputation," Philip said, interrupting Trevor's thoughts. "Just like Boatman, I was making a name for myself. But I was determined not to get caught for it.

"I started applying my mind as to how I could get to the others. If I waited too long, then the authorities might have forgotten about me. I was also worried someone would find the link between the victims, namely myself. So I did some research and found out where they lived and what they were doing for a living.

"Lucas was the easiest target on the list. He stayed alone, so all it took was quietly breaking into his apartment and injecting his leg with a drug that would make it swell up. When the call came in that he had reached the hospital, I had to work quickly. Before they could even take his body, I had it in the basement and did my work.

"I had planned to place it on display again, like the reception room, but getting out of the elevator with the bags this time was harder than before. So I decided to leave it there and make my way out."

"It sounds like it became trickier to just move the bodies."

"You won't believe how much the security picked up after that," Philip agreed. "And with the police starting to point fingers at me for being involved with every murder… well, I would like to say it scared me, but it became part of the thrill. To see who was smarter.

"Roderick's wife brought him in a few days later for a persistent fever. I knew this would be my one chance to get him. I had told the interns to put him in the examination room for me to inspect him. Of course, Roderick recognised my name and then realised who I was.

"I took pleasure in putting him down. He looked at me with pleading eyes as he fell asleep. I locked the room and went to work right there, knowing how hard it would be to transfer him out.

"Unfortunately, this pointed the focus more onto me, since the intern informed the police that I had asked for him to be moved to that room. I defended myself as much as I could, but I knew I had to either finish the game quickly or end it altogether.

"I went for Peterson myself. I broke into his home and injected the wife and kids with drugs to ensure they stayed asleep. But, I wanted him awake for this. So I grabbed one of their kitchen knives and tormented him for a bit, cutting into his arms. I wanted him to remember what they had done to me.

"I went as far as threatening to kill his family afterwards," Philip said, laughing. "But one of the neighbours had heard him screaming before I could shut him up and came to knock on the door. Knowing I didn't have much time, I put him to sleep with the same drug and left.

"When the ambulance collected him, I followed them until they got to the hospital emergency area. I received him from them, signing under someone else's name, and went to work. As I knew the bathrooms were the last place they would keep secured or expect to find him, it was the only option I had left."

"And that was it?" Trevor asked, frowning. "You dealt with all of them?"

"Yes indeed," Philip replied. "I started making plans to leave Ashbourne, as the police were hot on my tail after the last murder. The neighbour had caught a glimpse of a man my age rushing out of the backyard. Like Boatman, they thought they had their guy."

"Ok," Trevor said, processing all he had said and returning to his previous thoughts. "But why did you go to Emily?"

"Oh, that was all an act," Philip confessed. "I was hoping that the show of going for therapy would exclude me from the investigation. Emily seemed fairly convinced until the end that the killings had traumatised me, but I underestimated her interrogative nature."

"What happened?" Trevor asked.

"I had not expected her to look into my past," he replied. "I thought she would be like any other psychiatrist and simply nod and listen to my tragedy. But she was too intuitive and asked the right questions.

"In one of the last sessions I had in her office, I planted a bug under her desk so that I could hear if she was on to me. I heard her ask her PA to look into my past. When she came to meet me at the coffee shop before I left for Sacred Valley, I saw that she might have discovered something outside the office without me realising it. And then, just before I left, I heard her session with Caroline."

"Caroline?" Trevor frowned. "What has any of this to do with Caroline?"

"Oh, Trevor," Philip replied. "I really gave you too much credit. Did you not hear about my last victim? Have you not worked it out yet? Did you really think it was a coincidence?"

Trevor thought back to all the victims and one that he may have missed. It took him a moment to remember the one whose face had been bashed in.

"No!" Trevor shouted. "No, it can't be! What did you do to him?"

"Bishop was unplanned," Philip explained, looking back at the cooler box. "When Jay called and asked if I could take Bishop in quietly, it gave me several ideas. The first was that it would throw the police off my scent. Even if Emily produced evidence that I was connected to the other five victims, this would give them something to the contrary."

"But when we brought him to you, you checked him out!" Trevor argued. "You told me he was dead, that I had killed him."

"No, he had had a faint pulse," Philip said, smiling. "There was still some life in him. But I saw this as my way out, a way to get out of the investigation."

"You sick bastard," Trevor said softly.

"It was better that way," Philip replied. "If he had lived, he would have told Caroline everything. I'm surprised Jay didn't tell you."

"What? Jay knew?"

"Oh, dear boy," Philip laughed, "Jay isn't as innocent as you think. Who do you think I got to help me move those bodies around?"

"No. I don't believe it. Why would he help you?"

"Because I have some dirt on him that he would rather not have his colleagues find out."

Trevor stood still, trying to mentally consume what he had just been told. He had known Jay for many years; he was like a brother to him. For him to believe that Jay could be involved in killings was impossible.

"Of course, things with Bishop didn't quite go as planned," Philip continued. "When I was done cutting him up, I realised how stupid I had been. For all my intelligence, Bishop would have led the cops to me much easier than any of the other victims."

"How so?"

"Through my sister, Kathy, of course," he replied. "It's not a long stretch of the mind, actually. They would have discovered that you were having an affair with her eventually. And then it would take only a few more steps to conclude that Bishop had found out, and I helped you cover your mistake."

"You give the police too much credit," Trevor said.

"Oh, really?" Philip asked and then considered the statement. "It was too much to risk."

"What did you do?" Trevor asked, afraid of the answer.

"I got rid of all forms of identification. I believed it would still throw the police off my tracks, since Emily believed I had taken care of all the bullies. But I needed to remove all trace evidence that would help them identify everyone involved in Bishop's murder and who he was."

"Except that the police still found out. With all your and Jay's planning, they still found out it was him."

"Yes, that was a mistake on your part, and then mine," Philip sighed. "You see, when you had exacted your anger on Bishop, you had unintentionally dislodged some of his teeth.

"When they did the autopsy, they found it in his oesophagus, together with a small strand of hair. It was something I had not thought of checking on. When I heard from Jay what they had discovered, I immediately went to Emily's office and waited for her."

"And then you heard her final conclusions," Trevor said for him.

"How did you…." Philip asked, frowning. "Yes. From what she had said, I realised it was clear that her evidence was damning enough. So I kidnapped her."

"Wait," Trevor stopped him. "But the files still reached them. Jay told me Emily's evidence led them to me."

"I don't know how they came by that," Philip said. "By that time, I was already in Sacred Valley for… who knows how long."

"You never did tell me how you ended up here," Trevor said.

"I brought Emily with me to Sacred Valley. I had tried to restrain her with rope in my backseat, not realising that she was a cunning escape artist. She broke free as we passed Celestia Bridge and tried to push me off the steering wheel.

"The car careened down the bank's slope to the river, knocking me out. When I woke up, everything was foggy, and Emily was gone."

Trevor walked away. Pacing in circles, he considered everything he had been told and what he had discovered in the hospital. The weight of Bishop's death at his own hands was slightly off his shoulders, knowing now that Philip had delivered the final blow. Yet, there were still several things that made him feel uneasy about Philip's actions.

"You know, there was one thing that was quite peculiar to me," Trevor said, turning back to him. "The missing hearts."

"Oh yes," Philip said, turning back to the cooler and opening it up. He couldn't see what Philip was looking at. "That's something I've not had a chance to explain to anyone. But since I expect neither of us will be making it out here alive, I might as well share it with you.

"When I killed my first victim in that alley, his blood was all over my hands. There was something alluring about it. I decided to lick it off."

"Oh gross," Trevor said, stepping back in disgust.

"I can't explain the rush I got from the taste," Philip continued, taking something out of the box and holding it in his hand. "When I took the body to the warehouse after that, the hole in his chest just lay there staring at me.

"Something came over me. I wanted his heart, so I cut it out."

"Philip, please stop," Trevor said, putting his hand to his mouth in an effort to stop from throwing up.

"I just wanted a taste at first," he continued, revealing a heart in his hand. "The outer muscles were so good that I just carried on until nothing of the heart remained."

"You ate the whole damn heart!?" Trevor asked and then threw up between the steel under his feet.

"I know you don't understand," Philip said, running his fingers over the surface of the heart. "No one will. But with each killing, my craving for that taste came back, and I had to have it."

"So whose is that?" Trevor asked once he regained his composure.

"Bishop's," he replied. "I was saving this one for when I could actually enjoy it. I guess now it can be my final cigar."

To Trevor's utter surprise and revulsion, Philip bit into it. Whatever blood was left in it squirted out onto his mouth and nose, but he chewed into it like it was his last supper. Trevor clutched the axe, more for support than for any violent reason. He was unsure what to do, except turn around and run away.

As he ate, demonic wings broke out from his back. They looked like large bat wings with boils along the back of it. To complement this new look, Philip's lower body suddenly dropped off from his waist. The waist and legs fell to the floor, but the wings kept the torso floating in the air as he consumed the final part of the heart.

"Manananggal," Trevor whispered the mythical beast he recalled, just as Philip licked his fingers clean.

"And now," Philip said, turning his attention back to him, "it's your turn."

"Wait! Why me?"

"Your presence in Sacred Valley and me in this hell has made me realise something rather important," Philip said, flying higher up towards the ceiling. "I thought I was trapped here for my crimes, but now I am not so sure."

"What do you mean?" Trevor asked, hoping he would change his mind about attacking him.

"Everything was going well until you brought me Bishop," he explained, his upper canine teeth suddenly stretching out of his mouth like vampire fangs. "And nothing was happening with me in Sacred Valley until you arrived.

"I now realise that this all has to do with Bishop and that you are responsible for what is happening to me. I am being punished for your actions. So to get out of here, there's only one thing for me to do."

Trevor clutched the axe harder as the beast flew down. His fingers had become claws that aimed for Trevor's face. He brought the axe up as it slapped the claws to the side, but Philip flew up again.

"Just give into it!" Philip shouted, laughing like a maniac after that. "Your death is inevitable, whether it comes by my hand or another's."

It swooped down again. Trevor aimed and flung the axe up, but the vampire beast was prepared. It twisted its body and picked Trevor up by his clothes. Dragging him up into the air, Trevor was thrown against one of the cage walls. It hit his breath out as he fell to the floor below.

Unsure what else he could do, he simply stood and waited. Philip flew down again, and Trevor dodged to the side and struck. It bit into the beast's ribs, making it cry out in pain as he pulled it out again. The Manananggal flew up into the air, looking down at the injured side. Trevor watched in horror as the wound healed.

"HAHAHAHAHA!" the laugh filled the chamber. "You can't kill me, Trevor! No one can now!"

He ran low as the beast swooped down again, rolling away at the last moment to avoid having claws dig into him. The sharp nails clanged against the steel floor, sending sparks flying.

"There must be a way to kill you," Trevor muttered, watching as it turned around again for another strike. "There just must be."

Before he could formulate a plan, with decapitation at the top of his list, the Manananggal was on him again. Trevor parried and dodged again, but the claws bit into his left arm, making him drop the axe slightly. He had tears spring from his eyes in pain while he watched the beast go up again.

"Think, Trevor. Thi…"

His eyes caught the lower body of the beast on the floor beside the steel table. Suddenly, he remembered the one thing that could kill it. As it came down for him again, he rolled out the way and ran for the legs. When he reached it, he lifted the axe high above his head and brought it down on the body before him.

Once the axe sank into the flesh, a scream filled the chamber. Trevor looked around to see the Manananggal fall to the floor and roll around on its back in pain. Trevor ran towards it, hoping to drive the axe through its neck. When he reached it, he swung the axe up, aimed, and brought it down.

The beast opened its eyes at the last moment and struck with its claws. The sharp ends cut across Trevor's pants and into his skin. It didn't cut deep enough to stop him from walking, but the pain caused him to swing to the side instead. The Manananggal was up in the air again, flying away from Trevor.

It reached the ceiling as high as it could go and flew down at a tremendous speed. Trevor ran, hoping the change in angle would slow it down. The beast picked up pace until it was almost invisible and struck with both hands into Trevor. The claws dug into his abdomen just beneath his ribs and sent him flying forward before slamming into the cage floor.

Trevor opened his eyes. His belly was bleeding profusely. His eyesight was blurry, and he could no longer feel the axe in his hand. When he finally saw properly, he realised his arm was not paralysed. Instead, the axe had simply been knocked out of his hand towards the table.

The Manananggal seemed pleased. It grinned maliciously in the air above him, ready for the final slaughter. Trevor gathered what strength he had left inside, waiting for the right moment. As expected, the beast descended upon him, claws out ahead for the final strike.

He knew this was it. There would be no Lunar Nexus to save him now. With one deep breath, he waited for the claws to be above him before he rolled over his side several times. When he reached the axe, he lifted it up while groaning in pain from the effort. He brought it down to the waist and heard the beast cry out in pain once again.

Despite his exhaustion and agony, Trevor knew this was probably his last chance. He ran as fast as he could, ignoring the complaints from his body, and reached the Manananggal. Its heart was glowing a bright golden light, pumping hard and fast in its chest.

As its claws lashed out again, Trevor was the first to have an impact. The axe bit hard into its chest. The sound of cracking bones filled the chamber as it struck the heart. The beast gave one loud cry that shook the cage around them, lights of power and energy flaring up from the heart as it ruptured.

Finally, it exploded, causing Trevor to fall down beside it. He held onto the axe handle for as long as he could. The power thrummed against him, making it hard to determine what was happening. When he managed to squeeze his eyes open, he saw that the cage was caving in on itself. The steel was being crushed from all sides onto them.

At that moment, Trevor considered removing the axe from the chest to save himself. He looked at the place where the axe was embedded. A black circle was around the head of it, burning brighter than the golden glow all around it. Trevor pushed his arm forward into the maelstrom of energy, reaching out with his fingers towards the black Lunar Nexus.

As the metal around his feet started crushing his legs, his fingers touched the insignia. The world warped around him with the rush of sound that deafened him. Light brighter than the red Lunar Nexus entered his eyes and blinded him. He felt nothing and warmth at the same time. He screamed, but the surrounding noise killed any sound that could come from his mouth.

Trevor collapsed. It was gone. There was silence and stillness once more. He tried to open his eyes, managing just to get a slit of it open. He was back in the normal Ashenfall Hospital in foggy Sacred Valley, at the foot of the Bishop manikin's gurney in the Examination Room.

His hand was still clutching the handle of the axe. And next to him, under the head of the axe, was Philip's dead body.

ACT THREE

THE HORNED BEAST

26

SUPPLY STATION

Trevor stood like a zombie at the reception counter, staring down at the red Lunar Nexus. Philip's name had faded out in the bottom right of the symbol, just like Kathy's had been after her death. The only two names that still glowed brightly on the left side were Jason and Trevor.

He was unsure whether to be glad or confused about Jay's name still untainted on the sigil. On the one hand, it meant he was still very much alive, but on the other, it begged the question as to where he was. The only assumption he could make was that Jay had made it safely to the Police Station. Yet, it left him wondering why he had never let Trevor know.

After the Lunar Nexus washed over him and rejuvenated his body to full health again, Trevor checked his duffel bag. He had found it on the floor of the Examination Room, where he had dropped it just before awakening Bishop. The crowbar and shotgun were in their straps on the bag's sides, with the wrench still inside. The Beretta had been lost to Emily, which meant two things: he had to carry the torch again, and he had also lost the fifteen bullets he had placed inside the pistol when he reloaded.

Of the ammo, he had two boxes of shells left, two shells of which had been placed in the Citori. He had one and a half 9mm boxes left, leaving him with fifteen bullets in total. Thankfully, he still had the Ruger in the bag, so he had a pistol if needed.

Much to his dampened delight, the axe had come through with him from the hellish hospital. After several experiences, Trevor understood that as long as he was holding any items on him when the transformation between alternate dimensions happened, they came through with him.

All his notes and maps were still in place, as well as the mythology book. Of the medical supplies, he had three health bottles and one first aid kit left. He made sure his radio was on and headed towards the main entrance doors with only the street map in his hand. His desire to fight had gone, even with the knowledge that the Joro-Gumo spider lady could still be waiting in the front yard.

He opened the doors and stepped outside, not caring if he made a noise or not. The yard lacked any creatures, including the spiders he had killed before entering the hospital. The fog covered the streets again with its eerie blanket.

And still, Trevor made no attempt to take any of his weapons in hand. He simply listened to the silent radio as he left the yard and walked onto Shelley Street. Turning left, he made it to Emerson and headed right towards Celestia, where the bridge road led to the Police Station.

Everything was quiet in the mist. Trevor stepped louder on the streets, if only to make sure he had not gone deaf. His feet clapped on the pavement, but there was no wailing from the radio to accompany it. At any time before, the silence would have put him on edge. However, this time, he couldn't have cared less.

When he reached the Police Station on the northern corner of Emerson and Celestia, he took one last glance around. There were still no enemies lurking in the shadows of the mist and no indication of anything approaching him. He reached for the handle to the main doors when he heard a rattle in the lock.

"Trev!" Jay exclaimed as he opened the door. "I was wondering when I was going to see you! Come inside, please."

Not having much of a reply, Trevor followed him in. Jay locked the main doors again and proceeded to take him further into the building. It wasn't a very large precinct and had only a few rooms. They passed a secure room with a large metallic safe door. When they finally reached Jay's destination, and he sat down by a small police radio, Trevor noticed a red Lunar Nexus on a side wall.

"How long have you been here?" he asked, seeing the many files and papers that were in disarray on the main desk.

"Ever since I left you, basically," Jay replied. "I found a way down the riverbank to the bridge and then made my way here."

"Wait a second," Trevor said, rubbing his forehead and dropping his bag. "I thought you told me you were heading to the hospital."

"What? No, I clearly said I was coming here when I last saw you."

"Jay, after the school when I was on my way here... I got a radio message from you telling me you're heading for the hospital."

"No, pal," Jay said, raising his palms up in defence," that was definitely not me. I've been waiting here all along. Are you saying you went to the hospital first?"

"Yeah," he confirmed, "and met an old friend of ours."

"Who?" Jay asked, an eyebrow rising.

"Philip," he said, watching as the eyebrow went back down slowly. He could have sworn Jay's dark skin had gone slightly pale.

"What the hell is he doing here?" Jay asked, and then looked back out of the room. "And where is his sister, Kathy? I thought you went to the school to look for her?"

Trevor sighed. There was so much Jay did not know. He stared at his police friend for a moment, wondering how much he should tell him. It had become clear that Jay had not been completely honest about his relationship with Philip and Bishop's death. He suddenly remembered how secretive Jay had seemed when they had first walked through the fog-ridden streets together.

Starting with how he had reached Hollowbrook Elementary, he revealed what he had discovered about Caroline being Raven. He continued with the growing tension with Kathy and how it had led to the final showdown with the Inugami. He finished with how Kathy had informed him that the man with the twisted metal head was Bishop.

"You killed Kathy?" Jay asked with shock in his voice.

"I killed the Inugami," Trevor replied quickly. "I thought it would save Kathy."

"Clearly not," Jay snorted, and then sat quietly as Trevor stared hard at him.

"I found Caroline's house after that," he continued. "I discovered how close she was to Bishop and her reference to him being her guardian."

"Ok, so we're definitely dealing with Bishop then?" Jay asked.

"It seems so. Somehow, he has tapped into an ancient power here in Sacred Valley and is using it to get back at us."

"Back at us? You beat him to death."

"Nice try," Trevor said, sitting forward. "But Philip told me how he was still alive when we brought him in. He also told me how he executed Bishop to cover up our trail and how you were fully aware of it."

"Ahhh, I see," Jay said, looking away toward the radio beside him. "I'm sorry, I wanted to tell you. But Philip was convinced we should keep it to ourselves to protect you."

"You mean, to stop me from reporting you guys."

Jay had no further response. He kept looking to the side as if waiting for some reprieve from Trevor's accusation. Trevor sighed, sitting back in the chair and taking the moment to calm down. Jay must have sensed it, for he managed to look back at him again.

"What did you mean by ancient power here in Sacred Valley?" Jay asked, changing the topic.

"Did I ever tell you about Jeanette? The woman I met in that café on Hawthorne Avenue?"

"I can't remember," Jay replied. "What about her?"

"When I first met her, she told me how she was studying the occult and history of Sacred Valley," Trevor explained. "In the hospital, I discovered she was someone you may remember. Doctor Emily Hoffman."

"What??" Jay bolted forward in his chair. "The one who had submitted that evidence to the police?"

"The one and the same," he confirmed.

"What the hell is she doing here?"

"Hold on; one thing at a time."

Trevor told him what he could remember about the town's history and the ancient spirits. Jay sat and listened quietly, reclining in his chair again as if remembering some childhood tale. Once he was done, he informed him of his visit to the hospital and the details he had discovered about Philip and Emily.

"This is crazy," Jay said, rubbing his forehead while trying to process all the information. "So we're all tied to Bishop in some way."

"It looks like it," he said. "He seems to be the central figure in all of this."

"What about all these damn creatures, though?" Jay asked. "Where are they all coming from?"

Trevor reached into his bag and pulled out the school library book on mythology. He paged through it on the desk, stopping at certain places to quickly scan through the information.

"You see, there are some things I don't understand about them," Trevor finally replied. "Like I said before, I had only told Caroline about my love for mythology and the specific lore I had a fascination with.

"It would have been one thing if these were just random creatures. But the more I encounter them, the more I realise I know these beasts. I've intimately pointed them out to Caroline. So how does Bishop know about that?"

"She could easily have shared it with him?" Jay asked.

"Why? I'm sure it doesn't just come up in a conversation."

"You know, there is another possibility," Jay said. "We've been assuming that only one person is after us, but you've just told me that Emily is involved. Who says Caroline isn't in on this, too?"

It was Trevor's turn to go pale. The thought had occurred to him several times, but he had knocked it back. It was just easier to assume that someone else had wanted to pay them back for what they had done.

"If he has been able to harness this power, why not her?" Jay continued.

"I guess so," he replied, and then shook his head and rubbed it. "But that just makes it more confusing. Caroline killed herself. Why would she go to so much effort to punish us for what we did to him?"

"Hey man, she said it herself in that note you found," Jay said, leaning forward and gesturing with his hands. He seemed suddenly very convinced by his new argument. "They were close. She called him her guardian."

"Exactly," Trevor said, finding the part that confused him the most. "If he were her guardian and not the other way round, then why are they coming for what we did to him and not what had happened to her?"

"I think you're overthinking this," Jay said, standing up quickly. "They were siblings and looked out for each other. Take a break, man; you'll pop a vein."

Trevor sat forward with his head in his hands, trying to dispel his confusion and thoughts. Something inside him made it feel like he needed to solve the mystery soon. He pushed it down, trying to ease back to any form of serenity. He managed to just get the headache to subside when something slammed on the desk by him.

"I thought you might like that," Jay said, sitting down again. "Fuck, I'd love a beer right now."

The cursing was mildly ignored by the fascinating book beside him. He reached over and felt the damaged cover with the image of a single eye. In each corner of the book was a symbol, two of which he recognised. The first was the Lunar Nexus, while the other was the triangular symbol he had seen in both the school and the hospital.

"Where did you find this?" he asked, opening it up.

"In a safe in the chief's office," Jay smiled. "It seems we aren't the first to have these problems in Sacred Valley."

He looked through it. On the inside cover page, he saw an inscription that simply said 'Imanok'. Someone had taken the time to meticulously record other events that had happened in a place called Silent Hill. It seemed to be collated according to these events or the groups of people tied to them.

"Alessa and Dahlia," Trevor read the first section's notes out loud. "These names aren't familiar. There was also a Harry Mason who was looking for his daughter."

He went through several images of creatures that Harry had faced, as well as the locations he had been to.

"This is so strange," Trevor informed Jay. "He seems to have been through similar places we were. Then again, in Raven's journal, there was mention of a girl who was tormented for being a witch. But it wasn't Alessa. I can't remember the name, though."

He moved on to the next section, skipping the rest of the details. He saw a sketch of a man named James Sunderland. What followed was the same rough formula of creatures he had faced, the people he had met and the locations he had been to.

"Mmm, this one was looking for his dead wife," Trevor noted.

"Hey, you guys could go to a pub and talk it out about dead wives," Jay joked, and then sat back when Trevor glanced at him. "Just saying."

"He was directly responsible for her death, though," he said defensively, and then skipped to the next section. "I wasn't."

He saw Harry's face again and the mention of his daughter Heather. As he worked through the pages, he realised she had turned out to be Alessa. Frowning, he read through the section further until he could understand it better.

"This girl Alessa actually managed to get out of the other hellish world and this fog world into the real world," Trevor said. "Or at least be born through Heather into our world."

"Say what?" Jay asked.

"I don't know," he replied. "I don't understand half of what I'm reading. But something's bothering me. If she was really able to do this, then I wonder if that's what Bishop isn't up to."

"What do you mean?"

"I forgot to tell you about half of the things I needed to do in the school to find Kathy," Trevor explained. "One of those was dealing with historical paintings that had slightly been altered. Instead of the faces I was meant to see, I saw Bishop and all of us who were involved in his murder."

"Oh really?" Jay said, sitting forward in keen interest.

"I wish I had taken a photo of those paintings, though," he replied, closing his eyes. "But if I remember correctly, the images had to do with him killing us off and then being resurrected into the real world."

"Oh shit," Jay said, his eyes wide. "So... hold on a second. You're saying that in order for him to get his life back, he has to take ours?"

"I'm not saying anything," Trevor replied, looking up at him. "I'm just telling you what I saw."

"This is heavy, man," Jay said, standing up again and pacing up and down. And then he stopped. "Hang on. What if we stop him?"

"How? By killing him again?"

"There must be a way, right?" Jay said, sitting down and moving the chair closer to him. "I mean, they stopped Alessa in this other place. What else does that book say?"

Slightly excited by Jay's enthusiasm, Trevor worked through the rest of the sections. Next was a man named Henry Townsend, who was locked in a room where the only exit was through a hole in his bathroom wall. It seemed Henry's only connection to the murdered Walter Sullivan was that he was to be one of the victims in his ritual sacrifices.

The next section dealt with Travis Grady. It presented happenings from before the first section, when Alessa was originally burned. Wondering why it was not placed at the very beginning of the book, he decided to move on and find anything else that might be relevant.

He read through Alex Shepherd's section and the brief history of Shepherd's Glen before reaching another section on Harry Mason. The story seemed slightly different than the first, making Trevor wonder if someone wasn't just scribbling down thoughts instead of actually recording real events. When he reached the end of that section, he saw that it had been Heather Mason's recordings of what she had tried to remember.

The final section dealt with a prisoner named Murphy Pendleton and his involvement in a cover-up and police corruption. Trevor worked through the pages and then closed it when he was done.

"Anything?" Jay asked.

"Well, when Emily had said this is our personal hell, she really meant it," Trevor sighed. "What's strange is that none of the creatures I've encountered are in this book. As a matter of fact, they all are different for each case. Even the locations alter for each person. And some of them refer to the other version of this Silent Hill town as Otherworld. It sounds like Darcwurld; that's what Philip called it."

"Ok, so where does that leave us with taking care of Bishop?"

"I don't know," Trevor said, pushing the book across the desk. "I don't think that book will help us."

"And won't any of your mythology help us?" Jay asked, getting desperate. "You said it seems to revolve around your love for mythology and the supernatural. The only mythology I know is Greek; literally."

"Now that you mention it," he replied, standing up to walk around the room for a bit, "there is one thing that could help. There is a belief that if you burn the remains of a ghost or supernatural being, then the haunting or apparition will vanish forever. The only problem is, I don't know where Bishop's remains are."

"Awesome," Jay smiled with a huge grin.

"Wait, why are you so happy all of a sudden?"

"The one thing Philip never knew was that Bishop's corpse went missing from the police autopsy room," Jay replied. "The police were keeping it under wraps, not wanting the public to know just how inefficient they could be."

"You took the body?" Trevor asked, not believing his ears.

"Even better," Jay smiled even brighter. "I took it to the one place I never thought anyone would look for it. I buried it in the remains of Silverview Hotel, near the resort."

"What??" Trevor shouted, and then moved forward and grabbed him by the collar. Jay's back slammed into the desk, with his smile wiped off immediately. "You dumb idiot!"

"Hey!" Jay shouted, pulling Trevor's hands off his neck easily. "What the hell are you on about?"

"Do you realise that bringing the body here is probably the one thing that gave him the power to do all this!?"

"Oh," Jay said, looking down in thought. "No. Honestly, I really hadn't thought of that."

Trevor moved away from him and ran his hands over his face. Things were starting to make some more sense now. He looked at Jay while things worked through his mind and then took out both Central and Old Sacred Valley maps. He placed them on the desk.

"We need to get to those remains," Trevor said. "If we can find them before Bishop finds us, or finds out what we plan to do, we can burn the bones and maybe get out of this place in one piece."

"That's great. Sounds like a good plan," Jay responded, looking at the street layout. "But I'm looking at this map, and you know what I see?"

"What?" he asked, scanning it for anything that stood out.

"Many streets to get through, which means probably more creatures we would need to deal with," Jay replied. "More than that, if we head through the streets to the resort, Bishop might see us coming or know what we are up to."

"Alright," Trevor said, realising what he meant. "So what do you suggest? So far, he has had the upper hand, leading me to the school with Kathy and to the hospital with Philip. I'm up for any suggestions."

"Here," Jay said, pointing to the right of the police station. There's a small dock there, opposite the cemetery, that leads onto Silvercrest Lake."

"You want us to go near a cemetery in a town filled with monsters?"

"Just hear me out," Jay said, pointing a line down the map. "If we follow this coastline around the lake, it leads to a lighthouse near the hotel. It's much easier, quicker, safer, and Bishop won't know where we're heading until it's too late."

"Mmm," Trevor said, trying to find a hole in his theory. "You know what, that may just be your best idea yet. The only problem is, will there be a boat when we arrive?"

"At Ashbourne station," Jay replied, reaching up to a steel cabinet on the wall above the desk, "we were always told of a police patrol boat called Silver Sally that was the pride of the Sacred Valley precinct in the old days.

"Jay," Trevor started to stop him.

"It was one of the most beautiful patrol boats you could ever have seen," he continued, finding a key and then handing it to Trevor. "All I'm saying is, let's go have a look, and if it's not there, then we just pop back here and think of another plan."

Trevor looked down at the key and saw the words Silver Sally on the tag. He sighed deeply, and then looked down at his bag.

"We're going to need weapons, supplies," he said, still considering the option.

"Got that sorted," Jay smiled again, as if that would make up for bringing Bishop's body to Sacred Valley.

Trevor followed him back down the passages to the safe door he had seen before. It appeared as if Jay had been in there recently, as he pulled a large safe key out of his pocket and unlocked it. Jay opened the door and stood there with a beaming face that invited Trevor to go inside.

When he reached the door's threshold, the sight made him stand still. It was a weapon and ammunition armoury.

"What's wrong with them?" Trevor asked.

"Many of the weapons have been damaged," Jay replied, moving to the back of the room. "These are mostly ones that have been returned for repairs or replacement."

"Is there anything we can use here?"

Jay continued walking towards a steel cabinet that reached the ceiling and had three doors. Using a smaller key, he unlocked the doors and opened them up.

"While I was waiting for you, I've been tinkering with a few of them to see what I can put together," Jay said, taking out a pistol. "How's that Ruger working for you?"

"Well, I found a Beretta that I quite liked, but Emily took it from me," he replied.

"Here, try this," Jay said, handing him the silver stainless steel pistol. "It's a Smith and Wesson M&P9. It can take up to seventeen bullets, but I've extended the clip to make it twenty. I hate having loose bullets lying around when I empty a box into it."

"A box?" Trevor asked while inspecting the pistol. "Don't they usually have ten bullets in them?"

"Welcome to the big leagues, kid," Jay smiled, throwing him two boxes.

They were larger than the boxes he had become used to. He saw they contained twenty bullets, but he opened it up just to make sure.

"I've modified that Smithy in other ways, too," Jay continued to explain while returning to the cabinet. "There's a laser light and torch under the barrel that will help you with your aim, as well as an extra dual-illuminated RMR optic sight at the top there."

"Oh yes!" Trevor exclaimed while examining the top of the chamber.

"Yeah, I thought you might like that."

"No, this red dot at the top," Trevor showed him. "The one that lights up when the chamber is empty. I missed having that on the Beretta."

"Ah yes, of course," Jay replied, amused at his excitement. "The gun's already loaded, and here's its holster."

Trevor replaced the old holster with the new one, placing the pistol in it. Jay threw him a ballistic vest next. Even though he doubted any monsters would be throwing bullets at them, he put it under his top for extra protection anyway.

"That bag of yours is pretty small, so here, use this one," Jay said, throwing it over to him.

"It's like Christmas in Sacred Valley," Trevor laughed, inspecting the bag. It was twice as wide as his duffel bag and only slightly longer, but he could still strap it onto his back. There were four external straps, two on each side. "I can put the pipe and axe on this side, and the Citori on the other side."

"I doubt you'll want the Citori much longer."

Jay threw a shotgun with a silver chrome-plated barrel into the air. Trevor managed to catch it just before it hit the ground. It had a black pump-action forestock on the magazine, with matching black rear stock and recoil pad. The letters SXP were on the receiver.

"It's a Winchester Super X Pump Silvercrest Defender," Jay smiled. "Takes five shells, which I've loaded for you, but here are some extra boxes of twenty."

Jay threw two boxes in the air. Trevor caught them and placed them with the spare bullets in the bag. He was so mesmerised by the shotgun that it took some effort to finally strap it on the left side of the bag.

"What are you going to use?" Trevor asked, wondering why Jay didn't keep the firearms for himself.

"Oh, don't worry about me," Jay's eyes glinted as he took out another shotgun. "Say hello to the Remington 870, the love of my life."

Trevor only looked at it momentarily when something else in the cabinet caught his attention. A chainsaw was resting on its housing with the saw chain up against the back of the cabinet. There was some blood and meat on it from recent usage. On a shelf higher up, there was another firearm.

"Hey, what's that?" he asked, moving forward to inspect it further.

"That's a Colt M4 Carbine assault rifle," Jay said, taking it out and handing it to him. "I was building it up for us to use, but there are some parts broken that I can't find replacements for."

"Like what?" he asked, turning the weapon around in his hands.

"Well, the trigger is faulty, the bolt catch and magazine catch spring are missing, and there's no 5.56mm ammo anywhere."

"Can't we take it with us anyway? Maybe we'll find another supply store."

"Sure, if you're willing to carry the extra weight," Jay said, closing the cabinet and moving towards the door. "Come, there's one more thing I think you would like to see."

Deciding against keeping the damaged rifle, he put it back and followed Jay to the Chief's office. When he walked in, he did not need Jay to explain what it was that he needed to see. In a corner of the room, there was an armour stand with an ancient samurai suit on it.

"It looks a bit heavy to wear, though."

"Oh, I have no intention of putting that on," Trevor said, but moved towards it anyway. "But I definitely want this."

He untied the suit's scabbard and belt and pulled the katana blade out. The metal glinted against the office light. He felt the sharp edge carefully and saw a small strip of blood form on his fingertip.

"Oh man, this is well looked after," Trevor said in awe, before turning to Jay. "Can I take it?"

"It's all yours, man. The little I know about swords is dangerous."

In excitement, he strapped the belt under the holster and put the sword on his left hip with the pistol in his right.

"Alright," he said, blood boiling from anticipation. "Let's go find Bishop."

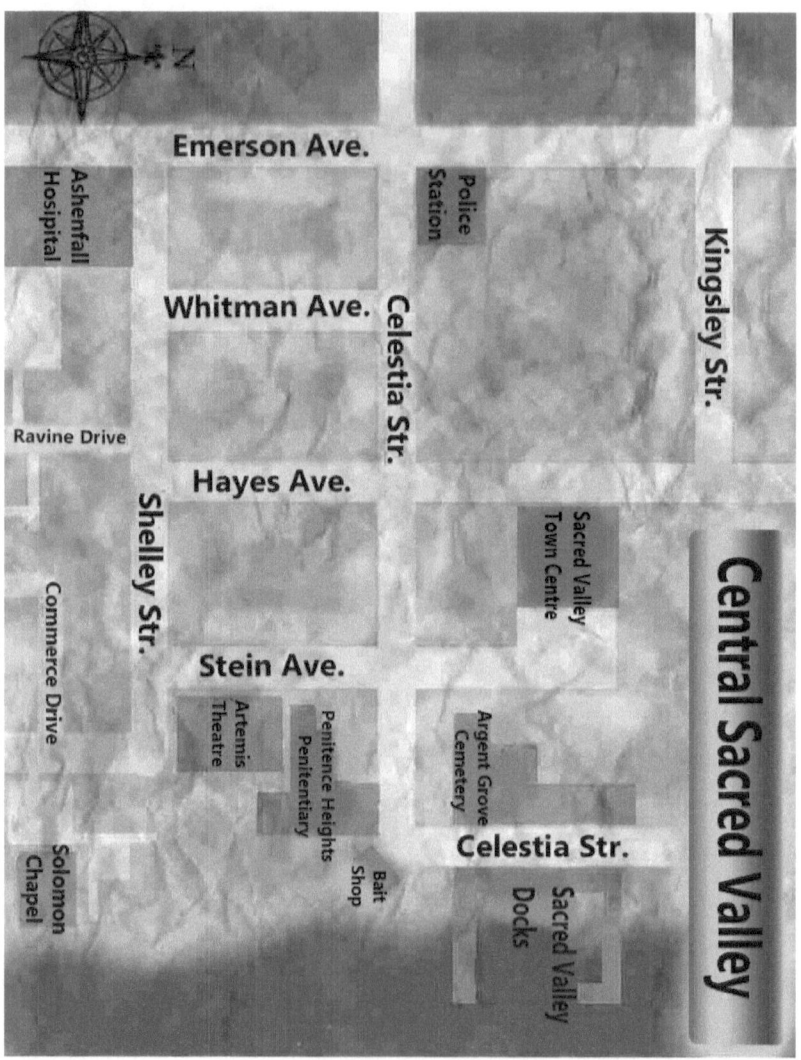

27

FINDING SILVER SALLY

Once Trevor transferred all his items from the duffel bag to the new police bag, handing Jay the spare gas cans for his chainsaw, they set out. They took turns touching the Lunar Nexus one more time before heading to the front yard. Trevor made sure that his radio was on.

Holding the M&P9 in hand, he shone the light ahead of him as they walked at a brisk pace towards the pavement and turned left onto Celestia Street. Jay had his chainsaw at the ready, not having anywhere else on him to put it. They had not reached Wilson Street yet when the radio started to crackle.

Trevor raised the pistol at eye level, making sure the laser was ready to aim at whatever creature approached. Jay put the chainsaw's motor on. The radio wailed slightly louder as the beast entered into view.

"What the hell is that?" Jay asked.

The creature walked on all fours. It was humanoid in shape, but the head was at the back of the beast. As it got closer, they saw that it was a nude man walking on his hands and knees in reverse. His butt cheeks faced them with a large eye between them where the anus should have been. Along its back, there were dome-shaped cancerous growths and two large mounds by the scapula.

"It looks familiar, but I don't have time to check the book now," Trevor replied and offloaded three bullets.

The ammo struck into its flesh, but the beast showed no pain from the impact. Jay moved forward and activated the chainsaw. Raising it in the air, he dropped it down on the beast's lower back. Just as the saw's chain reached the bulging eye, the buttocks and eye split open in two, revealing ferocious teeth within it.

The anal mouth caught the saw chain and made it stop turning. Jay tried to pull it back out, but the grip was too strong. Trevor shot five more bullets until he realised that it was not helping. The radio increased in pitch, and Trevor turned in time to see two more of the beasts to his right.

He raised his hand, but it was too late. The first beast lunged for his ankle and bit into it. The meaty flesh end eye innards wrapped around his leg like a parasite as Trevor screamed. He was easy prey for the second creature as it jumped over him with its buttocks and bit into his neck….

…his last gurgled cries echoing into the police station. He shook his head, wiping away the cobwebs of death as the warmth of the nearby Lunar Nexus washed him clean. He closed his eyes and held his head as the pain subsided. A thud brought his attention back to the room.

"They got you too, huh?" Trevor asked.

"Yeah, man," Jay replied. "Another two came from Wilson's side."

Trevor used the wall to help himself up and then offered Jay a hand. They moved to the desk where Trevor opened the mythology book. He worked through the contents until he found the section on humanoids.

"Where's your chainsaw?" he asked while reading.

"I had to let it go," Jay answered. "It was still in that thing's mouth…uhm, ass."

"Here we go," Trevor said when he finally found the relevant entry. "I thought I recognised it from somewhere, but the extra growths on its back threw me off."

"So what is it?" Jay moved closer. "More importantly, can it be killed?"

"It's called a Shirme," he replied, sliding the book to Jay. "The book doesn't have much to go on. It simply says an apparition of a man, having an eye where his butt is. There's no mention of those teeth. It seems this town has altered this monster a bit, too."

"It says here that there was once a samurai warrior who saw it, but the

Shirme ran away the moment he approached it," Jay read out loud.

"Yeah," Trevor said, wondering what he was going on about.

"Didn't samurai have swords like yours?"

Trevor looked at the sword on his hip and then brought it out, placing the M&P9 in his holster. It glinted in the soft light as he ran his fingers along the side of the blade's edge.

"It's worth a try," he finally said.

They prepared themselves and then headed back out. Checking his pistol quickly, he saw that the eight bullets he had shot before they had been killed were gone.

"I guess there are some things the Lunar Nexus can't resurrect," Trevor mumbled quietly to ease his tension.

As they advanced to the area where they had been killed, the radio picked up its noise again. Jay had his shotgun at the ready while Trevor held the katana before him. The first of the Shirme made an appearance. It moved towards Jay, who stepped backwards to let Trevor close in on it.

When the Shirme pounced towards Jay, Trevor struck from the side. The blade cut into its ribs, slicing a wedge of meat onto the road as the beast let out a horrendous scream. Not wasting time to let it recover, Trevor cut the blade through the neck, and it fell limp to the ground as the eyeless head rolled off.

Before they could congratulate themselves, another two approached. Jay shot at the one by him to stall it while Trevor dealt with his one. As it ran awkwardly on all four limbs to him, he hacked the sword into it until it fell down onto the road and died. He joined Jay, helping him out.

"Now I wish we had two of those," Jay said as they moved forward. 'I feel kind of useless."

"Don't worry. Just keep distracting them while I take care of them."

They found the other three that had killed Jay and Trevor, making quick work of them. He ensured they were dead by listening to the radio as it went quiet. They walked forward and saw two puddles of blood on the ground.

By the second puddle was Jay's chainsaw.

"Use that to keep them busy rather," Trevor said as Jay slotted his shotgun onto his bag. "Save your ammo."

They moved on further. Wilson Street branched off to their right, but they continued onwards towards the dock. The radio warned them of more beasts approaching just before they reached Simmons Street. Jay distracted the first Shirme with his chainsaw while Trevor took care of a second.

When both had been dispatched, they crossed over Simmons. They had hardly moved past the intersection when the road suddenly fell away into the abyss.

"Dammit," Jay cursed as Trevor took the street map out.

"We can go down Hayes, move along Shelley and hope for a way up Stein Avenue to the other side of this gap," Jay offered.

Taking his suggestion, they travelled on the route. They encountered three more Shirme before turning into Shelley. Halfway towards Stein Avenue, the road broke into the abyss again. Trevor stood there, looking over the rubble's edge before consulting the map again.

"That building there," Jay said, pointing at the indicated location, "the Sacred Valley Town Centre. It looks like it has a large parking lot behind it."

"What about it?"

"Maybe we can find a way onto Stein from there?"

"Well, it's worth a shot, I guess."

They travelled back to Celestia Street through Hayes Avenue again. They crossed over Celestia into the northern part of Hayes until the Town Centre was on their right.

"Should we check the other buildings up the road first, maybe find some more supplies?" Trevor asked.

"No," Jay said, heading to the front doors of the Town Centre. "The quicker we get to Silver Sally, the happier I will feel."

Trevor took a glance further up Simmons into the mist.

He had a feeling inside that told him there was something valuable up ahead, but he understood Jay's instinct to rather get to the patrol boat.

The door was unyielding. Jay thumped it door a few times, but no one came to their call. They searched the left and right sides until they found a gate that ran into the side yard. Moving along this path, Trevor cast his pistol down as he inspected their surroundings.

He stood still as the light touched the ankle-deep dead grass. Something was moving within it. The grass blades shifted ever so slightly and, for a moment, Trevor thought it was the shifting mist around them. He leaned down and shone the torch just above the grass. The blades continued to shift, but he could not see anything that was causing the movement.

Standing up again, he moved ahead until he caught up to Jay, who was waiting for him at the end of the path where the Town Centre building ended and the backyard began. They moved through the mist, hoping that the route to Stein was open.

Their feet touched soft sand as they walked over a small play area for children. There was a swing, seesaw, merry-go-round and jungle gym entrenched in the sand. Up ahead, Trevor saw a parking lot, just as Jay had predicted there might be. The mist was thinner in that area, and he could just make out wide open gates that led onto Wein Street.

Something creaked behind him as he stepped onto the paving of the parking lot. He looked back and saw that the swing was in motion. When it reached the front peak of its swing, he noticed the ghost of a young girl on it. When the swing moved back down, she vanished until it reached the other height of its motion.

The more he saw her, the more he realised that she looked frozen. It was not just the paralysed body language, but the ice that surrounded her ghostly form. He watched her for a moment longer, only able to see her at each apex, before he decided to move on.

The moment he turned around, the creaking stopped. He looked back to see that the swing was completely still, as if it had never moved in the first place. Shaking his head, he jogged to catch up to Jay. They crossed the parking lot and finally made it to the open gate towards Stein Avenue.

They stopped dead. The frozen apparition was before them. She was standing with her arms up in the air as if wanting to be held. Jay got such a fright that he brought the chainsaw crashing down on her head, sending the ice in shatters onto the road. The ice melted into the mist and was gone with no sign of the girl.

"What the hell are you doing?!" Trevor shouted, moving forward to inspect the spot she had stood on.

"Do you really think she needed our help?" Jay asked incredulously. "A frozen spirit, in a haunted town full of monsters? Come on, man, wake up."

Jay moved on, not waiting for a reply. Trevor followed shortly, the upper end of Stein narrowing into two lanes as they progressed further down. He spared one look back at the open gates, seeing the girl standing there. She had no ice on her this time, and her arm moved up freely as she waved at him.

The mist grew denser and moved like a cloud towards her. It swept over her, leaving a soft sigh in the air. Once the vapour mass had moved into the parking lot, he saw that she was once again gone.

Shining his light before him on the road, he saw movement beneath him. It had followed them from the parking lot and was moving towards Celestia. He realised suddenly what it was that had been moving in the grass.

"Hey, Jay!" he shouted. "Hold up!"

"What's wrong?" Jay asked when Trevor caught up with him.

"Do you see that trail of small black spiders?" he asked, shining the M&P9's light down.

"Yeah?" Jay asked cautiously, afraid of what he was about to say next.

"When I was on my way to the hospital to meet you, I came across the same spiders. When I reached the hospital, a woman was holding what looked like a baby wrapped in white linen. When she gave me the parcel to hold, I saw a load of eggs inside it."

"Ok, and I guess that has to do with the spiders?"

"It erupted with black wolf spiders," Trevor confirmed. "If you see her, rather avoid her or let's kill her immediately. It's a Joro-Gumo, and she likes to seduce men and then kill them."

"Ok, got it."

When they found Celestia again, they saw that they had indeed reached the other side of the abyssal gap. They turned left towards the dock. Trevor's nerves were taut. The radio was still silent, and he was unsure as to what that meant. It was too quiet for his liking.

The road took a left bend. They walked up to the huge dock gates that prevented them from seeing what was inside. Jay took a glance at the cemetery opposite the gates.

"You know, if the streets are this bad," he said, pointing at the cemetery, "I don't even want to know what is inside there."

Trevor inspected the bars of the gates. There was a large steel padlock closing it off from entry. He walked up and down both gates, searching for any clue for a key that may have been hidden nearby. When he reached the end of the right gate, he saw a note scratched in the wood:

The only way in is to take the bait

"Is that supposed to be some cryptic clue or something?" Jay asked.

"I'm not sure," Trevor replied, taking out his map. "There's a bait shop on the bend we passed."

"Do you think they meant that literally?" Jay asked, perplexed.

"We won't know until we go look."

Following Trevor's lead this time, they headed back. The radio was still quiet when they found the bait shop. He tested the door and discovered that it swung in at his very first touch. The door handle had been broken off, leaving the door to simply rest on its hinges.

"I don't like this," Jay said. "It should never be this easy."

"Maybe it's just a broken door," Trevor said snidely.

The bait shop was dark, and the light switches did not help the lack of illumination. Using the torches on their firearms, they searched the store until Trevor found a safe built into the wooden floor under the counter at the back. The fridges and deep freezers stood quietly with the remains of their wares within them.

"Anything?" Jay said when Trevor did not emerge from behind the counter.

"There's a safe here with a four-digit combination lock," he informed him.

"And let me guess, no combination code anywhere?"

Trevor didn't feel like the question required a response. Instead, he stood up and moved towards the freezers.

"The message on that gate said that we needed to take the bait," he told Jay. "Start looking through the bait boxes. Maybe the store owner wrote the code on one of them."

"Oh shit!" Jay said as he opened a fridge, clutching his nose closed. "This stuff honks to high heaven."

"Just go through it, will ya?"

Keeping his nose clutched, Jay continued to look in the fridges along the wall. At the same time, Trevor investigated the freezers in the centre. By the third freezer, he found what he was looking for. Underneath three tubs were written four numbers along the bases. The etchings of some of the numbers were split over the bases, so it was easy for Trevor to work out the order of the numbers.

"Here we go," Trevor announced, with a grateful Jay closing the fridge he was busy with.

Using the code, he opened the safe and found a single, long key inside it. Feeling triumphant and edgy simultaneously, he closed the safe and moved towards the shop door. The radio remained quiet as they moved back onto the misty road. They reached the dock gates with nothing disturbing them.

Trevor bent down and tried the key. It took a moment for the rusty lock to accept it and finally open up. They hauled the heavy gate open until they could both get through and then closed it behind them. The moment the two ends of the gates met, the radio started crackling softly.

"Of course," Trevor said, turning around to face the docks.

"Thought it was too quiet," Jay said, receiving a scowling glare from Trevor.

From where they stood, past the dock building before them to the left, they could see Silver Sally. She stood proud and majestic against a wooden berth, softly shifting against the lapping water of Silvercrest Lake. Dampened lights from light poles at the dock shone against the name of the patrol boat.

She had a silver sheen to her, her name painted in pink. It looked more like a luxurious yacht or cruiser than a patrol boat. They moved forward, Trevor entranced by the beauty of the boat. The closer they got to it, the more the radio rose in pitch, indicating that something was waiting for them ahead. Confirming his gut feeling, he shone the light down. The trail of black spiders marched ahead of them towards the dock.

Much to Trevor's expectations, the source of the radio's consternation was revealed. The Joro-Gumo walked into view between them and the ship as they passed the dock building. As before by the hospital, she had a package swaddled in linen in her arms.

"Are you sure she's a monster?" Jay asked, staring at her exquisiteness.

"Yes," he replied. "Watch out for the spiders, though; she uses that as her main attack before she eats her victims."

"Do you think the Lunar Nexus will return us if she eats us?"

"Uhm… good question," he answered, realising it might not. "Just don't let her eat you."

"I don't understand how something with such a small, beautiful mouth could eat us, though," Jay said.

The woman saw Trevor. By the expression on her face, he saw that she recognised him. Her eyebrows creased in anger, and she pointed at him, dropping the wrapping in her hands. It hit the floor with a crack, the liquid of the cracked eggs running down the concrete dock.

"Did she break the eggs last time, too?" Jay asked, with Trevor staring at her in confusion.

"Something's wrong," Trevor said as the radio started wailing like a siren suddenly.

Her lower body transformed. She rose into the air as eight hairy spider legs hoisted her up. Her face took on a more demonic look with sharp, vampiric teeth. Her hair sizzled like a medusa's snakes while her eyes burned the deep red of blood. Her gown ripped open, revealing eight large dark nipples on her torso in two vertical rows down to her belly. Her shoulders and back were covered in rough orange fur.

"What the fuck is that?!" Jay shouted over the wailing of the radio.

"You know, just because you're panicking doesn't mean you have to swear," Trevor replied, turning the radio off.

"Can you get over your petty hatred for cursing for one moment to just tell me what the hell is going on?!" Jay said, dropping the chainsaw and taking the Remington instead. "You never said she would turn into that."

"As far as I know, there's nothing in the Joro-Gumo legend that suggests she would," Trevor said, changing the sword for his shotgun too.

She towered over them, her belly at head height. They started shooting, and she rushed towards them, the shells ripping into her chest and legs. She staggered slightly, but kept moving closer towards them. The blood dripped off her body, but the shells did not slow her down.

When the shotgun ran out, Trevor jumped to the right side to avoid the first strike. One of her legs came down onto him. It was only when it struck the concrete beside him with a metallic shrill that he realised the legs tapered to a steel point. Jay rolled away as she struck him with a leg too, while Trevor loaded five more shells.

She turned to him as he shot into her side, giving Jay time to reload. Trevor had two shots left when she swiped the shotgun out of his hand. The firearm crashed into a garage door as he reached up to grab the axe. Another sharp leg crashed down, and he jumped back, striking into the upper meaty part of her leg.

The axe bit into the flesh, but she pulled her leg up and ripped the axe handle from his grasp. With it remaining lodged in her leg, she moved to him again just as Jay lifted the chainsaw and let it bite into one of her rear legs. The beast screeched, more in agitation than agony, and turned to smack Jay in his chest.

With her back turned towards him, Trevor reached down for his pistol when he saw something strange. The fur he had noticed earlier was striped like a tiger. This was further complemented by a tiger tail protruding out of her rear.

Trevor stepped back in thought. Years of mythological lore and study went through his mind like a library of books flapping before his eyes. He remembered a beast that had a tiger's body, spider ligaments and a demonic face. While she hit the chainsaw out of Jay's hand, he closed his eyes and tried harder to remember.

"Tsuchigumo!" Trevor shouted as it occurred to him. He unsheathed the katana. "Once killed by the most powerful samurai warrior ever known."

As if the mere mention of the tale awoke the legend, the sword suddenly vibrated in his hand. He could feel power thrum from his hands up the length of the blade as the steel glinted a cyan sheen. It felt like he was possessed by an ancient spirit as the sword lifted with the point towards the beast.

The sword recognised an ancient enemy. Trevor stepped onto the ground, taking a samurai stance. It felt like the samurai warrior was within him. Jay called to Trevor as Jay fell on his back with the beast lurching above him for the final strike. Trevor kicked against the ground and ran towards it.

As its leg came down towards Jay's sternum, the blade cut cleanly through one of her rear legs. It reared back and upwards like a horse, while the severed ligament fell to the floor. The Tsuchigumo landed back on the ground and attacked Trevor. It could sense the samurai warrior's spirit in the blade and raced to defeat it.

Trevor blocked up against a descending leg, swiping to the side as the two metallic objects met. The leg dislocated and then sliced off, making the beast stagger back and cry out into the mist. It was backing towards Silver Sally now, her legs near the edge of the dock.

Realising she would not last against his attacks, she took the offensive one last time. She rose up into the air on her remaining hind legs, the forelegs prancing before her. She prepared for the final drop, the three legs ready to strike onto him simultaneously. Trevor held his ground, the katana held firmly in his two hands as he watched and waited.

The legs struck down, and Trevor ran forward. As the legs crashed into the concrete, sending sprays of rubble into the air, he struck upwards. With her belly above him, the sword cut cleanly into her chest. He ran further, driving the edge along her body between the nipples. When he reached the end of the belly, he slipped the sword out and rolled away from her body.

Trevor sheathed the sword. The Tsuchigumo fell back, its forelegs lifting up in the air as its head angled over towards the patrol boat. Its innards started pouring out, collecting on the concrete in a large mound. Jay joined his side as its demonic head slammed onto the side of the boat.

"Are those …. skulls?" Jay asked, studying the objects that had fallen out of her belly.

"Yes," Trevor replied as he moved to collect his axe and shotgun. "One thousand, nine hundred and ninety skulls, to be exact."

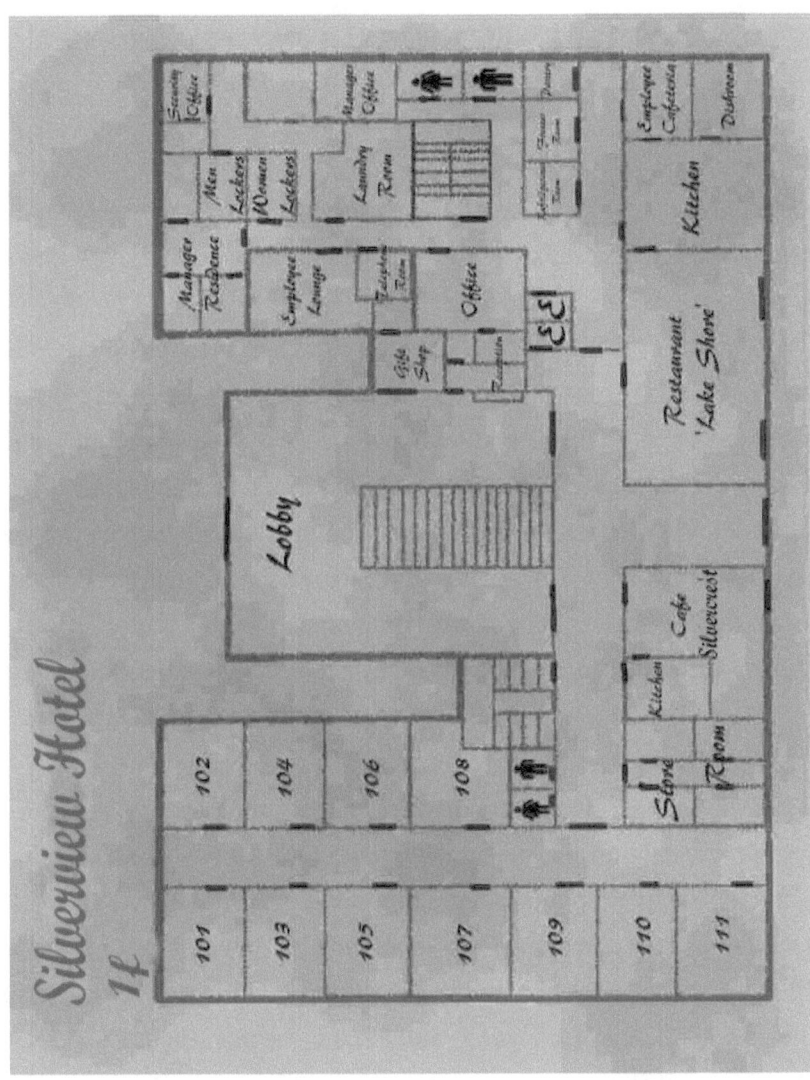

28

HAUNTING IN THE SACRED HOME

The boat ride was a quiet one. Trevor tried to enjoy the calm as much as he could. He watched as the waters lapped against the sides, the bow cutting through Silvercrest Lake serenely.

A towering object emerged from within the mist before them. Trevor stood up from his seat beside Jay at the helm. As they got closer, he realised it was a lighthouse with a pier at its base. The light was not operating, leaving Trevor to consider when it was last maintained.

Jay continued past the lighthouse. Trevor noticed that he was very much deep in thought. He wondered where Jay would set the boat in, as the only dock appeared to be at the lighthouse.

"Don't worry too much about the lighthouse," Jay said, as if reading his mind. "There is a small dock right in front of the hotel that I used when I came here to bury the bones."

Sure enough, a small wooden dock came into view. Jay pulled Silver Sally onto the side of the pier, manoeuvring her until she was settled in. Trevor assisted in tying the ropes up onto the moorings. Making sure they had their bags and items, they disembarked onto the pier.

"Let's just get the bones and destroy them," Jay said. "No side turns."

"Agreed," Trevor said, also wanting to destroy Bishop's bones as quickly as possible.

He held the pistol in his hands for the torch and security. Checking the mag, he saw that it was still loaded with eleven bullets, with one in the chamber. They progressed forward, Jay shifting his bag while holding the chainsaw. The radios remained silent on their sides.

They walked up the stairs leading to the hotel's land. Perimeter brick walls introduced the property of Silverview Hotel. They moved towards the wall until they found an opening and entered. Trevor gripped the pistol's handle harder, expecting trouble to appear.

They walked on a path between two square patches of lawn. Jay slowed his walk, frowning heavily as the hotel appeared before them. It towered three storeys high, with the hotel's name emblazoned on its walls.

"Didn't you say that you buried the bones in the hotel's remains?" Trevor asked, looking up the walls and down the sides. The mist hid how wide it was.

"That's exactly what I said," Jay replied, rubbing his palm on the entrance wall to make sure it was not an illusion. "The last time I came here, there was no building. It had all burned down."

"Well, I'm sorry to question your memory, but there's definitely a building here now," Trevor said. "Are you a hundred per cent sure this is where you buried it?"

Jay looked at him in doubt and then touched the entrance door handle. Trevor watched in anticipation when his hand turned, and the door opened. Casting Trevor one more look, he entered the hotel. Trevor gave the building one last glance before following.

The door banged closed behind them and locked. Trevor turned around quickly and turned the knob. When that failed, he tried to use his body to force it open.

"Move," Jay said. Stepping forward in big lunges, he stretched a leg and kicked at the door.

What would have sent any other door flying in splinters simply caused this one to vibrate. Jay recoiled backwards from the force and stared at it in defiance.

"I don't like this," Trevor said. "It's like the hotel doesn't want us to leave."

"A building can't think, man," Jay said, turning to look down the passage. "In all likelihood, Bishop's realised what we're up to and is trying to stop us from finding his remains."

"Well, if that's true, then he's succeeding."

"If I have to chainsaw through the floor to get it, then I will," Jay said, moving forward down the dark passage.

"Wait, hold on," Trevor said, finding something metallic embedded in the door's wood.

It was a disc with the same triangular impression he had seen at the school and hospital. Trevor wedged his fingertips on the outer protrusions of the design and carefully pulled it out of the slot. Hearing pages turn behind him, he spun around.

"I thought I told you to leave that behind," Trevor said, staring at the book they had found at the police station.

"I don't recall agreeing to you calling the shots," Jay replied, continuing to look through it. "Besides, it may have some clue as to what that sign is. Aha!"

Jay turned the book so Trevor could see the page he had found. A triangular symbol was in the lower left corner. Trevor stepped forward to inspect it when Jay simply turned it back around to read it.

"The Seal of Metatron," Jay read out loud.

"It looks similar to the one I saw, but not exactly the same. There's something different about it," Trevor said. "What exactly does it say the seal does?"

"Not much," Jay said, paging the book more. "It just says that the source of power is unknown and unquantifiable. It states that users of the talisman should be careful."

"That's great," Trevor said, stashing it in his bag anyway. "So we know it's something powerful, without knowing what it actually does, or what the one I saw is called."

Trevor provided light down the passage with the pistol. Everything about the hotel seemed normal. The walls were immaculate as if they had just been freshly painted and cleaned. Even the carpets beneath their feet looked as close to pristine as a hotel could.

The other things that caught his eye were the red Lunar Nexus and four picture frames on the left wall. Each frame had a floor map within it, from the basement up to the third floor. After both of them let the Lunar Nexus's sacred power wash over them, Trevor smashed each glass cover and removed the hotel maps. He put the street maps away for the time being.

Trevor noticed something strange about the hotel maps. Where the first and third-floor maps seemed intact, the basement and second-floor maps were not. The edges were burnt as if cast in a fire before being pulled out and saved. The maps were also more brown and yellow than the dark beige of the others.

"Those won't help you find the bones," Jay said, reminding him of their objective.

"No, but they will help us navigate the hotel while we look for it."

Jay simply nodded. They moved down the passage until they met with a wall and another passage perpendicular to the one they were in. On the wall immediately ahead of them, there were two large doors on either side. Trevor led them to the left, trying the doors of Café Silvercrest and the kitchen. They were locked.

The sound of a door creaking made them stop. Trevor shone his light ahead of them from the direction of the sound. A door to the left, just past the kitchen, bumped softly against the inner passage wall as it came to a stop. The pistol's light was trained on the opening as they waited for something to emerge. The radio remained silent.

Suddenly, a movement at the base of the doorway made Trevor shift the light down. A red, blue and white striped beach ball rolled into the passage before them. A child's laugh emerged from the darkness as the ball approached them. It swerved slightly to their left and then right, as if navigating an invisible slalom.

Before it reached them, it turned and rolled into the stairwell door. It bumped into it and rolled back, stopping before it headed forward and banged the door again. By the third impact, the ball remained still and waited. The door opened slowly, sounding like an aged man groaning with aches.

The ball rolled forward again, passing through the doorway and out of sight. Trevor moved swiftly after it, shining the light into the stairwell. The ball was bouncing steadily on each step towards the basement. Trevor moved forward, wondering if he should follow it, when the door slammed shut.

"What the hell?" Jay said softly, watching the open door from where the ball had appeared from.

Not wanting to appear ignorant or afraid in front of Jay, who had much less experience with the town so far, Trevor moved towards the door without responding. He shone the light down through the doorway, seeing a short passage with two doors on either side.

His light was trained on the object at the end of the passage, his finger resting on the trigger. A nude female puppet stood still, its skin made of brown sackcloth. The strings attached to its limbs stretched above it through the ceiling.

He moved further in, noticing that the radio had not set off any alarm just yet. There was something wrong with the puppet's features. Its breasts were absent, having domed indentations into the chest instead. Stitches lined the rims of the domes as if they had recently been repaired.

The puppet's face was a mess. Someone has slashed it with a blade. The white inner stuffing was showing through some of the cuts. More bizarre than that was the blade that was situated between its legs. The point was wedged into the sackcloth, which was red in the groin region.

"What is that thing?" Jay asked, entering the passage.

Trevor was about to turn and face him. He had a response laden with sarcasm about how he knew as much as Jay did, when suddenly the radio began to crackle. It rose steeply into a whine as the puppet jerked and moved. The strings wobbled above it, as if an unseen puppet master struggled to control it.

From its mashed face, the puppet cried out in muffled agony. Blood streamed down from the blade, running down the sackcloth legs and feet and forming a puddle on the ground. The stitches on the chest domes ripped apart as blood formed along the edges. The inner stuffing on the face turned a similar red that looked wet and drenched.

As if brought to attention, the puppet jerked its head toward Jay. It reached down and grabbed the blade, pulling it out of the bleeding sackcloth just as Jay started the chainsaw's motor. Trevor was about to shoot it, when it belted past him and ran for Jay. He fired two bullets, which missed the puppet and struck the passage wall instead.

When it reached Jay, he stopped shooting. He was too afraid the bullets would go through the sackcloth. Jay was prepared, though, driving the saw chain into her chest just as the blade came down towards him. The sackcloth tore apart and the puppet screamed, her cries filling the passage at a high pitch.

Pulling the puppet off the chain, Jay kicked it in the abdomen. It flew across the passage towards Trevor, where it slid to a stop at his feet. The head tilted on its side to the ground as the radio died. Jay bent over, breathing deeply from the short battle. Trevor moved towards him, testing the four doors as he did so and finding them locked.

"Let's get out of here," Trevor said to his recovering friend.

As Jay turned around to head out, the radio started screeching again. They turned around, the pistol's light shining back towards the fallen puppet. Where Jay had ripped its chest open, the stuffing was being pulled back in, and stitches formed around the opening. The strings from the ceiling pulled taught as it lifted the puppet back up.

With the blade still at hand, the puppet wailed again and ran for them. Trevor shot another three bullets, but they passed right through its head to the other side. He stepped back, fear written in his eyes as he awaited the onslaught. Yet, the puppet moved past him again towards Jay.

Reacting quickly, Jay shredded the shoulder blade of the blade-wielding arm. When the sackcloth broke off, he slammed his fist into its face and kicked it back to the ground again. As before, the radio died as the puppet lay still on the ground.

"Let's go before that thing wakes up again," Jay said, Trevor looking at the fallen puppet with a frown.

They left the short passage of the Storeroom, Trevor's hand reaching down for the door knob. He shone a light on the floor. The arm was crawling back to the puppet. Jay waited near the kitchen as Trevor saw the arm reach it and reconnect itself to the shoulder. The blade was still in its hand as the puppet stood up.

This time, the puppet remained motionless. The blade was dripping with blood in its hand, but the strings from the ceiling were slack. The radio was also inactive. Trevor moved back in to inspect it.

"What are you doing, man?" Jay called from the kitchen door.

Trevor walked right up to the puppet, the pistol placed against its head. He tapped it with the barrel, but the puppet did not move. A child's giggle came from the passage wall at the end. He shifted the light to find the source, but both corners were empty. The light caught small writing on the wall, scrawled in blood with someone's finger:

Leave now... she's mine

"Hey Trev," Jay called from the passage opening. "Are we going to get going or what?"

The radio awoke and trilled in warning. The puppet jerked to life and looked up at Jay. With the blade up again, it ran towards him.

"Jay!" Trevor shouted as a revelation hit him. "Shut the door!"

Frowning deeply, Jay banged the door closed just as the puppet was about to reach him. Trevor was alone with the puppet in the passage, hoping with all his beating heart that he was right. If not, he was stuck with a creature he could not kill.

He shone the light on the still puppet. The strings had slackened again, with the puppet's head dangling down in immobility. Trevor walked up to it again, ensuring there was no life in it anymore, before proceeding out the door and closing it.

"What happened?" Jay said to a bewildered man.

"It just…well, it's just standing still again," Trevor said, offering his best response. "I think it was after you, Jay."

"Why me?" Jay asked, scratching his head.

"Maybe because you buried the bones here?" Trevor said. "You are the only one who can find it."

"That's true," Jay said, sighing in relief. "That sounds logical."

Trevor observed Jay. Once again, he felt like Jay was holding something back from him. He knew better than to question him if he did not want to share it, but the need to know burned inside of him. Trevor decided to wait until the time was more appropriate or until Jay felt comfortable enough to share whatever he was hiding.

"Ok, look," Trevor said, focussing on their objective again. "Do you remember where exactly you buried his remains?"

"Give me those maps quick," Jay said. He took a moment to study the third and first floors before replying. "It's here, just underneath the Employee Cafeteria. The basement doesn't go that far, so I was able to wedge some rubble aside and get some good ground for it. Now, however…."

"We'll deal with it when we get there," Trevor reassured him while taking the maps back.

Not sure whether the pistol was defensively useful anymore, he kept it on him for the light anyway. They headed to the other end of the passage, ignoring the stairwell and lobby doors for the moment. Testing the other doors, they discovered only the Lake Shore Restaurant's door was accessible.

The restaurant was clean and well-lit with natural light. The area that they entered had chairs stacked neatly on their respective tables. To the right, there was another section with tables that had a large grand piano to the side. There were old paintings lining the wall with plants in potted containers that had too much life for a place that had supposedly burned down.

"Do you think we could smash our way out through here?" Jay asked, pulling Trevor's attention away from the ceiling fans he had been inspecting.

Jay was standing by three large glass panes that looked out onto the yard from which they had entered the hotel. The mist rolled past the windows, allowing some light to pass through and brighten the room. To the left of the windows was a door that led to the outside.

"Try that door; see if it opens," Trevor suggested.

"What are the chances?" Jay said, but walked to it anyway and tried it. As per his doubts, it was locked.

Trevor looked down at the tables between him and Jay and saw a key lying on one of them in the middle between the stacked chairs. He reached in, careful not to knock any down, and took the key. A coaster was under it with an image of two nude people holding each other in a loving embrace. Branches stretched out above their heads to form the upper foliage of a tree, while beneath them, the roots reached down into the earth.

"Maybe this key will help?" Trevor said, lifting the item to show it to him.

"No, I don't think so," Jay said. "It looks too small for this lock."

"Well, let's not break the glass unless we need to," Trevor said. "We need to find Bishop's remains first."

The door behind him creaked open. He spun around and aimed the pistol at it, ready to shoot anything that moved. Yet his determination to do so fell away when he realised that it was a short sackcloth doll standing at the door. It only reached Trevor's abdomen and not the full adult size they had encountered in the passage.

The button eyes stared between the two men before it, the head moving from side to side slowly. There was nothing on its body to clothe it, just the sackcloth material that covered it from head to feet.

"What are you doing here?" the doll said in a small boy's voice.

Jay and Trevor looked at each other, unsure what to say in response. Holstering the pistol again, Trevor moved forward to engage with it. The boy doll stepped back.

"She's been at peace for so long," the doll said. "Your presence is disturbing her. Please leave."

"Wait," Trevor said as the doll stepped out of the room. "Who is it we're disturbing?"

It was too late. The doll closed the door and left them alone in the room. Trevor ran for the door and opened it, staring down the passage. One of the doors opposite him slammed shut, the doll's face disappearing from view behind it.

He followed it without hesitating. Crossing the width of the passage quickly, his hand clutched the door knobs and turned it. The door opened to a large lobby with a single flight of stairs that led up to the second floor. The lobby was mostly empty, with a table surrounded by four blue single-seater sofas in each corner.

Trevor passed by the Reception and Gift Shop doors, finding both locked. He approached the entrance doors by the foot of the stairs leading to the hotel's northern yard. The table to the left of the doors had magazines stacked in three piles with a small box beside them. Hearing Jay close the passage door, he went to the table.

All three piles consisted of a collection of New Age Gaming magazines with various issues spanning over three years. Next to them were pamphlets advertising Sacred Valley Resort with a small map of the area, one of which Trevor pocketed.

The small box was made of dark wood with a golden clasp on the front. Someone had scratched the words 'In memory of our sacred home' on the lid with a sharp object into the wood. Trevor picked the box up, teased the clasp out and opened it.

There was a small pink ballerina on a rotating base. As soon as the ballerina popped up from the opening of the lid, it turned around to a soft, instrumental song. He couldn't recognise it and was about to ask Jay if he knew it, when he simply stared at him. Jay had gone pale.

"What's wro...."

His question was cut short. The window panes started rattling, and the front doors were raging against each other as if battling for release to be opened. The long drapes flapped into the lobby as if the windows were wide open and a strong gale was blowing in from the outside. The banging and rattling grew louder when a scream erupted from the second floor.

Trevor shut the box quietly, staring up at the second floor. As soon as the lid closed, the chaos all around subsided. No longer interested in the music box, he set it back down on the table and walked to the foot of the stairs. With the noise and disruptions gone and the lobby back to its former serene state, he stood entranced, looking up the steps at the ghastly scene above.

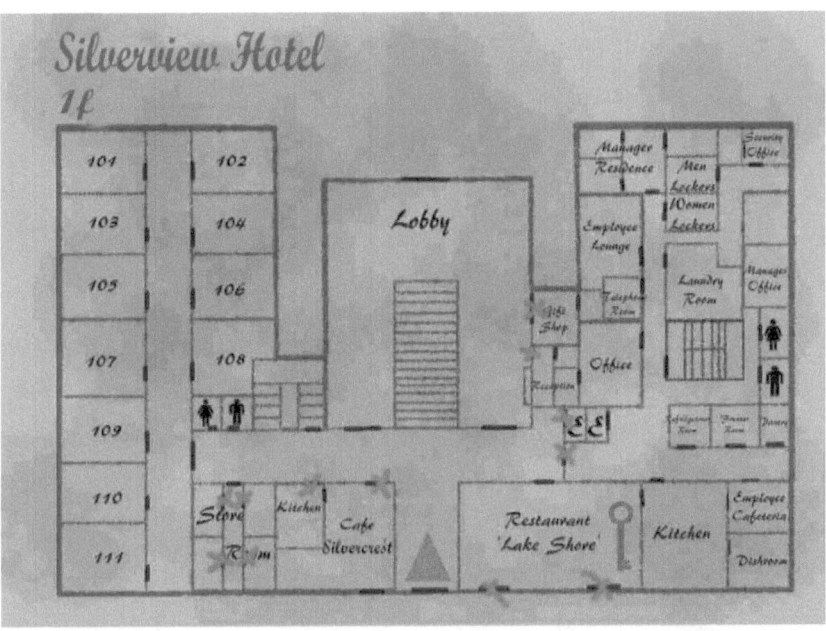

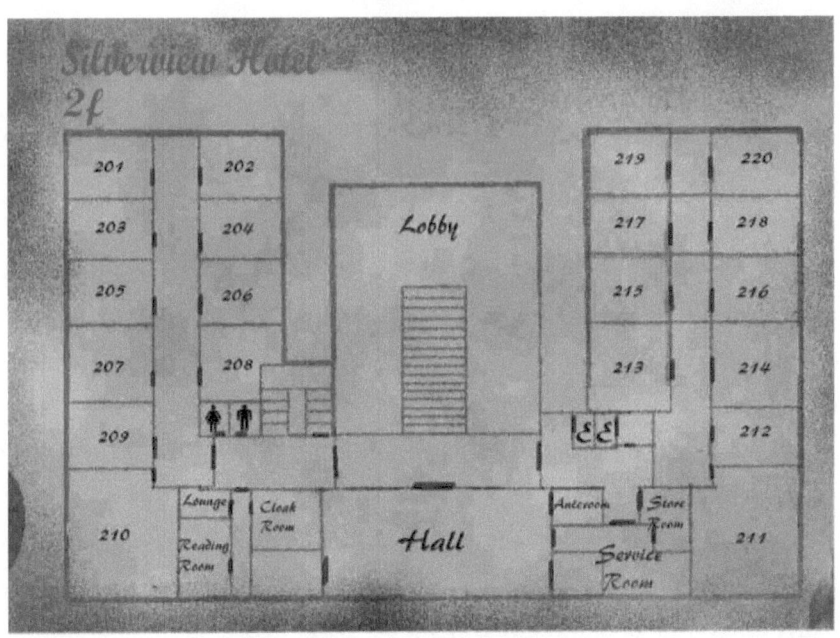

29

THE SECRET INVESTIGATION

The second floor was a complete contrast to the first. It seemed to be trapped in a demonic version of the hotel. The walls had been burned away, leaving the rusted steel formwork that Trevor had so become accustomed to. Traces of iron and blood drifted down the stairs towards them like an invisible mist of death.

The floor was also covered in darkness. The natural light coming through the windows did not seem to penetrate it as well as it did in the lobby. There was a faint red glow, though, but Trevor could not spot the source from his view at the base of the stairs.

"Is that the Darcwurld you told me about?" Jay asked softly as he joined his side.

"Yeah," he replied, unable to take his eyes off the dark floor above. "Listen, Jay, I need you to do me a favour."

"And what's that?" Jay asked apprehensively.

"Remember when I told you at the police station that Kathy and Philip's names were faded out on the red Lunar Nexus after they had been killed in the Darcwurld?" Jay nodded. "If I follow the pattern, then your name is next on that list."

"So you're saying Bishop could be after me next?" Jay asked, looking up the stairs again.

"I'm only assuming," Trevor replied. "I thought we needed the blue Lunar Nexus to go into the Darcwurld, but now I am not so sure. This hotel doesn't seem to follow the same patterns. Whatever you do, if you do see a blue Lunar Nexus, please just stay the hell away from it."

"Yeah, you definitely don't need to tell me twice," Jay said, throwing the chainsaw on the lobby floor.

"What are you doing?" Trevor asked as Jay pulled his Remington out.

"I'm tired of carrying it around. Besides, it doesn't seem to help much here."

Trevor checked his Smith & Wesson's mag and saw that he only had seven bullets left in it. Rummaging through his bag, he reloaded it quickly, ensuring his Winchester shotgun was still full. Using the pistol's light, he slowly made his way up the stairs.

The radio began to sizzle softly as he approached the landing. The light shone on the bars of eight large cages before him that stretched the length of the passage on either side. The cages replaced the walls that should have been there.

The cages swung and rattled with movement. In each of them was a woman's body, decayed with dried blood and fungating wounds. Open cuts on the flesh either crawled with white worms or had red and white spores along the malignant edges. Trevor would have all too readily called them corpses if it were not for their rabid movements within the cage.

Their limbs were also in the wrong places. Where the head should have been between the arms and the shoulders, their butt cheeks were showing with a deformed, bloated vulva leering towards the dark red ceiling. A black leathery thong around its waist stretched between the legs, but it did little to protect its privacy. The thong was split in the centre over the vagina by a long steel blade that rose out from within the sexual organ itself.

The head was between the legs, hissing and barking through the cage bars. The eyes had been cut out, the black depths aglow with the same redness that lit the floor. Its tongue lashed out as if trying to lick the air for a taste of their scent.

The arms were also wrong. At first, Trevor noticed that the thumbs were on the wrong side of the hands, but then he wondered if perhaps the arms had not been switched around. Looking at the legs, he saw that the toes were also the wrong way around. And just above the head, where the abdomen should have been, were deep cavities where he guessed the breasts once were.

"What are those?" Jay asked quietly as he stepped forward to inspect them further.

"I don't know," Trevor replied. Each of the creatures lurched against the bars. Trevor was not sure if it was an attempt to escape or attack them.

"Aren't they part of some ancient mythology you've studied?"

"None that I can recall that's as disproportionate as that," Trevor informed him. "I'll have a look at the myth book later. For now, let's move on."

Taking the maps out of his pocket, he studied the second-floor plan with the burnt edges. The bulk of the floor on each side wing was made of hotel rooms. Dead ahead of them should have been the entrance to a large hall, but as much as Trevor studied the cages, he could not see if the Hall still existed.

To his left and right, the doors were still intact, albeit in a decrepit state. He noticed a Storeroom to his left and wondered if there would be more supplies or clues as to the whereabouts of Bishop's remains. He put the map away and turned left, heading towards the door.

"No, let's go this way first," Jay said suddenly, pulling him back by his arm.

"Ok, sure," Trevor said, frowning as he complied with the request. "Any specific reason? I thought you buried the remains under the east wing?"

"I did, but I want to first see what's on this side before we head there," Jay said.

Trevor had that same instinctive feeling as before that Jay was hiding something but chose to ignore it again. The radio kept at the same low tones as they passed the wall of deformed bodies. Reaching the door, Trevor opened it up and swung it away from him.

Spotting an open doorway to the stairwell on his right, he checked it first. The further he moved from the caged beasts, the more the radio died down. The light broke through the darkness of the stairwell, revealing that there were no stairs at all.

Inspecting it further, he looked down at the edge of the landing and saw the first floor's steps. It rose up halfway between the floors before it stopped. There was no sign of damage or corruption; the steps simply proceeded no further. The stairs to the third floor were utterly destroyed, though. The concrete had been smashed by some blast before, and there was no way up from there.

"I guess we won't be going any higher up," Trevor said sarcastically to Jay as he returned to the passage.

"Why would we want to go up anyway?" Jay asked, his tone full of frustration with a hint of anger. "We're wasting time on this floor. The remains are under the east wing first floor."

"Well, clearly, we can't get it there," Trevor replied patiently. "If this town has taught me anything so far, finding these remains won't be as easy as we think."

Jay remained silent, yielding to Trevor's experience of the Darcwurld. Trevor moved to the small passageway behind Jay and tested the Lounge door on the right. It was locked. Trying the Cloak Room's handle, the door opened up.

Taking the cue from the silent radio that they were safe for the moment, Trevor moved in and studied the room. There were clothes hanging in a wardrobe nearby, but all the furniture and clothes had been burnt black. Trevor shone the light around until it lit something metallic on the floor under the clothes.

He knelt down and looked at the safe embedded in the burnt floor. Wiping some debris and dust off the surface, he noticed a small image to the left of the keyhole. The design consisted of the two symbols for male and female, with the circles entwined with each other. The male symbol's arrow pointed up to the right, and the female's symbol faced down.

Trevor remembered the image of the two lovers within the tree he had seen in the restaurant and retrieved the key from his pocket. He inserted it into the locking mechanism and turned. With a rusty clunk, the bars of the safe pulled open.

"What's in it?" Jay asked, peering over his shoulder.

"Another disc with that Metatron-like symbol that says Glyph of Aethertide," Trevor said, handing it over to him, "and a key to Room 203."

"Should we go take a look?" Jay asked, curiosity and relief silking his voice.

"It's our best lead for now," he agreed, stashing the seal with the first one in his bag.

The sound of metal clinking and dry hinges creaking open echoed from the lobby passage towards them. A low growl drifted through the darkness, followed by a soft crackle from the radio. As the groan came closer, the radio rose into a shrill pitch. Both men readied their firearms, Trevor stepping out of the claustrophobic room into the small passageway.

It was one of the caged female prisoners from the lobby passage. It had removed the blade from within her groin at the top and wielded the bloody weapon in its left hand. Slashing the air before it, the head snarled between its legs at the bottom while trying to bite into Trevor's knee.

He jumped back and shot into the head in panic. Two bullets hit the floor behind it, while the third crossed the right cheek. Jay offloaded a few shells into its bruised body, causing it to stammer backwards. Two more shots later finally gave Trevor a hit on its forehead. The beast fell to the floor, squirming and writhing in agony with a high-pitched wail.

Trevor unsheathed the katana and drove the tip into its neck. Twisting the blade, the neck snapped and the creature fell still. Blood leaked onto the burnt carpets beneath his feet. The radio died down.

Lifting the light to the wall beside him, he saw the door to the last room in the passage. The map identified it as the Reading Room. He tried the door, peeking past its edge as it opened inwards. Taking confidence from the fact that the radio remained silent, he stepped inside.

The state of the room surprised both of them. It was not pristine like the first floor, but the damage was minimal. There was a small desk with a neatly stacked pile of books on it, tainted only by the gathering of dust and the presence of small mounds of fungal spores.

On the centre of the desk was a note. The page had yellowed with time, but the cursive writing was still legible. He picked it up gingerly to avoid breaking it or causing it to crumble. As aged and fragile as the document looked, the paper felt strong.

"I know what I'm doing is wrong," Trevor read out loud to Jay, who was reloading his Remington. "He is so young.. I shouldn't be introducing these things to him. But whenever we're together, the smell of his skin, the touch of his hands…I don't want to break his heart."

"That's real sweet," Jay said, finishing up with the shotgun. "Shall we get going? Those bones aren't going to find us."

Trevor placed the page with his other notes and moved out. They stepped back into the main passage and tried the toilet doors, which were both jammed. The double doors opened into the west wing, revealing a passage that turned right into a row of hotel rooms.

He kept the torch steady before them, noticing how the walls were decayed with bleeding paint and bursting mounts of hyphae. These passages were more closed up than the school or hospital's had been, making him feel more boxed in than ever. The only sound he could hear was their feet treading on the worn floors and the locking mechanisms of each door that failed to open.

When they reached the end of the passage, Room 201 budged slightly open, but was barred from the inside. Walking back to 203, Trevor took out the key they had found in the safe and opened the door. They stepped inside, cautiously inspecting the interior until they confirmed it was vacant.

Both of them searched meticulously through everything, even checking under the bed. The wardrobe doors were thrown open, and the curtains were drawn apart to reveal a darkened mist outside. Trevor moved to the bookrack against the wall shared with 201, throwing the books on the floor until he found a small key behind one of them.

On the key were inscribed the letters EE. There was no note or tag to suggest what the key belonged to. He went through more of the books until it all lay in a pile by his feet, and he was sure there was no other clue as to what the key belonged to. He inspected the titles of the books, making sure there was no reference to the two letters.

"I know we said we should find his remains before he knows what we are up to," Jay said, turning his attention away from the bookrack. "I have a feeling we're too late. It still feels like we're being played…"

"Like puppets," Trevor finished for him.

They walked back towards the door, Trevor looking back at the bookrack, feeling like he had missed something. As the shadows caused by the light of his torch danced along the walls, he saw a slight crack between the rack and the wall shared with 201.

"Wait, hold on!" Trevor shouted, heading back towards it. "Help me move this quickly."

"I don't think it's the right time to redecorate the room," Jay said snidely, but moved swiftly to assist anyway.

They pushed the rack towards the window, revealing an opening in the wall that led into 201. The room was similar to 203 in most aspects, down to the decaying walls and foul stench. The main difference was the briefcase, pictures and notebooks littering the bed.

Trevor joined Jay in inspecting the photos. Someone seemed to have been spying on a young woman accompanied by a boy in his early teens. There were scenes with them relaxing on Silvercrest beach and in the waters, as well as scenes taken within the hotel and outside in the surrounding gardens.

Two specific scenes were disturbing. The two individuals appeared unaware that the images had been taken. The angle suggested that it had been taken from a ceiling corner, looking down towards the main bed. Both of them were naked above the blankets, enjoying pleasures reserved for a more mature audience.

Jay frowned heavily and took up one of the notebooks. Trevor took another and paged through it. From what he could tell, it belonged to a Detective Malone, who was a private investigator rather than working for any governmental or law enforcement agency.

Paging through the initial sections, Trevor came to a part where the detective had gone on vacation to the Silverview Hotel. He slowed his studious reading when he found the section relevant to the photos.

Today, I saw this young girl on the beach with a young boy, perhaps ten or eleven. In my usual casual nature, I expected his parents to show up at some point. They both left without any arriving, which I thought was strange. I don't know why I let it bother me, but I followed them.

I used my badge to discover from reception that they were staying in 211, a room they usually favour during their visits to the hotel, and always alone. The girl is his aunt, taking care of him while his parents are on holiday. There was a signed note from the parents that confirmed it. I guess I worried for nothing.

Trevor skimmed some more pages filled with the detective's idle musings until he found another excerpt pertaining to the two individuals.

My misgivings about that girl and boy may not have been misplaced. I was walking around the gardens tonight when I looked up and saw the light of Room 211 on and the curtains open. The girl appeared, completely nude, and closed the curtains. It worries me that she should be so unclothed with a boy that age.

No, I am not here on business. I'm sure she is just very comfortable with her own body, and it's all in my head. I think tomorrow I will gather the courage to go speak to that beautiful woman I saw at the bar today.

There were a few notes on a different investigation that followed before he continued with the couple the next day.

It's Sunday and my last day here today. That young girl and boy are still bothering me. After they left to go down to the beach today, I bribed a hotel employee to let me use the room before she cleaned it. There were not many clues that could have helped me discover anything devious, so I put a small camera in the smoke detector. Hopefully, it will help me work out if my suspicions are right.

Trevor hurried through the notebook, scanning pages quickly until he found what he was looking for. The detective had returned to his office the next day and had worked through his recordings.

I've been looking through the footage I took of that girl who stayed in Room 211, Silverview Hotel. There is no doubt in my mind that they have a sexual relationship. I'm sure if the parents knew of this, they would never let her look after the child.
I've printed stills of some of the images. She thought she was so clever, booking the room under a different name, but she used her credit card. I was able to trace her real name and address. I'm sure if I wait near her place, I will be able to see the child again and his parents. They need to know what's going on.

"What was that?" Jay said quickly, looking back into 203.
"What?" Trevor asked, watching as Jay rushed out of the room into the passage.
Paging through the last pages of the notebook, the only thing he could find was mention of the nights he spent staking out the girl's house waiting

for a sign of the child. Towards the end of the notebook, there was one last note.

I've done some more digging to find out who her siblings are, trusting that at least the information that she is his aunt is correct. She has one brother, who is listed as having a son. I've inspected the place and seen the boy. Tonight, I will confront them with the proof and inform them of what she has been up to. It will be up to them whether or not they want to lay charges.

My only hope is that they do the right thing.

Trevor closed the book and looked at the briefcase. There was a three-digit combination lock that was set to 3-1-5. An idea came to him. He turned the numbers until the lock read 2-1-1. The latch snapped open. The only object inside was another circular disc with the Glyph of Aethertide on it.

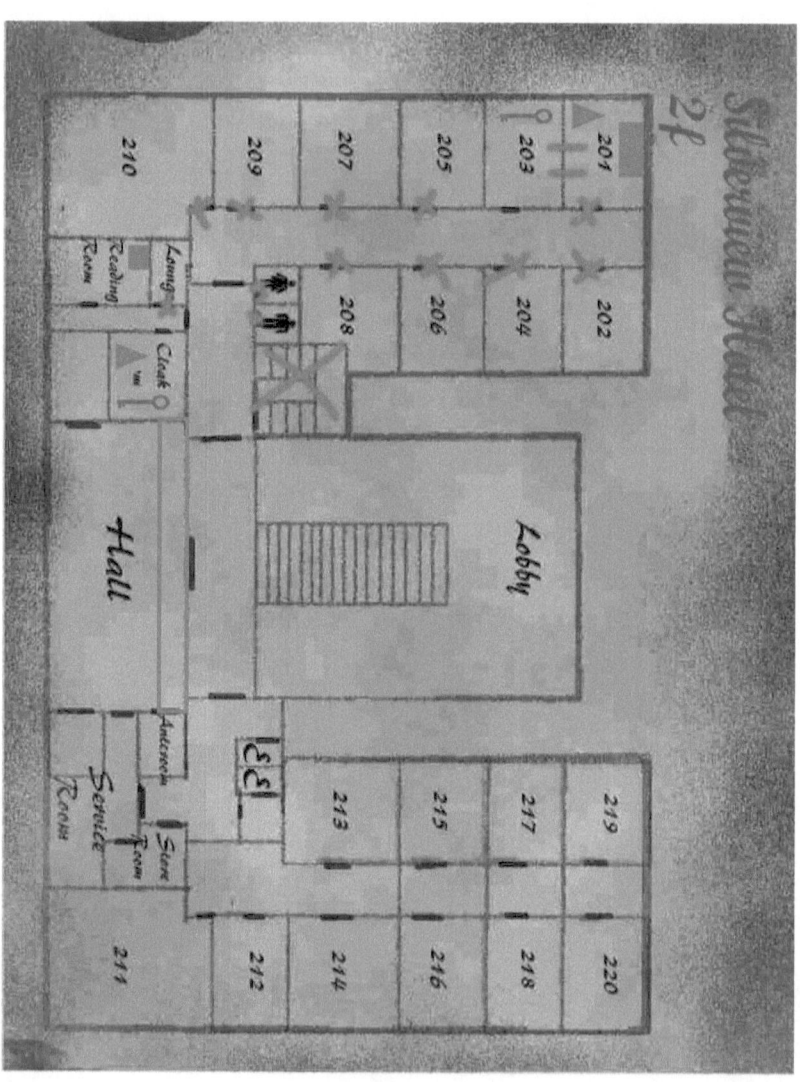

30

THE ROOM OF THE SALACIOUS AFFAIR

Trevor saw something move slowly in the shadows of the corner to his left. He cast the torch light up to it. The damp and metal spalling in the corner bulged inwards, but there was nothing there that could have made the movement. He brought the light down again, turning to leave the room, when he saw something shift in the shadows again.

"Why are you still here?" a boy's voice asked. It was the same voice Trevor had heard from the sack doll on the first floor.

"Who are you?" Trevor asked, shining the light back into the corner. The same decay showed on the walls. He waited for the boy's reply, but nothing happened. He turned the light down again and waited for the shadow to move.

"I don't like you being here," the boy replied. "You don't belong here. Get out, before it's too late."

The shadow moved back into the wall. When he shone the light back into the corner, he saw that the metal spalling and decay had melted back into it and was gone. When he was sure the boy would not return, he joined Jay in the passage.

"Why did you run out?" Trevor asked.

"I thought I saw someone watching us," Jay responded. "I thought it was that small doll again."

"Have you perhaps seen a ghost of yourself at all?" Trevor asked.

"No," Jay frowned. "That's an odd question to ask."

"Kathy and Philip both mentioned to me that they'd seen a spectre of themselves in the Darcwurld," he explained. "In mythology, this is known as a Fetch. It's usually seen by the person before his death."

"That's comforting," Jay said softly as they walked back towards the Lobby. "I'll let you know as soon as I see one."

"There are so many things that don't make sense," Trevor said. "None of the creatures here relate to mythology like the others. Bishop hasn't even made an appearance. And this hotel that's supposed to be burned down seems trapped between two different dimensions. It's like we're stuck in someone else's nightmare."

"I think it's best then that we don't dwell on it and just find a way out," Jay suggested. "I'm one for just forgetting about Bishop's remains and finding another way out of town. Take Silver Sally and see where the lake leads us to."

"Maybe," Trevor said, lost in thought about the girl and the boy. "I think we'll find the answers in Room 211."

"Oh, hell no!" Jay said, stepping away from him. "There is no way you're getting me to go there."

"Why not?"

"From what you've told me about the school and hospital, and from what I've seen, whatever is there will probably kill us."

"You're acting strange," Trevor said. "It's not like you to back out of anything."

"Have you seen where we are?!" Jay shouted, his voice carrying down the passage. "I think this would call for strange behaviour."

"Come on, man," Trevor said, continuing towards the Lobby. "Let's just go see what else we can find. If we don't find the remains, we break out of the hotel."

Not caring for an answer, he just kept walking. He was about to pick up the pace when he heard the sound of cage doors opening again. What concerned him the most about the noise was that it sounded like more than one clinking gate whining on its hinges. As if that had not been warning enough, the radio picked up in harmony.

They entered the Lobby, firearms ready to pummel bullets into any monsters that confronted them. The radio fell down in pitch but did not go quiet completely. The door to the east wing's passage ahead was open, as were three of the cages to their right.

"Where are they?" Jay asked.

Listening very carefully to the radio, Trevor walked towards the open door. At first, the radio lowered in volume, but it picked up again when he reached the door. Stepping back towards Jay, the radio fell again until it rose when he reached him.

"I think one of them went through that door, and the other one down the stairs," Trevor replied, pointing to the Lobby below.

"Well then...."

Jay's words were cut short. True to Trevor's suspicions, one of the creatures emerged from the east wing. Jay stepped forward with anger and revulsion as he offloaded shell after shell into its body. The beast recoiled, falling back into the passage as its screams rose into the air.

Trevor looked down the stairs, waiting for the other one. The radio increased its wailing despite the beast being forced into the passage away from him. He checked behind him, suddenly realising that the other one could have been hiding in the passageway by the Reading Room. The door swung slowly on its hinges as if recently disturbed, but there was nothing there.

The radio continued to warn him. The five remaining feminine beasts rattled their cages furiously. He wondered if they were causing the device to cry out when the thought of looking up occurred to him. Slowly, and with sweat travelling with the chills along his spine, he turned the pistol's torch up.

He had barely caught a glimpse of the beast clutching to the ceiling when it fell on him. Its hands held his legs to the ground as the face between its legs bit down into his neck. The sharp needle fangs caught some flesh as he forced the gun under its thigh and shot.

It cried out and reared up above him. Shifting his legs loose of the slackened grip, he caught the legs that kicked down on him and held them around the ankles. Manoeuvring his back on the ground, he kicked the beast over him towards the stairs.

He stood up quickly, lifting his pistol to fire when the sight caught him off-guard. As the creature crossed over the threshold between the first and second floors, it transformed. The skin pulled inward and then back outward until it was replaced with the same sackcloth as the puppets that they had encountered before. When it hit the lobby floor, the sackcloth body simply fell over and rolled towards the door, unharmed.

Thin white strings lowered from the ceiling above the puppet. Without too much difficulty, it attached to each leg and arm before the final one connected to the head between the legs. The strings lifted the puppet up until it was facing him again. The string pulled taut as the puppet was pulled back up to the second floor.

When the puppet crossed the threshold again, a reverse transformation happened. The cancerous skin returned with the putrid deformation of its joints and fangs. The indentations of the cloth returned to its bleeding flesh, its blade shimmering within its groin from the torchlight that shone towards it.

As it lunged up to strike at Trevor with its claws and fangs, he shot three bullets straight into its head. Its face had a ghastly expression of surprise on it as it closed its eyes and died. The body stepped back and fell down towards the Lobby just as Trevor grabbed its ankles.

"Oh no, you don't," he said, pulling her corpse back onto the second floor's landing. "You just stay right here and die like a good girl."

After a moment, when the corpse was done bleeding out, its skin turned to ash and faded into the carpet. Trevor turned around, ready to fire at the movement of the east passage door, when he saw it was Jay.

"What happened?" Jay asked. "I heard shots."

"This one tried to kill me from above," he replied, catching his breath. "Whatever you do, don't let them fall back to the first floor. They turn into puppets."

"No worries," Jay said, turning to the cages. "I'll just take care of them all right now."

Jay let loose a barrage of shells. Trevor was sure he was emptying whatever was left in it. The tungsten shot simply bounced off the cage's metal, spraying the area around it. When the shotgun was depleted, Jay dropped it and fired his pistol through a gap between the metal bars.

"Ahhhh!!!" Jay shouted, grabbing his right shoulder.

One of the bullets had ricocheted off an invisible barrier and hit him. Trevor moved over and inspected it. The bullet had gone right through the flesh and out the other side.

"Did you really think it would be that easy?" Trevor teased him, taking the last first aid kit out of his bag and applying it to the wound. "Try not to kill yourself before Bishop gets the chance, will you?"

Jay made a mock facial gesture with his face. Trevor laughed and finished up his work. They stepped through the door to the east wing, the body of the creature Jay had attacked to the left where the elevator shaft was. The elevator itself was missing, leaving a gaping hole in the wall with sparks showering light from the loose cables within.

Trevor took out the burnt second-floor map. A small passageway to the right led to a Service Room, which they found to be locked as was the Storeroom beside it. Further down the main passage was a doorway that opened up the east row of hotel rooms. The first room right behind these doors was Room 211.

The words 'Leave Her Alone!' were carved over the door. Eager to get to 211, Trevor pushed the door handles. His face slammed into the door before he could control himself. The bottom of the door moved in, but the top was locked from the other side.

"Dammit," Trevor cursed, inspecting the map again. There was an unnamed room to their left.

The lock was different to the others. Where the other doors had mortise locks beneath a lever handle, this one had a cylindrical lock set within a knob. Trevor removed the EE key and placed it within the knob lock, turning it. The latch unlocked on the inside, and the door opened.

They entered a small messroom with lockers lining one wall and a small elevator to the left. Trevor shone his light towards the empty shaft, noticing that it was also empty. Daring to look down, he saw the elevator resting on the ground floor in good condition.

"Hey, there are some supplies here," Jay said after opening some of the lockers.

There were five medicinal bottles and four first aid kits, which they shared between them. When they were satisfied that there was nothing else of use to them, Trevor pressed the elevator button. The lift clanked and ground against its gears until it finally rose up towards them.

As it passed through the floor levels, the clean lift transformed in the same fashion as the puppet creatures. They watched as the paint scraped off the metal. Years of rust, decay and burn marks appeared in a matter of seconds. When the lift stopped before them, all that remained was the outer shell and mesh netting for the floors, walls and roof.

"Our ride to hell is here," Jay said sarcastically, stepping in.

Finding the instrument panel, Trevor pressed the first-floor button. A short alarm bell indicated that the lift would not move in that direction. Pressing the third-floor button was more successful, causing the fenced doors to close. He raised his pistol to aim at the door, ready for anything that might attack them when it opened.

The elevator returned back to normal as they passed onto the third floor. The corroded metal was covered again with a clean, unspoiled coating. The light on the ceiling flickered back on as the lift came to a standstill. Jay had just finished reloading his Remington and was standing at the ready.

A woman's deep, evil laugh sounded all around them. The lift lurched before moving down again. Trevor grasped the rails on the sides to hold his balance just as the rusted formwork returned and the lights flickered off. Instead of seeing the hotel through the grids of the lift cage they were in, they saw a vast darkness all around them with soft red glowing clouds within.

The lights flickered again, and the lift returned to normal before flickering off and returning to the demonic state. The speed of the interchanges picked up with the increase in the lift's descent. Trevor bit into his teeth in anxiety, waiting for the final impact that would kill them both.

Through the narrow slits of his eyes, he saw a nude woman within the nothingness. She resembled the woman he had seen in the detective photos. She was disproportionately large, taking up most of the view before them. Her head was at least twenty times the size of the lift. She peered with one eye into the falling lift, even though she sat still in her cocoon of darkness and did not seem to be moving up or down at all.

Yet they could feel the gravity pulling them down, waiting for the fatal crash. The lights flickered so fast, and the interchange between the normal and damaged lift states was so quick that they could hardly tell one from the other. Trevor screamed, but all he could hear was the woman's laughter every time he opened his mouth. The pressure pressed so hard against his head that he felt like it would crush it.

The lift stopped so quickly that they collapsed, with their bags and weapons falling around them. The lift was normal again, and the number on the panel revealed that they had once again arrived at the third floor. Trevor threw up, clutching his stomach as he struggled to keep the nausea down.

He opened his eyes and looked around. Squinting and frowning, he saw that the weapons, bag and vomit were lying on the ceiling above him. When he felt the lift's light beside him, he realised that everything else was actually on the floor of the lift, and they were lying with their backs on the ceiling. He was about to warn Jay, when the opposing effects of gravity wore off, and they crashed onto the floor.

"Let's not take this lift again if we can avoid it," Jay said, grunting in between words.

The lift doors opened, and the alarm bell sounded. Trevor stood up, wondering why the lift was suddenly making a noise. He saw a notice above the instrument panel that was not there during its demonic state. It indicated that the lift could only take the weight of two people, showing the maximum weight it could take below it.

"Let's go," Trevor said.

They collected their equipment and stepped off the lift. The alarm bell ended, and the doors closed. They heard the lift move and saw it stopped on the first floor again. Jay tried to call it back by pressing the button. Nothing happened.

"Well, you got your wish," Trevor said, pulling out the clean third-floor map.

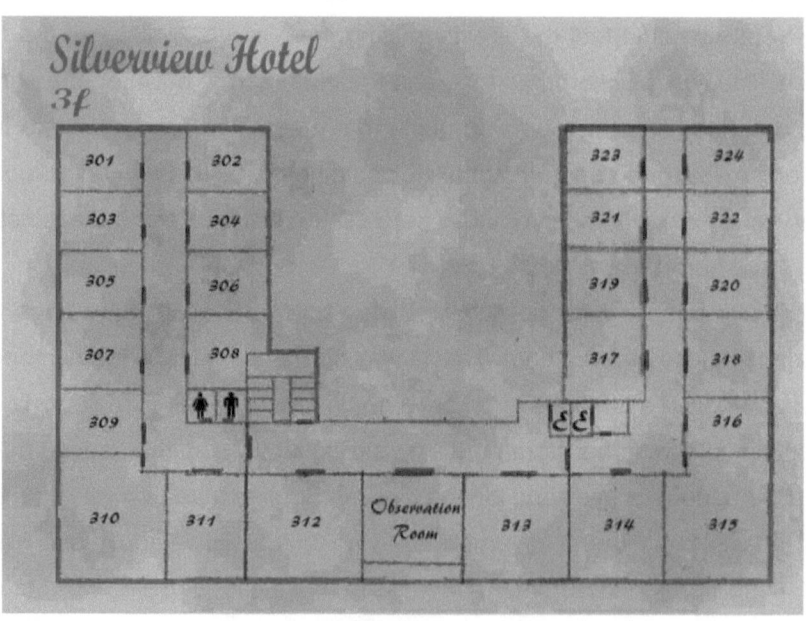

He noticed that the room they were in was in a good condition like the first floor. He opened the door into the east wing passage and saw that the rest of the floor was also in an untarnished state.

Wanting to inspect the east corridor first, Trevor checked Room 314 directly ahead of him. It was locked. He expected the same from Room 315, but found it opening instead. As soon as the door's outer edge left the frame, he heard cages creaking open from the Lobby below them. He peered into the room, not wanting to waste time going through each room thoroughly, when the scene inside caught his attention.

The room was well-lit from the large windows on the external structural walls, despite the fog still flooding the air outside. The few furniture items that adorned the room were tidily in place. The object that encouraged him to investigate was the four-poster canopy double bed in the centre against the south wall.

The curtains were neatly tied up to the posts, but the white sheets were in disarray as if recently disturbed. There was a pool of fresh blood in the centre with a sharp cutting knife beside it, the tip drenched in the red river of life. The left pillow at the headboard was white, while the right one was red.

On the red pillow rested a note. Trevor moved over to it and picked it up carefully. It resembled the handwriting on the note he had found in the Reading Room. He read over the words carefully a few times:

I fear it has all come to an end. I don't know why I've done what I've done. I panicked when his parents confronted me about our illicit affair. That detective had taken pictures of us. I was terrified. The only thing I could do was kidnap him and bring him back to our sacred home.

We chose a different room this time, but I can tell he doesn't know what's going on. He isn't used to this room. There's something… strange about it. As if we don't belong here. But I think it's my frantic mind playing tricks on me.

I've taken this too far. After he gets out of the bath, I need to explain that what we're doing is wrong and that we need to end it. I need to tell him that I will be going away for a very, very long time. He will see me again in the afterlife.

Please forgive me…

Trevor put the note down and looked back at the sheets. He imagined that she sat on the bed with the knife in her hand, driving it through her body before they came to arrest her. He wondered if the boy had witnessed the suicide, or if he had seen her body thereafter.

He realised that he was still alone in the room. Jay was still standing outside the door in the corridor, looking at the sheets in a blank expression. Trevor could not hold in his doubts and suspicions anymore. Jay had seen blood before, so there was only one reason that he had gone pale again.

"Jay, tell me what's going on," Trevor said as Jay finally entered the room and stood at the foot of the bed. "That boy… those pictures. Are we reliving your nightmare?"

Jay looked up at him with moisture filling his eyes. He opened up his mouth to speak, but choked it back instead. The Remington in his hands fell onto the floor.

"I…"

His words were interrupted. They both looked at the door to the room. The sackcloth boy stood there, once again with no strings attached. He stared at the sheets like Jay had a moment ago before addressing them.

"Why are you in the evil room?" he asked quietly. "I told you to leave her alone. I warned you. She knows you're here. I don't want you to take her from me."

The boy ran off into the corridor. Without warning, Jay belted after him. Trevor followed shortly, hearing a hard thud as he entered the corridor. At first, he thought it had been from the door opening to the central passage area, but he saw that Jay had dropped his duffel bag.

Trevor ignored it and followed the chase. The door was wide open as he passed through it into the passage area. He ran past the first closed door to his left and towards a second door that Jay entered after that. The sign on the door identified it as the Observation Room.

"Jay, wait!" Trevor shouted.

His call was ignored. There was a huge hole in the floor that led to the corrupted Hall below. Jay had already jumped down and rolled onto the floor, his police training saving him from breaking his legs. Without taking a breath, Jay raced on into an open passageway and out of view.

Trevor looked down at the floor, bracing himself. He held his breath as he jumped down while trying to roll like Jay had. He hit the ground too hard and collapsed more than rolled. The impact was not as hard as he had expected it to be, but he could feel that he had pulled a muscle in his left leg.

The Hall was blood-crusted with steel and formwork all around. The cages separated him from the Lobby this time. The remaining evil creatures within them leered at him from between their legs through the bars. He counted them quickly. Only two were left within their bars in the centre, with no sign of where the other three had gone.

The only opening available was the one that Jay had rushed through. From where he stood, he could see Jay shining his light on a wall inside. He checked the map and saw that the room was supposed to be the Service Room. The Service Room shared a wall with Room 211.

"What's going on?" Trevor asked when he reached Jay, referring this time to his study of the wall as opposed to the bloody sheets.

"Do you still have those Glyphs?" Jay asked.

He could see why. There was a painted portrait of two dark-skinned people. The woman was in her late teens, while the boy was about ten. They were both naked, and the boy was feasting between her legs. She was holding her exposed breasts in ecstasy, her eyes closed to the pleasure. Around them on the bed were blue-winged Jay birds.

The boy and girl's heads and her breasts were missing, though. Where they should have been were three round slots identical in size to the Glyphs of Aethertide. Trevor dropped his bag to the ground and removed the discs.

"Every time I've come across this symbol, it's brought me nothing but trouble," Trevor said, holding them in his hands. "You need to tell me what's going on before I even contemplate putting this in there."

His attention was drawn by the scuffling of feet across the floor behind them. Trevor dropped the Glyphs and raised his pistol instead, aiming the light at the boy who appeared before them now in his naked, human form. The boy moved beside Jay and looked up at him, holding his hand.

Without saying a word further, the boy dissipated like smoke and entered Jay's body. Jay's eyes burned a bright orange from a light that flared up from within before returning to normal. And then he looked at Trevor.

"I thought I had moved on," Jay explained, "blocked it out completely. There was a time when it was a haze of memories before I found some peace."

"Being molested can be hard to get over," Trevor consoled him.

"Yes, that's what everyone said," Jay continued. "When I was fifteen, I started getting dreams about it, and I wondered if the events had actually happened or if they had all been in my mind.

"In my twenties was when the depression really kicked in. Someone suggested I see a therapist. It is the most singular event in my life that really helped me move on."

"Why?" Trevor said, encouraging him. "What happened?"

"The therapist asked me one question; was I depressed and angry at what she had done to me, or rather at the fact that I had enjoyed myself."

"Excuse me?" Trevor asked, confused.

"She had been right," Jay said. "I had never fully understood the consequences of her actions. A child that young should never have to experience that. I blamed myself for what happened for so many years. And then there was her death."

"You can't blame yourself for her suicide," Trevor said.

"Suicide?" Jay said, frowning heavily. "Oh yes, I forgot she had wanted to take her life. That was her solution. The easy way out. I was so furious when she told me we had to end what we had."

Jay turned to the wall and ran his fingers over her face on the portrait. He sighed deeply, appearing to make some conscious decision.

"The thought of her leaving me was too much," he confessed. "That she would leave and we would never be together again. So, in my anger, I decided to help her along."

"What??" Trevor asked.

"I saw the knife she had wanted to use," Jay continued, still staring at the painting. It looked like he was in a trance, a soft smile of satisfaction on his face. "I took it and first slashed at her face in anger. She was screaming and in so much agony. Someone in the passage had heard and was trying to break the door down.

"Then I stripped her of her clothes. I took from her what she no longer wanted to give me, cutting into her breasts first. Then, when there was nothing left to call them breasts, I jabbed the knife between her legs. Constantly. Again and again. When I was done, only a lifeless form was lying there."

"Oh my G..."

"When the security eventually broke the door down, I was standing there with the blade in my hand, the blood dripping down my arms. I could not speak. The detective and police arrived and asked me if she had hurt me. All I could do was nod.

"To this day, they still think it was self-defence. I even convinced my therapist that she had attacked me and I had killed her as a reaction."

Trevor didn't know what to say. He could see the demons of his past haunting his eyes. Trevor had never experienced anything close to what Jay had done.

Jay leaned down and picked up the discs. Trevor simply watched, hoping that whatever was behind the wall would help him find absolution from his own inner turmoil. One by one, he placed the Glyphs into the slots, one between the legs, another over her breasts and the last on her face.

The wall shook as the portrait slid to the side, revealing an ornate red door decorated with gold, silver, and emerald trimmings. Jay slowly reached for the handle and opened it, Trevor moving behind him to get a better view of Room 211.

The room's arrangements were similar to Room 315 if one ignored the broken steel, floor, rust and decayed blood. The woman sat on the bed completely naked, her dark skin caked with coagulated blood. Her hair was a moppy mess, and her eyes burned red with demonic fever.

Jay walked in slowly, still in his trance state. As Trevor watched, wondering what he would do, she beckoned him with her hand to come closer. Blood and dirt peeled away from her breasts, leaving them clean as if she had just washed them. Her hands summoned him to them, and he kneeled down at her legs.

"No, Jay, don't!" Trevor shouted, realising suddenly that the blue Lunar Nexus was inked around each nipple.

Jay paid him no heed. His lips sank to the left breast, and he sucked on it hungrily. She closed her eyes, placing her hand on the back of his head to urge him to drink further. Black and blue veins spread out from her nipple to cover the rest of the breast. As he drank, she healed, and the years of dirt and decay washed off her body.

When Trevor saw the dark lines cross over Jay's face, he realised he had been paralysed by fright. He jumped into action, racing to pull Jay away as the blood and corruption started to change his face. Horns started pushing out on top, bulging from within the forehead. When the bone pierced the skin, Trevor touched his shoulder.

The woman's head jerked alert. She growled at him deeply and cast her hand up. Trevor flew through the air, pulled back by an invisible force as his back hit the floor, and he slid into the Service Room.

He regained his ability to move freely and ran back to the room. With another wave of her hand, the door slammed shut in front of him before the mesh and steel closed over it to stop him from barging it down. As he searched the wall for another way in, he heard her demonic laughter thunder from the other side.

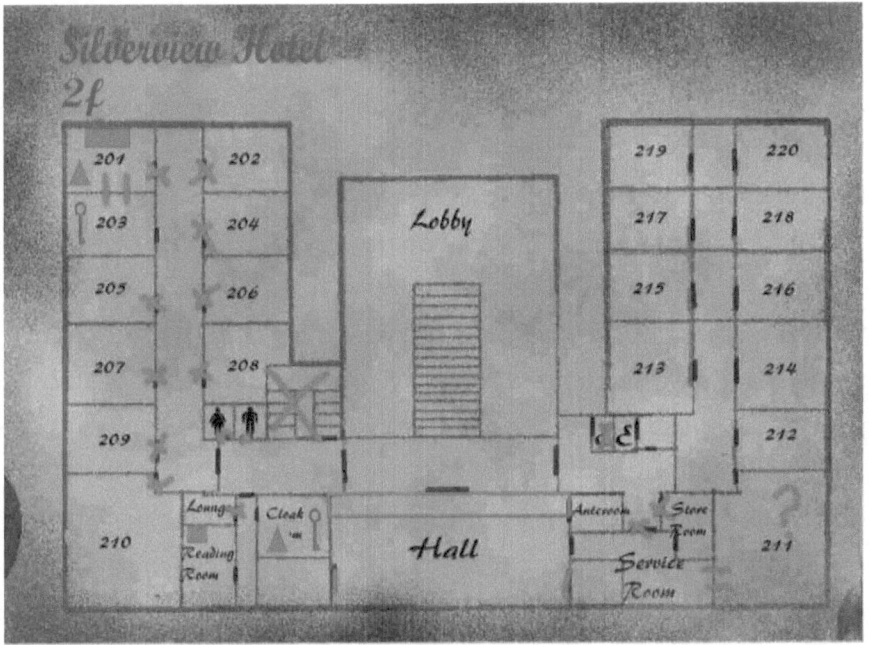

31

BURIED BLOWER'S BONES

He was unsure if the laughter had changed or if it was just his hearing, but there was a more masculine undertone to the rumble as it passed through the building. The sound shifted location until it seemed to be coming from the Lobby rather than the room.

"Heeeerrrrre's Johnny!" a voice boomed.

Trevor steadied himself as something exploded. He moved to his duffel bag and hoisted it up, equipping his pistol. Another boom exploded. Trevor made his way back to the Hall as cages creaked open again. He held his gun steadily ahead of him as he turned in the Service Room, ignoring the radio that wouldn't stop wailing.

Two disfigured creatures were in the Hall and making their way towards him. Trevor focussed on the closest one, shooting at its head between the legs until it fell. Another four shots later, and the second one collapsed, too.

Once in the Hall itself, he saw the two cages the creatures had emerged from. The gates were open on both sides, providing Trevor a way through to the Lobby area. He checked both sides of the passage area past the cages, ducking back when one of the beasts sliced a knife towards his face.

Trevor offloaded three bullets into it before it clicked without firing further. It was empty, the chamber's indicator changing in confirmation. The creature fell to the ground, its bleeding body writhing on the floor. There was no time to reload. He holstered the gun and reached for the axe, driving it down on the head between the legs until it remained motionless.

He felt an intense heat filling the building. He moved back into the passage and looked around. Instead of seeing more beasts charging towards him, he caught fire breaking through the walls and steel. Even the first floor's pristine walls were taking flame, the wallpaper burning like dry tinder.

The main entrance doors suddenly creaked open. Trevor wasted a moment to stare at it in bewilderment when another deafening boom woke him to his senses. He ran down the stairs, hearing the cries of the final two creatures somewhere on the second floor. His feet hardly touched the ground outside when a wild explosion hit him from behind, sending him soaring over the paving.

His head smacked the bricks. He groaned, trying to lift himself up. The fire raged behind him, burning the building down rapidly. He coughed as he inhaled the smoke and ran away as far as possible while watching the hotel vanish behind a wall of flames and blackness.

It was over in a matter of minutes. There was hardly anything left of it, the debris from the upper floors having collapsed to the ground. Trevor made his way back to the hotel's remains, searching for any sign of Jay.

The coals and ruins had gone cold. Trevor ran his hands over the burnt steel as the last of the fires faded away. There was no warmth in it anymore. He studied the ruins carefully. It was as if it had been burned down years ago.

Remember what Jay had told him before, he moved to the south-eastern corner of the hotel. He kicked and shoved some debris aside until he found a patch of disturbed earth beneath it. Putting his bag aside for the moment, he used the straight claw end of the crowbar to help him dig through it.

There was only one item buried in the ground. Trevor picked up the white object, realising that it was a whistle. He felt the material, running his fingers on all sides. It felt like polished bone. There were words scrawled in thin writing on both sides.

"The greatest crime," he read, turning it over to read the other side, "lay in the lie."

He frowned. He had no idea what it meant. He knew Jay had lied about the woman's death, but he could not work out what it alluded to. None of the actions in the hotel seemed linked to Bishop or Caroline, and the creatures were so different from the mythological beasts he had encountered. They were simply pure evil, deformed by the anger of the murdered woman.

The feelings of despair and loneliness filled him. Their last hope had been to destroy Bishop's remains and thereby escape Sacred Valley, which had been dashed by discovering that the remains were gone. He looked at the whistle one more time.

Having no other ideas, he blew on it. A deep shrill flowed out from it, which made him stop immediately. Taking a deep breath, he blew again, more prepared this time. The shrill sounded loud. He swore he could hear a woman screaming within it.

Trevor stashed the hotel maps away and inspected the crude Resort pamphlet map:

Welcome to Sacred Valley Resort!

He headed towards Stanson Lane, noticing that Hawthorne Avenue was on the east side of Silvercrest Lake's river. He wondered how long it would take for the road to lead him back to Old Sacred Valley. He could not drive the boat, so his only solution was to traverse the streets. One more person might have the answers, and he guessed that Emily was waiting at the church.

While heading down the street towards Hawthorne Avenue, he reloaded his weapons. There was no immediate threat, so he decided to keep his hands free for a change. Staring at the map would serve him no further purpose.

The Silverside Amusement Park appeared on his left. Trevor glanced absent-mindedly through the mist at the large wooden gates leading into the park when he realised they were open. Even though every fibre of his being told him that he was being led by someone again, steered like a cattle to be butchered, he wondered if going where they wanted might also help him escape.

It was a two-edged knife that he could use to his advantage. He decided to change his outlook on the situation; instead of being led to his death, he would follow the clues to his salvation. All he had to do was kill Twisted Bishop before it could kill him.

He entered the park, the pistol back in his hand again. The torch at the fore of the Smith & Wesson had become unnecessary. Huge lights led the way ahead of him, albeit still tainted with the veil of the fog. Within the park, the mist seemed to penetrate less, and the sky also darkened.

He passed benches on either side of the main walkway. At first, he thought people were sitting on them. He walked closer, his finger on the edge of the trigger, when he realised they were large sacks in the shape of adults. An array of male and female dolls sat slumped in their seats as if they were sleeping.

Trevor checked their limbs for any strings, but there were none. The light caught the necks of the dolls, and he saw blood and burn marks on them. He staggered back. They looked like rope burns.

He shook his head to clear it, reminding himself that Bishop was playing tricks with his mind. Ignoring the dolls, he moved further until he found the ticket booth and turnstiles. He jumped over the metal turnstiles and made his way into the actual park area.

There were several market stalls to his left and right. Most of them were empty or sealed shut. He inspected the locks and windows anyway in case there was anything useful he could find. The market section ended, and he found a road that snaked between trees.

He passed park rides, inspecting them for any sign of Bishop in his monstrous metal headpiece. The radio remained silent, adding to his trepidation again. He would have felt more comfortable if it sounded so that he could deal with whatever creatures the park had in store for him.

A movement on the sand behind the trees made him turn his gun towards it. The light caught the mist, struggling to penetrate beyond the trees. Trevor squinted, seeing further movement in the shadows. He moved the light down, seeing a foot that lay on the path with the rest of the body hidden in the long grass.

The radio started to sizzle softly. He lifted the torch again when a creature moved closer to the light shining from a pole above. Trevor recognised the beast from Ashenfall Hospital. It was the headless creature with its face set in its chest and the large gaping mouth in its belly.

"Anthropophagus," Trevor muttered as he watched it bend down to touch the lifeless body beyond the path.

It stood up. Trevor shot first at the Anthropophagus, hoping to stop it from reanimating anything else in the park. The bullets whistled into the night as it stepped back into the darkness. He shifted to aim at the mutilated sackman that stepped into the path before him.

He shot into its chest and shoulders. The stuffing flew out the other end, but the creature continued to limp towards him like a zombie. Trevor tried shooting its face, but the head simply snapped backwards. It stood still for a moment as the head returned into place, walking towards him again.

Trevor heard groaning further down the path he had come from. He saw further sackmen and sackwomen approaching. He realised that it was all the bodies he had seen sitting around the park.

He reached for his katana and unsheathed it, slicing through the neck of the sackman before him. The soft material of the cloth ripped open as the head fell to the floor. The rest of the body reached out its arms to grab him. Trevor kicked it away and ran up the path.

When he looked back, he saw that they were struggling to keep up. They had mobility in their limbs, but they were still lifeless. He slowed his pace, looking forward again as the radio died down.

In the swirling fog ahead, he saw more movement. Their limping suggested that they were more of the sackmen. He looked around for any building he could break into to hide from them so long until he could work out a way to get rid of them.

As he turned to his left, he noticed that the house's lights beside him had spotlights illuminating the name of the building on the upper wall. A chill went up Trevor's spine as he walked forward and studied the sign next to the door.

"Suicide Manor," he read out loud. "Only the sound of their screams will grant you entrance."

Trevor looked back at the sackmen closest to him. He wondered if that's what the sign referred to. He remembered slicing the head off the first one and could not recall that it had screamed.

"Maybe it couldn't scream because it had no head," Trevor said to himself, trying to unravel the mystery. "Let's try something else."

He moved to the creatures before him and sliced into their arms and chests. They continued to surround him, not one sound breaking from their cloth faces. He struggled against them, pushing free of their grasp and hitting them back again.

One caught him by surprise from behind and wedged his sack hand into his mouth, the other arm wrapped around his neck, trying to strangle him. Trevor coughed as his airways blocked up, swinging the blade behind him carelessly. He wondered if the manor had wanted to hear his screams instead of the creatures.

And then it dawned on him. As his life started to leave him, he realised what he had to do. With new determination burning through his veins, he rolled over his shoulders onto the ground. The momentum threw the sackman off him as the others turned to limply run after him.

Trevor waited until they had moved away from the manor and then pulled out the bone whistle. He blew hard through it, the sound of a thousand cries echoing along the path. He watched as the main door creaked open, waiting for him to enter.

The sheer exhilaration pressed him forward. He knocked the sack creatures out of his way as he sprinted for the door. It started to close just as he reached the wooden steps that led into the white house. As soon as his body made it safely inside, the door shut closed.

32

SUICIDE MANOR

There were three sources of light in the reception foyer he stood in. The immediate source was his torch, which he now switched off. The second, more indirect source was streaming in through the windows from the street lights outside. The final, softer light was from the red Lunar Nexus that glowed on the wall beside the door.

It was not painted on the wall this time. Instead, a pendant hung from a chain suspended by a nail in the wall. He pulled the chain loose and looked at the Lunar Nexus glowing in his hands before placing it over his neck.

He felt a twinge of relief. As much as he was gladdened to see the symbol, he was even more grateful to see that Jay's name was still burning within it unharmed. Kathy and Philip's names were dull and black. It gave him hope that he could still find his friend and save him. All he needed to do was locate a blue Lunar Nexus and transport to the Darcwurld.

After the Lunar Nexus rejuvenated him, he studied the room more closely. The light lit the stairwell on the right wall more than the actual foyer itself. There were three doors on the lower level: one to his left, one under the stairs on the wall opposite him and the last to the right.

He looked up to the walkway on the next level. There were four doors along the wall that he faced. Trevor looked on either side of the door behind him, hoping to see a light switch. Not finding one, he moved to the centre of the room, which was slightly darker than the wall lit from the outside.

As he stepped into the middle of the room, he heard a catch release. As he looked up, something creaked overhead and metal sliced through his head. He fell to the floor, his head spinning and aching as he tried to regain his senses.

Trevor stood up. He was standing by the main door again, his head intact. He put his torch back on, scanning the ceiling. A long chain was suspended from it, leading to the side wall. Attached to the end of the chain was a double-edged axe. He leaned his foot forward and pressed it over the centre timber boards.

The catch released again, and the axe swung to the other side of the room, over the rising stairs and back across the room again, where it slotted into place. A slit in the wall appeared to catch and hold the blade.

Trevor aimed his torch at the door to the left. He saw the light switch beside that door and moved towards it. He first tested the door and found it locked. When he switched the light on, he whirled around as the room changed colour. Instead of the slow transition into the Darcwurld he had grown accustomed to, the room switched over immediately.

The walls and floors were covered in rust and dampness. In the centre of the room, where his foot had triggered the axe, he saw a pool of black blood. He looked up, but could not find the cause of it.

The red Lunar Nexus burned brightly on his chest, trembling and shimmering against the darkness of the Darcwurld. Where his feet touched the floor, the timber looked as good and well-maintained as the manor had been before he switched the light on.

Shining the light on the opposite wall under the second level's walkway, he saw words written in the same black blood that read 'Dark Fables'. His study of the words was cast aside when he heard footsteps walking down the stairs.

"Put that damn light off!" a senior male voice shouted.

He heard the feet move to the light switch by him. It clicked, and the lights went off, returning the room to normal. His pendant also ceased its vibrations. A soft blue glimmer on the opposite wall past the axe caught his attention. Trevor stepped carefully over the spot where he had seen the pool of blood. The axe remained on the wall.

He knelt down as the ghostly figure became more visible. It was a woman, huddled against her knees and hiding her face from the world. Trevor recognised her body, even though he could not see who she was. He shivered slightly as he reached down to touch her shoulder.

"Caroline?" Trevor muttered.

She looked up at him with blue tears in her pale eyes. Recognising his face, she smiled at him softly. He fell to his knees, pulling his bag off and throwing it to the side. He held her tight, his arms passing slightly into her transparent form. He could feel her within him, cold as ice.

"Caroline, what are you doing here?" he asked, pulling away from her. Tears had now started rolling down his cheeks.

He waited, hoping she would finally provide him with the answers he longed for. She stared at him, still smiling up at him. He ran his fingers down her cheeks.

"Caroline, please," he said again, hoping to wake her from her stupor. "Can you see me?"

He could definitely feel her. The corners of her lips curled up slightly more, indicating a response to his words. He stood up, wondering what she wanted him to do for her to speak to him.

"Do you want me to apologise?" he asked. "Tell me, Caroline. How do we get out of here?"

She looked at him again, her eyes shimmering in the light from outside. She seemed anxious about something, casting her gaze around as if someone was approaching.

"Are we in trouble?" Trevor tried again. "Caroline, is someone coming?"

"It was the lie that killed me," she finally said.

As her words drifted through the room, she faded from sight. Trevor knelt down to investigate the spot she had sat, but it was empty. A loud, shrill cry sounded from the level above as one of the doors opened up. Trevor stepped back, looking up at the railings.

A woman crashed through the railings towards him. In fright, Trevor staggered backwards to avoid the body slamming into him. As his feet stamped on the centre boards, he heard the axe release. Before he could jump out of the way, it sliced through him again.

Trevor groaned as he stood up by the main door. The effects of the Lunar Nexus were wearing off. He didn't feel as rejuvenated as he usually did. He looked at the pendant resting on his chest, noticing how weak the glow appeared. It was losing its power with every reawakening.

He returned to the light switch, noticing that the railing the woman had crashed through was not broken. The axe was back in its place in the wall, but Caroline was no longer there. He put the light on, the room returning to the Darcwurld. His pendant vibrated less this time. 'Dark Fables' was still painted on the wall where Caroline had been.

"Fables?" Trevor thought out loud. "As in Greek Fables?"

He wondered if he had finally entered Jay's nightmare. Jay had been fond of Greek mythology, and the two of them had spent many drunken nights by a fire discussing the legends and lore as if they had truly happened.

He also considered Caroline's words. The bone whistle had said that the greatest crime had been the lie, and now she was referring to it too. He knew he had lied to her about Kathy. His stomach was bunched together with the tension, and he felt a sting through his side from the stress.

Putting the light back off, he moved carefully past the axe and tried the door. When it failed to open, he tested the final door in the room, which refused to budge. He looked up at the second level. All of the doors were closed. Deciding to try all of them, he moved up the stairs.

The first two were locked with no sign of possible entry. He reached the door where he had heard the scream come from. Carefully, he reached down for the handle, fearing what he might find inside. His fingers lightly touched the knob when he heard the same shrill cry as before.

The door flew open, and an apparition ran right into him. It pushed him into the railing, the two of them crashing through and falling to the floor. Trevor's back banged onto the floorboards, and he heard the familiar sound of the axe releasing. He rolled out of the way towards the main door quickly, the axe skimming over his back.

It cut into his flesh slightly, causing a searing pain as he crawled away. He stood up and looked back when he reached the main door. The axe was swinging from side to side until it slowed to a stop over the centre. The woman was dangling from a noose around her neck, the central wedge of the axe resting against her back.

The door that had opened was closed again. Trevor shone the torch on the axe's bevels that faced him. Words were etched into the metal on the left bevel. He moved closer to read it more clearly.

"For my dearest son," he said.

Trevor closed his eyes, pacing near the front door. It was clear now that he had to use Greek mythology to solve the riddle. He thought of any Greek lore that spoke of suicide by hanging. The words 'For my dearest son' reverberated in his mind, and so he thought of any male legends it could be linked to.

"Odysseus," he suddenly recalled.

He remembered how Odysseus had gone to deal with the Trojan War, leaving his mother Anticleia sick with worry. After a very long absence, someone had lied to her about his death. Not being able to bear the news, she hung herself.

"It was the lie that killed me," Trevor repeated, feeling excited by his discovery. "But what does Anticleia have…."

His words were cut short. At the mention of her name, the same door the woman had charged out of opened up again. The hanging body fell down to the floor and melted into the floorboards, leaving only the noose behind.

He picked up the rope and tied it over his left shoulder. He was about to move towards his bag at Caroline's spot when a movement out of the room caught his attention. The radio started singing in terror.

Trevor gaped at the horror above him. It was a large beast that had to bend down to make it through the doorway. It had long fur that covered its entire body. The torso was less covered by the hair, revealing dark nipples that protruded out of it.

Its feet were replaced by hooves, but the hands were human. The head was that of a bull with large horns that rose into the air. Around the Minotaur's left nipple was a Lunar Nexus tattooed with blue ink.

If that was not enough to strike fear into Trevor, the beast was transforming the room around it. As it walked towards the railing, the walls peeled off the plaster, with blood trickling down onto the second-level walkway. The blood dripped over the side through the wooden railings and onto the lower floor.

Yet the Minotaur only affected the room in its vicinity. The rest of the room remained intact. The beast jumped down over the railing and landed on the ground floor. Trevor watched as the upper level's walls returned to normal and the walls behind the beast changed. The words 'Dark Fables' were visible once again behind the Minotaur.

The pendant shook with the blue Lunar Nexus's proximity. He eyed his duffel bag by the beast's hooves, knowing he could not get to it now. The door the Minotaur had come out of was still open. As Trevor ran for the stairs, the beast grabbed the axe and ripped it off its chains.

Trevor reached the upper platform and turned around. He pulled out his pistol and fired at the Minotaur. The bullets ripped into the beast, causing it to step back at impact. Yet, it continued moving up after that.

"Of course," Trevor said, rushing for the room.

He entered it and shut the door, unsure what good it would do him. The radio fell silent, and the pendant rested quietly on his chest as if the Minotaur had simply vanished. The room before him was lit by moonlight from the open windows at the opposite end.

There was movement on the central bed, which was all Trevor could make out in the light. He reached up to switch the room light on and cast the room into the Darcwurld. The pendant vibrated again. Two demonic beasts with no skin were rolling around on the bed, engaged in passionate sexual activity. Their flesh rubbed against one another, the blood oozing out of veins and vessels onto the bed.

The male demon twisted its head completely backwards to look at Trevor. Its eyes shone a brilliant gold, and its long tongue lashed down past its chest. Trevor hit the switch again, returning the room to normal.

A blue glow appeared in the far corner of the room. Caroline was huddled and resting her head on her knees again. Trevor walked past the bed quickly, anxious to reach her. As his foot stepped on a switch midway down the width of the bed, Trevor looked towards the wall, where he heard something being released.

He woke up at the door of the room. He shone the pistol near the wall where he had walked but could not see what had killed him. His head was aching worse than before now, and the pendant had a very dull glow to it. He understood that he could not afford to be killed for much longer.

He walked to the glow in the corner again, hearing moans rising from the bed. The sheets and covers moved as if two people were rolling in ecstasy, but the torch revealed no one on the bed. Trevor carefully felt with his feet until he found the catch and watched as an arrow flew from a mechanism in the wall by the bed's headboard into the wall where he had stood.

"Caroline," he said when he reached her. "Sweetheart, can you hear me?"

She looked up at him again, this time with a sad smile. She reached up to him and stroked the side of his face.

"Please speak to me?" he pleaded, trying to pull her up. She slumped back down, refusing to stand. "Caroline?"

The moaning on the bed stopped. Trevor shone the light back on the bed. The sheets had stopped moving, but the indentation looked like it was breathing.

"Someone's coming," a young girl's voice said.

The bed shifted again, and the patter of small feet escaped the room. A man's voice was groaning on the bed. He shone his torch just above the bed and saw a shadow along the far wall. A man was kneeling on the bed, his hands on his face.

"What have I done?" the voice said.

The shadow drew a long dagger and aimed it at his chest. He lunged it inward, almost falling onto it, as the length protruded out of his back. His body went stiff, and he collapsed dead to the bed.

"Caroline, let's get out of here," he said, trying to hoist her up again. She held herself down as if there was an anchor attached to her legs.

She looked up at him, her eyes weighed down with sadness. He felt his guilt rise inside of him for what he had done to her, for the betrayal that had cost her her life. He reached down for her, touching her face.

"Caroline," he said softly, "I am sorry I betrayed you."

"Like a knife through the back," she said, vanishing into the floorboards like blue strands of dust.

He stood up again, sighing as he moved back to the bed. The sheet was now stained with red blood, with the words 'My loving daughter' scrawled in black. A small dagger was lying next to it.

It reminded him of a Greek legend Jay had once told him about. Knowing now what had happened between him and his aunt, he realised why it fascinated him. A king by the name of Cinyras had had an incestual affair with his daughter. The guilt of his actions had finally destroyed him, and he had killed himself by driving his dagger through his body.

"What was her name again?" Trevor said, thinking aloud. "Smyrna?"

The windows and door started rattling. He grabbed the dagger and tucked it in his belt behind the katana. The bed hopped up and down on its legs as if someone was trying to throw it over. This was followed shortly by the radio wailing again as the door burst open. The Minotaur stood there with axe in hand, staring into the room as if it had been waiting. The room changed around it again, shifting into corruption and corrosion.

With the door open, it charged in with the axe held high. Trevor fell to the ground and slid under the bed, determined not to die further and waste the Lunar Nexus's power. The bed came crashing down around him as the beast stomped on it.

He made it out the other end, the side of the bed falling behind him as he bolted for the door. He saw the broken railing as the fastest way down and jumped through it. He landed on the floor and rolled to the side.

The door to the right of the main door was now open. Trevor turned back to get his bag first when the Minotaur jumped down towards him. He ran backwards in fear, shooting at the beast to slow it down. Its shoulders jerked to the sides with each bullet until Trevor reached the door, entered the next room and shut it closed.

The radio fell silent again, the faint shimmering of the pendant falling still. He was in a large kitchen with a wide and long counter in the centre of the room. The walls held an assortment of built-in cupboards with a washbasin by the opposite windows.

Trevor saw the light switch beside the door. He was almost too afraid to put it on but decided to do so anyway. Clicking it transformed the kitchen into the Darcwurld, setting the stoves and counters aflame. Fire licked everywhere around him, the surging heat burning his skin.

He switched it off again. The wind blew through the kitchen, killing the flames as the room returned to normal. He looked at the windows, and the only other door in the room that led out the back, but none were open. The wind continued to blow, rattling the cutlery that hung from the elliptical metallic rail attached to the ceiling.

Trevor moved left first. He saw a small bottle on the other side of the counter where the stove plates were. He felt the floor carefully with his shoes, ensuring no traps were set within it. His ankle tugged against a wire between the wall cupboards and the central counter.

He jumped back quickly in fright. Flames erupted from a hidden exhaust set in one of the lower drawers. He watched as the fire burned the wood of the counter before it died down.

Bending the torchlight down, he saw the tripwire. He stepped over it gently. As he moved along the counter, the drawers and cupboard doors started banging open and closed. The cutlery rattled further until he reached the stove and picked up the bottle.

Everything died down. The bottle had a label with a skull and bones over it, indicating poison. The glass was a dark green, revealing a black liquid within it. Under the poison image on the label were the words 'My darling lover'.

A blue glow to his left lit up the glass bottle. Trevor looked down at the huddled Caroline. He sighed, walking towards her as he placed the bottle in his pocket.

"We can't keep doing this, Caroline," Trevor said. "Just tell me what you want. Tell me how to end your agony."

She looked up at him again. She seemed to have aged. Her face looked older, and she had no more joy left in her eyes. She scratched at her neck, which made Trevor realise that she now had rope burns on them.

"Caroline," he said apologetically, not sure what else he could add.

"With the fire that ate me alive," she muttered to him before vanishing again.

Trevor frowned. When he had spoken to her before, her responses had seemed relevant to what he had been saying to her. Now, her reply confused him. She appeared to be giving him clues rather than conversing with him.

The oven door of the stove began to rattle. He looked down at it, realising that smoke was pouring out of the sides and the top heat-release vents of the door. He bent over, looking into the oven. There was a body lying inside it.

Trevor reached for the door's handle, attempting to open it and save the person inside when the stove burst into flames. He fell back into the cupboard behind him, slamming the back of his head into it. The flames raged all around him until the counter's timber caught alight.

While he crawled backwards away from the flames and towards the other door, he quickly thought back on Greek lore. His mouth mumbled words inaudibly as he tried to find the relevance of what was occurring before him. It took him a moment before he applied poison and fire to darling lover, and then he remembered.

"Of course," he said. "Heracles had grown fond of Iole. When his wife found out, she doused his shirt with poison that burned his skin without killing him. Eventually, the suffering was so severe that he had his mortal body burned alive to stop the suffering. In the end, Deianira had lost him anyway."

When he said her name, both the door he had entered and the door behind him opened up. The Minotaur was waiting by the foyer door again as if he had not been able to gain access until that point. The head of the beast stared at the flames, its pupils reflecting the orange fire in its eyes before it turned its gaze on Trevor.

The Minotaur entered the kitchen, transforming everything around it into the Darcwurld. Trevor stood up and ran into the next room, closing the door behind him. Deciding to test something, he tried to open it again. It refused to move as if locked by some supernatural force.

He was in a large dining room with ornate colour-stained windows. The dinner table was laden with several plates of delicious food. They were so fresh that Trevor could smell their sweet scent from where he stood. Candelabra lined the centre of the table down its length between the two rows of plates.

What stood out was the woman at the head of the table. Her head was lying on the plate, her face pressed into the food. Near her head, by the first candelabrum, was a lighter.

"I wonder if this was used to light the candles," Trevor mused, picking it up and placing it in his pocket.

He switched off the lights. The candles went dark as the room was plunged into the Darcwurld. Trevor ignored the rusted windows and bleeding walls and focussed on the body. Fungus moulds were growing out of her flesh, beating like a heart to a sickly beat.

Her mouth was frothing as if she had been poisoned. Her head was jerking slightly. When he switched the light back on, the candles were burning again, and the body was still.

Caroline's apparition was sitting in a chair next to the body. She no longer huddled onto her knees but stared sympathetically at the body. He moved towards her, wondering how she would react this time. Even though he stood beside her, she didn't look up or indicate that she recognised his presence.

"Caroline?"

"The guilt poisoned me," she said, reacting the first time.

She vanished before his eyes again. Trevor frowned. Caroline had no reason to feel guilty about anything. It was Trevor who had wronged her. It confirmed his suspicions that the apparition was aiding him.

He turned to the woman and moved her head off the plate. He pulled the plate up, wanting to inspect it for any writing, when he felt how difficult it was to pull it up. He tugged hard at it, hearing a mechanism release from above. He dropped the plate immediately and jumped out of the way.

A kitchen knife had been released and smashed into the plate. It cracked into five pieces, the knife falling to the side. It was so sharp that he had no doubt it would have pierced the back of his skull. With the plate now smashed and the trigger wire underneath snapped off, he investigated the pieces individually.

Even though he never saw any writing, his fingers crossed a rough surface on one of the larger pieces. He traced it with his fingertips, realising that they were words. Getting an idea, he removed the poison bottle from his pocket and poured a small amount over the surface. The black liquid formed over the words, revealing what they said.

"Desire rejected," Trevor read, knowing exactly what it pertained to.

Caroline had gone to see a French play based on a Greek tragedy. She was so excited by the storyline that she spent the evening telling Trevor all about it. Theseus had been married to Phaedra, who had longed for his son. She had seduced him, hoping to sleep with him, but Hippolytus had rejected her.

Phaedra took her scorned wrath out on him, accusing him of rape to Theseus. Instead of killing his son, Theseus had him banished and invoked Poseidon to kill him.

"And so, racked with guilt," Trevor said, "Phaedra poisoned herself after confessing his son's innocence."

As soon as he had said her name, the two doors to the room opened. Trevor looked back at the Minotaur waiting at the kitchen door. They both moved simultaneously, Trevor stepping back as he eyed the beast.

The Minotaur roared in anger and charged. Trevor turned and ran as quickly as he could for the other door. The beast's speed was unbelievable. He had not guessed that it could move that quickly with such bulk and mass.

He felt the heat of its breath near him, the stamping of the hooves shaking the floorboards under him as he made it through the door. He closed it quickly, holding his shoulder against it as he felt the Minotaur ram it from the other side.

He was in a conservatory. The mist swept lightly around the glass wall, revealing the backyard that the room led to. There was minimal light in the room, leaving Trevor to resort to using his torch only.

A large fountain was set in the centre of the oval room. The water sprang from the top and flowed down to three different levels. Around the glass walls were vines and creepers with rich foliage that rose to the glass-domed roof.

Trevor searched around for a light switch, but the vegetation was so thick that he could not find one along the walls. He felt movement around his ankles and aimed the torch down quickly. The floor was bare around his feet.

Halfway to the door that led to the yard, he found a huge lever fixed to the ground. He fingered the top of the lever, wondering if it powered the lights or was another trap. He looked around further for a light switch along the walls but found nothing.

He moved back to the lever. Lying on the ground, he pressed his back against the fountain and kicked the lever over. He heard a mechanical sound as a sickle flew through the air and embedded itself into the thick stems of the vines before him.

"I guess that isn't the light switch then."

The lever reset itself. A blue glow guided Trevor to where Caroline stood beside the fountain by the exit door. She was resting her feet in the water, idly watching the water lap over her legs.

"Ok, so what's the next clue?" Trevor asked in a cocky tone.

Caroline continued to watch the water, no reflection visible on the surface. Trevor bent over and looked into her eyes. It appeared as if she did not know he was there.

"Caroline?" he asked.

She looked at him slowly, her eyes twinkling in his torchlight.

"Caroline," he said again.

She smiled at him this time. Her mouth remained closed as he waited for her to say something.

"Caroline," he said a third time.

"Your treachery drowned me," she said, her body vanishing into dust and swirling into the water.

"Well, that could mean anything," Trevor remarked, thinking back to any Greek lore where someone had drowned themselves.

He shone his torch into the water, hoping for further words. The water was still and calm, undisturbed by Caroline's latest movements in the water. Trevor shone the light up to the top of the fountain, where the water spouted out.

The torchlight caught a string attached to a light fitting in the glass ceiling. A cord switch needed to be pulled to activate the light. Trevor looked at the various levels of the fountain, realising that he would have to climb them to get to the switch.

"Yeah, as if that doesn't spell bad omen," Trevor said, amusing himself.

He climbed up anyway, guessing the answer was in the Darcwurld. His feet and hands slipped slightly on the first level until he grew used to the surface and clambered up. The water washed over his shoes as he climbed the next levels and finally reached the top.

Trevor took a deep breath. His fingers clutched the cord, but he was hesitant to pull it. Something told him that this was a bad idea. He tried to pull it thrice, building the courage to implement his idea. Biting hard against his teeth, he finally yanked it.

A flood of water broke into the conservatory. The fountain was no longer beneath him, and he sank down into the waters that crashed over him. He held his breath as it took him under, filling the room without breaking the glass.

The surge of the water's flow swung him around the room in circles. It felt like he was in a whirlpool with the eye in the centre of the room. He looked down at the submerged floor, spotting a lifeless woman at the bottom. She was the eye of the whirlpool, drawing everything to her.

Trevor kicked himself further down towards her, going with the flow rather than against it. When he reached her, he moved her onto her back, studying her body. There was a vial clutched in her right hand. With his breath running out, Trevor grasped at the fingers. He pulled them hard, eventually freeing the vial.

He swam back up hard, the whirlpool yanking him back down. His muscles bunched up as he kicked and swam harder, his expression raw with the effort it took to break free. The cord was just above him as he reached up.

Something wrapped around his ankles. Trevor looked down, seeing one of the vines pulling him back down. He placed the vial in a free pocket and reached down to break the vine free. He could hardly see with the water now rushing into his eyes as the vine pulled him down to the floor near the walls.

His breath was almost out. He could feel himself choking on what he had left. Bubbles escaped his mouth as his heart burned in his chest for oxygen. To make it worse, another vine wrapped around his neck and pulled him further away from the cord.

It was over. He could feel his life waning away. Deciding to let death take him instead, he looked down at the pendant on his neck. It was completely dead now, with no power left to revive him.

His last breath brought sanity back to his mind. Recalling that he had two bladed weapons on him, he drew out the dagger under his belt and sliced through the vine around his neck. As it drifted off, he bent over and sliced through the vines around his ankles. More vines reached out towards him, but he cut at them, causing them to pull back.

He let the current pull him to the centre and then swam up. He reached up with the last of his strength and clutched the cord. Yanking it hard, the cord broke off in his hand as the water descended all around him. He fell hard onto the floor, the dagger clanging out of his hand.

The room was back to its normal state, the fountain spurting water behind him. He stood up and saw that he was completely dry. Picking up the dagger, he took deep breaths of air, savouring every moment of it.

Trevor inspected the vial. There was a label on it with the words 'False Cupid'. There was only one Greek deity he knew of that could have any relation to Cupid.

"Aphrodite," he said out loud, watching as the door to the backyard opened.

He recalled a legend where Dionysus had loved a woman named Aura. As her name meant 'breeze', no matter how much he tried to court her, she was too fast for him. Dionysus then asked for Aphrodite's assistance, whose curse made her go mad until she gave in to him. Out of revenge, Aura drowned herself, after which Zeus turned her into a stream.

Trevor watched the door leading into the conservatory from the mansion and wondered why it had not been unlocked. More importantly, he questioned where the Minotaur had gone. He stepped out into the backyard and stared at the hedges all around him.

"Oh no," he said, realising what he had walked into.

.

33

MINOTAUR'S MAZE

There were hedges on either side of him, with only one way forward. Trevor could see paths further down that broke off to the right and left. The mist flowed over the high tops of the hedges and onto the path before him. He walked forward towards the first path that turned right and saw further hedges and paths breaking off within it.

"I am in no mood for a maze right now," Trevor said, returning to the house.

A loud bang erupted within the conservatory. He saw the Minotaur within it, bashing through the vines and walls, searching for him inside it. The beast looked up and through the back door, spotting Trevor between the hedges.

"I guess I don't have a choice," Trevor said, running to the end of the path and turning off into one that headed left. "Like a mouse, Trevor. Like a mouse."

He recalled an article he had once read about how mice had been placed in a labyrinth. The tests had revealed how the mice learned to just keep turning in one direction. He was going to keep turning left at every branch, and if he reached a dead end, he would just turn back and keep going left.

He checked his pistol's ammunition while he headed down his new path, which had some turns and paths breaking off to his right. There were nine bullets left in the magazine. He sighed heavily, realising that all his other ammunition was in his bag back in the manor.

Holstering the gun, he unsheathed the katana and walked to the path's end, realising no more branches were left. He turned around and headed back, going down a branch that had been his right before but was now his left. He investigated all the branches within it until he had returned to the main path again.

Taking the next path left, he searched through all the branches until he found a white marble pedestal at the end of one. It had a symbol of a water drop on the side facing him. The rest of the pedestal's sides were clear, with a protruding pad at the top like something had rested on there before.

"Your treachery drowned me," Trevor read the words inscribed beside the pad. "Those are the same words Caroline said in the Conservatory."

Trevor took out the vial of water, placing it on the pad. He waited a moment longer until he realised that it was not working. He retrieved the vial and uncorked it, pouring the precious liquid on the pad. This time, it sank down into the pedestal.

The portion with the words rose up from the pedestal until it popped free. Trevor picked up the small, rectangular marble slab. He removed the dagger and scratched '1' on the bottom surface.

Trevor placed the slab in his pocket and frowned. The hedge behind the pedestal was moving. The branches and leaves pulled to the sides, revealing a new path before him. He stepped around the pedestal and moved into the new area.

Suddenly, the radio started crying out. Trevor panicked and rushed to turn it off, afraid the Minotaur would hear it. He breathed heavily, listening around him. He heard a grunt on the other side of the hedge to his right just before the beast's axe started chopping into it. Trevor ran as fast as he could, turning back to see how the Minotaur's Darcwurld presence burned the leaves and branches as it passed through.

Sticking to his plan, he dived into the first left path he found. He raced down the path, investigating every turn he could find. Eventually, he returned to the path to the water pedestal and searched for a new left branch to turn into. Just as he was about to enter one, the Minotaur looked down the path he was in and saw him.

Trevor hurried. He realised suddenly that if he was in the wrong branch now, he would have to return to the path the pedestal was in, which meant passing the beast somehow. He kept turning into path after path, returning a few times until he found another pedestal.

This time, there was an image of a skull and bones similar to the one he had seen on the poison bottle. Next to the pad were the words 'Guilt poisoned me'. Trevor opened the poison bottle and poured it on the pad. As before, it sank into the pedestal, and the words propped out in a tiny slab. He marked it as the second item with the dagger.

The hedge behind the pedestal opened up a new path. Trevor stepped onto it, stopping for a moment when he heard someone move behind him. The Minotaur watched him by the only turn back to the maze's entrance. Trevor bolted forward with the Minotaur in hot pursuit, the hedge's leaves burning a sick purple colour wherever he passed through.

Forsaking his quest to stay to the left, Trevor darted into the right path that appeared before him. The Minotaur skidded past him, its axe dropping down and striking the ground. Trevor kept going, turning left, right, right and then left again.

He fell to his knees, catching his breath as he listened carefully. After a few minutes, the scrunch of leaves and twigs announced the beast's presence. Trevor dared to look around the hedge he was resting against. The Minotaur walked past the path that led to him, sniffing the air for his scent.

Not waiting to see if the Minotaur picked it up, he ran again. Even though his original plan was a mess now, he stayed on the left paths again. It twisted in and out again, and he found another pedestal. He sighed in relief.

"If I escape here alive, Jay can find his own way out," Trevor said. "I've had enough of this."

The pedestal revealed a noose. The words 'It was the lie that killed me' were next to the pad. Trevor removed the rope from his shoulder and placed it on the pad. Nothing happened. Bending over, he made sure the rope was tucked neatly around the pad and tightened the knot. He pulled it until the rope was choking the pad on all sides.

The pad sank into the pedestal, allowing the slab to pop out. Trevor marked it as the third item, placing the rope back on his shoulder. The hedge drew aside and allowed him through.

The Minotaur roared within the maze. Trevor could tell it was further away than the last time he had seen it but could not discern what upset the beast. Not wanting to find out, he moved along quickly onto the new path.

The hedge on his right before him shifted and shook. Trevor could hear the axe making a new way into his path. He frowned. He had been certain the roar had been very distant a moment ago. He looked back, wondering if he should head back the way he came.

Yet, he knew the way to the end of the maze was forward. The Minotaur broke through the hedge and stood before him, heaving his chest out from all the effort. Trevor saw there was no way past him now. He looked at the hole in the hedge that it had made and got an idea.

He ran back past the rope pedestal, trying to remember how he had gotten there. He stuck to the right paths this time until he reached the spot where he had knelt and watched the Minotaur pass him. He ran down to that path, and headed in the direction he had seen the beast go.

Trevor heard loud thuds behind him as the Minotaur hunted him down. Even though Trevor was faster, the beast had no trouble keeping him in view. Every time the Minotaur turned into a new path, it crashed with its shoulder into the hedge and then continued the pursuit. It was frothing at the mouth now, hungry for its quarry.

Just when Trevor was about to give up, he turned into a path that revealed the opening the Minotaur had made. He ran through it, seeing the rope pedestal on his left to confirm he was at the right place. He turned right and then into the first left branch he could find.

The Minotaur's hooves were not so close to him now. Trevor hid behind a hedge again to catch his breath. He watched as the mist rolled overhead and sank leisurely onto the path around him. His chest burned from the exertion, and he wished he had kept some water from the vile to drink. He looked down at his Lunar Nexus amulet, but its powers of rejuvenation were long gone.

The maze had gone silent. Trevor looked around the hedge to ensure he was alone before moving forward again. He searched every path and branch, continuing his left streak until he found the next pedestal.

The image resembled a bush of fire, with the words 'With the fire that eats me alive' next to the pad. Trevor took out the lighter and lit the air above the pad. The pad itself caught alight and sank into the marble. He claimed the slab that popped out.

Trevor waited long after the hedge had opened into the new path. There were still no signs of the Minotaur, no sounds to indicate that it had made a new way to him. He stepped forward cautiously and turned on his radio. The device was also quiet.

Not trusting the peace, he moved along quickly. There was only one path now, leading straight to a single end. It was a long path, taking at least two minutes for him to reach the pedestal.

A dagger symbol was on it, with the words 'Like a knife in the back'. He took the dagger out and placed it on its side. The pad didn't move. Trevor picked it up again and struck the point into the pad hard. It shifted down, but so did the dagger.

Trevor grabbed the handle hard, pulling with what strength he had left. The dagger was sinking into the pedestal itself, already a quarterway in. He placed his foot against the pedestal and pulled it again, yanking it out hard and falling on his back. As he returned to his feet, the slab popped out and fell to the grass before him.

The final hedge pulled to the sides. Immediately behind where it had been was an iron gate. There was one last pedestal before it. Trevor tested the gate hopelessly, knowing full well that it would not open.

He looked into the clearing beyond the gate. The hedge enclosed it, both circular sides ending against a large rock embedded in a rising hill. On the rock, directly opposite where Trevor stood, was a blue Lunar Nexus. The clearing itself was vacant.

Trevor returned to the pedestal. Five slots were in it, the same size as the rectangular slabs he had collected. He pulled them out, looking at the pedestal and the slots to see if there were any clues.

Deciding to follow the order in which he had found the slabs, he checked the numbers he had etched on them and placed the slabs in from top to bottom:

Your treachery drowned me
Guilt poisoned me
It was the lie that killed me
With the fire that eats me alive
Like a knife in the back

Trevor stood back, feeling triumphant. He was so glad that he had marked the slabs. He smiled broadly, looking back occasionally to make sure the beast had not followed him.

The gate remained closed. He pulled on the iron bars, but it was still securely locked. Trevor looked down at the words, hoping to place them in some logical order. No matter how he thought about it, the sentences could have been placed in any order and still made sense.

"Maybe I should place them in the order I entered the rooms," Trevor wondered, reclaiming the slabs. "First, I entered the foyer where the woman hung herself. Then it was the room where the father stabbed himself for sleeping with his daughter. The kitchen had the man who burned himself alive, and the dining room had the woman who poisoned herself. The last was the drowning. Rope, dagger, fire, poison, water."

Trevor placed the words in the new order:

It was the lie that killed me
Like a knife in the back
With the fire that eats me alive
Guilt poisoned me
Your treachery drowned me

He waited a few seconds again before realising that nothing was happening again. He kicked the pedestal in anger and moved forward to rattle the gate as hard as he could. Deciding to climb over it, he wedged his feet between the bars and moved up slowly.

The mist covered him completely. The gate and hedges appeared to rise up endlessly. Trevor looked down. The mist surrounded him so densely that he could not see the ground. He returned to the pedestal.

"I'm missing something," Trevor said, thinking hard about when Caroline had said the words to him. "There must be a reason Caroline gave me the words. "

He recalled how many times he had spoken to her in the foyer before it had evinced a response from her. It had annoyed him, but in the dining room, he had only said her name once before she responded. Deciding he had nothing else to try, he placed the poison slab's words first.

"When I first saw her in the foyer, I spoke to her the most before she responded, so let's put the rope message last," Trevor thought aloud. "In the conservatory, I said her name thrice in a row, so let's put the water message in the middle."

He was left with the fire and dagger slabs. He remembered that it had taken longer for Caroline to answer him in the bedroom than the kitchen, so he placed the fire slab second and dagger slab fourth:

Guilt poisoned me
With the fire that eats me alive

Your treachery drowned me
Like a knife in the back
It was the lie that killed me

The gate clicked and whined as it moved inwards. Taking the word slabs out again, Trevor walked through it. He closed the gate behind him again to prevent the Minotaur from entering, hoping it was strong enough to withstand the beast.

34

BETRAYAL OF THE BEAST

Even within the clearing, he could not see anything that stood out other than the blue Lunar Nexus. He inspected each part of the perimeter with his pistol's torch, keeping his radio on to remain alert. In the end, he stood before the Lunar Nexus once again. Jay's name was the only one within it.

"I never thought I would do this willingly, knowing what I do now," Trevor said, reaching out. "This is crazy."

His fingers and palm touched the centre of the Lunar Nexus. The amulet on his chest was too impotent to fight the transformation. He looked around, seeing the hedges catch alight and burn like walls of fire around the clearing. Rusted steel and rock, meshed into disfigured spikes, rose like thorns and barbs from the earth. Where they broke from the ground, the earth bled like pus from a pore's infection.

Where the gate had been before, Jay now stood. Trevor gaped, shocked at seeing his friend alive and well. He ran as the area's final transformation took place. Jay had his back to Trevor, standing naked in the clearing. His back has strange symbols and runes inscribed in black ink.

"Jay!" he called but slowed down when he reached him. The blue Lunar Nexus was around his nipple in the same place it had been on the Minotaur.

Jay turned around to face him. His expression did not express the same glee Trevor had had a moment ago. There was life in his eyes, but he looked mortified and defeated.

"Are you ok, buddy?" Trevor asked, watching as Jay blinked and then looked at him properly.

"Trev," Jay said coldly. "You made it. You found me."

"I wouldn't leave you behind," Trevor lied. "You know I'll always come back for you."

Jay looked at him suspiciously and then walked past him around the stony barbs. Trevor followed him, wondering what was wrong with him. Jay stopped in the centre of the clearing.

"The ritual is almost complete," Jay said. "There's no more time left."

"Wait, what ritual? What's going on?"

"There isn't time to explain," Jay said, turning back to face him. "But maybe there's enough time to make up for what I've done."

"You can explain when we get out of here," Trevor said. "We just need to find a black Lunar Nexus, and we can leave."

"No!" Jay said, grabbing his shoulders. "Listen to me!"

"Alright," Trevor said quietly.

"This isn't about Bishop," Jay said, looking around the clearing. "We've had it all wrong."

"But I saw him," Trevor argued. "He was in that twisted head thing."

"Yes, I know. But he isn't the one pulling the strings."

"Are you referring to your aunt who molested you?"

"No, man, will you shut up?!" Trevor looked at him, pursing his lips closed. "This place, this town, it makes us relive our nightmares. The sins we fear to have exposed. It feeds on what we have done, the guilt, to repay us for our crimes."

"Crimes?" Trevor tempted saying. "But all I did was have an affair."

"Don't you see?" Jay said. "Yours was the sin that started it all. Put everything into motion."

"No, I don't understand," Trevor said, shaking his head. "Kathy bullied Caroline and then stole me from her. Philip killed Bishop after we brought him in, and all those other victims."

"Yes, we would have all paid for our sins eventually," Jay said. "If we'd lived long enough, maybe in the afterlife. But you started the chain of events that brought us all together in one place, that brought us all to Sacred Valley."

"I still don't get it," Trevor acknowledged, feeling rather embarrassed at his inability to grasp what seemed obvious to Jay.

"When you slept with Kathy and Caroline found out, it reawakened the old anger she had when they were in school," Jay explained. "It reawakened Raven. And then you beat up Bishop, which landed him in Philip's hands. If it wasn't for you and your betrayal, Philip would have either gone on killing others or been caught. Bishop would never have been involved."

"Ok, I see where you are coming from with this," Trevor said honestly," but what the hell does your aunt have to do with this? And as far as I know, your only involvement with Bishop was to help me take him to Philip, and then bury his remains in Sacred Valley. That doesn't sound too serious to me."

"You aren't seeing the big picture," Jay said, looking down as tears filled his eyes. "And that's because I never told you the truth, Trev. I lied to you. It was that lie that killed her."

Trevor stood back, lowering Jay's hands off him.

"What do you mean?"

"My aunt was my sin, my great personal crime in life," Jay explained. "Just like Raven in Hollowbrook was Kathy's, and the victims in Ashenfall were Philip's. They were punished for their sins by being brought here to account for them, but the justice for what they had done to Caroline and Bishop, the affair and the murder, was delivered by your hand."

"What did you mean it was the lie that killed her?" Trevor said, ignoring his words.

"Remember the police report that stated she had hung herself in your apartment?" Jay asked, to which Trevor nodded. "I had written that report as the first officer on duty."

"What? I thought you had heard the report at the station. That's why you called me to tell me about it."

"I had heard about Emily's report on Philip and that she believed he had killed Bishop. I went over to your place to talk to you about it when I found

Caroline alone at home.

"She was packing her things, getting ready to leave. I asked her what had happened, and she said she had just heard from the police that they believed the corpse was Bishop. She told me about that phone call that Bishop had made to her when he walked in on you.

"She had heard you guys fight, heard Bishop screaming before everything fell silent. During the fight, you must have knocked the phone and killed the call. Ever since then, she had been waiting for news on Bishop. When she was told he was killed, she suspected you were involved."

"Why the hell didn't you tell me all this, Jay?!" Trevor shouted.

"Because I couldn't tell you what really happened, man," Jay confessed. "I lost it. I saw our futures falling before our very eyes. I knew if she implicated you in his murder, then it would eventually lead to me. I couldn't let that happen."

"No....."

"I did what I thought was best," Jay continued. "I calmed her down and told her to think about what she was doing. While she waited in the lounge, I went to your storeroom and took the rope…"

"No…"

"Caroline never killed herself, Trevor. I only made it look like that. It was me. I killed Caroline."

Trevor stepped back, a look of sheer horror on his face. Suddenly, a lot of Jay's actions, specifically since they had entered Sacred Valley, made sense. His back knocked into a protruding horn, and he rested against it.

"After all this time," Trevor said, "when for so long I've been filled with remorse for being responsible for her death, to find out how it was you. That's why you kept telling me to stop blaming myself."

The ground trembled beneath their feet as the horns, thorns and barbs glowed a dark black. It was like they were absorbing the air and light around them into them. Lines connected the protrusions along the ground. Trevor stepped out into the opening to study the image that formed underneath them.

"The Glyph of Aethertide," Trevor said, looking up at Jay. "It's for you?"

"I have to claim justice for what I've done," Jay said as horns started growing out of his skull. "And since you are the common factor in all our crimes, the spark that fuelled the fire, all I have to do is kill you, and I can be set free."

Trevor pulled his pistol out and aimed it at Jay, torchlight burying into the fur that grew from his chest. The rest of his body was covered in tufts of brown hair as Jay's face changed into a bull's. He grew in height, twice as large as Trevor.

"I'm sorry, Trevor," Jay said in a deep demonic voice. "But I don't deserve to be here for your betrayal."

Jay ran forward, leaning his head down to ram his horns into him. Trevor shot as quickly as he could, the four bullets either missing him or ricocheting off the horns and fur. He jumped out of the way just as Jay reached him and rolled to the side.

Trevor fired five more shots. Two hit his arm and flew out the other end. The blood rolled down his arms to his clenched fists. One hit the fur on his chest, and the last two almost hit his neck. The next time he pulled the trigger, the pistol simply clicked.

He threw the pistol to the ground as it was useless to him now. He unsheathed the katana, holding it before him. Jay ran to ram him again. Trevor jumped to the side and sliced his shoulder. Fur fell to the ground, but Trevor saw that the blade had bit into his flesh. There was a large open wound.

Jay grunted, steam rising from his nostrils. He shoved his huge hands into one of the large horns rising from the ground, breaking through the surface. The horn began to change around his fist. It melded with the skin of his arm until it became one with it. He ripped his arm out, holding onto the piece of the horn that came with it and completing the change.

It was a large chainsaw. Rocks and minerals were studded around where the saw chain should have been. The chainsaw replaced his arm up to his elbow, revving and spitting blood where smoke or oil should have been.

Jay ran forward on the offensive again. This time, he swung the chainsaw up and down. Trevor used the katana futilely to try and block it until the rock chain caught the blade and broke it in half. Trevor kept the other half at hand, hoping to still stab him when the chance came.

Jay ran to the attack. Trevor backed away slowly, waiting for the right moment. Just as Jay lifted the chainsaw arm to strike, Trevor dived at his feet and rolled. The weapon struck the barb where Trevor had stood, getting lodged within it.

While Jay struggled to free it, Trevor jabbed the short katana blade into his ribs. Jay cried in agony, howling into the dark fiery air as the pain seared through him. Trevor tried to wedge the blade back out, but it was stuck within him. Jay broke the chainsaw free and lashed out to his side. The rock and minerals cut into Trevor's chest, sending him rolling along the ground.

Trevor remained on the ground, holding his chest in agony. That one cut had done enough to make him almost black out. He looked up and saw the katana blade pass into Jay's body. His left hand transformed into the blade, the chainsaw on his right arm. He walked with the darkest of intentions towards him.

Looking around him, Trevor saw he still had one weapon at his disposal. The dagger was under his belt. Still on the floor, he pulled it out, looking at the steel of the dagger and hoping it was strong enough. And then his eyes went wide.

"Like a knife in the back," Trevor muttered to himself, looking up at Jay almost upon him. "Justice and vengeance."

Jay swung down with chainsaw and blade. Trevor rolled away, the katana clipping his arm. He cried out in pain but recovered quickly. Jay watched him carefully. He ran forward again, swinging both weapons in wide arcs.

Trevor jumped into a roll to the side and then ran up behind him. He drove the dagger deep into Jay's spine. Jay bent his back, his face howling into the sky as the pain coursed through every fibre of his being. Trevor pulled the blade out and was about to strike again when Jay twisted his arms around and knocked him backwards.

Jay limped towards him awkwardly, his spine in splinters. He revved the chainsaw, rushing to cut through Trevor's neck. Trevor slipped down to his knees, allowing it to pass over him and stood up behind Jay again. He embedded the blade into his spine again, this time causing Jay to fall to his knees.

Jay was breathing heavily. The Metatron lines on the floor glowed brighter as they fed him more power. Dark shadows flowed off from the barbs into his body. Jay stretched out his weaponised arms as it filled him with renewed energy.

Trevor looked at the ground and saw the rope behind him. At some point during the battle, it had fallen off his shoulder unnoticed. He reached down for it and threw it over Jay's head. He pulled the knot tight, the rope biting into Jay's fur and skin.

Jay gagged and tried to reach the rope with his hands, but he had no fingers to grasp it. Trevor pulled tighter, jerking the rope back to force Jay off his knees. Trevor jumped up into the air, used the rope to pull himself back down and planted his knees firmly on Jay's broken spine.

Jay collided face-first with the ground. The sick sound of metal slicing through flesh rippled into the air as Jay's body went limp. The rope snapped in two, causing Trevor to fall forward and hit the ground ahead of Jay.

When Trevor turned around to investigate, he saw that the katana hand had cut through Jay's neck. He had tried to cut the rope free, but the collision with the ground had forced it midway through. Jay's neck was now open and exposed, bleeding profusely onto the ground.

"Jay!" Trevor called.

Retrieving his gun, he approached the Minotaur's body and lifted it carefully off the blade. Jay's lifeless eyes stared back up at him, his mouth open but uttering no words. Trevor looked back at him, trying to feel remorseful for what he had done. He looked at the Lunar Nexus on Jay's chest. It was changing from blue to black. Carefully, he placed his hand on it.

The clearing began transforming back to normal. The horns, barbs and thorns sank back into the ground. As the mist returned, it killed the hedge's flames and brought the fauna back to life. The pus and blood oozed back into the hole just as Jay's body returned back to normal.

Trevor knelt down and held his former friend, closing his eyes as he mentally asked Jay for forgiveness. He felt very exhausted after the battle, with no sign of a red Lunar Nexus to replenish his health. He lay down beside Jay, placed his head on Jay's chest and rested. He no longer cared if Bishop found him. He needed sleep.

35

PENITENCE

He opened his eyes slowly. The mist swirled around him in a thick mass, covering him like a blanket. The ground beneath him was hard and pressing up against his chest. The air was thick with moisture with the scent of oncoming rain. A rumble sounded from the clouds somewhere overhead.

Trevor stirred his head, shaking it in an attempt to gain some sense of where he was. He heard a church bell ringing nearby him. It was the same bell he had heard from Hollowbrook Elementary. He looked down beneath him and saw a mound where Jay's body had been before. Looking ahead of him, he saw the wall of the mausoleum he had seen behind the church in Old Sacred Valley.

His body ached as he stood up. The cut in his ribs stung as the mist passed over it, the wound exposed through a gash in his clothes. Trevor took his pistol in hand and shone the torch around him and then down. The mound was the same unmarked grave he had seen in the church graveyard.

Trevor moved away from it, watching carefully around the graveyard. He inspected the gates of the mausoleum, but they were still very much locked. He walked with stealthy steps back to the streets. It was indeed Sacred Grove Church in Old Sacred Valley.

The church doors were wide open, inviting him inside. Trevor walked up the steps and saw the soft interior lights. Not wanting to be disturbed, he closed the doors behind him. Turning around, he surveyed the church's interior.

There were various rows of bench seats on either side of the centre aisle that led up to the altar at the head of the church. Candles were flickering on the altar, the wax ornaments still long as if they had recently been lit. A familiar red glow was emanating from the centre of the altar's surface.

Behind the altar was a large statue of a humanoid creature with wrappings over its face. It was on all fours, resembling the beast he had seen crawling above him in the Darcwurld version of Ashenfall Hospital. It was also the beast he had seen looking after the baby on the secret extra hospital floor.

On either side of the altar were pedestals made of black obsidian. Tall statues of men with triangular cloths over their heads stood on the pedestals with their blades in the outer hands closest to the east and west walls. The swords reached up to the roof as if supporting it.

Large paintings down the side walls caught his attention. He moved to the left wall first, approaching the painting closest to him. It was the image of a young woman kneeling in prayer with a golden Lunar Nexus above her head, giving her a saintly appearance. The plaque revealed that she was Emma Bennett.

The next painting was of an elderly woman dressed in a dark cloak, her wild white hair barely visible on the sides of her face. There was a darker, blackened Lunar Nexus just above the hood over her head. The plaque indicated that this was Seraphina Nightshade.

Third in line was a woman with a beautiful face that had faint indications of old burn scars. Her Lunar Nexus was the darkest, with tinges of red within it. Trevor ran his fingers over the name Selena Nightshade.

Moving to the fourth painting, he saw a young adolescent woman in Hollowbrook Elementary school uniform. She had long black hair, and seemed too mature to still be in the school. Where her mouth should have been was just skin, the lips completely absent. A misty Lunar Nexus whirled over her head. The plaque identified her as Jodelle Ferland.

There was one more painting on the east wall. Having grown used to seeing women in the paintings, the young man surprised him. He had long hair down to his shoulders with a long blue coat over his body. The halo over his head was silver, with jagged edges on the inner rim as opposed to the polished oval finish of the others. He was Sebastian Nightshade.

The penultimate painting was of a very young woman with red hair. She was looking up in adoration, her eyes feasting on something unseen. Her hands were held together before her chest in supplication. She held a rosary of beads in them, with the cross made out of two intersecting scalpels. The portrait indicated that she was Harmony Boatman.

Trevor frowned. There was no halo above her head. He remembered Philip mentioning a Doctor Boatman, but had been given the impression that it had been an older man, not a young, gorgeous woman.

Deciding to disregard it, he moved to the final painting. He did not need a plaque to identify the woman on it. Her hair was brilliant amber, the image resembling the painting he had made of her. She smiled beautifully at him, only her head above the neckline visible. Above her head, the halo was in the form of a looped rope, tied at one end into a knot.

"Caroline McKenzie," Trevor said aloud, feeling the weight of sadness awaken inside of him.

Trevor moved back to the altar. As he got closer to the main statue behind it, he saw the words 'Zephyranth, the Watcher' inscribed on the obsidian base. He scanned the altar's surface, expecting to see the red Lunar Nexus. He found more than anticipated.

The red glow came from a Glyph of Aethertide that covered the width of the white marble altar before him. In the top corner of the triangle within the sigil was a small red Lunar Nexus with only his name still glowing. The bottom left corner held the blue halo with only his name in it, and the bottom right had the black Lunar Nexus with all their names.

Afraid of what the Glyph might do, he moved his hand slowly onto the red Lunar Nexus. As always, it filled him with healing rejuvenation. Even the wound on his ribs closed as if it had never been there. When the flare of the red light was gone from his eyes, he noticed that the red light from the Lunar

Nexus was gone, the last of its power within him now. His pendant shimmered, filled with renewed energy that transferred from the altar.

"That's ok," he said to the now defunct Lunar Nexus. "I suspect this will be the last time I will need you."

He eyed the blue Lunar Nexus, wondering if that really was the only choice left. He looked around the church again in case he missed anything else. When he looked back, Caroline's white ghostly spirit he had seen at Suicide Manor was on the other side of the altar, the top point of the Glyph aiming straight at her.

"Set us free," Caroline said, reaching forward and touching the blue Lunar Nexus.

Trevor marvelled at how she said 'us'. Even after everything, she still wanted to be with him. She wanted him to find a way for him to break Bishop's hold on them so that they could be together again.

He smiled and placed his hand over hers. It went right through and touched the Lunar Nexus. Trevor waited for the walls, ceiling and floors to become corrupted by the power of the Darcwurld again. He looked around and expected the blood and rust to overpower every sense of sanity he had left.

Instead, the altar split in the centre of the Glyph, breaking the triangle in half. It moved to the sides, scratching against the wooden floorboards and revealing stairs that led beneath the church. Caroline's spirit vanished, the statue of Zephyranth looming over him and the new entrance.

With an abruptness that almost gave Trevor a heart attack, the two large statues to the sides swung their blades inwards and pointed them towards the entrance. They were once again motionless, their masks facing him. Trevor stepped down into the dark staircase, aiming his torch down.

As he walked down, the walls changed from regular plaster to the rusted steel formwork he had expected before. The stairs felt like they were descending forever, the heat rising the further down he went. The more he pressed on, the more the amulet around his neck vibrated. Eventually, the power of the darkness overcame it, and the pendant shattered, falling onto the stairs at his feet.

When the walls opened to reveal further corroded steel and earth, he saw a large chasm filled with burning fire. There was a massive being in the fire. Its head was wrapped like the Zephyranth statue, but it had a large gaping mouth filled with stalactites and stalagmites of fangs on the upper and lower gums. It roared at him, bathing in the lava and fires surrounding its lower body.

Eventually, there were just the stairs left beneath him. The walls and roof fell away, and he could see the fires burning below. The large entity roared again to the side, making the stairs quake beneath his feet. He ran forward along it while trying to step as lightly as he could.

He could see a single door ahead of him now. It stood on a prominent rocky spire that rose from the lava bed below. He reached it quickly, afraid that the huge beast would kill him if he hesitated. When his feet landed on the spire, he turned the knob and opened the door.

Trevor stepped in quietly, not believing his eyes. It was his apartment in Ashbourne Heights, the one he had shared with Caroline. Closing the door, he investigated the lounge thoroughly, seeing the painting of Caroline he had done before she had died. The same smile that the portrait in the church had exhibited looked back at him now.

He walked to the bedroom very slowly. He knew what he would find there. This was his nightmare, his crime, his sin. He had to face the guilt he had felt ever since Caroline's death, knowing full well that the affair had killed her emotionally. Even though Jay had confessed to suffocating her and faking her suicide, he knew she had been long dead inside before then.

The door handle was ice cold when he touched it. When he opened the bedroom door, the chill of a freezer blasted against him. He walked inside, looking up at the ceiling above the bed. The noose was there, but Caroline's body was not.

Trevor investigated the room first. Nothing was out of the ordinary. It was exactly as he remembered it when he had come home and found her hanging corpse. The noose swayed slightly, inviting him to get onto the bed and hang himself, too.

He walked up to it, placing his feet carefully on the mattress. His hands teased the rope's fibres as his fingers traced the inner rim. There were specks of blood and raw skin on it as if Caroline had only hung there five minutes before.

He pulled the rope down, testing if it would hold his weight. As the rope moved down like a switch, the bed suddenly fell away beneath him. Trevor grappled with the rope, holding onto it with every bit of strength he had left. The floors and walls gave way, opening up to a dark pit with a cloud of smoke at the very bottom.

His arms ached as he looked up. The ceiling was peeling away in the same way the plaster and paint from the school and hospital had peeled away whenever the Darcwurld took over. It moved towards the rope in the very centre until there was nothing but a small circlet left around the rope. And then it was gone.

Trevor fell into the darkness. He aimed his pistol's torch down. The light shone brightly before flickering and dying out. He was cast into the shadows once more, nothing visible but the swirling clouds beneath him. He held his breath as if it would save him when his body hit the mist.

His body collided with a hard thud onto an obsidian floor. Trevor rolled to the side, his shoulder throbbing from where he had crashed. Even though he had felt the impact, he knew he should have died from the fall. Something had cushioned the blow.

And then he looked up. He was in some sacred chamber with large torches on tall stands within it. There was a huge circular design made from obsidian stones that rose like steps around him. Before him was another altar, this one washed by blood all over. The more he looked at the altar, the more it looked like it was made from a large slab of blood in stone form.

There was a strange sigil design on the side of the altar facing him. It resembled neither the Lunar Nexus nor the Glyph of Aethertide. Above the sigil sat a large demon with wings on either side, his seven horns rising from his demonic head in huge curls and twists.

"Beautiful, isn't it?" said a female voice.

Caroline stepped out of the darkness beside the altar. She had a malicious grin on her face with fires that burned softly in her eyes. He could not tell if it was a reflection of the torches or from something more sinister within her. Even though he saw Caroline before him, it was not the woman he had originally chosen to love and spend his life with.

"Who are you?" Trevor said, standing up and aiming the gun at her. "You're not Caroline."

"Are you sure?" she said, her voice becoming more demonic before returning to normal. "Do I not look like her? Do I not have the same appeal to you?"

"There's something different about you?" Trevor said, keeping the pistol on her as she walked around the altar to stand before it, blocking the demonic sigil.

"I am your dear Caroline," she responded, licking her lips with a black, forked tongue, "yet I am not the part you remember. This is the darker side of me, the part you awoke with your actions and betrayal."

"Raven," Trevor whispered.

"Very well done," she said, clapping her hands in applause. It echoed around the chamber.

"What is this place? Where am I?"

"You're in a very dark place, a place even the most horrid demons fear to tread. It is both everywhere and nowhere at the same time. It is a place so hallowed that no name will suffice to title it. It is the birthplace of god."

"God? What the hell are you talking about?"

"Not hell, but a new heaven," Raven explained. "Our new saviour will release us from these prisons and take us to our new homes in Sacred Valley."

"Why have you never used the black Lunar Nexus?" Trevor asked. "It seems to take me out of this place easily enough."

"Unfortunately, the power that traps me here cannot be undone by that sigil," Raven replied. "Those of you who can still return to your true world are the only ones who can use that key to traverse dimensions."

"So that's all you want?" Trevor asked, confused. "To get out of this darkness?"

"For now, but we do desire a deeper purpose," she replied. "We will start with reclaiming the town that is our soulrite, the holiest of sacred places, before we move on to the surrounding villages and then the world."

"Who exactly are the 'we' you are speaking of?" Trevor said, remembering what Emily had told him in the graveyard. "Is it the group called The Zephyrite Conclave?"

"Our goals are similar, but no," Raven replied. "From the ashes of what once was, we are something new. You see, for eons of time, god has been trying to be born on the earth, to give new life and light to the people on it. They worship false beings, entities that pale in comparison to her splendour and glory.

"The Sect of the Twilight Covenant attempted it, first through Selena. Unfortunately, they failed, misunderstanding the sacrifice that needed to be made. Willing and pure. Then there was the Sect of the Holy Father with their orphanage that moulded young Sebastian's mind. Yet, even with the aid of Zephyranth, they could not succeed."

"Please don't tell me, after failing so many times, that you're going to try to raise this god of yours again," Trevor said, not realising that he had slackened his grip on the pistol.

"Where the others have failed, The Zephyrite Conclave will not," Raven said confidently, pacing up and down. "From your betrayal and the darkness you have weaved in the hearts of others, you unintentionally provided the perfect opportunity for god to be born, for us to realise our dreams."

"I don't understand," Trevor said, lowering the pistol. "How could anything I've done have aided you?"

"The pure side of me was right not to trust you with the truth," Raven said, moving towards him. She floated over the stones with a dark, misty cloak around her as she pressed her face seductively close to his. "You never even suspected."

A cry sounded from the altar. Trevor looked past Raven's face and saw a baby's hands reaching upwards, its feet kicking out playfully. He moved up the stairs to the altar. As the baby was nude, he observed that it was a little girl.

"Caroline was pregnant?" Trevor asked, his heart sinking in despair.

"She only found out a week before she was killed but was struggling with how to tell you," Raven explained. "She knew you were sleeping with Kathy too. That betrayal cut deep. She did not know if you would care enough to leave Kathy, or if you would choose rather to leave her and your child. Unfortunately, Jay spared you that decision."

"I would have chosen my child," Trevor said.

"Easy to say that now," Raven said, a hint of doubt in her voice.

"How is it that this child is alive?" Trevor asked, staring into the baby's eyes. "She should have died in Caroline when she was killed."

"She died in the real world," Raven said, walking to the other side of the altar, "but I kept her alive here. I gave her the power to be born from me. The essence of god is within her now. Zephyranth has been watching over her, waiting for the rebirthing ritual to be complete."

Trevor remembered again seeing Zephyranth on the hospital's secret floor. It had walked towards the baby. Trevor had thought it had meant to do her harm.

"Why have I been spared?" Trevor finally asked the one question lingering on his mind for a long time. "You could have had me killed since I entered Sacred Valley."

"Killing you was never my intention," Raven remarked. "Emily was meant to bring you here from the start when she met you in Sacred Valley.

For some reason, she chose not to."

"Emily works for you?" Trevor asked. "Hold on, she was the one in the twisted metal covering that knocked Kathy out and took her into the school."

"Yes, although that was just an illusion. Emily was introduced to our religion by her brother, Edward. Ever since his death, she has been a willing servant."

"Did Emily introduce Caroline to you?"

"No," Raven said, shaking her head. "Like I said, I am Caroline, and yet, I am not. I am the darkness born in a time of sadness and loneliness. It was in Hollowbrook Elementary that I first formed within her, although my only influence at that time was to guide her. She believed she was Raven, and that helped her through her troubled times."

"There are so many things I still don't understand," Trevor said, looking down at the baby again. "The most burning question I have is what I'm doing here?"

From the shadows to the side, Trevor detected movement. He saw the Twisted Guardian step into the light of the torches, revealing his large blade in hand. In fright, Trevor stepped away for a moment but then stopped when he realised Bishop was not moving any further.

"Ah yes," Raven said, "ever loyal Bishop. When he left his father's house in Sacred Valley and then the army, it was to meet with a religious group he had heard about. That was where he first met Emily. They introduced him to the hallucinogens the group was using, a mild alternative to White Selena created by Harry Boatman called the Pink Princess.

"Bishop grew interested in the active Zephyrite sect members up there. It was through them that he received that branding on his arm. His distance from Caroline was to protect her from them, but that isolation only caused her to rely more on me."

"Why is he wearing that helmet?" Trevor asked.

"It's a symbol of Zephyranth, an image of justice and retribution, but twisted to reflect the injustice done to him," Raven explained. "Members of the cult usually hide their faces to resemble the face of Zephyranth, but Bishop had seen this image in some designs by the cult members. He had taken to it quickly, and it became his favourite. When I chose him to be the god's guardian in this world, that was the face he wanted to portray."

"This does not make any sense," Trevor said, studying Bishop some more. "This is not the Caroline I know. She would never give in to this, into this demonic ritual. She was a good woman. Even with a troubled past, she would never betray her purity."

"Your faith in her goodness is not far wrong," Raven said, smiling maliciously again. "With her soul taken by betrayal, I offered her the chance of vengeance, not only for her but for Bishop, too. When it came to Kathy, Philip and Jay, it was easy for her to succumb to the desire, but not when it came to you.

"Even with what you had done to her, she wanted you spared. I offered the chance to spare your child, and she welcomed it."

"She could not have known what you were planning to do with the baby. To allow your god to be born inside of her."

"That was my only request in exchange for offering her justice and saving you and the little girl. Eventually, she made her bargain. It was done."

Trevor considered her words. He found it hard to believe that Caroline would give in to such a demand, but with Bishop simply standing there and the baby before him, he could not doubt Raven's claims. Yet, Caroline's spirit had asked him to free them. He now understood that she had meant her and the baby. Raven was holding them both hostage.

"You used me," Trevor said, realising what Raven's purpose for him had been. "You used me to kill them."

"That wasn't the plan initially," Raven confessed. "Like I said, Emily was meant to bring you to me while I helped Caroline exact her revenge on the others. Yet, your desire to save those you cared about got in my way. I had to send Bishop to stop you.

"But as you travelled into their nightmares and fought the creatures each of them conjured up through the power that flows through Sacred Valley, you played right into my hands. You became my Executioner. By trying to save them, you inadvertently became the blade by which justice prevailed. You enacted your own penitence for your betrayal of Caroline."

"No," Trevor said, shaking his head. "I did not agree to serve you."

"You didn't have to," Raven smiled. "You were more than willing, especially when you learnt what Jay had done."

"Fine," Trevor acceded. "So why haven't you released your god from this world? Why are you still here?"

"There is one final part of the ritual that is required," Raven said hungrily. "She requires the blood of her father."

"My blood?" Trevor frowned. Why?"

"Your sacrifice will give her the power to release her from this prison," Raven explained. "You can either offer it willingly, or we can take it from you."

Trevor looked at the baby before him. She was quiet now, staring up at him with eyes that reflected the pure Caroline within them. Set us free, Caroline's spirit had pleaded. He now understood why she had helped him and that it must have been her who planted the red Lunar Nexus around the town. She had regretted the bargain and wanted him to save them all. He had failed her.

He was not going to fail her ever again. He knew what he had to do. The dagger was still hidden under his belt. The baby smiled up at him, a darkness taking over her eyes. Caroline was bound to their child in the fog-ridden Sacred Valley, while Raven was tied to her in the Darcwurld. There was only one clear way to set them free, even if that meant sacrificing his own life in the attempt to do so.

36

JUST REWARDS

Trevor reached for the dagger and swung it up in the air. As he brought it down on the baby, Bishop's blade pierced the air above the child and blocked his strike.

Raven was furious. Fire broke out around her as her demonic wings spread around her back. Trevor stepped back down the stairs as Bishop held his blade between them just as Raven wrapped her cloak around the baby. Trevor watched as his daughter vanished into the flesh of the demon into her womb.

"To hell with the bargain!" Raven shouted and pointed at Trevor. "Bring me his blood! If you want your resurrection, Bishop, then you need god to release you! Finish the final sacrifice!"

The Twisted Guardian moved forward. He brought the heavy blade up effortlessly and struck. Trevor jumped back and hit the edge that banged on the ground with the dagger. The small blade vibrated, sending spasms up his arm.

"Alright, so you won't do me much good here," Trevor said, tucking the dagger away and feeling stupid for trying.

He raised his pistol and started shooting. The gun clicked. He had forgotten entirely that he had already run out of ammo when fighting Jay. Using the pistol as a torch instead, he ran away from Bishop, hoping to find something else he could use.

As he ran back, he saw he was in an aisle with monstrous benches on either side. It reminded him of the Sacred Grove Church, albeit much darker and larger. Bishop was scraping his blade across the floor, not in a rush to pursue him. Trevor didn't blame him; there was nowhere to go.

There was no exit. The walls of the dark church simply closed before him where the doors should have been. He ran to the sides and then stopped in his tracks. Where the portraits had been, the real people were now standing. They were hidden in the darkness, and as the torch passed over them, they simply turned to stare at him. They were waiting for something.

He ran past them. Bishop used his blade to smash the benches between them out of his way. Trevor scanned the floor, hoping there was metal somewhere that he could use in defence. All he saw was the black obsidian rock on which the church stood.

Trevor stood at the altar, taking the dagger out again. Raven was in the left corner near him, watching in anticipation. Bishop picked up his blade and charged towards him. Trevor waited until the last moment and then jumped out of the way. Bishop crashed into the bloody obsidian altar, his loud moans crying out as his shoulder broke on impact.

"The rock," Trevor said, looking around him. "I need to use the rock."

"Get after him, servant of Zephyranth!" Raven shouted.

Bishop stood back up, and rammed his shoulder into the altar again. It clicked back into place. Grabbing the blade with his other arm, Bishop ran towards him again. Trevor held his small dagger before him, waiting again for the right moment.

As Bishop sliced through the air horizontally, Trevor fell to the ground and lashed out his leg. Bishop tripped over it, toppling to the ground as his helmet collided with the obsidian floor. It cracked through the side seams where each plate of the twisted object met.

Bishop grabbed the helmet with his hands and pulled it off. He now stood before Trevor with nothing to hide his damaged and slaughtered face from him. He picked up his blade again. Instead of running, he moved forward carefully and swung his blade in X formations before him.

This time, there was nothing Trevor could do. The large blade covered any angle Trevor could have used to bypass him. He stepped away, his back moving towards the altar. He realised that even if he ran to the sides, it would just be a chasing game that would only keep him alive longer.

Deciding he preferred the latter to be skewered on the altar, he ran to the right side and made his way back to the end of the dark church. Bishop ran down the centre again, determined to kill him. Trevor simply stared at the blade swinging over the air before Bishop, twirling like a fan to cut his head off.

Trevor wished he had spent more time finding Bishop's remains. If he could have just burned his body, then he would only have had Raven to deal with. As Bishop was about to strike at his head, he realised he had just solved the problem.

He smiled and rolled to the side as Bishop's blade clanged against the hard wall. He sprinted for the altar as fast as possible, grabbing one of the torches off the walls. Raven frowned as she watched, wondering what he was up to. Trevor reached the altar with Bishop halfway back towards him.

Trevor pulled the bone whistle out of his pocket, causing Bishop to stand still. He put the torch onto it, ensuring the fire licked around it on all sides. Bishop's horrid cries filled the church, his skin suddenly breaking out in flames. Trevor removed the torch, the bones warm to the touch as he grabbed it and dropped it onto the cold floor.

The fires were dying from Bishop's skin, but he was still screaming. Trevor used one of the benches to hoist himself up into the air as he drove the dagger down into his chest. Bishop cried out and hit Trevor with a heavy arm. He kept his grip on the dagger as he soared back into the air and slammed into the wall near Jodelle's portrait.

The fire on Bishop died out completely as he picked up his blade again and charged harder towards Trevor, who was still recovering from his fall. He saw the bulge of his body about to slam into him, when he rolled out at the last moment. Bishop crashed into the wall and fell back, the force causing him to collapse onto the benches on the side.

Taking the closest torch, Trevor burned the whistle again. Bishop went up into flames. Trevor left the bones in the torch's fire on the ground this time and ran for him. He jumped into the air again, driving the dagger clean through his throat. The fire caught on Trevor's clothes as he jumped away, Bishop's head rolling down the middle aisle to the altar's steps.

"Impressive," Raven said as she emerged from her shadowy corner. "I honestly did not see that coming. You really are determined to live."

Trevor stood there staring at her as she transformed. Her demonic wings stretched out on either side of her as her body changed into that of a dragon's. Her tail stretched out with spikes along the upper central line, with her claws reaching out from each digit the length of Trevor's torso.

"I will never be fascinated by mythology ever again," Trevor said. "You just ruined my favourite mythological creature for me."

Ignoring his quippy remarks, Raven opened her maw and blasted a ball of fire into the air. Trevor jumped out of the way just in time as some of the flames burned onto his right arm. He cried out in pain and then repeated the cry when his shoulder broke into a bench from his fall.

"Brings new meaning to fighting fire with fire, I guess," Trevor said, laughing at himself despite his dilemma.

"You think this is funny!?" Raven roared in a deep, guttural voice.

"Well, if I'm going to go out, I might as well go out laughing," Trevor replied.

Raven stomped the ground, crushing the benches as she moved towards him. She swung with her claws, scratching his legs as he rolled again. Before he could stand up again, she grabbed him in her huge hands and stared down at him defiantly. She opened her mouth to bite down on him with her vicious, black teeth.

Trevor lifted his blade and thrust it into a space between the fangs. Raven roared and stepped back in shock as he fell to the ground. He ran around her, his body aching as he made his way to the altar.

He held the small dagger before him. Raven laughed at him, seeing the small weapon in his hand. She ran forward at full speed, blasting a wall of fire before her towards him. The fire scorched at the altar as she stood over it, the flames heating the obsidian rock beneath her.

Raven stopped and closed her mouth. The altar was vacant before her. She looked behind her and saw that he had dived under her. He had stabbed the dagger into her belly where the baby was being protected, but the shell was too hard, causing the dagger to bounce back off.

"There must be some way to kill you," Trevor said softly as he stared down at Bishop beside him.

He dropped his dagger and reached for Bishop's large blade. It was heavier than anything he had ever tried to pick up, but he pulled at the handle with everything he had left. Raven grunted, staring at the sword. She weaved to and fro, uncertain of herself now against the blade of Zephyranth.

Despite her concerns, she breathed fire again and ran forward. Trevor moved out of the way and drew the blade across her legs. The sharp edge cut through her legs cleanly, leaving her to fall on her face and crash into the wall. Trevor lifted the blade again as Raven roared in agony.

She flapped her wings hard and used her forearms to lift herself off the floor. She rose into the dark air above, with no sign of where the ceiling limit was. Trevor listened to the flaps, using them to help discern her location. The flaps grew closer, and he rolled to the side just as she clawed the space he had been standing in. Two of the claws hit the floor and broke off against the obsidian.

Raven rose into the darkness again. Trevor listened intently again. A ball of light emerged from the void above and hit him full in the chest. Trevor crashed to the floor, the fire burning his skin. Trevor rolled on the floor as he skid to the wall, killing the flames before they could do more damage.

He had lost the blade. It was lying where the flames had hit him. Breathing heavily, he limped back to the blade and picked it up, wincing as every bone in his body complained. The flaps grew louder as she descended again.

Trevor watched carefully. He saw the area he wanted to strike. She descended with fury and fire, opening her mouth as she drew her fangs to devour him. The flames burst over his body as he lifted the blade up. Raven's belly drove right into the upright sword, and she crashed into Trevor as they went sliding to the wall.

Trevor groaned. Raven was lying beside him, her body heaving up and down from exhaustion. She hardly moved, and he wondered just how badly he had wounded her. Her collision with him had killed the fire that had almost consumed him, but the flames had done their part. The skin on his arms, chest and face was terribly burnt and bleeding.

Just as Raven sighed her last breath, he heard a small cry amid the church. He walked towards the baby lying in the blood of the dragon's womb. The blade had cut the scales open and caused the child to fall to the floor. The blood looked like shimmering rivers of gold that led to the altar.

Trevor picked up his daughter and carried her towards the altar, collecting Bishop's large blade as he did so. He could barely pick it up this time. He was unaware he was bleeding profusely over her from his latest injuries. He dragged the huge blade behind him, much like Bishop had done before, placing his daughter on the altar.

She was still crying from the latest collision with the floor. Trevor looked down at her, tears welling in his eyes at what he would have to do.

"I'm sorry, my little girl," Trevor said. "I would have loved to watch you grow up."

Trevor lifted the blade high up into the air just as he heard Raven's desperate roar behind him. He twisted his body in panic and drove the blade down in a wide arc. The blade bit with a sick sound into Raven's scaly neck and sliced right through it. Raven's body crashed into the left wall, the obsidian breaking all around her.

Bishop's blade clanked down the stairs and onto the floor. Trevor was too exhausted to pick it up this time. Instead, he strolled down the aisle to where his dagger was and picked it up. He made his way tiredly back to the altar, limping at a very slow pace.

The baby was on all fours now, looking at him as he approached her.

She had a gorgeous smile on her face. Trevor smiled back but could not feel the same joy. He had to kill the evil she had inside of her.

With no more paternal words to give her, he raised the dagger just as she crawled to the side and touched the altar with her palm. The air around her hand lit with a dark, black aura. Trevor stood dumbfounded, waiting to see what the child was up to. Only then did he realise that his blood was on her.

When she lifted her tiny hand, a new black sigil unknown to him was imprinted on the obsidian altar. He could not believe his eyes. Somehow, she had created the symbol by herself. She reached for the sigil, her fingers open wide.

"No!" Trevor screamed, bringing the blade down on her tiny body.

The dagger shocked through his body as it collided with the altar. His daughter had vanished from his sight.

"She must have gone to the misty Sacred Valley," Trevor said out loud. "She has taken the evil with her."

Trevor reached out to touch the new sigil. His palm was inches away when Bishop's blade passed through his back and out his chest. He coughed blood out of his mouth that spilt onto the altar. It seeped along the surface towards the sigil, feeding it and causing it to glow more.

"You might have postponed the rebirthing ritual," an old man's voice said, "but you have released god out of this world at least. That's good enough for now."

Trevor collapsed onto the stairs, staring up at the ceiling as his life started leaving his eyes. An old man walked past him, looking down at Trevor. His eyes went wide. He recognised the old man as Doctor Boatman.

"I've been waiting for this moment for a long time," the old man said, looking around at the others along the sides of the church who watched him in anticipation.

As the last of Trevor's life escaped him, the final thing he saw was Doctor Boatman touch the bloody sigil on the altar and then disappear...

ALTERNATIVE ENDINGS

PARENTAL GUIDANCE

(Good Ending 1)

The baby was on all fours now, looking at him as he approached her. She had a gorgeous smile on her face. Trevor smiled back, but could not feel the same joy. He had to kill the evil she had inside of her.

With no more paternal words to give her, he raised the dagger just as she crawled to the side and touched the altar with her palm. The air around her hand lit with a dark, black aura. Trevor stood dumbfounded, waiting to see what the child was up to. Only then did he realise that his blood was on her.

When she lifted her tiny hand, a new black sigil unknown to him was imprinted on the obsidian altar. He could not believe his eyes. Somehow, she had created the symbol by herself. She reached for the sigil, her fingers open wide.

"Wait," Trevor said calmly.

His daughter looked up at him, seeing the loving care that suddenly shone in his eyes. She stayed her hand and reached up with her arms to him instead.

"Let's get out of here together," Trevor said, reaching forward and embracing her.

He looked down at the altar, knowing that he was taking the evil with him, but deciding he would find another way to rid her of it. He pressed his palm firmly on the new sigil, holding her tightly. They vanished like black clouds of smoke into the altar.

From the darkness of the church, there was movement. Into the light, Doctor Boatman walked up the bloody steps and reached the altar.

"I've been waiting for this moment for a long time," the old man said, looking around at the others along the sides of the church who watched him

in anticipation. Doctor Boatman touched the black sigil on the altar and then disappeared....

Trevor opened up his eyes from the light that had blinded him. He was back in his apartment room. He got up quickly and opened the curtains, staring out at the mist that rolled past the window.

A cry sounded from the living room. He rushed out and then slowed down when he reached the lounge. Caroline was sitting on the sofa, breastfeeding their daughter.

"Look, it's daddy, our saviour," Caroline teased, smiling at him as tears of joy rolled down his cheeks. "Looks like we're in for bad weather."

Trevor had no response. He simply moved towards them and sat down beside Caroline. He wrapped his arm around her, feeling her skin press against his.

"Welcome home, my love," Caroline said, resting her head on his shoulders.

And still, the mist swept past the windows, keeping them in its chilly embrace.

RAVEN'S VENGEANCE

(Bad Ending 1)

The baby was on all fours now, looking at him as he approached her. She had a gorgeous smile on her face. Trevor smiled back, but could not feel the same joy. He had to kill the evil she had inside of her.

With no more paternal words to give her, he raised the dagger just as she crawled to the side and touched the altar with her palm. The air around her hand lit with a dark, black aura. Trevor stood dumbfounded, waiting to see what the child was up to. Only then did he realise that his blood was on her.

When she lifted her tiny hand, a new black sigil unknown to him was imprinted on the obsidian altar. He could not believe his eyes. Somehow, she had created the symbol by herself. She reached for the sigil, her fingers open wide.

"Wait," Trevor said calmly.

His daughter looked up at him, seeing the loving care that suddenly shone in his eyes. She stayed her hand and reached up with her arms to him instead.

"Let's get out of here together," Trevor said, reaching forward and holding her in his embrace.

He looked down at the altar, knowing that he was taking the evil with him, but deciding he would find another way to rid her of it. He pressed his palm firmly on the new sigil, holding her tightly. They vanished like black clouds of smoke into the altar.

From the darkness of the church, there was movement. Into the light, Doctor Boatman walked up the bloody steps and reached the altar.

"I've been waiting for this moment for a long time," the old man said, looking around at the others along the sides of the church who watched him

in anticipation. Doctor Boatman touched the black sigil on the altar and then disappeared….

Trevor opened up his eyes from the light that had blinded him. He was back in his apartment room, staring down at the bed beneath him. It took him a moment to realise that he had a noose around his neck attached to the ceiling. He choked and coughed, kicking the air as he tried to loosen the rope.

When he cast his eyes on the wall ahead of him, his vision blurring, he saw the image of a raven set in black on it. A deep laugh broke out, followed by the giggle of a small child.

Trevor twisted his body around. A girl who appeared to be over seven years old looked at him, pointing and laughing at him. Caroline's features dominated her face, and he guessed that it was his daughter.

His life waned, and his arms fell slack at his side. An old man appeared behind her in the room and watched as he died.

"Don't worry," Doctor Boatman said. "I'll look after her."

NEW GUARDIAN

(Good Ending 2)

The baby was on all fours now, looking at him as he approached her. She had a gorgeous smile on her face. Trevor smiled back, but could not feel the same joy. He had to kill the evil she had inside of her.

With no more paternal words to give her, he raised the dagger just as she crawled to the side and touched the altar with her palm. The air around her hand lit with a dark, black aura. Trevor stood dumbfounded, waiting to see what the child was up to. Only then did he realise that his blood was on her.

When she lifted her tiny hand, a new black sigil unknown to him was imprinted on the obsidian altar. He could not believe his eyes. Somehow, she had created the symbol by herself. She reached for the sigil, her fingers open wide.

"Wait," Trevor said calmly.

His daughter looked up at him, seeing the loving care that suddenly shone in his eyes. She stayed her hand and reached up with her arms to him instead.

"Let's get out of here together," Trevor said, reaching forward and holding her in his embrace.

He looked down at the altar, knowing that he was taking the evil with him, but deciding he would find another way to rid her of it. He pressed his palm firmly on the new sigil, holding her tight in his arms. They vanished like black clouds of smoke into the altar.

From the darkness of the church, there was movement. Into the light, Doctor Boatman walked up the bloody steps and reached the altar.

"I've been waiting for this moment for a long time," the old man said, looking around at the others along the sides of the church who watched him

in anticipation. Doctor Boatman touched the black sigil on the altar and then disappeared....

Trevor opened up his eyes from the light that had blinded him. He was back in Sacred Grove Church, with the mist swirling outside. His daughter was held warmly in his embrace as he removed his top and covered her with it. He stood there, holding her lovingly against his nude chest.

The altar lurched behind them and closed, sealing the doorway to the Darcwurld dimension. The two statues moved their huge blades back to support the roof.

As Trevor was about to leave, the massive bulk of Zephyranth suddenly moved. The faceless entity stared down at them, seeing the baby in his arms. Zephyranth reached with its giant arm and pulled the head off the left statue. The remaining body crumbled down into stone on the obsidian plinth.

Zephyranth held the metallic object over Trevor, and he understood. He knelt down as Zephyranth opened the sides up and planted it on him. The bolt screwed in, sealing his head within it. The Paternal Guardian walked out of the church into the mist that consumed them, ready to protect the god from any that wished her harm....

ETERNAL DAMNATION
(Bad Ending 2)

The baby was on all fours now, looking at him as he approached her. She had a gorgeous smile on her face. Trevor smiled back, but could not feel the same joy. He had to kill the evil she had inside of her.

With no more paternal words to give her, he raised the dagger just as she crawled to the side and touched the altar with her palm. The air around her hand lit with a dark, black aura. Trevor stood dumbfounded, waiting to see what the child was up to. Only then did he realise that his blood was on her.

When she lifted her tiny hand, a new black sigil unknown to him was imprinted on the obsidian altar. He could not believe his eyes. Somehow, she had created the symbol by herself. She reached for the sigil, her fingers open wide.

"No!" Trevor screamed, bringing the blade down on her tiny body.

The dagger shocked through his body as it collided with the altar. His daughter had vanished from his sight.

"She must have gone to the misty Sacred Valley," Trevor said out loud. "She has taken the evil with her."

Trevor reached out to touch the new sigil. His palm was inches away, when a sound behind him made him turn around quickly. He turned his body as Bishop's blade passed him, almost skewering him on it. The old man holding the blade staggered slightly and fell over.

Not giving him another chance, Trevor grabbed the blade from his hand and lifted it up. The blade sang through the air as it cut through Doctor Boatman's neck, the head rolling down the stairs to meet Bishop's.

The beings on the side walls floated up into the air like wisps and transformed back into paintings. Trevor turned to face the altar, laying his hand on it once more when he saw that the sigil had vanished.

"What?" Trevor said.

He inspected the red obsidian surface again, but the symbol was definitely gone. He had taken too long to activate it. Turning around, he saw the hole in the wall that Raven's dragon form had created. He walked through it, seeing small islands suspended in the lava. He left the hellish church behind to journey through the Darcwurld....

SURREAL ENCOUNTER

(Joke Ending)

The baby was on all fours now, looking at him as he approached her. She had a gorgeous smile on her face. Trevor smiled back, but could not feel the same joy. He had to kill the evil she had inside of her.

With no more paternal words to give her, he raised the dagger just as she crawled to the side and touched the altar with her palm. The air around her hand lit with a dark, black aura. Trevor stood dumbfounded, waiting to see what the child was up to. Only then did he realise that his blood was on her.

When she lifted her tiny hand, a new black sigil unknown to him was imprinted on the obsidian altar. He could not believe his eyes. Somehow, she had created the symbol by herself. She reached for the sigil, her fingers open wide.

"Wait," Trevor said calmly.

His daughter looked up at him, seeing the loving care that suddenly shone in his eyes. She stayed her hand and reached up with her arms to him instead.

"Let's get out of here together," Trevor said, reaching forward and holding her in his embrace.

He looked down at the altar, knowing that he was taking the evil with him, but deciding he would find another way to rid her of it. He pressed his palm firmly on the new sigil, holding her tightly.

The church started trembling. His daughter looked up at the roof, causing Trevor to look up, too. The roof ripped off the church until it was lifted clean off and tossed aside.

The sky was dark, except for the bright lights that shone directly over them. Several flying saucers were hovering above them, the lights under their bases spinning in rapid circles. On the sides of the UFOs, Trevor managed to just make out large Aethertide symbols.

"What the…." Trevor said, looking down at his daughter.

Her eyes were golden orbs. She smiled at him as the light from one of the saucers enveloped them, consumed them and brought them up into it. The UFOs hummed with power and then flew into space….

THE WINDFARER

Book 1 of the epic fantasy series
The Celenic Earth Chronicles

CELENIC EARTH: A WORLD OF MIGHT, MAGIC AND MYSTICAL
CREATURES

A shadow lurks over the earth, as foul creatures attack the villages. The leader of hurorcs and purorcs commands them to attack the southern tribes, and is captured. But Mercius, once known as the Windfarer, finally breaks free after years of imprisonment and sets his sight upon the Asbec College of Elements where an ancient power is rumoured to be hidden.

Shadowolf is in his last year of studies at the Asbec College of Elements when word of the escape spreads. Strange things happen and he becomes entwined in a world of mystery and murder, using the power of the elements to survive. And as war erupts, Shadowolf returns home and does everything in his ability to protect the five southern wolf tribes. For his effort he merely frustrates Mercius's plans, but significantly learns that Mercius is subservient to a dark lord; someone more powerful, known as Le'Mar.

Between the protection of his family, the loyalty of the Shadow Clan and the new-found love of his life, can he pull himself away to stop Mercius from reaching the potent power node? For neither the elves nor the dwarves can stop him should he gain the power he seeks. Even the dark lord seems troubled.

The Masaran Phenomenon approaches, and the "Prophecy of the Windfarer" is upon them.

REVIEWS AND PRAISE

"Jooste's imagination has depth of both scale and scope, with parallels between this imaginary world and the real world, characterised by an interesting contrast between the industrialised evil forces and the 'natural' forces of good..."

THE DRAGONRIDER

Book 2 of the epic fantasy series
The Celenic Earth Chronicles

DRAGONS ARE COMING TO CELENIC EARTH TO END A WAR
RAGING ON FOR CENTURIES

Pernonil was lost to the Elves....the southern lands forsaken by the tribes....Chenesia lost to the Vale...Shadowolf lost to the world...

It has been two years since Shadowolf released the power node and destroyed Mercius; since he had been mysteriously taken by a dragon to Bentley Strip. But rumours of the dragons are stirring in New Avalion, and one of them is that the son of Nighthale has returned.

The Shadow Clan reform and set out to him in the Strip, and they meet a man wiser and more powerful than before. They quickly learn that Shadowolf had been in another world with Asgorna the Dragon King in what is called the Dragon War, a war that has leaked into Celenic Earth and that the dark lord Le'Mar plans to use to his advantage. Ursula the unicorn joins their Clan, and urges Shadowolf to find a horn lost in the Battle of T'Mar's Scourge. The horn holds untold power and would assist in defeating the dark lord. But on their way they find many obstacles, including the undead, witches, the Butcher of Philagis and Firestroms.

Quietly, Le'Mar is preparing his new champion for the War, Sonersaat the

DragonRider. As his quest grows larger, Shadowolf decides to enter Eldor's Forest, find Eldor and Masara and await Le'Mar. It is a war the earth has been anticipating….and it is a war with the direst consequences.

The "Prophecy of the DragonRider" is upon them…

REVIEWS AND PRAISE

"Fans of high fantasy such as Tolkien, Terry Brooks or David Eddings will be well pleased with Jooste's first novels and foray into the popular genre…He is finding his rhythm and style, doing a great job of making the reader care for the hero and characters; these books will be in my rotation of heavily reread fantasy novels in my bookshelf."

THE SADGI

Book 3 of the epic fantasy series
The Celenic Earth Chronicles

LE'MAR THE OMNIPOTENT, THE OMNIPRESENT, THE OMNISCIENT…..

The Battle for Eldor's Forest cost the world not only the elvin forest, but also every chance they had of standing up against the dark lord. The Southern Wolf tribes live defenseless in New Avalion, their walls shaken to the ground and the art of the elements forbidden. The mer-Kingdom was defeated in Avalendil, with no knowledge of where the survivors reside. And the elves have left for the Far Isles, leaving the ancient forest to the rule of Le'Mar's new servant, Darcwulf.

And all across the land lies Le'Mar's fog, his ever-present window to all that is happening on the land. The people of the earth have lived in relative peace in the two year's since Shadowolf's victory over Sonersaat the DragonRider, a victory that had almost cost him his life when he challenged Le'Mar thereafter. With no knowledge of where the hero escaped to and under the watchful gaze of Le'Mar and Darcwulf, the earth makes no move to retaliate against the dark lord.

It is to such circumstances that Shadowolf returns with powerful allies at his side. Determined to take back the world from Le'Mar's clutches, he begins his quest for four powerful artefacts encrusted with the tomes of time. Entwined in this quest is his personal mission to find and reclaim those he loves and lost. Yet, the greatest undertaking he faces is to convince the world to fight for their freedom. This time, Shadowolf is taking the war to Le'Mar.

The Masaran Phenomenon approaches again, and the "Prophecy of the Sadgi" is upon them…

REVIEWS AND PRAISE

"If you are looking for an epic, sweeping expanse fantasy book to read, then this is it. Congratulations Shaun Jooste for entering the world of print in the fantasy genre with a tale that will be picked up again and again just so I can immerse myself into his richly described world that is Celenic Earth."

www.ingramcontent.com/pod-product-compliance
Lightning Source LLC
Chambersburg PA
CBHW030538020726
47494CB00005B/1420